To Agnes,
Enjoy this
Giveaway
Douglas E Cameron
2/22/2019

Predator Island

By

Douglas Ewan Cameron

W & B Publishers
USA

W & B Publishers

For information:
W & B Publishers
9001 Ridge Hill Street
Kernersville, NC 27284

www.a-argusbooks.com

ISBN:9781635541359

This is a work of *fiction.* All of the characters, organizations and events portrayed in this novel are either products of the author's imagination or used fictitiously.

Book Cover designed by Dubya

Printed in the United States of America

Dediction

To my daughter Laurel Gray Shurlow, without whom the idea of this book would never have crossed my mind.

TO THE READER

One of the questions an author is asked is "Where did you get the idea for this story?" In this case, I was walking through Wildlife Zoo & Aquarium in Phoenix, Arizona with my daughter Laurel and her husband Rex. We were between exhibit areas and there was nothing really to see. Nearby was an area with a train for kids to ride around an enclosure that had donkeys, flamingos and other non-threatening animals. I said, "They ought to put a predator in there and play musical train, stopping the train every so often." My daughter laughed at the absurdity of it, but she and I started talking about the idea with predators, and when we got back to her house, I started writing.

The result was *Predator Island.* I describe the book to people as a combination of *The Hunger Games* (the use of television and drones to watch the game, only here, the participants are animals – except for one), *2001: A Space Odyssey* (because of the computer Hal); and a short story *The Most Dangerous Game* by Richard Connell (1893-1949). It wasn't planned this way, but it is what happened. Some people suggest *Jurassic Park* and my answer is that my animals exist now without cloning.

This story starts with an uninhabited, unimproved small island off the coast of Brazil and ends with the island having an infrastructure of dirt roads, electricity provided by solar panels, running water, a harbor for shallow draft boats, and a five-star headquarters inside a volcano. To get there it is necessary to tell some of the problems that were encountered in completing the infrastructure. In particular, there is the digging/drilling of a quarter mile long tunnel through the side of a volcano for access to the volcano's crater floor. Many of these things are necessary because of the importance they play in the story of what happens when the infrastructure is complete – and that's what the story is truly about. There may be times when the reading seems technical and unnecessary but when the story winds to a conclusion, I think you will agree that it was worthwhile. And everything done in this book has been done or is being done elsewhere in the world. So don't give up. The "tough read" isn't that much and in the end you'll be glad you persevered.

Douglas Ewan Cameron
Spruce, Michigan
Summer 2018

Prologue

"Good evening, America. Jamie Sherrod here with tonight's edition of CBS National News."

On the television screen, viewers saw a petite pretty African American woman with medium length black curls, rosy pink lipstick, and otherwise flawless makeup. She was wearing a royal blue Calvin Klein dress with simple jewelry. The background behind her showed a rocky coastline with palm trees.

"We start tonight with an interesting development in the wake of Hurricane Davido. You will remember that in a season of few tropical storms, Davido rose up traveling south of the usual hurricane path and smacked the small island of São Rochelle which lies one hundred miles east of the Bay of Olapoque which is where the Oyapok River empties. The Oyapok River forms the border between French Guiana and the Brazilian state of Amapa."

The view changed to a group of palm trees being battered by rain and winds with waves battering the beach in front of the trees. In the background was a modern building.

"The island's twenty-seven inhabitants had all fled the island before the hurricane. The population reached a maximum of eighty-two in 1898 but difficulties and the lure of broader horizons drew them away. This is a strange island in that its inhabitants had always retained their independence despite the territory being claimed by Brazil. Since it is of little value, the Brazilian government has let it alone."

The view switched to a ship's tender near a shore with people wading out in the water and being helped aboard the tender. The short loop ran several times as Jamie talked.

"The island has no tourist value as it has only one small port, if you can call it that, and the water is too shallow to permit boats of any size to land. Where one might find beaches as on most tropical islands, São Rochelle offers only a rocky coast: the west, northwest, north and northeast sectors of the island are rocky slopes, with the tallest slope on the boundary of the north and northwest sectors being fifty feet. The one access where a small boat could land is on the boundary of the northeast and eastern sector where the height of the northeast slope drops sharply down to near sea level. There cruise ships' lifeboats – called 'tenders' when used to transport tourists from ship to land – could make a landing if some kind of pier was reestablished. The dock that had been laboriously constructed by the inhabitants to help them have access to the outer world was destroyed in the onslaught of Davido as was all the habitation that the natives had for centuries made to house themselves. Truthfully, once ashore, there is little of interest for tourists to see and there is little if any infrastructure. The island's arable land had been hard to come by due to it's rockiness, yet vegetation and trees have managed to find a foothold and the wildlife that exists is of a small nature. Of course, there are birds, none native to the island, and naturalists have made a study of the island's animal population. The largest animal is a green monkey that apparently was brought to the island from the Old World at some point. The devastation of Davido made the inhabitants eager for an easier life and that is where the Billionaire Bundle came in."

The view switched to a lion attacking a gazelle. Then to a tiger chasing and catching a small deer. Again these film clips ran several times as Jamie continued.

"Seven billionaires, as yet unidentified, purchased a 10-year lease on the island for fifty million dollars. But why, you might ask, just as we did? The answer came from a source which refuses to be identified. The plans are to stock the island with predators from all continents, except Antarctica of course, and see which one survives. It will be televised in a weekly series showing how battles for food ensue because there won't be much there for big predators such as lions and tigers to eat. Our source says that they will turn against each other in a fight for survival until only one is left – the Deadliest Predator."

PART I

CONCEPTION

Boutique Hotel First Floor

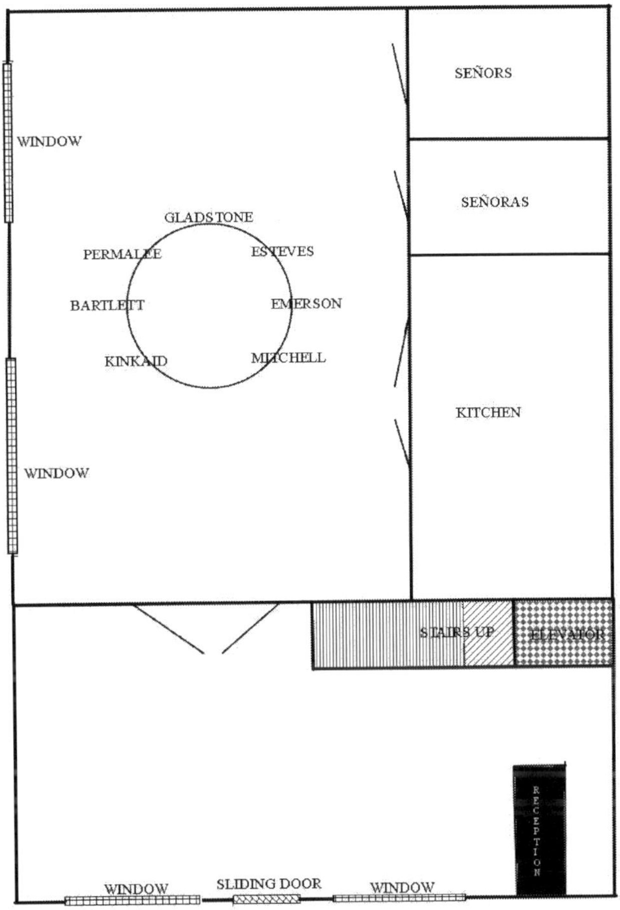

Chapter 1

The building in which the meeting was held was being developed as a small boutique hotel in the host city. At the time of the meeting, the hotel had been vacant of guests for six months as renovations were being made. Entrance to the lobby was through two bulletproof glass doors which were opened when the card that was sent to the invitee – with other directions at the time of the invitee's acceptance of the invitation – was detected by a scanner within the designated five-minute period. Unknown to the invitees was that all windows and doors on the first floor were bulletproof, and state-of-the-art electronics prevented any snooping either visually or electronically.

The meeting room was the hotel's dining room off the lobby and an invitee was admitted after both a thorough electronic scan and a physical body search in the lobby. The only furniture in the dining room were the table and chairs. The round tabletop – reminiscent of the Round Table of King Arthur – was one solid piece of alternating one-inch strips of ebony and cherry, sanded and handfinished with wax. When it had been installed in the room, it had been covered with one piece of glass ostensibly to prevent any watermarks or senseless doodling. There was no concern with a doodling problem this day because no implements of any kind were permitted in the room. All participants had been told in advance, and no one had argued because of the subject matter. Still, everyone had been thoroughly searched and again no one had complained although one said, "I have never before had a search in which everybody part was touched. My only regret is that the searcher was a man." Watermarks would have been a concern because everyone had a crystal glass with ice and a liquid of choice. The person who brought the glasses and refilled them was only permitted in the room before the meeting started and during the ten-minute break every hour, just like a classroom, except there was no teacher. The seven chairs were all wooden armchairs which reminded some of the Bundle of university chairs. The chairs were made like the table but with black leather cushions on the seats. On the table in front of each seat was a small plastic package containing an earbud with a short extension not more than an inch in length that was obviously a microphone and an antenna. An engraved card with the package told the person to put the earbud in when he/she sat down.

The first man to enter the dining room was Harvey Gladstone. He had arrived at the door to the hotel at 7:59 a.m. and stuck his card into the slot. But nothing happened. His directions had been clear: "Use the enclosed key card to enter the hotel doors between 8:00:00 a.m. and 8:04:59 a.m." He looked at his watch and waited. When it changed to 8:00:00 a.m., he stuck his card into the slot and the doors slid open quietly, and he entered. After clearing security, he had entered the meeting room through the double doors which opened automatically and then closed behind him. He was short – if five feet eight is short – and weighed two hundred fifty pounds. His friends called him "Stubby" because he looked like Stubby Kaye and his ringtone was "Sit Down You're Rocking the Boat." He was wearing a dark suit bought off the rack at XL & More Men's Store. He had money enough to buy custom-made suits from anyone he wanted, but clothes were not important to him. As he said, "You put a Gucci suit on a snowman, it's still a snowman." He was a well-to-do real estate developer who was already wealthy when the 2005 recession hit. At the low point of the recession, he gambled and bought real estate for a quarter on the dollar. One of his buys was in north Phoenix, Arizona where he bought a large development intended for fifty million-dollar-homes, but only four lots of the hundred had been sold and houses built. He got the development rezoned, divided the lots in half, and sold them for the original price with homes going for $450,000 to $750,000. The owners of the four mansions in existence when he had purchased the remaining lots were not happy when the value of their investments was cut in half.

Assessing the table setup, Harvey Gladstone chose the seat facing the door, so he could see his fellow invitees as they entered. No sooner had he settled himself, then the butler set down a crystal tumbler half filled with ice and then filled it three quarters full of Jack Daniel's Tennessee Fire.

"If you need anything else, Mr. Gladstone, my name is Stefaan Declercq." He pronounced his name as DE•clerk. "People call me 'Declercq.'"

Gladstone picked up the glass and took a sip. "How did you …," He began and then stopped when he realized that Declercq had already disappeared back into the kitchen through one of the doors on the left as Harvey sat. He sat alone for almost twenty-five minutes because invitees were admitted in twenty-minute intervals – a five-minute interval to present their invitation, ten minutes to pass security, and five minutes to spare. Harvey had been punctual presenting his card at ten seconds past eight o'clock and had entered the meeting room at 8:11 a.m. The next guest would not be able to enter the hotel until 8:20 a.m. and had until 8:24:59 a.m. or the front doors would not open.

Monica Bartlett was the second to arrive. She was twenty-three and was the newest rock sensation from England. She had won *Britain Has Music* in a landslide with her original song "The Slag Has Heart." Four record companies vied for her contract with Detroit's Soul Mate Records hocking its soul to give her a $350,000,000 signing bonus. They made it back quickly with *The Slag Has Heart* hitting platinum in a week, and her next two *I'm No Slut* and *He's My Cocksman* following the platinum ride. Her video for *I'm No Slut*" featured her in a skintight silver mesh dress which left nothing to one's imagination, especially the fact that she was a true redhead. Her first U.S. tour was a sellout at all sites within minutes. The crowds, while enthusiastic, were well behaved after an incident at the first stop in Yankee Stadium when a fan tried to get on the stage after disrobing revealed body paint saying "Slut Mutt" on his back. Once he had been secured and removed to the cheers and jeers of the crowd, Monica had said, "Any more uncivilized displays and I'm leaving, and I won't come back." She opened her next show in Cleveland two days later with the debut of *Act Nice or I Won't Be Back* which rocketed to #1 and platinum in record time.

She didn't belong in the group that was assembling in the room mainly because of her age, but she hoped that she had sense enough to keep her mouth shut and just listen. Expressing her youth and status, she wore cherry red leather pants, black crocodile knee high boots, and a black leather jacket over a skin-tight black tank top.

Entering the room, she evaluated the situation and chose a seat at what she thought was the eight o'clock position assuming that Gladstone was at twelve o'clock. She observed Declercq dressed in a black tuxedo and wearing white gloves emerging from one of the kitchen's doors with a silver tray bearing two crystal glasses. Her eyes followed him, and he circled the table and stopped behind her. Soon his arm and hand appeared on her right side and placed a crystal champagne glass filled with champagne in front of her as he introduced himself as he had to Harvey Gladstone. The arm and hand vanished and then reappeared with a crystal tumbler full of ice and water. The arm was withdrawn, and she watched as he reappeared on her left and walked back to the kitchen disappearing through the other door.

"Is that what you wanted to drink?" Harvey asked.

"Well, I don't usually drink alcohol in the morning," Monica replied, "but I think I will make an exception today."

She picked up her champagne glass and took a sip.

"Fantastic," she said and proceeded to tell Mr. Gladstone the vintage.

As she did so, Declercq reappeared from the kitchen bearing a single glass on his silver tray. He approached Harvey's seat from behind, picked up the glass from the tray and placed it on the table on Harvey right side. Stepping to the left, he removed the first glass which Harvey had drained, placed it on the tray and headed for the kitchen.

"Could I have some water, please Declercq?," Harvey asked after him. There was no sign of acknowledgement from Declercq, but shortly after disappearing into the kitchen he reappeared with a single glass on the tray. Shortly he set down a tumbler-sized glass of water and ice, and then, as silently as before, disappeared into the kitchen.

"Sometimes I wonder if he can speak," Harvey said, and Monica giggled.

"You don't go to high class restaurants, do you?" Monica said after taking another sip of champagne.

"No need," Harvey said. "I can get the food I want at a tenth of the price and enjoy it more."

This elicited another giggle from Monica.

"What do you do that got you invited to this meeting?" Harvey asked.

Monica looked at him in amazement.

"You don't know who I am?" she said.

"I am afraid not," Harvey Gladstone said, "Any more that than you know who I am. By the way, I am Harvey Gladstone and I deal in real estate."

"Glad to meet you, Harvey Gladstone. I'm Monica Bartlett and I won *Britain Has Music* this year."

"Sorry," Harvey said. "I am not a music buff. Especially this modern stuff. No offense."

"None taken," Monica said and the two were silent awaiting the arrival of the next invitee.

Chapter 2

Issaack Kincaid was the third of the "Billionaire Bundle" – as they would become known – to enter the room. If the two already in the room had been watching the time and had known the time interval being used by their host, they would have known that he entered the meeting room at 8:57 a.m. with only three minutes left in the allotted twenty. He was dressed in a black denim three-piece suit which looked like it had been designed by Burberry and it had. The material had been dyed to match his hair. Under the vest he wore only a silk white t-shirt. Black glasses with round lenses made him look like an owl, which his green eyes only accented. He wasn't much older than Monica. He qualified for the group when his fledgling Foto-Grotto social page went from infancy to full blown viral sensation with its ability to upload images and film clips at unprecedented speed, combined with a censoring ability that stopped 99% of anti-social blogs, murders, and eroticism. Anything hinting at unlawful content was sent to the FBI and CIA for proper handling. Google tried to buy him out, but he wouldn't sell until Microsoft and Apple entered the bidding for not only the dot com but for Issaack's forte - programming. However, he wasn't willing to sell himself, only his progeny. With the sale consummated, he walked away with his next project ready to launch, but there was no hint in the media as to what it was.

Issaack stood just inside the doors and surveyed the room. Then he walked to and took a seat at what would have been several minutes past the six o'clock position and faced Harvey with Monica on his left. No sooner had he sat down than Declercq appeared bearing a tray with one glass upon it. Monica watched it and guessed that it was beer. Declercq stopped behind Issaack, picked up the glass from the tray, set it down on Issaack's right side as he introduced himself. He then continued on around the table glancing at each individual's glasses to ascertain the need for replacement and then disappeared into the kitchen.

"I am not accustomed to drinking at this time of the day, but I need this," Issaack said and picked up the crystal beer stein, lifted it toward each of them in silent salute or toast, and took a deep draft. When he replaced the glass on the table, it was half empty.

"You're Issaack Kinkaid, aren't you?" Harvey Gladstone said.

"Yes, how did you know?" Issaack acknowledged.

"I watch the news and follow the stock exchange," Harvey Gladstone answered. "That's all television is good for. I'm Harvey Gladstone. I'm in real estate."

"Pleased to meet you," Issaack said. "And you're Monica Bartlett. I love 'The Slag Has Heart.'"

"Thank you," Monica said. "Are you a fan?"

"No, I don't really have time for music," Issaack said, "but I watched you win *Britain has Music.* Your presentation of the song was fantastic."

"Now I know who you are," Harvey said. "I saw that video where you were … uhh … well, sort of showing everything."

Monica blushed. "I'll never do that again. I didn't realize I would look so nude. My parents will never forgive me."

"They will if you give them some of the money," Harvey said.

Monica looked at him with a mixture of disdain and questioning.

The three of them talked for a few minutes and then heard some kind of commotion coming from the lobby. Heavy metal shutters covered the windows in seconds and the lights increased in brightness. Issaack started to get up when Declercq appeared from the kitchen and walked rapidly to the door and stood off to the right side facing the table. If they had really paid attention they would have noticed the slight bulge suggesting a shoulder holster, but only one of them did.

"Please don't get up," Declercq said. "There is nothing to worry about. Just a misunderstanding with the meeting's regulations."

Issaack sat back down and glanced at each of the other two. Monica appeared apprehensive and Harvey Gladstone had finished his Tennessee Fire.

In few minutes, the shutters opened silently, the lights went back to their normal illuminations and Declercq walked around the table glancing at glasses. "Everything's fine," he said and disappeared into the kitchen only to reappear with another glass of Tennessee Fire and another beer for Issaack. He then disappeared into the kitchen with the empty glasses.

It was a silence-filled fifteen minutes before the next person entered the room. Harvey Gladstone recognized him and knew that he was the reason why the meeting was being held in Cartagena, Colombia. Ramiro Esteves was the head of one of the biggest drug cartels in the world. This was his first public appearance in five years because he risked being killed or kidnapped by his rivals or arrested and deported to the United States. His reception in the anteroom of the "Board Room," as it came to be known, had been anything but civil. His arrival was heralded by two swarthy clean-shaven men of dubious origin dressed in dark pants and coats entering through the double doors. Simultaneously heavy deadbolts shot from the floor and into the dual doors leading into the Board Room rendering the steel doors virtually impenetrable. The noise of the bolts was the noise heard by those already in the Board Room. Declercq had been alerted from the moment the two men had entered the lobby.

Underneath the coats of the two bodyguards were sparkling white starched shirts accented by white leather belts indicating shoulder holsters by the bulges in their jackets – the one on the right bulging on the left and the one on the left, on the right. Their progress toward the Board Room was halted by two equally impressive guards, who were not nearly as swarthy but taller, heavier, and more threatening because they were armed with Uzis. Between them was Symon Sheetz, who towered above his compatriots by a head. He was dressed in a black suit, black silk shirt with a black silk tie, all exquisitely tailored, and made one wonder whether he should be in the Board Room rather than checking and supervising the security clearance of those who were invited to the meeting.

"Gentlemen," Sheetz began, in unaccented Portuguese although it pained him to address them in such a manner, "you are not on the list, so I must ask you to leave."

The swarthier of the two bodyguards, who were stopped by the imposing barrier of the three, looked at the other, shrugged and both started to pull their weapons out of their holsters. Their movements were halted by two simultaneous events, one physical and one vocal. The physical action was the two Uzis being thrust violently yet non-lethally into their chests pinning their gun hands to their chests just shy of their guns as the two security guards stepped forward. The vocal action was a strong voice uttering ***"NÃO"*** ("No" in Portuguese). Both actions brought everything to a halt as Ramiro Esteves entered the room through the double doors which had closed behind the swarthy two. Just as Symon Sheetz was dressed all in black accented by a head of perfectly coiffed white hair belaying his age of thirty-five, Ramiro Esteves was dressed all in white. The material was linen and his hair an unruly yet oily mess of natural black. As much as Symon Sheetz towered over the swarthy duo, they towered over Ramiro Esteves. His brown eyes peered out from under a heavy brow. Between his eyes was the start of a hawk nose, which had been broken numerous times in his youth. Under the nose and above a perpetually smiling mouth exhibiting perfect brilliantly white natural teeth was a razor thin mustache that only close examination would reveal was not penciled on. The real fault of an otherwise impressive face was the chin or lack thereof. It was this fault that had precipitated the fights in his teen years in which his nose had been broken. These fights had continued until an aggressor had discovered a line of blood seeping across his knuckles. Ramiro Esteves was standing with empty hands beckoning his attacker to return for more. No one could figure out how he had done it or would venture to see whether it would happen again. As the mystique surrounding Ramiro Esteves increased, so did his power. Even now, thirty-two years after he received his nickname of Switchblade, no one would mess with him. Until now.

"My men merely wizh to azcertain that the room is zafe for me to enter." He said switching to English which had been specified as the official language of the meeting. He didn't like English because the malformation of his jaw gave him a terrible time with English esses.

"Señor Esteves," responded Symon Sheetz. "If you do not believe that your host has made the meeting place perfectly safe as was guaranteed in your invitation, please feel free not to attend. If you choose to attend, your ..." Sheetz looked at the swarthy two as he searched his English vocabulary for a proper word and chose "… assistants will have to depart the premises until you ask us to summon them either when the meeting adjourns, or you choose to leave."

Ramiro Esteves stood as though considering the obvious affront to his stature and whether it was worth his time to adhere to the conditions as set forth in the invitation or to turn and leave. At this point, the latter would mean only an affront to his dignity and mystique. Also, and most important, at least in the eyes of the inviter, it would mean not knowing what opportunity he was missing. The invitation had read:

> You are invited to attend a meeting to provide you with a unique business opportunity. This proposition, should you decide to accept it, is potentially not one which will provide a return on your investment . If successful – and that is by best estimate a 70-30 proposition – at worst, you will earn a place in history of scientific investigation. At best, acclaim in the world press and perhaps a partial recoup of your investment.
>
> Your acceptance of this invitation will necessitate a deposit of

> one hundred million dollars U.S. in a secure account, method of deposit to be given to you upon your acceptance. After attending this meeting, those funds will remain in the account to be used in the advancement of this project for ten years. If you choose not to participate, the funds will remain gathering interest for ten years which is the anticipated time frame for the project. If you have remained silent about this project during this time, your deposit will be returned to you with interest estimated to be a minimum of ten per cent.

The remainder of the invitation held the conditions under which the invitee must comply to attend: No other person(s) allowed on the premises in which the meeting would be held, no electronics or mechanical devices of any form, no cameras, no methods of recording any portion of the meeting other than one's memory.

His mind having raced through the options, Ramiro Esteves shrugged and said, "Paz."

The swarthy duo immediately relaxed, and the Uzis' pressure lessened enough for hands to be removed, but not enough for pistols to be withdrawn from holsters. The swarthy duo separated, turning left and right, and passed through the doors and out into the sunshine of the early morning. After submitting to the security examination, Ramiro Esteves entered the meeting room through the door held open by Symon Sheetz. Turning around after closing the door, Symon

Sheetz saw that the next guest was already standing inside the double doors.

Chapter 3

Entering the Board Room, Ramiro Esteves made a counterclockwise circuit of the room, finding the doors to the kitchen unresponsive, first to his touch and then his push. Continuing on to the restroom doors marked "Señoras" and "Señors," his efforts to open the door to the Señoras failed. The second opened under his touch, and he went in and inspected it finding nothing unusual. He continued on to the windows, rapping on them and peering at them. Apparently satisfied with his inspection, he turned to the table and saw the three looking at him.

"You may call me Juan," he said as he proceeded to the chair at the approximate two o'clock position so that he could get a better look at Monica.

"We will call you 'Juan,' if that is what you want," Harvey Gladstone said, "But we all know who you are."

He looked at Monica and Issaack who nodded their agreement. At this moment, Declercq stopped behind Esteves to his right and introduced himself as he set down a crystal tumbler filled with a clear reddish-brown liquid.

Esteves looked at it and then picked it up, holding it up to the light. Lowering it, he swirled the liquid gently in the glass and then lifted it to his nose.

"I would be glad to test it if you want, Juan," Harvey Gladstone said. "Havana Club Máximo is one of my favorite rums."

"I don't like rum," Monica said. "Gives me the hiccups."

"A little rich for my taste," Issaack said. "I don't mean I can't afford it, but the taste."

As Esteves had listened to this comradic banter, he had lifted the glass to his lips and taken a taste. Lowering the glass, he seemed to be swirling the rum around in his mouth before swallowing it. He let it sit in his stomach for a moment and then shrugged and downed the entire glass. Then he smiled and said to them, "As you wish. I am Ramiro Estevez."

At this juncture, the doors from the lobby opened and they all looked to see who was coming in.

Phillip Parmelee was so brown one would have thought him a native of some Caribbean or south sea island. Actually, he was 100% Caucasian (he had his DNA tested and knew this for a fact) and was brown only because of the extensive amount of time spent in the sun despite his fastidious use of sunscreen. He was six feet three inches and two hundred pounds of muscle with 1% body fat. His manner of dress exhibited his preference for the out of doors. This may have been a business meeting, but no dress code was given, and he had come dressed as he usually did going out in public. He wore a Caribbean blue t-shirt on the back of which was a map of the eastern Caribbean islands of Dominica and Martinique. And between the islands was a graphic of what was obviously a sunken ship with the words Santa Teresa written under it in gold. On the front of the t-shirt, over the part of the chest where a pocket would be, was replicated the ship and its name although smaller this time. On his feet were thongs. His one acceptance of the fact that he was attending an extremely important meeting was that he was wearing long pants – a new pair of khakis that he had taken the tags off this morning. The belt that he used to hold the pants up was a piece of hemp rope and it was used only because the pants would have slid down his bony frame within ten steps without it. The t-shirt was the reason for his invitation. Not the shirt itself, but the ship that was emblazoned upon it. When asked about it, he would tell the following story, "*I had been scuba diving in international waters along an isolated reef off the southwest coast of Dominica. With me was Bill Rutgers, my business partner, who had already started for the surface when a great white shark had made a run at me. Or at least I thought he had. Neither of us had done anything to provoke the fish, but I am a firm believer in running away to live to fight another day. A quick look around had revealed a hole in the reef that looked big enough for me to fit through and toward it I went, kicking my flippers wildly. Reaching the hole, I grabbed the sides and pulled to help propel myself in, quickly stretching out an arm in front to prevent crashing into a wall. I was expecting to find a small cave, but when I stopped, I realized I was in a room. I turned on my light – always carry one when diving – and realized that I was in a ship. I could make out chests and other things lying around. I knew that my time was short, so I gathered a few things in a net bag I always carry and then carefully exited the ... well, I exited what turned out to be the Santa Teresa. Jaws wasn't around – at least that I could see – and I surfaced quickly but cautiously. When I pulled myself up on the dive platform at the back of the boat, I yelled for Bill, but there was no answer. When I climbed up on deck, I didn't see any sign that he had been there. I looked around the boat and over the side for signs of him, but there was nothing. I put the net bag down without looking in it, changed air tanks, grabbed two spear guns and went back in the water. I searched around for half an hour and found nothing, and I was nearing my physical limit as well as my time underwater. Back on the boat I called for help over the radio. A Dominican Coast Guard boat with divers came out, but nothing was found."*

That was his story and he was sticking to it, but there were always questions about what really happened when he revealed that he had discovered the *Santa Teresa*, a Spanish treasure ship on the way home to Spain from Mexico. Apparently she had been in a storm and sunk to settle to rest next to – and becoming part of – the reef. It is possible that she was attacked by pirates and scuttled to save the gold, but there were no signs of any damage other than what age would do. The find was worth 2.5 billion dollars and being in international waters, it was all his.

The truth of the story is that Bill Rutgers had discovered the hole and had come out with the bag shaking it to show Phil that there was something important and headed for the surface. On their boat, they discovered that what the bag held was a gold goblet and plate and several doubloons. They had danced and celebrated and gotten drunk, all while still in their wet suits. Well, at least Bill had gotten drunk or drunker than he should have. Phil was sober enough and selfish enough with the thought of fame and enormous riches to take advantage of the opportunity. Seizing a gaff from the rack and swinging it, he hit Bill in the head with the metal handle and knocked him unconscious. Working quickly, he marked the site with an underwater beacon, and moved the boat several miles away into deeper water. He used fish they had speared for dinner as chum. When several sharks had appeared and were sufficiently frenzied (and it doesn't take much when a shark is hungry) he had slit Bill's hands and let the blood drip into the water to add to the frenzy. Then he rolled Bill – whom Phil had made certain would not regain consciousness – into the water clad in his scuba gear and let the sharks finish their feast. The reason that no sign of Bill was found was that when Phil called for help he was anchored sufficiently close to the reef to make his story plausible but was two miles from where he had dumped Bill.

He stood just inside the doors to the lobby and looked at the assemblage. Then he pointed and said, "Ramiro Esteves, Issaack Kinkaid, Monica Bartlett, and …"

"Oh, I'm Harvey Gladstone, real estate," Harvey said, a bit miffed that he hadn't been recognized.

"Oh, yes. 'And the devil will drag you under by the sharp lapels of your checkered coat'…"

And Monica, Issaack and Harvey chimed in "Sit down you're rocking the boat." And they all laughed.

"What'z zat," Ramiro said, "Zome Broadyway zhow zong? I donz't know Broadyway."

"No matter," Phil said. "We'll explain it to you when we have time."

Phil laughed under his breath and walked and took the chair at approximately the ten o'clock position. No sooner was he seated than the entry door to the kitchen opened and Declercq entered the Board Room bearing several glasses on his tray. He stopped between Monica and Phil, introduced himself, and lowered the tray for Phil to see.

"I'm sorry, sir," he said. "We were able to narrow your likes down to these three, but you don't seem to have a preference."

Phil looked at the selection and pointed: "Knobs Creek on the rocks, Macallan Single Malt on the rocks, and … I don't know what that is." Phil pointed at the third glass containing a dark red liquid in an amber glass.

Declercq appeared surprised at Phil's reaction. "I'm sorry, sir. That was one of the three on the list I was given."

"Well, what is it?"

"Why Dead Man's Chest Rum, neat," replied Declercq.

"What is this? Some kind of a sick joke?" Phil sounded and appeared to be incensed.

"Oh, no, sir. I … there must be some kind of terrible mistake. I will take it back."

"Relax, Phil," Issaack said. "Mistakes happen. That happens to be one of my favorites and if you don't want it, I will take it."

"Me too," Gladstone said. "I like that."

The bluster seemed to go out of Phil and he relaxed and smiled. "I've never tried it." He looked up at Declercq whose face showed that he was troubled, and it was a look that not even the best actors in the world could give easily. "Relax," Phil said. "I'll take all three. I sense it might be a hard day."

The tension in Declercq's face disappeared, and he put the three drinks on the table in front of Phil. Monica reached over and took the glass of Dead Man's Chest.

"May I?" she said.

Phil smiled.

"Indeed you may, Ms. Bartlett. Indeed you may."

Chapter 4

The tension within the group was completely gone eight minutes later when the door opened, and the sixth person entered the room. Her entrance was like her – there but not overpowering.

Unlike the others in the Billionaire Bundle, Gloria Grendel Mitchell was not self-made, but her wealth was in family money and she was currently the power behind Family Dollar Tree, a growing chain of merchandise marts. She was five feet nine, one hundred forty pounds tending more to flab than muscle, with non-descript features and a figure that said she was female but wasn't the kind to draw attention. In her mid-fifties, she wore her hair short and was considered a dyke when people first met her. However, her three children by three different husbands – all of whom barely lasted past birth of their progeny – showed that not to be necessarily true. Put in that perspective, her name should have been Gloria Ann Grendel Wallace Forsythe Mitchell.

She was wearing a dark gray department store bought pants suit with a long sleeved pink blouse with a ruffle down the front and fire topaz cufflinks rather than buttons. She was carrying a large shoulder bag that had taken ten minutes to go through even though the scanner and all the other electronic gear installed for this meeting had indicated that she was clean. Symon Sheetz was leaving nothing to chance. Upon entering the room, she had looked at the table and then chosen a seat opposite Monica Bartlett.

"I'm Gloria...," she began when the sound of gunfire could be heard and immediately thereafter, shutters closed over all the windows and the room's illumination brightened. None of this was noticeable to the people at the table because to a one they were now under the table. Almost simultaneously with the closing of the shutters, there was the sound of a silver tray hitting the floor and the crash of at least one crystal glass. Declercq had just come out the kitchen door when the gunfire had sounded. He had let go of the tray and gone back into the kitchen, then returned with an automatic rifle in his hands and a bandolier with extra clips and what appeared to be hand grenades over his left shoulder.

"You're safe in here," Declercq said, only to have the period at the end of his sentence punctuated with an explosion that shook the room. "That's a handheld missile of some type," Declercq said as he took a stance beside the two doors from the foyer, the bolts of which had been thrown when the shutters started closing.

"What's happening?" Issaack asked as he got up from the floor and started toward the doors.

"Stay at the table," Declercq said, turning so that his weapon pointed in Issaack's general direction. "You can't do anything, and you are perfectly safe."

In the background of Declercq's words, the sound of more gunfire and sirens were evident.

"I'm too young to die," Monica said, tears starting to pour down her face.

"Don't worry, miss," Declercq said, "You're not going to die today."

He stood still listening and then said, "It's over."

As the rest of the Bundle started to get up, the bolts in the door were withdrawn and Symon Sheetz came through the door followed by one of the security guards. Like Declercq, Symon Sheetz was armed with an automatic weapon, although his was an Uzi.

"Everyone okay?" Sheetz asked.

"What the hell is going on?" Gladstone demanded.

"We suspect that there was an assassination attempt on Mr. Esteves," Sheetz responded. "We had hoped that he hadn't been followed, but either they're very good or Mr. Esteves was a little sloppy in his travels."

The look on Ramiro's face showed that he was not happy with the latter of the two choices.

"Who's they?" Gloria asked.

"I don't know for certain, maybe Mr. Esteves has an answer. We were aware that something might happen and were prepared as were the police. The assassination team – if that's what they were – got off one round and then were silenced."

"What if there are more?" Gloria asked.

"We doubt that there are, but, if so, they have seen some of what we can retaliate with and will probably take off."

"Well, regardless, I need to use the restroom. Can someone point it out?"

Declercq pointed to one of the two doors at the rear of the room on the same wall as the kitchen and Gloria started for them.

"I'll come also if you don't mind," Monica said. She giggled. "I haven't peed in my knickers since I was … who knows, I was young that's all I know."

"We apologize for this unfortunate event," Sheetz said. "Your host will understand if any of you decide to withdraw at this time. If you do, your deposit will be completely returned."

"Withdraw!" Phil exclaimed. "Hell, I came here for some excitement although I wasn't expecting this. I thought I might be on the shooting end, not the bullet end. Next time, give me a weapon. I know how to handle guns."

Symon Sheetz smiled. "That may be so, Mr. Parmalee, but I think it will be best to leave any armaments in the hands of professionals."

His statement was punctuated with the shutters over the windows opening and the room's illumination returning to its former brightness.

"Now, if you will excuse me," Sheetz said, "I will go and see to our last invitee who had just gotten inside when the fracas began."

He turned and walked through the doorway followed by the security guard. Declercq started for the kitchen as a woman dressed in a mid-length black dress with a white lace apron came out of the kitchen with a brush, dustpan and rag and started to clean up the mess from Declercq's tray.

"I think a break to relieve myself is in order," Issaack said and started for the restroom.

"Sounds like a plan," Gladstone said.

"Certamente (certainly)," Ramiro said.

Phil Parmalee was left alone at the table – all of his glasses empty in front of him.

Chapter 5

"Anyone hurt?" The last invitee had taken a chair in the hotel's foyer as he had been instructed and watched and listened to the sounds of the invasion. He heard the sounds of the shutters being opened in the Board Room and watched the ones being opened on the lobby windows. He looked up as he heard Symon Sheetz and the security guard return through the doors from the Board Room. The other security guard had been standing behind a section of the outside wall next to the exterior doors, weapon at the ready, eyes moving, alert for any attempt at intrusion.

"No, just disquieted a bit," Symon Sheetz replied. "Sorry for the delay, Mr. Emerson. Now if you will please step over here and empty your pockets." As he was talking, Symon Sheetz had put his Uzi and bandolier on hooks behind the desk where he would have sat if he had had time which he hadn't since the first guest arrived.

Ralph Waldorf Emerson was an electrical engineer with a degree from M.I.T. He had gone to work for an automobile battery company where he had helped develop a longer lasting battery for electrical cars. Having to share his patent with his coworker Julian Hitchcock and his company did not make him happy. So, he borrowed money and started his own battery company using a much better variant in his batteries and then moved on to the place where the batteries were being used – electric cars. His first car was small but ideal for people who lived in cities and just needed a runabout. Though expensive, its sleek design, long battery life and fast recharging made it appeal to yuppies and it was difficult to keep up with the demand during the first year. At the end of the year, he released his bigger SUV and they sold like hotcakes. The IPO of his company's stock made him a billionaire overnight and he began to enjoy life and the excitement that it offered.

As he had been instructed, Waldo – as he was referred to by his friends – walked over to the desk and put his wallet, change, money clip and handkerchief into a dish which Symon Sheetz put into a small scanner. As the disk disappeared through the small doorway carried by the conveyor belt, Symon Sheetz motioned that Waldo should step into the state-of-the-art body scanner. Waldo complied, raised his arms and stood motionless for the required three seconds. Then he exited and one of the security guards passed the handheld scanner over Waldo and then set it down.

"Body search okay, Mr. Emerson?" the security guard asked.

"Whatever you need to do," Waldo said. "Can't be any worse than the one I had at the Dubai airport."

When the guard finished the body search, he handed Waldo the dish with his belongings. As he was putting them into his pocket, Symon Sheetz asked, "What was this 'body search' at the Dubai airport?"

"Well, it was equaled here" Waldo said. "Every part of my body was touched."

"We leave nothing to chance," Sheetz said. "Our host requires that."

"Bet the women must have been a little upset with the intrusion," Waldo said.

"Not at all," Sheetz said, "Gretel searched the women," he indicated the other security guard. Waldo looked and realized, upon more than a cursory examination, that the other security guard, while as big as her male companion, was indeed a woman.

"I would guess that your name is Hansel," Waldo said to the guard who had searched him.

"No, but that's what they call me when I work with Gretel. My given name is Harry."

Waldo laughed and said, "Why didn't they call her 'Sally'?"

Then, without waiting for an answer, walked through the doors into the meeting room as indicated by Symon Sheetz. His entry wasn't dazzling although his Honolulu Blue shirt under a dark blue sport coat, charcoal black Lee jeans and black topsiders with white socks wasn't exactly subdued. He was greeted by six pairs of eyes fixed perfectly on him. "Hello," he said feeling stupid as he said it, "I'm ..."

"Ralph Waldorf Emerson" came out of five of the mouths. Only Ramiro didn't know who he was. There was one seat remaining between Ramiro and Mitchell. He noted that, other than the six at the table, the only other person in the room was a woman dressed in black with a white bib apron with large straps over the shoulders. She was offering a tray filled with pastries to the beautiful blonde woman seated almost straight across from him. He did the math - seven people. 8.57 minutes per person. Using Harvey Gladstone as 12:00, he was sitting at seventeen past, so she was seventeen till or forty-three past, give or take some seconds either way. Pulling out his chair and sitting down he turned to his left to introduce himself to the dowager lady sitting there when he felt a presence behind him and to his right. Startled, he turned that way and bumped

Declercq's arm as he was setting down as glass in front of him.

"I'm sorry, sir," Declercq said as some of the liquid spilled on Waldo's pants.

"My fault actually," Waldo said. "This is polyester, and it won't sink in."

"If you'll let me, Mr. Emerson," Declercq said as he set the wine glass on the table and picked up a white napkin off the silver tray he held in his left hand. He quickly wiped the liquid sitting on Waldo's pants and then disappeared. Waldo tried to see where he had gone, but his vision was blocked by a dream in black and white. The waitress was standing between him and Esteves and holding a tray down so that he could see the pastry selection.

"I'm afraid the croissants are gone," she said with a sultry voice that caused his toes to tingle and his manhood to start to harden. She might as well have said, "*Why don't we go to your room and get acquainted.*"

"That's fine," he managed to say. "What I would prefer is some brie with crackers. Maybe some cherry preserves."

"*Oh, the cherry's been gone a long time,*" he expected her to say and had to blink and take a deep breath to get back to reality.

She picked up a saucer from the other side of the tray and set it down in front of him. A nice wedge of brie with four Townhouse crackers, and a tablespoon of cherry preserves. Then she put a white napkin on the table and set a cheese knife on top of it.

"Can I get you anything else, Mr. Emerson?"

"Uhm …" he couldn't say anything without making it sound stupid. "No, I'm fine." *For now - but come back later … and bring your sister.*

And just like a wisp of smoke up a well draught chimney, she was gone and replaced by Declercq who set down a fresh glass of Chateau Ste. Michelle chardonnay and like the waitress vanished like a magician's illusion.

It was just a little too much for Waldo after the gunfire and … he turned back to the table and was reaching for the second glass of wine – the first glass having gone with Declercq – when a voice seeming to come from the center of the table said, "I would like to welcome you all. Thank you for coming."

Waldo noticed that the others seemed to be looking around for the speaker but seeing no one.

"Look down in front of you," the voice said.

They all did and saw the image of a man's face looking up at them from the table's glass cover in the place where their dinner plates would have been placed.

Chapter 6

Monica giggled. "He looks funny."

Her comment was correct because the face they saw was not a real face but more like a cartoon drawing.

Harvey Gladstone said, "Who are you?"

The head laughed. "I am your host. Or, as I guess you would say, your host's avatar."

"Well, what is your name?" Phil asked.

"You can call me … Horus."

"Why did you pause like that?" Monica asked.

Horus looked abashed. "Because I was going to make a bad joke at the expense of one of you."

"I like a good joke," Monica said.

"Then lean closer, so the others cannot hear," Horus said softly, and a hand appeared on Monica's screen as Horus disappeared from the others. The hand beckoned her to come closer.

"What happened?" was heard from several of the Bundle. "Where did he go?"

Monica leaned close to the table and turned her head so that her right ear with the ear bud was almost touching the glass top.

"I was going to say," she heard, "You can call me Juan."

Monica shrieked in laughter and sat upright.

"What's so funny?" Gloria asked.

"Him. Horace," answered Monica.

"I didn't hear anything."

"You weren't supposed to," Monica said.

Meanwhile, Horus appeared in front of Phil.

"Mister Parmelee, I must apologize for the drink order. It was not meant to upset you, but our research suggested that it was a favorite drink of yours. You might want to check the security on your computers."

"Not a problem, Horace," Phil said. "Looking back on it, it was funny. That's water over the dam."

"Or under the bridge," Horus said, and his face appeared on all the screens.

"How you do zat?" Ramiro asked.

"Do what?" replied Horus.

"Appear on the table in frontz of uz and be able to talk individually to each of uz."

"Oh, that. Cool, isn't it."

"Yes," came a chorus of voices from the Bundle.

"How come zey can all hear ziz when I waz talking to you?" Ramiro said quizzically.

"Because I felt that your question was one that everyone had and so I wanted them to hear the answer."

"Hear! Hear!" said Waldo.

"Under the table in front of each of you is a black box about the size of a small box of wooden matches, if you can relate to that. Or the size of some of those soap bars in some of the cheaper establishments. There is a small hole drilled in the table – I think 1/32nd of an inch in diameter and a fiber optic cable leads up to the top of the table where there is a network of very thin cables which permit the picture to be shown. Of course, the sound comes from the earbud and the built-in microphone is how you can communicative with me and others. No need to shout.

"Are there any other questions?"

There was a murmur of no's and then Issaack said, "What are we here for?"

"Right to the point as usual, Issaack," Horus answered. "No time for chit-chat. Okay. First, we will talk for fifty minutes and then take a ten-minute break for you to use the restroom and for Stefaan to replenish your drinks."

"Who's Stefaan?" Gloria asked.

"The waiter," Phil said, not waiting for Horus.

"Yes, the waiter," Horus agreed. "His full name is Stefaan Declercq. He prefers to be called 'Declercq.' You might as well know, because he will be around for the entire project. Your waitress's name is Carmen Domingo, she is also the cook and will be around for the entire project. If you want something to eat simply say, 'Carmen, I would like a cookie' or whatever and she will get it for you.

"Lunch will be at 1:00 p.m." A menu appeared on the screen. "Take a look at the menu. Not many choices, but we want to reconvene at 2:00 p.m."

"How long iz ziz meeting going to take?" Ramiro asked.

"That depends on you and by that, I mean all of you. When we need to adjourn for the evening, each of you has a room upstairs. There is a change of clothes for cocktails and dinner, sleepwear, and clothes for tomorrow if needed."

"Wow," Monica said. "I'm impressed."

"Thank you," Horus replied. "Now, while you look at the menu, I am going to take a short break because I have been sitting here since Harvey arrived."

"Wait," said Monica.

"Yes," replied Horus.

"Where's 'here'?"

"Where I am," Horace said.

"That's not an answer," Monica said.

To that question, there was no answer, and Horus vanished from all screens.

And as silently as he always was, Declercq appeared with his tray laden with drink refills and behind him, the waitress who they now knew as Carmen Domingo, with her tray laden with an assortment of pastries and other eatables they might want.

"He said that I should check out my computer security," Phil said. "It seems to me that since he knows what we drink, eat, and wear, we all should be worried about our computer security."

"Not I," Issaack said. "Mine is impenetrable."

Phil laughed. "Did he get your drinks right?"

"Of course," Issaack replied.

"And your food," Monica asked.

"Yes."

"Then I guess your computer isn't as secure as you thought," Waldo said.

Issaack shook his head in disagreement. "There are lots of ways for him to learn about favorite drinks. Good security checks learn that kind of thing. Bartenders know, your tailors know your clothes likes and dislikes, where you eat can give you food preferences. He isn't perfect. Look at how he screwed up with Phil's drink order."

"As you said," Phil answered, "He could have learned things by asking the right people. In my case, maybe he asked the wrong person or asked someone who wanted to be funny."

"Or had a grudge to bear," Waldo said.

As silently as Declercq and Carmen had appeared, they went just as silently. No sooner had the door to the kitchen closed than Horus reappeared.

São Rochelle Post Hurricane Davido

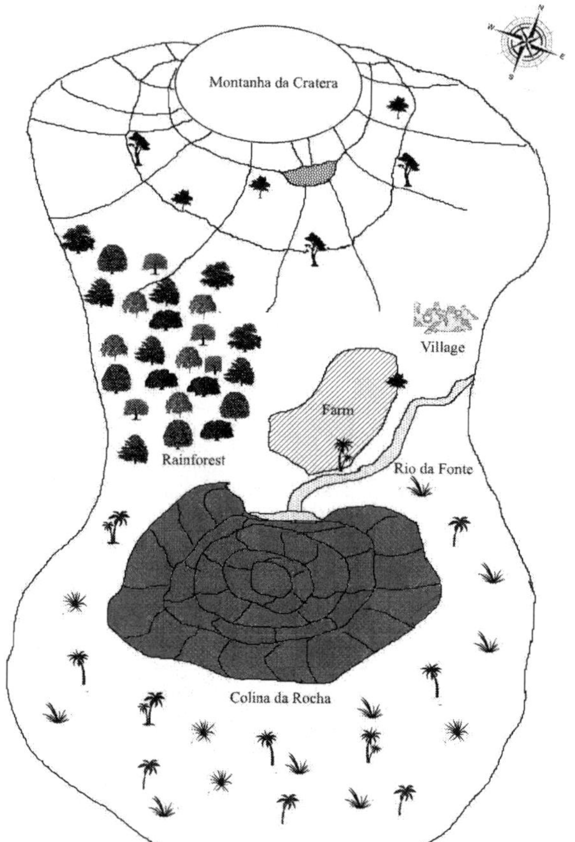

Chapter 7

"Well, I hope we are all ready to start," Horus said. "But first, I realized during the break that there might be a little misunderstanding with my name."

"I doubt it," Monica said. "Horace is easy to remember."

"Well, then," Horus said. "Let me ask you to spell it."

"I – t," Harvey Gladstone said and there was a smattering of laughter.

"Ha, Ha," said Horus. "Spell my … no change that. Spell 'Horus.'"

"Let me," Gloria pipped in. "H – O – R – U – S."

Monica giggled. "That's wrong. H – O …"

"She's right," Horus said. "It is not 'Horace' as in Horace Mann, U.S. Representative and Educator, or Horace Greeley, Editor and Journalist; or Horace Andy…"

"I know him," Monica chimed in. "He's a Jamaican singer and songwriter. He wrote *Skylarking*."

"True," said Horus. "But I am Horus as in the Egyptian tutelary deity."

As he spoke a picture appeared on the table screen in front of them. It showed an ancient Egyptian depiction of a man with the head of a falcon wearing a red and white crown known as a pschent.

"Oh, I get it," Waldo said. "You are leading this session, so you are our teacher or tutor and the name Horus is really the name of the avatar, not your real name."

"You get an A on this little quiz," Horus answered. "Now, let us get back to the reason you were all asked here."

The avatar known as Horus was replaced with a video showing an island surrounded by bright blue water so clear the bottom could be seen quite a distance out.

"This is São Rochelle," the voice of Horus explained. "It is a small volcanic island approximately one hundred miles east of the Bay of Olapoque, which is where the Oyapok River empties. The Oyapok River forms the border between French Guiana and the Brazilian state of Amapa. São Rochelle is four miles by two miles with the length oriented in a north by north-east direction. The water around it is extremely shallow reaching a maximum depth of twenty feet for a quarter mile and fifty feet for half a mile and then it drops quickly."

"That doesn't make it easily accessible by cruise ships, so we aren't talking resort here," Phil said.

"That's correct," Horus said.

"I remember that island," Gloria said. "Hurricane Davido basically obliterated it forcing the population to evacuate."

"Yes," Horus said without the slightest indication of being bothered by the interruptions. "The island is well off the normal hurricane track but somehow Davido didn't adhere to the rules. Now continuing with the island... its only access is on the northeast side where the small Rio da Fonte (or Fountain River) flows into the Atlantic Ocean."

The view changed to a lower view.

"This is the view from a drone starting at the southwest end of the island and proceeding up the middle to the north end. This will give you a quick view of the island.

"The south of the island is basically grass with a few trees. The edge of the island is for all intents and purposes rock anywhere from five feet tall to ten feet tall. As you can see there are rocks everywhere. Not much arable ground to be seen."

"That wouldn't even be fun with a dune buggy or ATV," Waldo said. "Way too many rocks."

"That is an astute observation," Horus said.

"Wow! What's that?" Monica said.

What appeared to be a big pile of rocks appeared in the picture.

"That is Colina da Rocha or Boulder Hill," Horus explained. "It appears to be a solid piece of granite just poking up out of the ground. It is one hundred fifty feet tall. The base is virtually circular with a radius of three-eighths of a mile or a circumference of almost 2.356 miles. If you want that in feet, it is 12,440 feet or 4,147 yards."

The video continued as the drone crossed the top of Colina da Rocha. There were gasps from the Bundle's members as water appeared to be pouring from about three quarters of the way up the side of the rock hill. The water cascaded down into a pool about a third of the way from the bottom.

"The pool is approximately thirty feet long and ten feet wide. Reports are that it is at least twenty feet deep," the voice of Horus intoned over the oohs and aahs. "The water then pours out of the pool and falls straight down into another pool which is more semicircular with the outer edge being carved out of earth and rock. It had been accurately measured as being thirty-five feet deep at the point where the water hits the ground. The water then flows as Rio da Fonte or Fountain River from the base pool across the island to the point where it empties into the Atlantic making the only feasible access to the island."

"What good iz it zen?" Ramiro queried. "Doesn't lookz like you can grow ztuff zere."

"Basically that is correct, Mr. Esteves. There is a small arable portion along the north side of the river where the inhabitants raised enough food to subsist along with the fish which they caught in the ocean and the fish were quite plentiful. Enough to feed them but not enough to make it worth trying to sell."

"It would be difficult to get the fish off the island and into any kind of refrigerator ship," Issaack said. "And you can't have a trawler there because the water is too shallow to make port unless you had a super long pier."

"Quite correct, Mr. Kincaid, and that is the reason the island has never been commercialized. The population at its maximum in the mid-1800s was eighty-two and when the population was evacuated because of the threat of Davido there were twenty-seven people. None of them wished to return."

"How did they get off?" Monica asked.

"The *Caribbean Isle* sent a tender in and took them and their immediate belongings off. It was a good thing that they did because their homes were wiped out."

As Horus was speaking the video showed the remains of the village in which the inhabitants had lived. It was nothing but piles of rough sawn wood timbers and what appeared to be thatching.

"The homes were made from the deciduous trees and few firs that were on the island and the roofs were thatched. There are sufficient palm trees on the southern end of the island to provide fronds for the thatching."

"What's going on?" Phil said as the island started to grow smaller under them.

"We are approaching the volcano," Horus said.

Chapter 8

*"**Volcano!**"* came from the mouths of almost all of the Bundle's members, the exception being Gladstone.

"It's extinct," Gladstone said. "I remember the news when they showed the inhabitants being evacuated. There's no smoke and no sign of activity."

"That is correct," Horus said. "Montanha da Cratera or Crater Mountain, rises three-eighths of a mile above sea level and is two miles across at its base. The crater mouth is a half a mile across. The crater base is one thousand feet below the rim and is solid. There is heat felt there although not too hot to walk on. The temperature at the crater floor never drops under 80° Fahrenheit or 27° Celsius. The floor appears to be solid and the inhabitants thought about building homes there except for access, distance and lack of water. Basically they left it alone. It has trees growing on its slopes and on the Caribbean side there is a small rain forest that provided the population with fruit and some meat from the small rodents and snakes which live there."

"Speaking of wildlife, what happened during the hurricane?" Gloria asked.

"Good question as you will shortly learn," Horus said. "As far as can be determined by our flyovers, some of it survived. We have seen several cows and a horse or two that the people had. We figure they were freed before the evacuation and most likely moved up the slopes of the volcano. The island is so rocky that the water from the rains simply ran off and didn't sit there. All the damage was done by the winds and storm surge. It will take some time, but the island's flora and fauna will recover.

"Any other questions at this point?"

Hearing no one respond, Horus continued, "Then as it is twelve minutes before the hour we will break until 11:00 a.m."

People began moving their chairs back.

"But, the break is not scheduled until ten before the hour, so you must stay seated until then."

"What?" several of the Bundle said.

"Just joking."

Monica giggled, but the others remained silent. Arising from her chair, she caught Gloria's eye and nodded toward the woman's room. Inside their private facility, Monica said, "I'm trying to figure something out about this system Horus is part of. When we go back, you sit where I did."

"I've been doing some wondering also," Gloria agreed. "I think that Horus is a computer. If I am right, it is a pretty smart computer. So, let's try to find out. We can meet back here next break."

"That's a plan," Monica said.

The two left the ladies room and headed back. Gloria reached the table first and went to where Monica had been sitting. There was a fresh glass of champagne there indicating that Declercq had been busy. Across the way where she had been sitting there was a fresh glass of Bodegas Hidalgo La Gitana Manzanilla Sherry. Monica reached the seat and sat down, pulling the chair up to the table and eyeing the glass of sherry. She looked over at Gloria who was sitting at the table and holding up the glass of champagne up as in a toast. Monica lifted the sherry in a similar motion and then took a sip. It was cool and delicious as it slid down her throat. She smiled at Gloria.

When the men were all back at the table, the visage of Horus appeared in front of their places. Monica watched him carefully. He appeared to look at her and then left and right and then back at her.

"You are not in the correct seat, Ms. Whitmore," Horus said. And almost simultaneously, Gloria was told "You are not in the correct seat, Mrs. Mitchell. This is not a game of musical chairs. But if you wish to stay where you are, I am fine with that."

"Gee, Horus," Monica said. "I didn't know that the seats were assigned. I thought we chose where we wanted to sit, and I wanted to talk to Waldo a bit."

"Fine. Anyone else want to change seats?"

Everyone else just heard the second sentence of the last interchange. The others indicated they were perfectly happy being where they were.

"Now, the question to be asked or answered, is 'So what is the interest in São Rochelle?' Is that a correct assumption on my part?" Horus began.

There was a response chorus of yesses from all except Ramiro.

"Mr. Ramiro, is there a problem," Horus asked him.

"No, I am juzt waiting to zee where all ziz iz going." Ramiro responded.

"You are welcome to leave," Horus said, "But because we are already talking about the focus of this meeting, your deposit will be held as was stated in the contract you received."

"Contract?" Ramiro questioned.

"Yes, it was not a signed contact but the conditions that were stipulated went into effect when you accepted the invitation."

"Well, let me azk you zen," Ramiro said. "Doez ziz plan for the izland have anything to do with my buznezz?"

Horus smiled. "You think we would be going into competition with you?"

"I had begun to conzider zat."

Horus laughed. "I am not making fun of you, Mr. Esteves, but nothing could be further from the truth. We are going into competition with no one. Well, maybe one if it were part of the real world. Are you ready to continue?"

"Sim," Ramiro said. "Yez, let uz continue."

Ramiro sat back in his chair and realized the other six were looking at him.

"What?" he said. "Canz't man have opinionz?"

Everyone smiled, nodded or said yes, and seemed to relax a little bit. The way Ramiro had looked had caused them to wonder what was going on because they were not privy to the conversation between him and Horus – at least on the part of Horus because people close to Ramiro could hear his part of the conversation.

"Pardon the short delay," Horus said to everyone. "Mr. Esteves had a slight problem, but now he understands."

"Butz I have another question. I do notz underztand ziz São Rochelle. You zay itz part of Brazil butz ze name, it iz notz Português."

"You mean that the name is not proper Portuguese."

"Sim. 'São' is Português. It mean 'zaint', but diz 'Rochelle.' I know no zaint Rochelle."

"You are correct. Let me give you the history of the island. It is very interesting.

"In the late 1600s, it was reported that a fabulous vein of emeralds, diamonds and gold had been discovered in Minas Gerais, a region in Southeastern

Brazil. Fortune hunters came from all over and artisans (carpenters, stone masons, members of the arts, etc.) headed for Brazil to build the necessary infrastructure for cities in Brazil's interior. In Portugal, one enterprising sea captain started using his ship to carry these immigrants to Brazil. His second trip encountered a terrible storm, perhaps not unlike Hurricane Davido. Winds and waves tore the sails off and demasted the ship, which was left to flounder. After a day, the ship was cast upon rocks in the middle of the night. As the waves beat upon the ship, the passengers and crew began to feel that all was lost. Talk was of taking to the lifeboats as the only alternative. The passengers and crew were praying for deliverance. Then in the late hours of the night, a light appeared in the dimness of the approaching dawn. Looking at it through his telescope, the captain reported that it appeared that a man had built a fire upon a beach and was waving his arms trying to get their attention. The three remaining lifeboats were launched and filled with passengers and guided by the light, made it to shore. When they got there, a fire was burning low, but there was no sign of the man. A lull in the storm enabled the crew to bring the rest of the passengers and most of the supplies ashore before the storm increased intensity and forced the passengers and crew that were ashore to seek shelter on the island's interior. When the storm abated, the ship was gone along with the captain and part of the crew who – hoping to save it – had stayed aboard. No sign of the ship was ever found. The survivors built huts using what wood was available but mostly using the plentiful rocks on the island. They had no mortar so the stones were put together by the stone masons and topped with thatched roofs.

"The island was not visited by another ship for over fifty years and most of the survivors had passed on and their progeny had adapted to life on the island. The two lifeboats that had not been destroyed were used as fishing boats and a couple of new ones were built. When a ship finally appeared – and it was a Brazilian ship – most of the populace was happy with their lives and stayed although some of them left with the ship following their parents' dreams."

"Interesting story," Issaack said. "But what about the name?"

"I was just getting to that," Horus said. "The owner of the ship – and the captain – was French from the city of Rochelle and that is what he named his ship: *Ville de Rochelle*. The religious survivors felt that the man who saved them was giving them a sign that this was where they should stay. They believed that he was an angel sent by God but at best he was a saint for saving them and so they named the island after him and the ship that had brought them there: Saint Rochelle or São Rochelle."

Ramiro laughed and the other six looked at him.

"Zat'z a good ztory. I likez zat. Now I underzstand."

Chapter 9

"Now let's get back to why São Rochelle is of interest to us.

"As you could see from the video, this island basically has many of the earth's livable zones. Excluded are the Arctic and Antarctic because they are not habitable within normal means and only one creature there would be of interest at all, but we will get to that."

"Penguins," Monica said.

"No, Ms. Whitmore, not penguins. Remember that penguins exist in places beside the Antarctic – Australia and South Africa, for example."

"But there's no snow or ice in those places. Is there?"

"Penguins don't always live in places with snow and ice. Believe me –we can talk about this at a later time – but penguins are not under consideration here."

"Then it must be …" Harvey Gladstone began.

"Please, Mr. Gladstone. Let me present the case and we can discuss it at that time."

Gladstone sighed. "Very well."

"With these zones, it is ideal for our proposed project. Remember I said that there were horses and cattle on the island. They have no natural predators here. The largest predatory animal is the prehensile-tailed hutia, which resembles a coypu or nutria. That said, they are basically rodents – rats, if you will. They are mostly herbivorous but do eat small animals. They nest in trees or rock crevices and that explains why they survived the hurricane's waters.

"What we – I, if you wish – would like to do is to stock the island with fourteen of the world's most dangerous predators and see which one or ones survive."

"Lions, and tigers and bears," came out of the mouths of Gloria and Monica almost simultaneously and a chorus of "Oh my" came from everyone except Ramiro. This was followed by giggles and chuckles.

"What'z ziz?" Ramiro said. "Another Broadyway joke?"

"What's the joke?" Horus said. "Have I missed some… oh, I see. *The Wizard of Oz*."

"*The Wizard of Ooze*!" said Ramiro. "I doon underztandz."

"It's not a short story," Waldo said. "I'll explain at the next break."

"Está bem (Okay)," Ramiro said.

"If you're ready to continue," Horus said, not sounding the least bit perturbed.

"Where are you going to get these animals?" Phil asked. "I think I can name a lot of them, but it won't be easy."

"How do you get them to the island?" Issaack asked.

"I meant it won't be easy acquiring them," Phil said. "It is easy to name a bunch."

"We will get to all that," Horus said. "Just let me continue."

After murmured assent from those with questions, Horus continued.

"First, let us talk about apex predators. These are predators at the top of their food chain upon which no other predators prey. They are also called alpha or apical predators."

"One would be the lion," Phil said. "Nobody messes with the King of Beasts."

"The Polar bear has to be another," Harvey Gladstone said.

"That is most likely true, Mr. Gladstone," Horus said. "But on the island in consideration, there is not a suitable habitat for the polar bear because it spends most of its life on snow and ice and its main prey is seals. Also because of climate change or global warming or whatever you want to call it, the polar bear is losing its habitat and is considered a vulnerable species. I have chosen to avoid any species that is in anyway endangered. Beside it would be difficult to legally obtain such creatures."

"Who said anything about legally?" Phil said. "You need 'em, you get 'em."

"That would draw attention to us. In addition, there is a good chance that we can make a televised series out of …"

"Predator Survivor," Gladstone pipped up.

"Perhaps," Horus said. "But back to apex predators. The lion is an apex predator and resides in central, southern and eastern Africa and the Gir Forest in India."

"I've never heard of a lion in India," Waldo said. "Tigers are in India. Say, that's another apex predator, isn't it?"

"Yes, it is," Horus said. "And lions are in that one place in India and are referred to as Asiatic lions. And before anyone asks, the Gir Forest is a national park and wildlife refuge in the northwest part of India bordering on Pakistan and the Arabian Sea."

"I don't recall any big predators from Australia," Issaack said.

"Well, there is one," Horus explained. "It is the only surviving carnivorous marsupial and is both a scavenger and predator. Anyone know?"

"This is getting to be like a classroom," Waldo said. "But the answer is the Tasmanian devil, which is not on the Australian continent proper but only found on the island state of Tasmania."

"I've seen those," Harvey Gladstone said. "They have a ferocious bite but wouldn't survive with either a lion or a tiger."

"Unless they could get at a spot the lion can't reach. When they bite, they can really hang on."

"Well, we are not including the Tasmanian devil for that very reason," Horus injected. "It would not survive the competition for very long."

"I'll take a grizzly for my predator," Phil said. "Those beasts have nasty claws and teeth and great protection in that fur coat."

"Correct," said Horus. "They are brown bears and would naturally be one of the animals we would choose. Also, black bears need to be considered because they are omnivores. They are smaller than the brown bear but certainly deserve a shot at the title."

"They aren't apex, are they?" Gloria asked.

"No, but many of the animals we would include in this competition are not apex either," Horus said.

"This whole thing sounds like a dog fight," Issaack said. "They're outlawed in the States."

"Cock fights are too," Phil said, "But they're big in Puerto Rico."

"Gentlemen," interrupted Horus. "While you are both correct, let me remind you that São Rochelle is not in the United States. It is a sovereign island under the protection of Brazil. There are no restrictions to what we are going to do." There followed a brief pause that many would term "pregnant." "That is if we do it."

"I'm game," said Phil. "Sounds like an interesting experiment. Those animals having never encountered the other. Say, are there tigers living where those Asiatic lions live?"

"No. That region of Indian is not suitable for tigers because it is too dry, just like where the lions live in Africa.

"Now if we may move on to some other animals."

"Not juzt yet," Ramiro said. "I like diz idea. We got the bull fightz and I likez them but ziz iz a bit more natural and iz – howz you zay – only the bezt zurvive."

"Survival of the fittest," Issaack answered. "But that's not really what this is." He paused. "No, I guess that is what it is. That would be a good name for the series, unless it has already been used."

"Not that I could find," Horus said. "Now can we…"

"Not yetz," Ramiro said. "I have not queztioned yet. Before we decide what animalz we will uze, how do we get them there? They needz beeg cagez and lots of menz or a cranez to lift them off boatz. No airplane can land, could be helicopter but be beeg helicopter."

"I agree with 'You can call me Juan,'" said Harvey Gladstone smiling at Ramiro, who scowled in return. Obviously, he did not like to be the brunt of a joke. "How do we build the pier? How do we move the animals around? There is a lot of infrastructure needed. How's that going to happen."

"I suspected that someone might have that question," Horus said. "First though, is everyone in on the idea of the project. See who the best of the best predators is?"

"I'm in," Gloria said. "I need a little excitement in my life. I judge that we'll be able to watch it."

"Not in person, but over television."

"That's better than nothing," Gloria said. "One vote for."

"Make that two," injected Harvey Gladstone. "Provided the rest of the project is satisfactory."

"Three," Waldo said. "There's no gas on the island, at least I didn't see a BP station. There's going to be a need for transportation, and I guess that's where I come in. We can charge batteries solarly. That island has to get a lot of sun."

"I'll be four," Issaack said. "Computers are my forte and there's going to be a lot of need for that because you're going to need to track animals."

"Five," said Phil. "I've got money dying for a use. I've been playing with drones recently and I can see a use for them in this project. I'd like to be there to see it all."

"I don't like the idea of killing animals," Monica said. "But I think it's a fun experiment. Count me in."

"That's six," Gloria said, showing all the fingers of her left hand and the thumb of her right. All eyes turned to Ramiro.

"You waiting for me?" he asked. "Az long as I doon getz killed, it zoundz like fun."

"We're agreed," Gloria said. "So tell us how to prepare the island, Horus, or whoever you are."

Chapter 10

"I must admit that I wasn't totally prepared for this at this time," Horus said. "I thought it would come after lunch. So we'll take a break, it's almost time anyway. I'll alert Declercq and Carmen. See you at noon."

Monica was moving her chair back, when something made her look at Gloria, who was giving a one-sided nod at her. Monica realized what she wanted and headed for the ladies' room.

"You think its bugged in here?" Gloria asked.

"It better not be," Monica said, "Remember when I had to take my knickers off and wash them out." Monica had hung them off the end of a sink and now she looked at the sink and saw the knickers lying folded on the sink's ledge. She walked over and picked them up. "Oh, my goodness. They're dry," she said. "Give me a minute and she entered a stall, closing and locking the door. Gloria could hear her boots being removed and set on the floor, then the cherry red leather pants were hung over the door. There was a pause, the toilet flushed, the pants were removed and shortly, the stall door opened, and Monica walked out.

"Feels much better," Monica said. Then stopped. Gloria was indicating not to say anything and had her invitation card held out to Monica. The light dawned quickly, and Monica pulled hers out of a pocket in her jacket and they exchanged cards. Gloria winked at Monica and they exited the ladies' room. Waldo and Ramiro were standing about ten feet away and Ramiro was laughing and saying, "Lionz and tigerz and bearz! Oh my!"

Monica and Gloria went back to the seats just before the break ended and sat down. At precisely noon, Horus's face appeared in front of Gloria and said, "Monica, you're back in your seat."

Gloria smiled and said, "No, she's not."

Horus's face vanished and reappeared in front of Monica. "Enough games, young lady. You go back to your original seat and give Gloria her card and get yours."

Horus appeared in front of Gloria and said, "You get your card from Monica and go back to your seat. Enough games."

The two did as bidden, with the other five watching curiously.

"Okay, you two," Waldo said. "What's behind the games?"

"I just wanted to learn if Horus could see and how he knew who was where."

"You could have asked," Horus said, and then explained to everyone. "This system isn't to the point yet where I can see you and, as you might suspect from the shenanigans that have been going on, I rely on your cards to know where you are. Those cards are your identification and keys while you are here, so if you want to maintain your privacy and security, please keep them with you and don't give them to anyone.

"Now, are we ready for the infrastructure lecture?"

Everyone said they were. The screen showed a graphic representation of the island as seen from above and as they watched it zoomed in on the area on the other side of the pool at the bottom of Boulder Hill.

"This is the area that the population cleared over the years to grow wheat and other staples needed in their lives. It wasn't easy as some of the stones were large, but these were cut and used as tile in the houses and as a foundation for the walls. The first houses were much cruder and as things progressed they were replaced. What is important here is that the field is clear. It won't permit a plane to land, a large helicopter could, but that won't hold what is needed to get started: a bulldozer and not just any bulldozer but the size used in strip mining. There are two under consideration for the job: The Caterpillar D9T dozer and the John Deere 1050k Crawler. The D9T has an operating weight of 106,000 pounds and has 460 horsepower. The 1050k Crawler operating weight is 95,000 pounds and has 350 horsepower. We still have a lot of research to do before we make a decision."

The screen now showed a graphic of a big plane approaching the island.

"That's a C-130 Hercules," Phil said, "or something like it."

"Again," Horus said, "the dozer we will use and the plane have not been decided yet. This graphic was done to show you what we expect to happen. Nothing more."

The plane approached the island at a low altitude with its cargo doors open and they could see a bulldozer just inside the open doors.

"We haven't worked out all the details yet because the dozers aren't very fast. We may have a catapult propel the dozer out but hopefully this is what will happen."

The video showed the dozer exiting the cargo hatch and several parachutes opening and the dozer floating down to the ground and making a landing on the farm land. There was applause just as though it had really happened.

"We might get two or three down depending on how well they work on the island. The first step will be to make a road to the dock site. Then to make a road like a figure eight with the cross piece running through the arable land and the outside being on the edge of the island except at the volcano end where it would be along the base."

The video showed the little bulldozer plowing to the dock site and then the road around the island as described by Horus.

"Once the dock is built, we will be able to land more equipment using something like an LST. It would be built while the initial construction was under way and would make the run from Belém, but of course the weather would have to be good."

The video showed the LST coming to the dock and offloading some other equipment.

"What's that equipment needed for?" Waldo asked.

"Our headquarters."

"Where's that going to be?"

"In the volcano," Horus said.

Chapter 11

They watched as the new pieces of equipment followed the bulldozer counterclockwise on the road from the dock toward the volcano and then up the slope. The bulldozer made a road going back and forth making switchbacks until it was nearly at the top of the volcano. Then, as if by magic, a tunnel opening appeared, and the dozer went through followed by the equipment. When they disappeared into the tunnel the view moved upward until they were looking down into the volcano where there was a building.

"That is the proposed headquarters. We don't have it completely laid out yet, but it will have work areas as well as living quarters for twenty to thirty people. Once the animals are released, all of us will be sequestered in the headquarters until the winner has been decided."

"How will you know when that is?" Monica asked.

"Every animal will have a chip inserted that will not only transmit its GPS location but monitor the animal's health. We will know when and where it dies. Or doesn't, depending. We will have antennas all over the island able to relay the data, plus we will have video cameras and, as Mr. Parmelee said, we will be flying drones."

"What's to keep the animals out of the volcano?" Gloria asked

"There will be a gate at the tunnel's entrance they will not be able to get through."

"But what if they come over the rim?"

"There is no reason for them to and if one does reach the top and can make it down the slope to the crater floor, we will have weapons to kill it if it cannot be chased off."

"What happenz to ze winner?" Ramiro asked. "How do you zay, to the winner goez ze prizez?"

"It's 'To the victor go the spoils'," Horus said. "I don't expect that the island's entire wildlife will be depleted but .... I believe the saying is 'We will cross that bridge when we come to it.'"

Monica sat up straight and said, "Well, I for one, not being totally comfortable with this whole killing thing – although I am willing to go along with it– would like to see that the survivor or survivors are properly cared for medically and nutritionally."

"I agree with Monica," Gloria said. "It is the only humane thing to do. Getting to that point won't be very humane, I agree, but once...," She glared at Horus even though she knew he couldn't see her, "...that bridge has been crossed, kindness needs to be applied. I want your building to have a large animal veterinarian and proper facilities. I am certain that you plan on having doctors and facilities available for your people, don't you?"

"In Belém, the closest city in Brazil, yes. We will have a helicopter landing pad within the volcano and will be able to fly anyone who needs assistance to Belém."

"Even so, you minimally need EMTs on staff."

"I have noted your point and it will be considered."

"Considered?" Gloria was irate. "It needs to be implemented, not considered."

"So noted. Any other questions about the proposed infrastructure?"

"What about food, water, electricity?"

"Good question, Mr. Kinkaid," responded Horus. "We will have stocked water and food prior to the sequestering. We feel that the process should take a month, no longer, but we will have supplies for three months. Electricity will be done by solar panels on the south side of the volcano.

"Other questions?"

"How long will this infrastructure construction take?" Waldo asked.

"We anticipate five years. The first part will be slow because of the rocky condition of the island. The rocks will be picked up and used to build the dock. We didn't say but in addition to the bulldozers there would be trucks and workers. We will have to build quarters for the workers which will be done in the area of the original village so that we don't disturb the environment any more than needed. Supplies will be airlifted either by helicopter or dropped by plane. Gasoline will be a priority for the equipment unless there are electrical dozers and trucks by the time they are needed."

"When do you expect to be able to start the construction?"

Horus was silent for a moment. "Within a year, two at the maximum."

"Is this all within your original time frame?"

"No, the time frame starts when the bulldozer and crew are on the ground. We will have dropped what is needed for shelter prior to the crew being on the ground. We want to be able to drop prefabricated sections of the housing from helicopter, but the range will be a problem. Our best bet would to fly them in from a ship sitting off the island."

"And the cost?"

"Covered by your contributions," Horus said.

"And what are you contributing?" Ramiro asked, having sat straight up in his chair when the talk of money started.

"The idea behind the project and the ability to make certain that it happens." Horus responded in the blink of an eye.

"How do we know that our money will be safe?"

"Your money went into a fund in a bank in Panama. You were all given a password and username. You can keep tabs on the money twenty-four seven. Monthly expense sheets will be provided, and you can match them with the money in the fund and the withdrawals. A fee for our services of $250,000 per annum will be withdrawn at the beginning of the fiscal year."

"When does this fiscal year start?"

"When you have approved the plan."

"Are there any more questions at this point."

There weren't or at least they weren't asked.

"Then we will take a break for lunch and reconvene at 2:00 p.m."

Chapter 12

Declercq and Carmen came out and asked everyone to move away from the table for five minutes, so most of them made for the men's or ladies' restrooms to relieve and/or freshen themselves. Monica and Gloria were happy to be alone again.

"I was right," Monica said, "He can't see us and knows where we are through the cards. I don't know how they can read the cards, but they can."

"I think there is a GPS chip in the card that tells your location."

"Sure, that's it. What an idiot I am! Tell you what, let's see if after lunch we can go upstairs and find our rooms. I want to see what they look like and what clothes they picked out for me. I tell you, I find their ability to give us what we want to drink and snack on uncanny. They must have done some deep work."

Gloria laughed. "With you, it's easy. All you need to do is read the magazines and listen to interviews."

"Yeah, but they don't know what color my knickers are or whether I wear a bra or not. I've never said that."

By the time everyone had finished and returned to the table, it had been covered with a gigantic white linen table cloth that hung evenly all around and there wasn't a wrinkle or crease in it. Each place was set perfectly with sterling silver and white linen napkins.

Lunch started with soup: onion, minestrone, or consommé; followed by beef bourguignon, chicken parmesan or blackened red snapper. Accompanying the entrées were parsley potatoes, green peas with tiny onions, carrots; and either a leaf lettuce salad with choice of dressings, Caesar salad, or shredded head lettuce with oil and vinegar; dessert was apple pie, chocolate cake, a cheese plate or a fruit plate. Conversation was lively with people talking to each other, getting to know them. Not a word was mentioned about what had transpired prior to the luncheon.

Gloria and Monica had kept an eye on the time and excused themselves at 1:35 p.m. and walked to the doors leading to the hotel's foyer. Looking through the glass they could see no one in the lobby. Monica pushed on the left door and it didn't give. Gloria pushed on the right with the same effect. Monica rapped on the door, but not one showed themselves.

"Is there a problem, Ms. Bartlett?"

Declercq had come up behind them as silently as a cat, which is the way he always seemed to be. Monica whirled around. "Yes, there is. I wanted to see what my room is like and maybe catch a breath of fresh air."

"I'm sorry, miss, but no one is permitted outside the confines of the meeting room until today's session is over. It's a security issue after the attack this morning."

"But they weren't after us. They were after … Juan." She couldn't help but giggle.

"Yes, miss, but if you were taken hostage then they could get at … Mr. Esteves."

"Oh, feck," Monica said. "He doesn't give a fat trump about me."

"Excuse me, miss, but I am not certain what you meant."

"Oh, ahh, to trump is to pass gas through one's arsehole. I believe you Americans say 'fart.' So he doesn't give a big fart about me."

"I see. Thank you for that elucidation. And I am not American, I am Dutch."

"Oh, from Holland."

"No, miss, from the Netherlands. North and South Holland are two of our twelve provinces. I am from Utrecht."

"So we've both learned something but that doesn't help ..."

Declercq had whirled around and started off for one of the windows where Ramiro was standing with a lit cigarette in his hand.

"I'm sorry, Señor Esteves, but smoking is not permitted inside."

"I don't care. I am nervouz and I needz a cigarette. You juzt go tell your Mr. Horuz or whoever he iz that if I cannot go outzide for a zmoke, I am going to zmoke in here. I am certain that it'z not going to bother anyone."

Declercq was silent for a moment and then he said, "Very well, sir. I understand." And he walked to a panel in the wall beside the doors leading to the foyer, inserted a key into the glass cover, opened it and pushed a red button to prevent the smoke detector from going off and turned a dial one click to the right which turned the circulation fan up one notch. Closing the panel cover and locking it, he turned around and saw with satisfaction that the smoke was being drawn up and that Carmen had arrived and given Señor Esteves a crystal ashtray.

"Thank you, sir," Declercq said seemingly to no one and returned to his duties, noting with satisfaction that Ms. Bartlett and Mrs. Mitchell were conversing with Mr. Kinkaid and Mr. Emerson. On the other hand,

Señor Esteves, Mr. Gladstone and Mr. Parmelee were in a huddle near the window. One was good; the other bode evil. How evil only time would tell.

Chapter 13

"Welcome back," Horus greeted them precisely at 2:00 p.m. "I trust you all enjoyed your meal. I think we are done with the infrastructure unless there are further questions."

Horus paused but no one said anything.

"Hearing no questions, let us proceed. We have the lion, tiger, brown bear (which will be a grizzly), and black bear. Except for the lion and tiger, we will proceed through my prepared list alphabetically. Please note that some of these entrants you might not back as the potential winner, but we want to have a big enough pool to make it interesting.

"The caracal is a wild cat native to Africa, the Middle East, Central Asia and India. It is a medium-sized cat of sixteen to twenty inches at the shoulder and weighs between eighteen to forty pounds. It is a carnivore preying on small mammals, birds and rodents. It can leap higher than 9.8 feet and catch birds in mid-air. It stalks bigger animals until within sixteen feet and then runs the prey down and kills with a bite to the throat or back of the neck."

As he was describing the animal a brief video of it was shown although none of it included it hunting. Videos or pictures would be shown for each of the animals being discussed to help the people who didn't know about them familiarize themselves with the animals.

"It is an ideal predator for the fauna of São Rochelle," Horus concluded.

"I like the way it gets birds," Monica said. "I can hardly wait to see it in action."

"It doezn't ztand a chance in the competition," Ramiro said. "It iz too zmall and would be eazy prey for a lion or tiger."

"Could be," Phil said, "but they have to catch it first."

"Although it may not win, I think it deserves a chance," Harvey Gladstone said.

"Me, too," Gloria said.

"Majority rules and the caracal is in," Horus said.

"The next one I am certain is familiar to you all," Horus continued. "The cheetah. This speed demon lives in eastern and southern Africa and a few places in Iran. Characterized by a slender body, deep chest and spotted coat, it stands twenty-eight to thirty-five inches at the shoulder and weighs between forty-five and one hundred fifty-nine pounds. This puts it bigger than a leopard (which we haven't gotten to yet) and much smaller than a lion. Specializing in speed, the cheetah hits forty miles per hour in a sprint but can go seventy miles per hour for a short distance. This is the reason for its hunting technique which is to stalk its prey to within three hundred thirty to nine hundred eight feet and then chase it down. Its usual method of kill is to trip the prey and bite it in the throat, holding that bite until the animal suffocates."

"Bigger than a panther? Really?" Harvey Gladstone said.

"Perhaps I misspoke," Horus said. "It is taller than the leopard."

"Well, since you brought in that comparison, tell us about the leopard," Phil said.

"I agree," Ramiro said. "and alzo, ze panther. Let'z get all ze catz taken care of – at leazt the big catz."

"Then add in the jaguar. That's my favorite," Issaack said.

Everyone voiced agreement.

"Then we move forward with the jaguar which is next alphabetically and therefore easiest to find on my list," Horus said. "The jaguar is the only member of the Panthera species in the Americas. The other members are the lion, tiger, snow leopard, and leopard."

"The cheetah's not a panther?" asked Monica.

"It is another species," Horas said "and is the only member of that species we are considering. And before anyone asks, the cougar – also known as mountain lion, puma, and catamount – and also panther is another species: the Puma."

"We will include that in the discussion though, won't we?" queried Waldo.

"Yes, we shall. Can we move on now to the jaguar?"

Assent heard from the bundle (except for Ramiro), Horus continued.

"The jaguar is seen very many places in the Americas: ranging from Argentina and Paraguay north through Central America and Mexico to the Southwestern United States. Its numbers are third behind the lion and tiger. El Tigre, as it is known in Mexico, weighs between one hundred twenty-four and two hundred eleven pounds. It only stands twenty-five to thirty inches at the shoulders but varies from 3.7 to 6.1 feet in length even though its tail is the shortest of any big cat being only eighteen to thirty inches in length. It is a stalk-and-ambush rather than chase predator and will even go into the water after prey. One of the amazing features – at least to me – is that it has a very strong bite and can pierce the shell of armored reptiles.

Its favorite killing method is to bite through the skull between the ears of its prey and into the brain killing it."

"Ugh," Monica said. "That's deadly. With the stalk-and-ambush style, that's my choice. Scary."

"Any other comments about el Tigre? Mr. Esteves, you have been exceptionally quiet at the table."

"I am juzt liztening and learning. My Englizh is not zo good and I am liztening hard to underztand."

"Would you like a Portuguese translation?"

"That iz out boundz for diz meeting. I am doing hookay," Ramiro said.

"Then it's time for the leopard which has a wide range in the part of Africa below the Sahara and in parts of Asia. It is similar in appearance to the jaguar but not as heavy, relatively short legs although a long body and big skull. Preferring prey weighing between twenty-two and eighty-eight pounds, …"

"What's it do, carry a scale and ask potential prey to step on it?" Harvey Gladstone said.

This brought a smile to Ramiro's face but not too many noticed.

"That's a joke, right?" Horus said. "What it means is that it knows what it can attack and doesn't go after things that are too big. That size range was given in the research material that I consulted."

"I understand," Harvey Gladstone said. "I was just trying to make a funny."

"I likez ziz funny," Ramiro said.

"Okay. Done with that?"

No one said any more.

"The leopard stalks the target animal trying to get within sixteen feet … No tape measure needed, Mr. Gladstone … before pouncing and killing by suffocation, biting small animals in the back of the neck and larger in the throat. Small animals are eaten on the spot, but larger animals are dragged away and hidden to be returned to later. Leopards are strong enough to drag a young giraffe weighing two hundred seventy-six pounds nineteen feet into a tree. This has been documented."

"Zat'z zome ztrength zere," Ramiro said. Members of the group were surprised at his understanding when he has just pled difficulty understanding.

"Although we have already included the lion in our list because of its status as an apex predator, let me make some comments. Lions prefer prey weighing between 420 and 1,210 pounds and have a preference for wildebeest, buffalo, zebras, giraffes and gemsbok. You might think that an animal that size might give a lion trouble but males can weigh five hundred fifty pounds and where possible hunt in prides, the name for a group of lions. In the hunt, lionesses are given the privileged position of being on the flank of prey and as a rule, males do not participate in group hunts. They are not known for their stamina and tend to run fast only in short bursts so it is necessary to get close to its prey before attacking. Since we are going to try to limit ourselves to one of each kind, we are most likely going for a male lion since they prefer solo hunts."

"Good choice," Phil said. "Serial killers hunt alone and are most always men."

Chapter 14

"Are you inferring that women are not capable of killing?" Gloria said. "Because I take exception to that inference."

"Does that have anything to do with the fact that two of your husbands died shortly after you divorced them? I believe that the divorce agreements stipulated that in such a circumstance you were the prime beneficiary."

*"**You bastard!**"* Gloria was livid. Her face turned bright red and her hands were clenched. "I was never – never – considered as a suspect in their deaths, which were never considered as homicides. One was a heart attack and the other an automobile accident."

"Still, accidents can be made to happen," Phil said.

"You mean like the shark killing your partner?"

Phil started to rise from his chair and surprisingly Harvey Gladstone reached an arm out to stop him.

*"**That's enough,**"* Horus said. "If you two have differences you cannot iron out, then I suggest you withdraw from this group."

"I apologize," Phil said. "I think it is the excess alcohol with which I am being plied. That Dead Man's Chest rum carries a big kick."

"It doesn't give me the hiccups," Monica said quietly.

Gloria said nothing but just glared at Phil.

"May I continue?" Horus said and did. "The snow leopard's territory is the mountain ranges of Central and South Asia. On São Rochelle, we will place it on the volcano's slope, but it will have to come down for food. Although they kill their prey for the most part, they are not above eating carrion and will hunt domestic animals. They kill animals two to four times their own weight. They weigh between sixty and one hundred twenty-one pounds, but males are known to weigh as much as one hundred sixty-five pounds and females under fifty-five pounds. They have a stocky build and are short legged, standing only two feet at the shoulder and a body length of thirty to sixty inches. Add to that a tail that runs from thirty-one to thirty-nine inches and they appear bigger. Their kills are impressive for their size including horse and camel. Because they live in mountains, their modus operandi is to attack from above, usually lying in wait. Interestingly a kill lasts them for a while. A yearly kill of twenty to thirty adult sheep suffices for one adult."

"And it's such a cute animal," Monica said. "I've seen them in several zoos."

"From such a small animal, let me say something about the tiger. While the lion has been given the title of The King of Beasts, the tiger is the largest cat species. The male Bengal tiger, the kind most people think about when you say 'tiger,' will have a nose to tail tip length of one hundred ten to one hundred twenty inches and in the range of four hundred nineteen to five hundred sixty-nine pounds. In contrast, the Siberian tiger has a head to tail tip length between seven-five and ninety-one inches and weighs between three hundred ninety-seven and six hundred seventy-five pounds."

"These guys are fat," Harvey said, patting his own stomach as though associating himself with the Siberian tiger.

"They are nocturnal hunters for the most part and ambush their prey using body size and strength to knock the victim off balance. With larger animals, they get a bite on the throat and then hang on with their powerful front limbs until the prey is suffocated."

"Suffocation seems a popular killing method with the cats," Monica said.

"It's a popular method of killing anyway," Issaack said. "When a person is sleeping, it's easy to place a pillow over the victim's face and hold it down."

"Is this said from experience?" Waldo said with a grin.

"I won't comment on that," Issaack said, making a gun out of his right hand and mimicking shooting Waldo who threw his hands up and played dead for a few seconds. Then both men laughed.

"That finishes the Panthera group," Horus continued unmindful of the horseplay. "To remind you, they are the lion, the tiger…"

"Not the bear," said Gloria and an "Oh my," came from Monica. Then they both laughed.

"… jaguar, leopard, and snow leopard. Should we keep them all?" Horus asked.

"Can you get one of each?" Waldo asked. "Some of them are endangered to some degree."

"That is true. But there are cats who go astray, and people would like to get rid of them for the sake of population safety. We will do our best which is all we can hope for," was Horus's response. "And that is the case with any of the animals. The list has already been shortened quite a bit. Of course, there are no reptiles, no aquatic predators.

"Next on the list … let me see … ah, yes, the cougar."

"You made that sound almost as though you were human, Horus," Waldo said.

There was a pregnant silence, but no pin dropped.

"I don't understand," Horus said.

"Well, you paused, as though you were searching for something. But it's all on the computer – right at your fingertips, like they say … whoever they are – and you don't have fingertips. Do you?"

"I don't think that a discussion of who or what I am is appropriate at this time. Can we just proceed?"

Monica noticed a wisp of a smile flicker on Issaack's face and then was gone. *I wonder what he thought was funny?*

"Certainly. That comment was not meant to insult. Rather it was … oh, forget it."

"Forgotten. Earlier we mentioned the cougar but did not talk about it. This well-known cat has a range from the Yukon in Canada to the Andes in South America. It is a secretive, solitary creature. Like many of the cats, it attacks from ambush. They are the fourth largest cat, with the adult male standing twenty-four to thirty-five inches at the shoulder and are 7.9 feet from nose to tail tip, of which twenty-five to thirty-seven inches is the tail. Better said is that of the 7.9 feet, two to three feet is tail. Males weigh between one hundred fifteen and two hundred twenty pounds. This said, it is not the apex predator throughout its habitat. It gives way to the jaguar, gray wolf, American black bear and grizzly bear. I personally think that it would like the chance to prove it is the apex predator where it lives."

"I agree," Phil said. "Count that critter in. Now what's this about the gray wolf? We haven't talked about that, have we?"

"No, that's next on my list," Horus said, "but does everyone agree that the cougar deserves to be in."

There was a chorus of "yesses" from all, even Ramiro.

"Nice to hear from you, Mr. Esteves," Horus said. "Do you have a special affinity for the cougar."

"Ef-fine-ate-tee? I do not understand this word. I hate thiz cougar. It killz too much liveztock no meu fazenda (on my ranch) and I want zem killed."

Everyone laughed.

"'Affinity' means 'afinidade,'" Horus said.

"Ah, sim. Hookay. I have not affinity for diz cougar."

There was a chuckle from Horus. Monica and Gloria looked at each other and shrugged. *Always expect the unexpected*, Gloria thought.

Chapter 15

"I believe we are done with cats," Horus said.

"Then let's go to the dogs," Waldo said with a big smile on his face.

Several of the Bundle cracked smiles, but there was nothing from Horus.

"First, on the list – again we are going alphabetically – is the coyote. One of my favorites," Horus remarked.

Monica noticed that Gloria raised an eyebrow at this.

"The coyote fills the ecological place that the jackal does in Eurasia. It is smaller than the gray wolf – we haven't talked about that yet – and actually is a close relative. A male averages eighteen to forty-four pounds with the female just slightly smaller. It eats small animals and the occasional deer. Interestingly, man is the coyote's greatest threat and, of course, man means civilization. In the animal world, cougars and gray wolves are tops on the coyote's threat list. It hunts in pairs or in groups and approaches the prey from the front trying to bite the prey's head and throat."

"You said that they don't hunt alone," Phil said.

"Not typically," Horus answered.

"Does this mean that we get a pair?"

"I think that it makes sense in this case, because of what we are doing, to get a couple."

"Right, we get two."

"Well, two or three, maybe four. When I say a couple, I am using the word as an idiom and that means two or more."

"Okay, I think I can agree that since this is a pack animal, getting just one would put it out of sorts. Therefore, I move – makes this sound more businesslike – that we get two or three coyotes. Four would be too many." Phil smiled when he was finished.

"I agree," Issaack said.

"As do I," chirped Gloria.

"Sim," Ramiro said.

"Right on," Monica said.

"Then we're agreed," Horus said, sounding a bit pleased. "Now to the coyote's cousin, the gray wolf, which – interestingly enough – is native to Eurasia and North America. It is also known as the timber wolf or western wolf. Males weigh ninety-five to one hundred pounds with females about fifteen pounds less. It is a social animal and, interestingly, an apex predator throughout its range. The biggest threats to it are tigers – where they exist – and man. We've already talked about its attack method, coming from behind an animal. It tries get the prey to run so they can chase it and try to trip it or cut its hamstring, I think. If the prey stands its ground as elk or moose do, the wolves don't like it. It seems to be the chase they like."

"You said it is a social animal. Does this mean it hunts in a team, like coyotes?" Harvey Gladstone asked.

"They seem to be most successful when they hunt singly or in pairs," was Horus's answer.

"Then I move we go with one. We can make the coyote an exception to the rule," Harvey Gladstone said.

"All those who agree…"

A chorus of "yesses" rang out before Horus could finish.

"Then we are down to the last predator that we offer for consideration…"

"You keep saying 'we'," Gloria said. "Who's 'we'?"

Horus almost looked pensive.

"I think that Monica can explain," Horus said.

Everyone looked at Monica, who laughed.

"You want me to explain why he says, 'we offer' or 'we have.' Is that it?"

There was a murmured affirmative.

"It's easy. It's the royal 'we.' The way the queen talks."

Several people laughed.

"Ha," Phil said. "Horus thinks he's royalty. Well, it's not worth a long debate. We think we should move on to consideration of …"

"The spotted hyena," Horus finished. "Or more popularly, the laughing hyena. Since we have been considering whether the animals hunt in groups, the spotted hyena hunts alone, in small groups or large groups. An adult is between twenty-eight and thirty-six inches at the shoulder, is between thirty-seven and sixty-five inches in length, and weighs between eighty-nine and one hundred-twenty pounds. They have extremely strong front quarters and much more underdeveloped rear quarters. Their heart is about 1% of their body weight which makes them able to run long distances in the chase. And they basically run their prey into the ground and when it tires, it's dead."

"I don't want to ever face one of those," Monica said. "They're ugly and nasty. But I think it stands a chance. Let 'em in."

"Agreed," said the others.

"Well, that's it then. We have …"

"No, zat'z not it," Ramiro said. "You left out the mozt important one."

"I don't understand," Horus said. "I offered everyone on the list. No one was left out."

"Sim, zere waz," Ramiro said. "Zhe mozt dangerouz predator in ze world. It livez on every continent. It livez in every environment. It haz conquered everyzing on ziz world and beyond."

"You don't mean…"

"Sim, I do. Man. You have to include man."

"No. That is unacceptable," Horus sounded perturbed. "We will not put man in the contest. It would be …"

"What? What would it be?" Phil chimed in. "Man is a predator. Man is the apex predator. Isn't that what we are really looking for. The one predator that is at the top of all the food chains. In a way, it's almost ridiculous to even have this contest when we know who the winner will be."

"I don't agree," Gloria said. "We are talking about predators in the natural world. Man doesn't count in that world. Man is above all the animals because …"

"You're wrong," Harvey Gladstone said. "And you are right. Man has shown himself to be better than all the animals in each of the places in the world. But this is different. We are taking the best from North America, South America, Africa, Europe, Asia. We're leaving out Australia because nothing there is big enough to fight lions and tigers and bears …"

"And wolves, and cougars, and hyenas," put in Phil. "And there aren't any land predators in Antarctica and the climate on São Rochelle is not amenable to host anything from Antarctica or the Arctic. That's why we are leaving out the polar bear. São Rochelle is outside the polar bear's environment. That's why we're leaving out sharks and whales and aquatic predators. But other than that, man is not out of his environment in São

Rochelle. I second Ramiro's nomination. We need to include man in this."

"That's crazy," Monica said. "A man wouldn't stand a chance against a tiger or a lion."

"Certainly he would," Gladstone said. "One shot from a thirty aught six and a tiger is history."

"There'll be no guns," Horus said. "That's not natural."

"Well, there's been a nomination," Phil said. "We've discussed it. Now let's vote."

"Show of hands," Gloria said.

"No," Issaack said. "We ask – Horus asks – each person in the order they arrived. That's the way to do it."

Everyone seemed to agree so, Horus started.

He appeared on the table in front of Harvey Gladstone.

"How say you, Mr. Gladstone?" Horus intoned.

"Guilty," Harvey said and laughed. "I am in favor of including man in the mix."

"How say you, Ms. Bartlett?" Horus said as he appeared in front of Monica.

"No. Man is not to be included." Monica answered.

"How say you, Mr. Kinkaid," Horus said.

"I vote to exclude man from consideration," Issaack said.

"What say you, Señor Esteves."

"Sim," Ramiro said, "Man is always in the discussion."

"What say you, Mr. Parmalee?"

"I vote yes. I would volunteer."

"What say you, Mrs. Mitchell?"

"No, I object. It would be cruel and unusual punishment."

"It's tied," Gladstone said.

Everyone looked at Waldo.
"What say you, Mr. Emerson?" Horus asked.
Waldo looked around.
"I vote the way my mind says is right, I vote …"

Chapter 16

He'd been in place since the mid-morning and was growing weary. He hadn't had a shot when Esteves got out of the limousine, there were two bodyguards in front and two behind. Although they weren't tall, they had blocked him. He could have taken one or both of them out but that was all, and he wouldn't have gotten away. He had followed Esteves from the airport where he had flown in two hours before his arrival at the meeting hotel. He had known there was a meeting; that's why Esteves had left his Brazilian Ranch and flown to Cartagena. It had to be important to get him out. All the contact had known was that he was going to Cartagena and that he would arrive early that morning. An informant in the airport's ground crew had told him via a text message that Esteves's plane had landed and had described the limousine, including a picture showing the license plate clearly.

The stop at the restaurant had been a surprise and Esteves was out and inside before he had a chance to do anything. The limo sat there idling with two of the bodyguards around keeping an eye on the outside of the restaurant and the limousine. When Esteves came out and got in the limousine, a shot, if he had wanted to take one, would have been impossible. So he waited and followed him to the meeting place. It was a small building with a patio on one side and an alley on the other. The walls on both sides of the alley were free of windows on the first floor. There were doors leading into the building, but he couldn't get to them because both ends of the alley were gated with security cameras and there were security cameras on the hotel. After a quick walk-by during which he had discovered the security devices in place (and there were probably many more) he had found a place from which he could watch three other people arrive. One came in a limousine, one in a cab and one in an UberSelect. Being a meticulous person, he noted that there seemed to be an almost precise twenty-minute period between arrivals. The vehicle would drive up and sit idling until the passenger got out and entered the building after showing a card to an electric eye. Two were men, one woman and most were dressed for business except the first who was wearing a T-shirt and Dockers.

The attack that had occurred after the woman arrived took him by surprise. A car had driven down the street past him and he had noticed that the windows were down on his side but up on the other side. Two men sitting on his side were wearing dark glasses and peering out the windows looking ahead – when they started shooting he realized they were waiting for the target to appear. Almost immediately, there was an explosion and then more automatic fire from the far side of the small hotel where he realized there was a small yard and probably a veranda for the hotel's dining room if it had such. Simultaneously when the men in the car opened fire at the hotel, return fire came from the second-floor windows. It came with such ferocity that the driver of the car picked up speed and the car disappeared. The same thing happened after the explosion and the violence was over quickly. He was surprised when the Cartagena police didn't show up but from he what had heard, the police were more interested in payoffs than law enforcement. Undoubtedly one of the two sides in the dispute – which certainly was a rival cartel hunting Esteves just as he was – had paid the cops off. The tit for tat that he had witnessed convinced him that he did not want to complete his hunt here. Good planners never show all their cards at once, so he was certain that there were other defensive pockets around that he hadn't seen yet. He had been surprised when the first fusillade had come from the front of the hotel. The windows had opened so quickly he hadn't seen them. In fact, he was wondering if they were there at all. He would have to check his camera. But he had really been looking at the car not the building and by the time his vision shifted from the car when it started pulling away, he was certain that all the windows were closed.

An hour after the third person had shown up, he realized the meeting was small. He had no idea when it was going to let out. Never knowing what was going to happen on a job like this, he was prepared with food and drink and was using a catheter with a catch bag on his thigh. He had moved the car twice and had only driven by the building once. His surveillance tour had been on foot. At 5:30 p.m., he was beginning to wonder what was going to happen when a van pulled up in front. Four young people – two men and two women, got out. The men were dressed in tuxedos with aqua blue ruffled tuxedo shirts and dark blue bow ties and cummerbunds. The women were wearing black dresses with what looked like a string of aqua pearls around their necks. They went around to the back of the van and opened the door. They reappeared carrying black cases. He identified the instruments immediately and realized that the four were a string quartet: two violins, a viola, and a cello. That signified one thing to him. There was a banquet that evening and, more than likely, everyone was staying the night even though none of the people who he had seen entering the building were carrying luggage of any type – not even phones or computers of any form. *Strange*, he thought.

Boutique Hotel   Second Floor

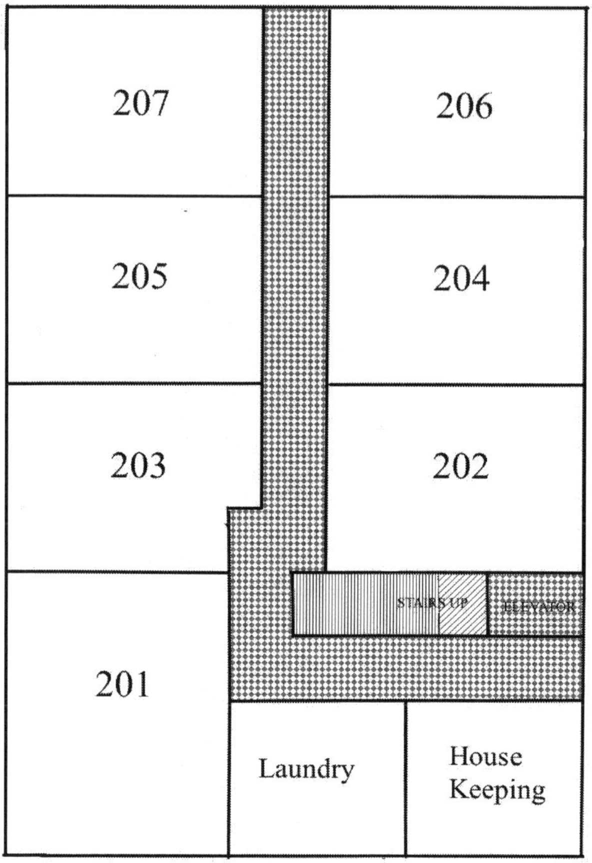

Chapter 17

Monica and Gloria were the first out of the meeting room and headed straight for the elevator.

"What's your room number?" Gloria asked.

"207. It is in a back corner. What's yours?"

"206. It's across the hall."

"I just hope we are not close to Juan."

The two ladies laughed as they reached the elevator, the doors opening. Entering, they turned around and saw the doors closing and then the elevator started ascending.

"I've never been in a lift without buttons," Monica said.

"I'll bet it's the card. You don't have one, the door won't open. And it won't let us go to any floor but our own unless someone on it has a room on that floor."

"I like it."

The elevator stopped, and the doors opened. In front of them was a pale pink door with white molding with a nameplate shaped like an orchid Cattleya trianae, the national flower of Columbia, and mauve lettering reading "Housekeeping." The carpet on the floor was a mauve plush, the walls were a pale pink, the ceiling a brilliant white. That was the only way to describe it because it seemed to glow. When they stepped out of the elevator, lights turned on somewhere because the hallway brightened yet there were no lights to be seen. The only way to go was to the right. Just past the elevator on the right was a landing and stairs going up. As they continued a few steps, they could see another doorway on the left with an orchid nameplate reading "Laundry" and in front of them, a doorway with an orchid nameplate and mauve number 201.

"I like the color scheme," Gloria said. "The pink on the walls looks like the pink of the orchid."

"Yes, it's really relaxing. And the door handles are all mauve matching the carpeting," agreed Monica. "They may call this the Orchid Floor. That would be in keeping with the boutique idea."

Turning right they passed the top of the stairs leading up from the lobby. As they looked down the stairway, they could see that the carpeting at the bottom was white about halfway up it had changed to dark pink and at the top of the stairs it had become the mauve of the floor carpeting.

"If the stairs are like that going to the third floor, the carpeting is going to be black," Gloria said.

"That's radical the way that changes," Monica said.

On the left just past the stairway was another door labeled 203. The wall jutted out about two feet just past the doorway and so they jogged with it and saw a doorway labeled 202. Turning back to the left they could see a window with mauve floor-length curtains at the end of the hallway showing the buildings outside but as they continued down the hallway they realized they weren't actually seeing the buildings outside because in what looked like the distance was the Eiffel Tower. The lighting seemed to follow with them because Monica turned around and saw that it had darkened behind them.

"It's like we're in a cone of light coming down the hallway," she said to Gloria.

"Yes, it's fascinating."

"Hey, here's mine," Monica said, stopping at a door labeled 207. "There's no card reader." She had been carrying her identification card assuming that it doubled as a keycard for the room.

"Grab the knob," Gloria said.

Monica turned the knob and the door opened.

"Mine's across the hall. Try it."

Monica crossed the hall, grabbed the knob to 206 and tried to turn it.

"It won't budge."

"That'll keep Juan out of your knickers."

Monica giggled.

"The only one I would let in my knickers is Issaack. I think he's cute."

"Well, I going to take a bath and lie down for a bit. See you about five of six."

"Sure."

Stepping into her room, Monica found herself in a hallway about eight feet long. It had the same pink walls and mauve carpeting and was well lit apparently in the same manner as the outside corridor.

"I wonder how you turn the lights off," Monica mused half aloud and suddenly found herself in partial darkness, the only light being the sunlight coming in the window in the wall straight ahead. What she was seeing in the window would have "knocked my knickers off" she would later say because it was as though she was standing at the foot of London's Big Ben looking across the Thames at the London Eye, the 443-foot tall Ferris wheel which debuted in 2000.

"Lights," she said, and the room was brilliantly lit, not overpowering but bright enough. She walked down the hallway and found herself in a room that took her breath away. On the right was a king-sized bed with a cream-colored bedspread decorated with American Beauty roses. Over the head of the bed was a valance the color of American Beauty roses with drapery trimmed with the cream-colored lace. The head of the bed was covered with throw pillows in a variety of pinks and reds and in the middle was one large cream-colored pillow. On either side of the bed were ebony nightstands each with a mauve digital clock, the one on the right showing local time and the left, London time. Draped across the foot of the bed appeared to be three dresses. She had to gasp as the one in the middle appeared to be the silver mesh dress she had worn in her "I'm No Slut" video. Upon closer inspection, she realized that the other two were basically silk slips made to go under the mesh dress. One was black and the other was American Beauty red. Obviously, she was supposed to wear the mesh dress with one of three under options – black, red or skin tone. Well, enough of the nudity bit – she'd done that on a dare. And the red didn't go with her hair. She picked the mesh dress up to check for size and under it was a third slip – this one silver. She picked up the third slip and walked to the window to compare colors in the daylight. When she got to the window, she realized that close up it looked just like an ordinary window. She also saw other parts of the room which, even though obvious, had escaped her attention. To the left of the window was a black writing desk with a black mesh office chair. On the right was a sitting area with two black recliner chairs with a black coffee table in front of them. Her decision about dresses made, she turned around to go back to the bed and saw that the other side of the entry hallway wall was the bathroom. Half the area was blocked by a wall behind which were the toilet and a bidet. Then there was a square bathtub which she knew was a whirlpool and in front of the sink area with dual sinks. She looked at her watch and saw that she had plenty of time for a leisurely bath. She was about to remove her clothes when she remembered the window that looked straight into the open bathroom. Starting to go to the window to close the curtains she observed that there were no curtains.

"I can't close the curtains," she said wanting some privacy for her bath and the window went black.

"Wow," she said.

"All you have to do is ask," a female voice said.

"Who are you?"

"Aphrodite," the voice answered.

"Where are you?" Monica whirled around looking for a box or something that would be the source.

"Everywhere and nowhere," Aphrodite said. "I am your virtual maid."

"Well, I am going to take a bath."

There was a sound and Monica turned to see water running into the tub.

"If it's too hot or too cold just let me know."

In a few minutes, Monica knew that it was juuuust right.

Chapter 18

Issaack waited until all others left the meeting room and then he went out into the lobby and walked toward the elevator waiting for him, doors open like a dutiful wife awaiting her husband's return at the end of a long day.

The doors closed, and the elevator started upward. As it slowed to stop at the second floor, Issaack said, "Base." The elevator continued to the third floor. If anyone else had said "Base," nothing would have happened.

There was really no difference in appearance between floors two and three except for the numbers on the rooms. Issaack walked to room 301 and opened the door. The room was filled with computer hardware, servers in two floor-to-ceiling stacks around the room, and a man was sitting at a desk in the middle of the room. If he stood, he would have been six foot four and weighed two hundred pounds. His curly red hair always looked unkempt. He looked up as the door opened and cracked a smile showing brilliant white teeth under a hawk's nose above which two gray green eyes seemed to dance among the myriad of freckles on his face.

"Going well, isn't it," Siegfried Schmidt said,

"Horus is better than expected at this point," Issaack agreed. "His learning is astounding. I'm going to have to build some more servers."

"Wish I could have seen Phil's reaction to the Dead Man's Chest."

"It was priceless. I don't think he had ever heard of it. But by the look, I am certain that he is guilty," Issaack responded. "Wish Horus had been up at the time, he might have had some great reaction."

"I almost fell down when he told Monica and Gloria to quit fooling around and go back to their places."

"You didn't tell him what to say?"

Siegfried shook his head no.

"I don't know where he picked that up, but he is definitely learning," Issaack replied. "Any problems with the software?"

Issaack wasn't referring to computer code or program; instead he was referring to Siegfried's brainchild, organic memory.

"Not a bit. It's holding up well."

"Only took ten tries, but you've done it. Now we are ready to start the long test and see how Horus will handle the island."

"Won't be a problem," Siegfried replied. "When we are done with the testing in five years, we can announce both your A.I. (Artificial Intelligence) and my organic computer."

"Those remote control windows and guns in the Laundry on the second floor and in 305 worked well. I was monitoring them and only had to press one button."

"Fortunately we knew enough about the man to be prepared. A little damage to clean up but nothing extensive."

"Better that than dead," Siegfried said with a smile.

"Just give me a call if there's a problem. I've got to change for cocktails and dinner."

"Wish I could be there."

"Someone's got to be here for now to babysit your brain child. Beside you weren't on the guest list."

Chapter 19

It was almost six o'clock when the next attack occurred. Gerallt Cearrach knew that one would be coming and was wondering when and where. He saw the van in the rearview mirror moving slowly toward him. It was too slow. Whoever it was had a timetable he was trying to keep. Gerallt looked in front and saw another heading toward him, but a little further away. It flashed its lights and the one behind answered. Bingo. The game was afoot as Sherlock Holmes used to say.

He was parked twenty feet past the hotel on the right if one were standing in front of it looking at it. The building itself was situated thirty feet back from the road, with a small plaza in front giving room for a vehicle to pull in and unload. It also would give ample time for a vehicle to turn and accelerate before smashing into the building, with the doors being the most probable target. *Lots of luck,* he thought, thinking of the metal discs he had seen in the pavement every three feet across the plaza's opening just three feet off what normally would have been the sidewalk area.

Reaching under the seat, Gerallt pulled out his Sniper Grey Beretta 92FSR-22. Opening the glove box, he removed the suppressor and screwed it on. Then he pulled back the slide and slid the first shell into the chamber. He rested the pistol on his lap and prepared to watch the attack unfold.

The tan van eased past him with only a quick sidewise glance from the driver who had only seen someone sleeping, straw hat pulled down over his eyes and head back on the seat. Mouth open. Obviously snoring. The head back position gave Gerallt the advantage of being able to keep an eye on the area in front of him. Ten feet past him and ten feet to the hotel's plaza opening, the van's engine roared and the vehicle began to pick up speed. Five feet past where the plaza started, the van turned toward it and started moving toward the hotel. When the van's wheels hit the pavement that indicated the start of the plaza, the circular metal caps Gerallt had seen on his walk-by shot upward and became pillars. Too late the driver saw them, his brake lights flashing on just as the front end smashed into the pillars bringing the van to a rapid and destructive halt.

As soon as the van had started its acceleration, Gerallt was out of his car and running toward the plaza with the Beretta held down to his side in his right hand. He was ten feet away when the van hit the balusters. Another five feet, he raised his pistol and fired two bullets, his hand-loaded ammunition punching through the van's window. Reaching the window, Gerallt used his left elbow to smash in the glass. The driver was slumped over the wheel, blood dripping from his head. Cracks in the driver's side window told Gerallt that his two bullets had missed. So he raised his pistol and put two into the driver's head to ensure that he could not push the plunger on the black box lying on the seat beside him. Gerallt was certain that the wires attached to the box led to explosives in the back of the van.

At that very instant, a fusillade of bullets came from the other van where the occupants, having seen that the demolition part of the attack had failed, were firing parting shots as they zoomed past. Moving quickly, Gerallt got to relative safety at the front of the damaged van and could only watch as the other van disappeared down the road. He stood up and took a step back toward his car when he heard, "Don't move a muscle, mate. Drop your weapon and step back three steps, then get on your knees."

Having seen what happened in the morning, he knew better than to chance anything, so he complied. A tall person wearing electric blue pants and shirt and a black Kevlar vest over the shirt, and a black helmet with an electric blue shiny visor, stepped into his vision and picked up his pistol. Simultaneously he felt a barrel in the small of his back.

"Now lie down with your arms in front of you."

Gerallt complied and felt himself being patted down.

"Put your arms behind your back," he again complied and felt his hands behind bound together with flexi-cuffs. Then each of his arms was seized by a hand and he was jerked roughly to his feet, turned to face the tan van and pushed up against it. Hands went over him again, then turned him around and did a thorough search on his front side leaving nothing to speculation. It was then that he got a look at his captors – twins in almost every respect, both standing at least six foot three. Every respect except the one on the right had a physique, mainly the hips, that bespoke of femininity although he wondered how much of that she actually had.

"What's your business here?" the male asked.

"The same as yours," Gerallt answered.

"Don't get smart," the male said.

"I'm not. You're here protecting the people in the hotel."

"And who are you protecting?" the female asked.

"One of the people who was, I think still is, in the hotel."

"Who?"

"Does it matter?"

"If you want to walk away, it does."

"Ramiro Esteves."

"You're one of his?" the male said, sounding incredulous. "Thought he only hired his own kind."

"He does," Gerallt answered. "I am not one of his."

"Then why are you protecting him?"

Gerallt sighed. He hadn't wanted it to come to this. The answer might seal his fate fatally.

"Let just say I have a score to settle."

"So did they," the male said indicating the van behind him.

"Why didn't you let them settle your score for you?" It was the female this time.

"It's personal. His drugs killed my brother. I am going to kill him, and I will do everything I can to be certain that he doesn't die at someone else's hand."

The female held up his wallet and passport.

"This really you?"

"Yes."

"Pretty blatant of you to be using your real name."

"He knows I am coming after him. I've told him enough times."

"You tried before?"

"No! Never had the chance. I learned he was coming to Cartagena and was hoping to get a shot at him."

She stood listening for a moment.

"He's capable," she said to the male. "British Special Forces. Sniper. Three tours in Afghanistan.

Seventy-five confirmed kills. Honorable discharge. Is your brother why you left?"

Gerallt nodded.

"Turn around," the male said.

Gerallt complied and felt the flexi-cuffs being cut, falling to the ground.

"Turn around," the female this time.

The male had stepped back six feet and was pointing his weapon at him. The female handed him his wallet and passport, which he put back into place. Then she handed him his Beretta, suppressor first.

"Leave this area and don't come back until Esteves is gone. When he is away from here, he's yours but as long as we can see him, he's ours and you're not."

Gerallt took the pistol, thanked them and walked away, never looking back. He reached his car just as a tow truck came down the street. No police in the vicinity but the van would be removed and in fifteen minutes the incident would only be a memory. But for Gerallt, not forgotten.

"He's a strange duck," Gretel said as they watched Gerallt walk away.

"Yes," Hansel agreed. "But he knows his business."

"We had better keep an eye out for him."

"Already been noted. Horus is double checking."

Chapter 20

It was 5:55 p.m. (1755 military time) when Monica Bartlett, bath and nap refreshed, knocked on the door of Room 206. It swung open almost immediately to reveal Gloria Mitchell standing dressed in a long black gown with long sleeves. It was adorned with silver sequins and she was wearing silver flats and carrying a silver handbag.

"Wow," they both said as they saw each other. Monica had selected the black sheath under the silver dress and had found silver heels and a silver handbag in her closet which was part of the wall hiding the bathroom.

"Someone knows how to treat a lady," Gloria said as she stepped out of the room and the door closed behind her.

"My window showed London," Monica said as they walked down the hallway.

"Mine was New York," Gloria said.

"I was guessing Washington, D.C.," replied Monica.

"My bed looked like it was a half poster," Monica said. "I've seen something like it somewhere but don't know what it's called."

"It's a half tester," Gloria said. "I had the same thing," and she described her room that matched Monica's.

"Good nap?"

"Yes, and what a nice bathtub. I would have stayed in there until I was a wrinkled prune."

"The towels were exquisite."

"Nice and soft. Not too rough on one's..."

Gloria paused in her speech as Issaack stepped out of Room 201. He was dressed in a black tuxedo, with a gray tux shirt, matching bow tie with silver specks hanging around his neck untied. Around his waist was a matching cummerbund.

"Don't you look smashing," Monica said as she stepped up to him, took hold of the tie and quickly tied it perfectly. "There," she said patting his chest in a surprisingly motherly fashion, "Now even more so."

"Thank you. And you two look exquisite, I must say."

"Who made the choices?" Gloria asked.

"I have no idea. Someone was hired to study your likes and dislikes."

"And how about you?" Monica asked.

As she finished the question they arrived at the elevator whose door was standing open.

"Ladies," Issaack said, extending his arm toward the door which at the instant closed quickly.

"What happened?" Monica said. "Did the queen arrive?"

Issaack looked quizzical and then said, "Must be a malfunction."

"So how do we call it?" Gloria asked.

"We don't," Issaack said. "A sensor reads your card and opens the door."

"And then slams it on you like a guillotine?"

"I am certain that it wouldn't do anything like that," Issaack said.

"So what's for dinner?" Monica said. "I'm suddenly hungry."

"Don't know," Issaack said. "Carmen wouldn't say and Stefaan just smiled when I asked."

"Are they a thing?" Gloria asked. "They are both so darling."

"Haven't the faintest. I hired them, but they weren't asked about relationships. Neither is married or at least won't admit it."

At this moment, the elevator door slid quietly open, and Issaack, as though expecting it, extended his arm inviting the ladies to enter. Both looked at each other as though making a choice. Maybe that was "who would be the first to run the gauntlet." Then Gloria entered followed by Monica, then Issaack. No sooner had Issaack cleared the entrance, then the doors closed just as a voice was heard "Waitz a minute."

Gloria and Monica looked at each other and mouthed "Esteves" just as Issaack said "Ramiro." Then the three of them laughed.

When the doors opened, they exited. Monica noticed that Issaack looked out the window and did the same. There was a tan van sitting at the entrance to the drop off area with three people off to the side. All were tall.

"Is that Hansel and Gretel?" Gloria asked.

"Looks like it," Issaack said.

"What are they doing?"

"Maybe the motorist is lost and asking for directions."

At this point, the third person walked away to the left and left Hansel and Gretel standing there.

"Well, if that person was driving the van, he isn't going very far with the front end smashed in like that." Gloria said.

Declercq was standing at the doors to the dining room and opened them as they approached.

"Good evening, ladies and sir," he said with a smile on his face for all of them although he was looking at Monica.

"Good evening, Declercq," Gloria said. "What was the hubbub out front?"

"Hubbub? I'm afraid I don't know, madam. My concerns are for my duties and they are only inside and dealing with the dining room."

Then what were you doing with that weapon earlier this afternoon and how did you know that the explosion was from a handheld weapon? Gloria wanted to say but didn't because she knew the best she would get would be a blank look.

They entered the room and heard the quartet which had set up in the far left corner playing something quiet and classical. A bar had been set up to the right and Symon Scheetz was standing behind it. Already available were several glasses of champagne and white and red wine.

"I can make you something else if you'd prefer," Scheetz said.

"What's the white wine?" Monica asked.

"One is a chardonnay from California and one is a Riesling from Germany," Scheetz said indicating which was which. "The red is a French Merlot."

Monica selected champagne, Gloria chose Merlot and Scheetz handed Issaack a glass of amber beer. Monica and Gloria looked at each other with raised eyebrows.

Harvey Gladstone and Waldo were standing next to the table where there appeared to be an assortment of hors d'oeuvres. The three started to walk over just as Ramiro and Phil burst into the room with Ramiro making a beeline for them.

"Whatz you meanz not holding the door?" he snarled up at Issaack and it wasn't a question.

"There are no buttons to push in case you haven't noticed," Gloria said.

"I wazn't talking to you, puta," he said turning to her and then started to turn back to Issaack when Gloria grabbed his arm.

"But I was talking to you," Gloria said.

"Don't you touch me, puta," he said, pushing her arm off and then brushing the sleeve of his white tuxedo.

"Well, don't spit in my face," Gloria said as she wiped it with a silk handkerchief she had gotten out of her purse.

"Now, both of you calm down," Issaack said, stepping between them. Monica took Gloria's arm and led her away.

"And you should have better manners," Issaack said. "There are no buttons and the doors were already closed before I could stick my arm in to stop it. So go have a drink and put it on my bill. Oh, look, here's Phil with one for you already."

Issaack turned and walked away as Phil came up with two drinks. He handed one to Ramiro who glared after Issaack.

"Em breve… (Someday soon…)," Ramiro muttered under his breath.

Chapter 21

Despite the rough start to dinner, things calmed down by the time the meal was served although seating was not as before, but the change was minor. Monica Bartlett and Issaack Kinkaid switched seats so that Monica and Gloria were sitting between Issaack and Waldo. Thus, neither woman was seated next to an antagonist – meaning someone in the Bundle that Esteves had befriended and voted in favor of his controversial motion. Conversation was basically kept between the two groups. Dinner was served by Carmen and Declercq who wheeled out a great cart laden with plates and serving dishes for vegetables. A white linen tablecloth covered the round table and it had obviously been made to fit. The entrée was a choice of surf and turf: whole lobster and prime rib, or they could be had separately; red snapper crusted with parmesan; rack of lamb with gravy and mint jelly. There was a choice of tossed salad with five dressings: creamy Roquefort, peppercorn ranch, green goddess, Frisky Italian (it had a bite), and balsamic vinaigrette; peas with baby onions, parslied carrots, pan roasted potatoes, candied yams, and pickled beets. Dessert was orange sorbet, strawberry chocolate cheese cake (the pie crust was chocolate), key lime pie, or chocolate mousse. Just as after dinner drinks were being served, the string quartet, which had been playing light classical before and during the meal, suddenly changed and a lilting rock tune arose.

Monica was shocked to hear a fantastic string version of *The Slag has Heart* arise. She noticed that all eyes were on her, Ramiro was leering, and then the other members of the Bundle started applauding. She had no choice but to rise and go stand in front of the small orchestra and break into song

Melinda was a harlot, a prosty, a whore
It wasn't for money, it was just for the cock
Melinda loved it heaty, always wanting more
Men who had her numba, didn't go by the clock
Chorus
The poor are just as needy,
They cannot do their part
The poor they are not greedy
That's why the slag has heart
Melinda had one rule, a reg she neva broke
Payment was in cash up front, thirty quid plus five
Melinda kept thirty, it went into her poke
The five went in a pocket, neva was it rive
Chorus
Melinda wasn't cheap, she spent her income well
Sunday going to church, she duly paid the tithe
Melinda did due penance, so not go to hell
But once between the bedsheets, then she'd really writhe
Chorus
Melinda walked the lanes, for sterling by the night
She answered to no pimp, she always worked alone
Melinda walked the lanes, by daytime doing right
She neva told her name, they called her Cherry Stone

Chorus
The fivas in her pocket, list'ning for a plea
"Me luck is down," "Me health is rot," "Can't do me part"
She drops a fiva, sometime two, or perhap three
She hears him say, "God bless you ma'am. That slag has heart"
Chorus

When she finished there was stunned silence especially from those who had never heard her sing before. Hearing her beautiful voice, they could understand how she had won the contest and the hearts of the world's youth. When she sat down, Gloria reached out and grabbed her hand and whispered "That was fantastic."

"Thank you," was all Monica could say.

Dinner broke up about nine, they all said their good nights and goodbyes and left the dining room in ones and twos. All had promised to get together as needed but would also welcome Facetime or Skype meetings. Gloria and Monica walked to their rooms with hardly a word but had exchanged contact information.

Chapter 22

Each had made their own transportation arrangements to and from Cartagena and they were so spaced that each left separately. Monica was up at 5:00 a.m. and out the door to a waiting limousine at 5:29 a.m. The only people she saw were Hansel, Gretel and Symon Sheetz. Hansel and Gretel were standing out by the street and Symon was the doorman. Symon took the bag containing her clothes from last night and put it in the limousine. Monica had found a black calfskin leather carry-on bag with silver buckles on her bed when she walked into her room after dinner and the bed had been turned down. She had set the alarm and slept the sleep of the dead until the alarm chirped gently at 5:00 a.m. She'd been offered breakfast to take with her on the way to the airport, but she'd get something in the first class lounge while she waited for the plane. And she didn't like drinking tea from Styrofoam cups. It wasn't a success thing, it was that she never had. Didn't like that cardboard type of cup either. Besides, the road to the airport wasn't all that smooth.

As she sat back and relaxed, she thought about the previous day and realized that she liked everyone but Ramiro. Him she hoped never to see again but realized that was a vain hope considering the situation. Although she didn't like the premise of the enterprise, she was excited because it was something different. Something she could use to get her mind off touring and songwriting every once in a while. After all, there were more things in the world besides music.

The second person to leave was Ramiro Esteves. He was actually up at 4:45 a.m. and at 5:15 a.m. when Monica was stepping out of the shower, he was sitting down alone at the table. On the left side was a tall glass of fresh squeezed orange juice and on the right a pot of freshly brewed rich dark Brazilian coffee – no fancy flavors for him. The glass of orange juice was finished in one drink and he had just poured his first cup of coffee when Declercq emerged from the kitchen with a silver tray with glass dome atop it. Under the dome was a china plate with an eight-ounce ribeye grilled medium, two sunny side up eggs cooked as one, hash brown potatoes with "juzt a little crizp" and one slice of untoasted white bread buttered and cut diagonally. Carmen got a food order and it was done to the letter. Declercq removed the cover and set the tray and china plate in front of him just as he had ordered. Then like a wisp of smoke, Declercq was gone as silently as he had approached.

Ramiro had finished his breakfast and was just pouring his second cup of coffee "No worry, I do myzelf" when Monica exited the building at 5:29 a.m. At precisely 5:45 a.m., a black limousine pulled into the hotel's drop-off area with the driver's side next to the building. Two bodyguards got out of the passenger side and stood shoulder to shoulder covering the rear passenger door. The driver was out and looking over the top of the car toward the street and the bodyguard who sat in the middle seat facing backwards was holding the door when Ramiro emerged, his gleaming white suit offering an easy target to anyone wishing to take a shot. One person did but wasn't in the proper position and was without a long-range rifle. All Gerallt could do was watch and wish. He wasn't about to test the defenses of the small boutique hotel. Ramiro got into the car followed by the bodyguards and the driver, the doors were closed, and the limousine pulled out quickly going back the way it had come. No sooner had Ramiro sat down than his secretary, sitting on the passenger side of the middle seat handed a sheaf of papers containing reports of things that had occurred in his empire in the past twenty-one hours. He had no further thoughts about the meeting and its participants until he was on his plane and then that was only to label The Good (2), The Bad (2), and The Soon to Be Dead (2).

Issaack Kinkaid was next, simply to fill the illusion that he was one of the "guests." Knowing that, because of the security in the building and the order and timeliness of the departures, no one was about, he was dressed simply in tan Dockers, a Dodger Blue tee shirt bearing the appropriate logo and tan topsiders with no socks. He had gotten up at 5:30 a.m., showered, dressed and gone downstairs at 5:55 a.m., gotten into the hired limousine and gone for a one-hour ride. When he returned he and Siegfried, Hansel, Gretel, Symon Scheetz, Declercq, and Carmen would have breakfast (made by Carmen and served by Declercq before they both sat down) and talk about the past twenty-four hours, what went wrong and why, and what didn't and why.

Gloria Mitchell was next. She was up at 5:15 a.m., showered and dressed and downstairs for breakfast just after Ramiro Esteves had departed. It was a light breakfast of orange juice (also freshly squeezed but not necessarily required), coffee (nothing special specified except "Not Decaf") with sugar and cream, a pastry (not overly sweet) with butter and berry preserves ("Not jelly"). She ate leisurely thinking about the past day and her new "friends" and their project. She knew that she and Monica had bonded; she was friends with Issaack and Waldo, acquaintances with Harvey Gladstone and Phil Parmalee and despised, bordering on hatred, Ramiro Esteves. He, she knew, was a party with whom to be reckoned. She didn't know what to expect from him, but it couldn't be good.

Her breakfast complete and the dishes cleared away by the ghostly Declercq as soon as the last crumb had vanished, Gloria stood, surveyed the room so she wouldn't forget it, and walked to the front door, the dining/Board Room doors opening automatically. Symon Scheetz was standing inside the front door and greeted her cordially, his attention from the drop-off area diverted only for that instant. Thirty second later, her UberSelect pulled in, Symon Scheetz opened the front door and she exited, followed by Symon Scheetz who opened the rear door of the UberSelect Cadillac and she got in, Symon Scheetz handed her the black leather carry-on she had left with him as she passed going to breakfast, shut the door, and the UberSelect Cadillac drove away heading for the airport.

Harvey Gladstone was third to last. He was riding standby because it was cheaper. He'd left his evening clothes in the room along with the black leather suit bag. Just something extra to worry about and added an unnecessary expensive look to his persona. His alarm went off at 5:30 a.m. and he was in the dining room by 6:00 a.m. His breakfast order was like everything else in his life – simple and straight forward. Eggs – scrambled or fried over easy, bacon crisp, buttered white toast, orange juice, black coffee. He ate fast and was out the door to get his taxi at 6:20 a.m. On the way to the airport he thought about the events and the people. *Gloria was a bitch – not major but still a bitch. She needed to be watched. Monica was a low-class cunt with a great body and fantastic voice. Even with the black slip under the silver mesh, he could visualize her body from the video. Issaack was smart. He had a lot going for him but didn't show it. He could be behind the entire thing. Waldo – now there's someone who knows what to do with his money. It's all been reinvested in his companies and it just keeps rolling in. Wow, I should be so lucky! Hmmm, guess I am. Parmalee – he killed his partner. I know he did. Ha, whoever thought of that Dead Man's Chest Rum for him was a genius. Yep, that's the kind of thing that Issaack would do. Don't want to get on Phil's bad side. Basically he's a wimp but deadly when he strikes. His partner should have been more aware and maybe he'd still be alive.*

Phil Parmelee was right behind Harvey Gladstone. His alarm rang at 6:00 a.m. and at 6:30 a.m. he was in the dining room having left his bag with Symon Scheetz. His breakfast was different – people would have been surprised: a slice of Virginia ham with redeye gravy, two fried eggs sunny side up but basted, grits and biscuits with butter and honey, no juice but black coffee. He ate slowly savoring every bite and was in the foyer by 7:00 a.m. His limousine was punctual. When Symon Scheetz opened the foyer door, Phil took his bag from him without a word exchanged, opened the limousine's door himself, threw the bag in and followed it flopping onto the seat as he drew the door closed. He leaned back, and thoughts of the past day ran through his head. *Ramiro didn't get under the table as fast as most of us. In fact, I think he was last. I pictured him as more of a coward. Or did he know something we didn't? Monica is a knockout but a bit uncouth. Needs some couth lessons. Love to give it a try. Flat on her back with me on top. At least for starters. Gloria's got a real bitch tone. The way she handled Ramiro was straight out of the bitch handbook. Watch out for her! Harvey's a dweeb. Won't worry about him one way or the other. Waldo and Issaack both are really driven. They know what they want and where they're going. Wouldn't be surprised if either or both are behind this.*

Waldo was last in and last out. He was up at 7:00 and in the dining room at 7:20 a.m., ten minutes before he said he would be. "Sorry," he had said to Declercq. "If I could get some coffee with a little cream, I'll manage just fine." Declercq brought the pot and a cup, "Cream's in the little pot, sir." Breakfast came out punctually at 7:30 a.m.: two sausage patties (hot as in spicy); three pancakes with real maple syrup, if you please; small glass of orange juice; half a grapefruit. He ate leisurely mulling over the past twenty-four. *Issaack was right. Most of the group is perfect. Ramiro is the one to watch out for. He's needed because Brazil owns the island. He'll get it for us and take a cut off the bribes. You know there'll be bribes. Monica will just ride along. Gloria – she's tough. She could have her own ideas about things. Already trying to take command. Harvey – milquetoast, that one, but he sided with Ramiro. That was a surprise! Phil – definitely a killer, at least of one. He'll go with the winner though. Watch him switch now that Ramiro's lost his entry. Came close though.*

Finishing his third cup of coffee just before eight, he walked out of the dining room just as his limousine pulled up. He let Symon Scheetz carry his bag to the limousine and open the door. Do all the footman things. Once in the car, he settled back for a nap that would last until the airport.

PART II

CONSTRUCTION

Chapter 1

The next meeting of the self-named Billionaire Bundle was 7 months, 9 days later in the same spot. Entry was the same although new cards had been issued and the entry times changed by lot – except for one, Ramiro Esteves. This was because of the incidents that had happened the time before. Ramiro Esteves had been handpicked to enter last. Well, actually Siegfried and Issaack had been talking about it where Horus could hear.

"With all that went on last time," Issaack had said, "We need one of three things: 1) Esteves doesn't attend; 2) Esteves comes first with a delay for any attack; 3) Esteves comes last with an hour delay between the last person and him."

"How are you going to explain that to him?" Siegfried said. "You know he's going to be upset."

"True but he'll just have to live with it."

"Based on what we know," Horus said, entering the conversation uninvited, "the probability of another attack is less than 5% or the odds are 19:1."

Siegfried and Issaack looked at each other. Both shrugged meaning "Don't ask me." And Siegfried mouthed, "I didn't program that" and Issaack replied, "neither did I."

Horus continued, "And here is the arrival schedule with Esteves arriving last which is best."

And the printer spit out two sheets of paper. Siegfried and Issaack both took a copy, looked at it, agreed and that was that. Both noted that Esteves's arrival was just fifteen minutes after Gloria Mitchell's, the sixth to arrive.

By chance (or at least by Horus's chance), Harvey Gladstone was first to arrive, and he did punctually at 8:00 a.m. Directions were the same as the first time although the new keycard each billionaire received had a notation that "the old one will not work." He completed the screening process in five minutes and walked through the door into the dining room, which was set up with the round table as before. Stefaan Declercq greeted him with his silver tray bearing a crystal tumbler half filled with ice and then filled three quarters full of Jack Daniel's Tennessee Fire.

"Good morning, Mr. Gladstone," Stefaan said.

"Good day, Stefaan," Harvey Gladstone said amenably as he took the crystal tumbler and had a sip. "Is seating as the first time?"

"Nothing was said, sir," Stefaan said, which is what he was told to say. "So I suspect you may sit wherever you wish."

And where Harvey Gladstone preferred to sit was exactly where he had the first time. In fact, as the rest of the Bundle arrived, each sat precisely where they had the first time. Because the security equipment had been updated and was the best that was available, the arrival times had been pared down to fifteen minutes, so Esteves arrived at the outside door at precisely 9:30 a.m., but this time with no bodyguards. Well, at least none that tried to come in.

And basically, everyone came dressed as before and was greeted with his or her preferred beverage. Harvey Gladstone was wearing a gray suit with a blue shirt and dark blue tie with Daffy Duck on it (he mentioned he got it at Goodwill). Second in, Phil Parmalee had a plain gold tee shirt, black Dockers with a gold leather belt (big change for him), the buckle of which resembled an open but empty treasure chest with a skull in it (his answer to Dead Man's Chest rum), and his habitual thongs. Waldo Emerson, the third to appear, was wearing a white button down shirt, robin's egg blue Dockers and his traditional black top-siders with white socks. A lightweight dark blue sport jacket was folded over his left arm because he had taken it off to make the body search easier. Arriving just before her time was up at 8:49:50 in fourth place, Monica Bartlett was clad in a white leather jacket, crimson skirt and white patent leather knee high boots with a skin tight black top. She looked tired having flown from Lisbon on a private jet after finishing a show at 1:00 a.m. She eschewed the champagne asking for a double English Breakfast Tea – not Earl Grey. Issaack Kinkaid strode in fifth wearing a dark blue Levi jacket and pants with a silver polo shirt showing no identifying logo. Gloria Mitchell had toned down a bit (or brightened up a bit depending on your point of view) wearing a pink short sleeved blouse with a blood red skirt and red cross trainers explaining that her feet had been killing her. The first six were finished with their croissants, Danish, or donuts when Ramiro Esteves, dressed exactly as before, came in, gave the room a once-over as he had the first time and sat down without a word. A quick glance and a nod passed through the other six and in unison, they welcomed him with "Bom dia, João."

He looked at them and went back to his pastry and Havana Club Máximo.

"Good morning, everyone." Horus's voice came through their earbuds which they, except for Ramiro, had all put on when they sat down. As before, Waldo picked up Ramiro's and handed it to him. In return, he received a noncommittal look, but Ramiro did put it on.

"We have a lot to talk about today and at least one of you has asked for an early day, so we had better get started."

"That's me," Monica said. "I have a show in Naples tomorrow."

As the meeting began, on a rooftop two blocks away, Gerallt Cearrach was putting away his rifle. Although he had been ready, the bodyguards were too good and had Ramiro Esteves's back covered from the car to the door where they had handed him off to Hansel and Gretel. It had been a long shot anyway – not the distance but the opportunity.

Chapter 2

Horus began, "It's taken a while and it hasn't been cheap, but we have the property. We tried to purchase it outright but because it is a territory of Brazil they wouldn't sell, but they were willing to give a ten-year lease which was approved for fifty million dollars. All infrastructure improvements – roads, buildings, etc. – are to be left. The ten years was more than was to be required, but it was felt prudent to leave some kind of leeway. Of course, the fifty million was just the legal fees. Whenever there are politics and money involved, there will be bribes. Yes, that a nasty word, but that's business and we were prepared."

"*We?*" Phil mouthed at Ramiro.

Horus continued, "However, there were some things that happened before the lease was approved.

"Because we want to build headquarters in the volcano's crater, we asked permission to do a survey prior to the start of negotiations. That was approved – for a price – and Mr. Kincaid and Mr. Parmalee accompanied by two surveyors, four volcanic experts, and a videographer made a trip by helicopter."

The Eurocopter EC145 dubbed Surveyor I for the purpose of this trip entered the one-thousand-foot cone of Montanha da Cratera at 11:19 a.m. (1119 military time) on the agreed upon day and started a counterclockwise tour of the area. In two revolutions they corkscrewed down to two-hundred feet above the crater's floor. The sides of the crater were relatively smooth and getting down from the rim to the crater floor on foot would require an experienced rock climber or rappelling with a very long rope or making the descent in stages – if any of those were possible. The remains of the vent could be seen in the center of the crater's floor. From that height, it was obvious that the floor was covered with vegetation. There were even two sizable trees and many small ones.

"Drop down to about fifty feet and take us around again," Issaack instructed. He was in charge of this excursion as everything else in the program.

Raoul Sanchez, the pilot of the rental Eurocopter, followed his order and flew around the crater slowly letting everyone get a good look.

The members of the Bundle watching the proceedings via digital recording on a large screen television set between the two windows of the hotel's dining room were enthralled.

"Looks good and solid," said Mike McCormick, one of the two volcanic experts.

"Fairly level," Virginia Columbine, head of the surveyor team, said. "You shouldn't have any trouble with construction."

"If we can get a tunnel through the mountain," Issaack said.

"It's not the tunnel that's the problem," Phil said. "It's getting the machinery to the spot."

"Looks like a good spot to put down," Issaack said. "There on the left."

The chopper went into a counterclockwise turn and Raoul Sanchez looked at the area Issaack had identified.

"Looks good to me," Raoul said. "Let's put this bird on the ground."

As the Eurocopter started dropping down to the crater floor, a small flock of birds took flight from the area that had been designated as the landing area.

Monica laughed. "Look at those boids scatter."

"Looks like we're not the first bird to set down," Raoul said.

The Eurocopter settled peacefully on the crater floor, and Raoul shut the engine off.

"It's 1207. Lift off for the trip back is 1700," Raoul said.

Everyone hurried to get out of the chopper because each had tasks to perform and wanted as much time as possible. While everyone was gathering whatever equipment they wanted, Phil and Issaack got two freezer chests out.

"The blue one is water and the green is food," Issaack said. We've got sandwiches: chicken salad, ham salad, veggie subs, turkey subs, salami subs, and roast beef subs. Each is labelled appropriately. There's also a platter with cheeses, pickles and olives and mustard, ketchup and mayonnaise. Help yourselves and don't leave any trash."

Phil looked at Issaack as though to say "*Do you think that last was necessary?*" and Issaack mouthed "*You never know.*"

"Where do you think you'll put the headquarters?" Virginia Columbine asked Issaack.

Issaack pointed and said, "Over there. It's flat enough and should be big enough."

"You got it," Virginia Columbine said, and she and the other surveyor took their equipment and headed for the indicated spot.

The four volcanic experts had handheld augers with which to drill as deep as twelve feet down and bring back core samples. They broke up into two teams and one team took off for the opposite end of the crater while Mike McCormick and the other team headed for the area where the surveyors were setting up.

Issaack and Phil each picked up a sandwich from those left, fixed it with cheese and condiments, added a bottle of water and started walking, followed by the videographer.

"Mine was a veggie sub," Phil said.

"Lah di dah," Gloria said.

Phil looked at her and shrugged.

"Be certain to get pictures of each of the teams and what they're doing," Issaack said to the videographer, who touched a finger to his cap brim and went to where the closest team of volcanic experts was drilling a hole.

Chapter 3

While the team from Surveyor I was doing their business in the volcano, a second Eurocopter C145 dubbed Surveyor II was setting down on a plateau on the south side of Montanha da Cratera. The two helicopters had travelled together from Belém, Brazil. The Bundle team in Surveyor II was headed by Harvey Gladstone and Gloria Mitchell. Harvey Gladstone was dressed in a brown guide shirt with khaki cargo shorts, white athletic socks and hiking boots. Remarkably the hiking boots had been purchased new from a top flight outdoors store. With them were six surveyors, two volcanic experts and a videographer. Their duties were to survey the plateau and the incline leading up to it so that plans could be made for the tunnel through the mountain.

With the chopper on the ground, everyone alighted, and, except for four of the surveyors and one volcanic expert, the others retrieved their equipment. As with Surveyor I, there were two freezer chests with food and water and everyone got sandwiches and water. The four surveyors and one volcanic expert got back into the chopper and with the ground teams clear, the chopper fired up its engine and took off for a short flight to the bottom of Montanha da Cratera where the four surveyors would determine the best route up to the plateau.

On the plateau, the volcanic expert start taking core samples and the remaining two surveyors set to work mapping the plateau. When they were finished, they would start working their way down the mountain to meet up with the other team. Harvey Gladstone pulled out a GPS that had a contour map of the island. It said that he was 872 feet above sea level. That matched the GPS map, so he began to have some confidence in that.

"So what's the plan with this tunnel?" Gloria Mitchell asked. She had volunteered to be the second Bundle member on Surveyor II.

"It will link the crater basin with the rest of the island. The crater's basin has a lot of potential for agriculture once we get water there," Harvey Gladstone explained.

"And how do we get water there?"

"Through the tunnel. We run a pipe through the concrete in the tunnel – it may be possible just to have the hole in the blocks and the seal between blocks will be watertight. That is yet to be investigated."

"So the basin is for the future of São Rochelle – beyond our use of it?"

"As is the entire infrastructure that we construct. It will all be left for Brazil to do whatever they want with it."

The two had started walking around the plateau. Gloria had her hands in the pockets of red cargo shorts and was wearing a beige nondescript blouse. On her feet were white cross trainers with tennis shoe socks. As she walked, she was kicking small rocks and watching as they careened off bigger ones which dotted the plateau as they did the rest of the island. Suddenly she raced after a rock she had just kicked. She bent down and picked it up and then screamed, ***"A snake!"***

Harvey laughed. "I don't think so."

"I do," Gloria screamed. ***"It bit me."***

Gladstone hurried toward her as did one of the surveyors who had heard her scream and the videographer. Gloria was holding her hand out in front of her looking at her wrist. The surveyor looked at her wrist and then said, "¿Donde está la serpiente? (Where is the snake?)"

Gloria pointed (it was easy to understand "la serpiente") and both men looked and could see a snake about five feet long moving away. It had two dark stripes running on the length of its back.

The videographer had been filming the two billionaires and had caught the snake perfectly. Gloria cringed.

"Cascavel," said the surveyor. "We must get her to hospital."

"Cascavel?" said Harvey Gladstone. "I don't understand."

"Very poisonous."

"Well, don't just stand there, get the helicopter," Gloria said.

The surveyor had taken a handkerchief out of his pocket and was tying it around Gloria's biceps.

Harvey Gladstone finally snapped out of it and used a walkie talkie to call the chopper pilot. Within seconds the sound of the chopper's engine was heard roaring to life. Several minutes later, the Eurocopter settled on the plateau and the two billionaires hurried toward it just as the other surveyor came up holding a plastic bag in his hand.

"What's that?" Harvey asked.

"Serpente … fix," the man stumbled grasping for the proper words in a language he didn't speak too well.

"I don't know how…," Gladstone began.

The man opened the zip lock bag, pulled out a piece of paper and handed it to Harvey. Harvey looked at it and saw printing but not in English – Spanish, he judged.

"I don't read … no entiendo," he said pointing at the paper.

"It fix bite," the other surveyor said as he grabbed the bag, shouted something at his partner, and started to get into the Eurocopter with Gloria.

"You come?" he said to Harvey Gladstone.

Harvey was going to say "No" and then thought that he shouldn't leave Gloria alone at this time and got in the chopper, which lifted off immediately.

On the television screen, the Eurocopter faded into the distance and then the video stopped.

"Why it stopz?" Ramiro asked.

"The videographer had to get down the mountainside to the other surveyors and didn't need to film his twenty-minute trek," Gladstone said as the video came back on and showed two of the surveyors conferring over a map. One of them pointed up the mountain and the other started in that direction.

In the chopper, Gladstone got on the radio and called Issaack.

"Gloria got bitten by a snake. We are going to a hospital in Belém. The surveyors said that it's poisonous. One of the men had a snake bite kit. I have one of the surveyors with me because the instructions are in Spanish and I'm monolingual."

"As you can tell, they made it to the hospital in time," Horus said. "While the surveyor, Luis Garcia, read the instructions, Mr. Gladstone, an admitted haemophobe, did what the instructions said to do. The doctors told him that he may have saved her life or at least prevented some severe damage.

"The snake was identified as a tropical rattlesnake or scientific name Crotalus Terrificus.

Unlike most rattlesnakes, it strikes with little or no warning. The venom is extremely toxic and has haemotoxic and neurotoxic components that can damage tissue and paralyze the central nervous system."

"Excuse me, Horus," interrupted Phil. "How was the identification of the snake made?"

"The surveyor left behind on the plateau was very familiar with the snake and its habits. In his equipment, he had a machete and, after catching the snake, he cut the head off and put it and the body in a bag."

"That man is to be congratulated."

"Yes, because the hospital required accurate identification before administering the anti-venom serum and with the body and head, he was able to answer the question. He was fortunate to have a satellite phone provided by his company and his partner gave them the number. I think we should thank Mr. Gladstone for overcoming his fear of blood."

The other members of the Bundle applauded Harvey and Gloria.

"Just to conclude the story of the day," Horus continued, "Mrs. Mitchell's son flew down to Belém the next day and escorted her home. The Eurocopter dubbed Surveyor II, refueled and Mr. Gladstone and Senor Garcia flew back to São Rochelle to pick up the rest of the crew and then returned to Caracas where they were reunited with Mr. Kincaid and Mr. Parmalee. The results of the day permitted us to proceed apace with the lease negotiations."

Harvey looked at Gloria and thought *She didn't bother to mention that stone she had picked up and held onto so tenaciously. I wonder why not.*

Chapter 4

"Now that we have the property, we can begin planning the construction phase. The first item on the agenda is to get two construction bulldozers onto the island. With no boat access, they will have to be air dropped."

The lease began April 1, and on the evening of March 31, a container ship anchored as close to the shallows as the captain felt it was safe. The ship was loaded with containers, all of which were bound for the island in one way or another. Part of the ship had been made a helicopter landing deck and on it was securely fastened a CH-53E Super Stallion, the U.S. military's largest helicopter in use. It could carry up to 14.5 tons externally. It was intended to bring containers from the ship to shore and to place them where they are needed.

These were the ones that were to be used for housing for the construction crews. For now, the containers have food and fuel and appliances and furniture to make the working crews living quarters. One container with fuel would be lifted ashore on the first day. Other containers have to wait until the bulldozer was dropped and prepared the ground for containers in the area where the old village was.

The Stallion's first trip was a cargo of men and four dirt bikes. Six of the men were surveyors and would quickly lay out the landing field and mark it with a big plus sign made out of orange nylon. This was the target for the C-17 to drop the bulldozers on. The construction team had decided that things would go faster with two. The people who comprised the construction team were 90% men. A betting poll was already awaiting the drop of the first Caterpillar D9T. Whoever guessed the correct distance from the cab of the bulldozer to the middle of the plus sign – without going under – would be the winner of the pot. Toby Tyler didn't care if he won or not. He just wanted to survive the drop. He was one of two drivers of the 106,000-pound D9T Caterpillar medium sized bulldozers and by lot he had "won" the right to ride down with the behemoth dozer and release the chutes after the dozer was safely down. His only hope was that he would live to spend the hundred-thousand-dollar bonus for taking the ride. At the time the Stallion landed on São Rochelle the first time, he was sitting at an airport in Belém waiting for word that the Boeing C-17 Globemaster III could leave on its mission.

The other men in the first group were carrying picks and shovels. Once on the ground they headed for the site chosen for the first two containers. One was fuel. The second (and to the workers definitely important) was the kitchen and mess hall. Its first offering would be lunch and they were bound and determined it would get there on time. The two sites for these containers had been picked earlier. Using a hand-held GPS, Kirk Donahue led six of the men to the site of the island's first gas station. The area was quickly marked off and the team set to work digging and moving dirt to get a sufficiently level spot. Since the choice of the spot had been made earlier, the ground didn't need much leveling but did need rocks removed – rocks that would become part of São Rochelle's pier. The site for the Rochelle Deli was one hundred feet away and another team of six men quickly got busy leveling it.

These two sites were at the eastern end of the drop zone and, if all went well, would not be impacted (pun intended) by the landing of the dozers.

The landing site was ready quickly and word passed to the C-17 crew that all was in readiness, at least on the island. Not as ready was the C-17 because a thunderstorm was temporarily halting its takeoff.

The gas station's site was the first ready and the King Stallion headed ashore with the container. It, as all the containers, was specially made. The sides were destined to be walls of the construction office. When the container was in place, workers with battery powered ratchet hammers attacked the outer shell, revealing a 4,000-gallon tank containing diesel fuel weighing 28,000 pounds. As said, the walls and top which had been removed would be used for other buildings.

The second trip ashore by the King Stallion was with the Rochelle Deli and when it was set in place, the men cheered, and the cook unlocked the door. The men entered and helped unpack and organize the furniture while the cook got busy preparing lunch, which having been fixed on the ship, required very little preparation.

The four dirt bikes would be used for a perimeter tour of the island south of the volcano, but it wouldn't be a fun ride. Their task was to mark the path of the perimeter road. It didn't have to be fancy, it just had to be feasible for the bulldozers. Two bikes started where the dock was to be constructed and went clockwise ending up where the bulldozer was supposed to land. The other two would start at the same place going counterclockwise and their road was infinitely more important because it was the road which initially would be used to get construction vehicles and materials to the base inside the volcano once the tunnel was dug. Their task was not expected to be completed this day and they would be joined by the two other surveyors when their task was completed.

One hour after the deli opened for lunch, it was announced that the C-17 was almost to the island. All who could gathered to see the drop and most crossed their fingers, not that they'd win the jackpot – although many had that thought – but that Toby Tyler would land safely.

Chapter 5

The big doors of the C-17's cargo bay opened slowly. From his seat in the dozer, Toby watched the view change from that of gray rain-laden clouds to gorgeous azure blue with patches of fluffy white clouds. To his left stood Jeff Lyons, the cargo master of *Super Sue*, currently named for the pilot's wife although rumors had it that status of the marriage was iffy. Jeff was really a U.S. Air Force Master Sergeant, although for this operation an agreement had been reached that the crew of the C-17 would wear civilian clothing. They felt this was better for their work at the airfield they were using as a base for this operation. All Air Force insignia on the plane had been painted over. The only insignia – other than the plane's number – was the head of a Tyrannosaurus Rex on the tail. That was the logo which had been taken for this project. The Caterpillar wasn't fast enough to propel itself out like the cars used in *The Fate of the Furious,* but the idea was the same. The dozer was sitting on a wood pallet to which it was fastened. Lines from sixteen parachutes were fastened to the pallet and the dozer. The fastening cords led to another pallet in front of the dozer on which were the sixteen chutes. In front of that pallet was the drogue chute which was attached to the parachute pallet. At the proper moment, the drogue would be released from the cargo hold. When it deployed, it would pull out the parachute pallet. When the sixteen chutes on that pallet deployed, the combined strength would pull out the pallet on which the dozer sat and in the dozer sat Toby. Toby knew that the scene he was looking at was basically what he would see until he was about to land in the middle of the plus sign on the cultivated land on São Rochelle.

As he waited for the signal from Jeff Lyons, Toby went over and over the process he had been through twenty times in the simulator. He had some control over the chutes and could do some steering and could see the predicted landing of the dozer on a hand-held tablet about the size of a smartphone. There were five buttons on the touch screen of the device: four buttons that controlled the chutes and one button – green – released the chutes from the dozer when it was firmly in contact with the soil of São Rochelle. In the twenty simulations, the best he had ever done was eighteen inches away from dead center of the plus sign. By watching the altimeter readout on the device, Toby would start the engine of the dozer when he was five hundred feet above the ground and could get it moving immediately.

His thoughts were interrupted by the changing of the red of the ready light to yellow. That meant less than thirty seconds to launch and almost meant that it was too late to call it off. Giving a thumbs up to Jeff, Toby said a silent prayer to his god (or maybe "gods" because he wanted all the help he could get) and turned his attention to the landing device. Then he sensed that the parachute pallet moving and looked up. Somewhere behind the plane, the drogue was deployed and was pulling the parachute pallet out. Even as that thought hit him, he saw the parachute pallet leave the plane and watched as the parachute packets stretched into the distance and then opened and just as suddenly as that happened the dozer was moving. Almost before he knew it, he felt the dozer tip forward and he was falling. There was supposed to be a five second delay from leaving the plane until the dozer had fallen enough for the parachute cords to be extended, the sixteen parachutes open and stop his fall. It would be sudden and almost instantaneous. Mentally counting to five, Toby waited for the jerk that would signal that the dozer pallet was under the parachute umbrella and the 106,000-pound D9T dozer was being lowered safely to São Rochelle. Reaching five, he tensed himself … but there was no jerk. That meant that something had gone wrong and the dozer was plummeting unrestrained toward ... well, it didn't matter where it was plummeting because upon impact it would be rubble and he would be dead. He had one chance and that was to get out and use his emergency chute before the speed of his fall became such the chute would be ripped to tatters when it opened.

The almost instantaneous decision made to release the buckle on the safety harness holding him coincided with a loud ***BAM***, temporarily deafening him. The jolt of the dozer's fall abruptly slowing rattled his senses. He looked at the screen of the landing tablet and saw that his rate of decent was faster that he would have liked but within the parameters that he had been told were his safe landing figures. He knew that it would be several seconds before the computers had a read on his trajectory and breathed a sigh of relief when the numbers flashed onto the screen that they had him just one hundred feet from his target.

The four control buttons were set in a square around the green button in the center of which was the projected landing spot. The upper left one pulsed meaning that the computer had determined a course correction, and Toby hit it. Then the upper right, and he pressed it. Distance now eight hundred eighty feet. The upper left button pulsed again, and he pressed it. Then the lower left and he pressed it. He had said after his sixth simulation that it was like a game of Twister. His attention to the pulsing was interrupted by a beeping signaling that the dozer was five hundred feet above the ground. He started the dozer's engine and was thrilled to hear it roar to life. That beeping also signaled that it was too late to make any more changes – the dozer and he would just have to ... *BUMP*. He was jolted at the sound of the dozer pallet hitting the earth, but he sensed he was still moving. He knew that he was not to hit the green button until he felt his downward trajectory halted – just like you know your car has come to a stop when you can feel your forward trajectory stop after applying the brakes. He sensed that the front of the pallet was still moving down, and, in that instant, it hit the ground with a loud *BANG* and all sensation of movement stopped.

Reaction honed by the twenty simulations, he pressed the green button on the landing device, and heard the thunderous *POW* of the chutes being released from the dozer as he put the machine into first gear and started it forward. As he grinned widely at the sudden thought that he had survived, there was a pounding on the window to his right. He looked and saw his friend Tommy Lee, standing on the dozer and holding onto the door handle, screaming something at him. He listened and heard **"DEAD CENTER!"**

Chapter 6

Although the weather on the island remained perfect, the weather in Belém wasn't and the second drop was delayed day after day. Jason Beanne, who was to ride the second dozer down, was understandably nervous despite the fact that Toby had made it through. Like Toby, he had made numerous simulations, although not as many as Toby. He was more proficient with the landing tablet and had managed to hit the target within one foot seven out of eighteen times. While waiting for the second drop, Toby had made a rough road from the edge of the landing zone to the pier area and then from the pier area to the village. In the village, he had leveled areas for the buildings which would become home to the workers.

It was midmorning of the fifth day that the C-17 Globemaster lifted off from Belém and headed for São Rochelle. To say that Jason's stomach was uneasy would have been putting it mildly. He didn't have butterflies, he had bats – hundreds of bats … thousands of bats. A Carlsbad Cavern full of bats. He had been walking around the cargo area trying to calm his nerves, but it wasn't helping. At last the time came, and he climbed into the cab.

With Jason securely strapped in the cab of the Caterpillar D9T, Jeff plugged in and stood waiting for the command to open the cargo doors. When it came, he pushed the button and the giant doors began opening.

He turned his attention to Jason and saw that he was completely calm. Somehow he had gotten hold of himself. When he heard the order to drop the package, he pressed the button starting the conveyer and changing the ready light from red to yellow. He looked, and Jason was giving him a thumbs up and smiling. *He's good to go*, Jeff thought. The drogue chute shot out of the cargo bay, deployed with a pop that couldn't be heard over the roar of the plane's four engines. With that pop, the connection to the parachute pallet tightened and the pallet raced out of the cargo bay and disappeared. Almost immediately the sixteen parachutes deployed, the connecting line to the D9T pallet tightened and, like the parachute pallet, the Caterpillar pallet raced out of the cargo bay. Jeff breathed a sigh of relief and turned back to his job as the cargo doors started to close. He was glad to have this job over with. In hindsight, he wished he had been able to watch the drop in its entirety.

Jason was elated as he watched the parachute pallet exit the cargo bay. He saw the sixteen chutes open and before he knew it he was out of the cargo bay and falling earthward. He didn't even have time to start counting when he felt the jerk as the chutes took control of the heavy dozer's pallet. "Yippee ki yay," he yelled in his best imitation of Bruce Willis and bent his head to look at the landing tablet. He was happy to note that unlike Toby's drop, his descent speed was well within predicted limits and he was ready to make adjustments, at which he was good. He had figured out the maneuvering the first time in the simulator and after seeing the first two adjustments made by the computer was able to adjust on his own. Well, at least he was on the simulator. When the first adjustments came, he used them and when he saw how the landing spot had moved, he predicted the next adjustments and was correct.

Okay, I'm on it now, he thought. *But I'd better wait.* No, he had been correct in the next prediction too.

The landing spot was steadily advancing toward "ground zero" as the center of the plus sign was called. What he failed to notice was that the last adjustment had not moved things as much as before. Unknown to him, there was a wind current near the ground that was affecting his drift. Therefore, when he put in what he felt were the next changes, the effect was drastic, and the landing site jumped halfway to the river. Originally the site was a quarter mile from the river and now it was an eighth of a mile. *Holy shit*, he thought, *I'm going to get wet*. And he was correct. Even using the corrections as given by the computer, he drifted steadily toward the river.

On the ground, the reception committee was in a panic. No one knew anything about the river except that one spot where the dirt bikes had crossed it was fairly shallow and that was closer to the pool for which the dozer was headed. Plans were to build a bridge, but the bridge would not support the weight of one of the Caterpillar D9T bulldozers. As the computer tablet held by Toby Tyler indicated, the landing spot was at least a hundred yards from the crossing.

"The best he can hope for is to land as close to the southern side as he can," Toby said. He typed a message into the tablet knowing that Jason would see it.

"SHOOT FOR THE SOUTH SIDE" was what Jason read. The altimeter was saying he was under a thousand feet and he didn't have far to go before further adjustments would be futile, so he punched two buttons and there was a slight shudder in the dozer. On the ground they saw that whatever Jason had done had semi-collapsed one of the outside chutes causing the dozer to drift toward the pool at the bottom of the water wall.

"CHUTE FAILURE HEADED FOR FALLS POOL" was sent by Toby. Both men could see that the rate of decent had picked up.

"TRYING SOMETHING" was what Jason sent. The dozer canopy of sixteen chutes seemed to dip on the falls side of the canopy and almost instantaneously the partially collapsed chute filled again. Jason felt the shake and noticed an immediate decrease in the rate of descent and the movement toward the falls seemed to hesitate.

"Passing five hundred feet," Toby intoned, and everyone knew that the die had been cast.

Everyone except for Jason it seemed, because there was a sudden movement of the chute canopy and the dozer seemed to be more aligned across the river. At the same time, the roar of the diesel reached them and with that the crowd broke and headed for the river, watching as they ran.

In the dozer's cabin, Jason had the cabin door ajar because if the dozer went down in deep water he was getting out. He also had pulled his hunting knife from its sheaf to cut parachute cords if necessary. He was as prepared as he could be. Now all that was needed was the green button to release the chutes. He would know almost immediately when the dozer hit the water whether there was bottom because the speed of the dozer and its weight could sink it quickly and that waterfall pool was reported to be deep. It was eerily quiet except for the roar of the waterfall.

Then he heard the splash and felt the front of the dozer hit something and then the rear and the green light came on. BAM the chutes were gone and in a moment the shadow was replaced with the warm glow of the sun. He looked around and saw the waterfall on his right. Turning left he saw the river and on the bank behind him a crowd of men standing and cheering and then one of them stepped forward and entered the stream. He walked over to the dozer and looked up at Jason. It was Toby giving him a thumbs up. He yelled at the men and they immediately entered the water. With Toby pointing and yelling directions they formed two lines in front of the dozer extending it toward the lowest part of the bank. The bank was barely wide enough to get the dozer on it sideways. Jason could tell by the depth of the water on the men that it got deeper closer to the shore. Crossing his fingers, he put the dozer in gear and began moving slowly between the two lines of men. He was moving about three miles an hour when he reached the bank and the dozer didn't pause but climbed the bank slewing left as it clawed its way upward and was soon out of the water and headed downstream. He continued on until he was past the rock mountain before stopping and then he was out and knelt down and kissed the ground. Those of the crowd who were following him yelled their approval. Then he stood up and started to remove his pants.

"Hold on," Toby said in a surprised tone of voice, "What are you doing?"

"After what I've been through, wouldn't you have a load in your pants also?"

The crowd laughed and Jason rebuckled his belt.

"Tell me," Jason said. "What was that last maneuver for?"

"The way the dozer was oriented, the front was going to be over the pool and the back in the riverbed. We would never have gotten the dozer out of the pool but stood a chance in the riverbed. I knew that part of the river was probably bedrock like the hill and took the chance."

"Well, I'm glad it was you and not me because the dozer would be at the bottom of the pool," Toby said. "In a way you're lucky you could get out. That area of the bank is the only one you could crawl up. To get the dozer back to the dock area, you are going to have to go all the way around Colina da Rocha."

He pointed at it to let him know what he was talking about.

"You'll leave the dozer here and work on this side. I keep my dozer on the other side and work there until the bridge is made. That will be our first concern. Let's get you back to Rochelle Town. Tomorrow we begin some serious work."

At this prophetic point, there came a pulsing roar from the direction of Colina da Rocha, faint at first but increasing in volume. The men looked around wildly. Some cried "Earthquake," but, if it was, the ground wasn't shaking at all. They could see and feel nothing and after about two minutes, the sound died completely as suddenly as it had begun.

"What the hell was that?" Jason asked.

"Don't have the faintest," Toby answered. "But we had best report it when we get back to base."

Chapter 7

Horus continued the discussion about the construction of the island's infrastructure, "After getting the living quarters set up, one of the first items of importance was to rid the site of the need for fossil fuel as much as possible."

The dump trucks and pickup trucks that were brought ashore by the helicopter from the anchored container ship were designed and made by Waldo Emerson and ran on electricity. The heavy-duty machines, like the two bulldozers and the six backhoes, ran on diesel. They had the one diesel tank and there was a second on the ship but those were not going to be enough to fuel the machines and the generators to recharge the trucks. Until another source was installed, these vehicles would be charged by diesel powered generators. So two of the primary installations were solar panel farms on the southeast and southwest sides of volcano. These would not only take care of the current need for the vehicles but provide the source of power for the Bundle's headquarters when it was built. The volcanic mountain had already been renamed Vulcan's Forge and the headquarters to be built inside was Vulcan's Roost. The latter's name was not in great keeping with the idea of the Roman god of fire which included both volcanic fire and the fire of forges, but it was apropos. Other solar panel farms were set up on the south end of the island and would provide power to the village as well as to vehicles.

It had been decided that Toby's bulldozer would work on the road up Vulcan's Forge to the Northeast Olympus Solar Farm and then on past the plateau where the entrance to Vulcan's Roost would be dug and finally on to the site of the Northwest Olympus Solar Farm. Jason would make the road south from the proposed pier site near the mouth of the River Styx (which had been called Rio da Fonte or Fountain River) to the Southeast Hades Solar Farm, across the south end to the site of the Southwest Hades Solar Farm and up the west side past Prometheus's Aerie (which Colina da Rocha or Boulder Hill was renamed) and back through the former farm area to the proposed pier site.

"What's the significance of Prometheus?" Monica asked. "I'm not much into Greek gods."

"He was a Titan, a second-generation divine being and ancestor of the gods on Olympus," explained Issaack. "He is credited with the creation of humans from clay..."

"You mean like the Christian God created Adam?"

"Yes, but the Christian God is also the Jewish God, so let us not forget that," Waldo injected.

"Always have to be politically correct, don't we," Phil countered and received a glare from Waldo.

"Back to Prometheus," Issaack said giving both men a warning glance. "Yes, what he did is like the biblical god. There are many instances within modern religions of events from the Greek (and by assimilation the Roman) Gods. What Prometheus is best known for is giving fire to people he created. As punishment for his crime, Zeus sentenced Prometheus ..."

"Wait a moment," Monica interrupted. "You just said 'Zeus sentenced Prometheus.' A moment ago you said that Prometheus was second generation and an 'ancestor of the gods on Olympus.' Zeus is one of those and he sentenced one of his ancestors?"

"They were all basically immortal," Gloria explained. "The Olympian gods ruled them all."

"Oh, I see," Monica said. *But I don't,* she thought.

"I'll recommend some reading for you," Issaack said, little knowing that he was inspiring her next hit *Titans, Olympians and Fire.*

"But continuing, Zeus sentenced Prometheus to eternal torture for his crime by binding him to a rock and every day an eagle (which is the emblem of Zeus) would feed upon the liver of Prometheus and every night the liver would grow back."

"Gross," Monica said. "That's like the guy Sisyphus who had to push a rock up a hill and when it got near the top it would roll back down."

"Exactly," Gloria said. "That was a favorite method of punishment. There was a guy named Tantalus who – for a crime I will not go into – was sentenced by Zeus to stand in a pool of water under a grapevine. Whenever he would reach for the grapes to eat, they would rise out of reach and when he bent to drink, the pool would recede."

"Evil people those Greek Gods," Phil said.

Issaack continued, "The names Styx and Hades were chosen because Vulcan's Forge was more like Olympus and it only made sense that the river should be the River Styx and beyond it must be Hades."

But of course with Jason's dozer across the river, what was planned was not going to happened so Jason would start on the road from the River Styx and Toby would begin with the road south to the River Styx. When the road reached the River Styx, the bridge was brought by the Super Stallion. At the time it arrived it was just pieces of metal and nuts and bolts.

Cleve R. Barker, from New Jersey, had one job to do on São Rochelle's new infrastructure – supervise the construction of the Charon Bridge. He would never use that name, and, in fact, it would not have a name other than "The Bridge" during the construction phase. Although at times, it was called the "Off Balance Bridge" but only when Jerónimo Romero was around, but we're not ready for that yet. To explain the name of the bridge, how did one cross the River Styx? In a boat propelled by Charon, the ferryman of Hades.

Cleve preferred to be called Ron after his middle name Ronald because Cleve Barker seemed so much like Clive Barker, the British writer known for his horror stories. But when people learned his first name was really Cleve, that was what he was called. The bridge that Cleve was here to build was to be positioned just before the River Styx made a turn north before a turn east to empty into the Atlantic Ocean and help provide the only reasonable harbor for the small island.

The first items that had to be built were the abutments on both sides of the river and that required concrete and a fair amount of it. Therefore, the Super Stallion brought in a concrete truck and lots of bags of concrete. There was going be a plant made which would be able to fill the trucks with water and concrete for later projects, but that wasn't ready yet. When it was ready, it would make concrete railroads ties that were needed for the railroad to get the tunnel digger up to the plateau and also to move the concrete pieces made by the concrete plant up to the tunnel but that was still in the distant future. Water was put into the concrete truck by a hose set in the river and a gasoline powered pump.

For this project the truck didn't need to move and could pour the concrete into the form on the north side of the river without moving the truck. To get the concrete into the form on the other side of the river, required brute force and a line of men standing in the water passing five gallon buckets half full of concrete from the north side to the south side and another line passing the buckets back. This took thirty men, the entire labor force at the time, an entire day. Every half hour, the two lines changed duties because two and a half gallons of concrete weighs fifty pounds. Slowing the whole thing down was the fact that they only had ten empty five gallon pails. Fortunately for the men standing in the water, it wasn't cold, and the temperature was something that they couldn't explain but would be discovered later. Needless to say, at the end of the day everyone was tired and ready for bed after a big steak dinner. This was a small glitch in the program not because Issaack neglected to look closely at the river, but he figured that the concrete truck would be able to drive around Colina de Rocha although it might take a while. The motorcycle surveyor team had come back with a negative on that point – at least until the road was made and that was going to take a while.

While they waited the two days for the abutment forms to be built and the reinforcing rods put into position inside the forms and the two days for the concrete to cure, ten men who were basically laborers – but well-paid laborers – were being taught how to put the parts of the bridge together. The bridge was the Mabey Compact 200 HS25, a one lane bridge designed to carry ninety thousand pound three-axle vehicles which was enough for a conventional loaded concrete truck. It was akin to a bridge built from erector set pieces. When Issaack and Siegfried went looking for a bridge, Paul Orr, an engineering friend, suggested that they consult the Mabey Company.

In 1923, Guy Mabey registered Mabey & Johnson Ltd as a general building supplies business servicing new construction in South East England. In 1940, Donald Bailey designed an alternative to the Inglis Bridge system which was considered to be overly complicated and expensive. When the full prototype of the Inglis Mark III Bridge failed during testing, Bailey was given the go-ahead to develop his new bridging concept. The first prototype Bailey Bridge was successfully load tested and delivered to troops in the field during December 1941. The Mabey Super Bailey Panel was launched in 1967 when Thomas Storey's sole rights to manufacture panel bridging using the Bailey concept expired. It quickly proved to enable construction of stronger bridges to carry bigger earth moving equipment. In the mid-seventies, development of the Mabey Universal Bridging System began and in 1988 the Compact 200 system was introduced. Mabey bridges were used world-wide and the U.S. military used them in Iraq and other Middle East countries.

Chapter 8

The galvanized steel parts for the bridge were brought to the Plains of Olympus side of the River Styx by the Super Stallion helicopter. Cleve Barker had gone over the plans with Walt Jefferies, the construction project supervisor. It was easy enough. The parts were put together with nuts and bolts using pneumatic powered hammer drills. In a way it was like assembling a child's toy on Christmas Eve:

Tab A goes into slot BB on part CC. Remember to insert the peg into the hole in tab A *after* it is through slot BB.

As you probably remember, if you (or whoever put the toy together) perform that step improperly and no matter if you do all the rest of the procedures exactly right, the toy won't work the way it was supposed to. What the workmen had to do was to construct nine rectangular boxes called bays, each ten feet long by seven feet high by ten feet wide. The second ten feet was the width of the bridge and was made by two ten-foot transoms between two ten-foot long by seven-foot high preformed panels. There are other pieces but with unfamiliar and possibly strange names: raker, bracing frame, vertical frame, end post, chord reinforcement,

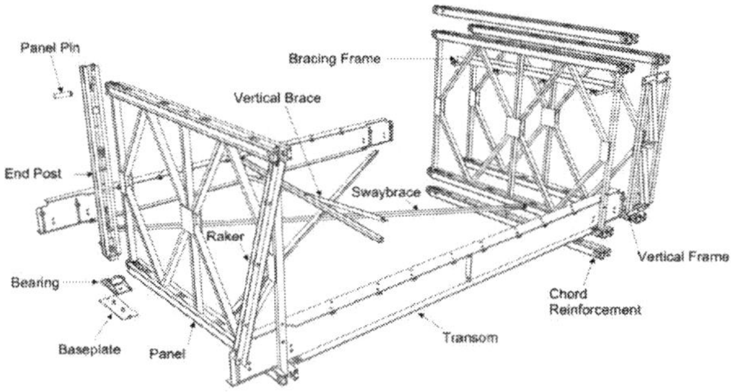

etc.

But they are all attached together with nuts on bolts. Oh, yes, there are male and female ends of the box, and the first one made – pointing south across the River Styx – has to have the male eye on both sides pointing across the river. South is what was called the "Direction of Launch" because the Mabey 200 bridge is shoved out in stages over the river from the launch side to the other side. That's the job of Toby Tyler's D9T Caterpillar bulldozer on the north (Plains of Olympus) side. So the ten-man bridge crew spent four days practicing putting rectangular boxes together: First one and then the one connecting to it. And then taking them apart because they couldn't be moved as they weighed eight tons each. Because of the weight of the pieces (the panels weighed 1,600 pounds each and the transoms 950 pounds each) two backhoes were used to assist in moving the parts.

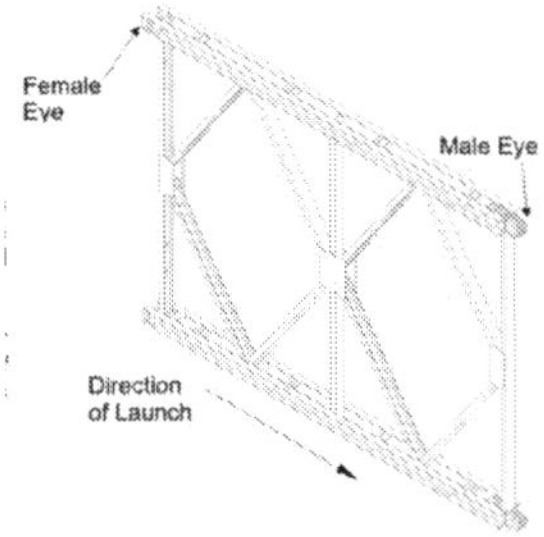

Finally the morning was here for construction to begin.

The first four bays that were built were part of the "launch nose." The method of getting the bridge across the river is called "the cantilever launch." When the bridge is ready to be launched (be pushed by the dozer), the first of the bays is lifted at an angle and held in place on either side with a piece of metal and two pins called a launch link. This is to enable the nose to hit the landing rollers a little low. The landing rollers tilt (the launch rollers don't) because the metal bridge is heavy and there will be a little give and the front will sag. The launching rollers were placed first and then the landing rollers were positioned on the south side using laser range finders.

The first four bays have one panel on each side because they are only temporary and will be removed when the bridge is in place. The launch nose is normally two-thirds of the length of the bridge so that the nose hits the landing rollers with just a third of the weight of the bridge over the river. However, with a forty plus foot span requiring five bays, two-thirds is between three and four bays, thus four nose launch bays were used. After the four nose launch bays, five bridge bays were made with two panels on each side with bracing frames top and bottom. No decking was installed at this time because it would only add to the weight.

Because the construction crew was untrained, and the pneumatic tools being used were to be powered by only one air tank, the decision was made to move the equipment a minimum number of times, so they started making three bays and would launch one bay out over the river at a time until necessary to move and have more on land. The first bay started on the launch rollers, its female end on two timber cribbing towers shared with the male end of the second bay. The female end of the second bay was on rollers atop two other timber cribbing towers and this process continued during the construction. When the first three nose launch bays were completed, it was time for the first launch. Recall that this necessitated the first being raised at an angle of six degrees with a launch link holding it in place and then the assemblage was pushed ten feet by Toby's dozer, and the fourth nose launch bay constructed. And then another push and two bays were over the river and two bays on land. All this was to be carefully done because the center of gravity had to be kept behind the leading edge of the launch rollers or the bridge would tilt and end up in the river.

But this was the time – before construction could start on the first bridge bay the next day – when Jerónimo Romero earned his claim to fame or notoriety – your choice. To be totally truthful, it wasn't all his fault because the second push of the nose launch had gone just a bit awry – by six inches. However that caused the center of gravity of the build to be six inches in front of the edge of the launch roller. That's one twentieth of the length of the bay but left the transom just in front of the launch rollers and the transom weighed nine hundred fifty pounds. That's more than one tenth of the weight of the entire bay in one twentieth of the space. That gave the over-the-water portion of the nose launch section that much more weight and moved the center of gravity forward of the balance point, the forward edge of the launch roller. You couldn't tell, but the nose launch was "thinking" about moving.

It had been a long hot day and the water in the river looked so inviting to Jerónimo Romero that when Cleve Barker called an end to work, Jerónimo Romero quickly removed his boots, socks, pants and shirt and climbed up onto the abutment, onto the side of the second section of the nose launch build and started making his way out over the river. He was quite agile despite his size (five foot ten but two hundred thirty pounds) and he quickly moved to the front of second bay and was ready to move up the slight incline of the first nose launch bay. His intent was to get to the front transom and jump into the river. The river wasn't really deep here – eight feet – and he probably would have been okay with a drop of about ten feet, but he never got to find out that day. As he moved out over the river, his weight kept moving the center of gravity a little bit further toward the river and away from the fulcrum (the front of the launch roller.) He was receiving cheers from his compadres and Cleve Barker was standing there laughing when suddenly … the nose launch structure started moving down.

Cleve Barker saw it and yelled at his men, "get on the bridge" pointing at the last bay made. Jerónimo Romero had started moving back, but the bridge had momentum and it was moving – albeit slowly. Suddenly the noise of Toby's D9T Caterpillar bulldozer's engine broke the air. He had seen what was happening and had quickly climbed on the dozer he had moved twelve feet back from the bridge and set the blade down for the night. Putting the dozer into gear, he started the blade moving up and the dozer forward advancing at an angle toward the bridge. The men who were climbing onto the last bay stopped and hurried to get out of way of the dozer, setting off another change of the center of gravity but only by a bit. Fortunately, by the time Toby got his dozer close enough, the blade was high enough that it was eighteen inches or so over the transom, Toby stopped the dozer and started lowering the blade of the 108,000 pound dozer. When the blade made contact with the transom, all that weight moving down to stop the transom moving up caused the bridge to shudder and Jerónimo Romero lost his grip and he half fell, half jumped, into the river making a belly flop which would have brought the jeers from his compadres had they seen it, but they were busy with other things. When the blade had brought the bridge back down to "solid ground," Cleve Barker organized the workers who carried sections of road decking, each weighing seven hundred twenty pounds, which were stacked on the last bay until Cleve felt that the structure was secure enough that it wasn't going to move.

In order to insure no further problems in the launch, three bridge bays were built and then the last of the nose bays launched. However, before the launch, with the nose launch held firmly in position, Jerónimo Romero, followed by the members of his team, made their way out and up to the furthest transom and dropped into the River Styx. Then the last two bridge bays were built, and the entire launch finished. Once the bridge was in position, each end was raised separately with two hydraulic jacks, the launch rollers removed, and the bridge lowered into final position. Then a concrete wall was poured at each end before the road was graded to meet the bridge. The decking was on the bridge before the walls were poured and wheelbarrows of concrete were taken across the bridge to pour the south wall – no bucket brigade needed.

Fortunately, there were no further problems with the construction and soon the Mabey Compact 200 bridge was complete and concrete trucks (but not the Caterpillars) could move south to provide concrete for the Southeast and Southwest Hades Solar Panel Farms.

Chapter 9

While the bridge was being constructed, Jason turned his Caterpillar D9T south and started making the road around the southern end of the island, up the west side past Prometheus's Aerie (formerly Colina da Rocha) and then back to the northern side of the bridge.

Once the road reached the site of the Southeast Apollo Farm and the backhoes could reach it, work started on the farm and Jason continued with the road across the southern end of São Rochelle. The soil was only a foot deep at the south end and so the backhoes would clear the area for the solar panels and the concrete foundation would be built right on the bedrock. Digging the trenches for the power cables was to be done by Caterpillar Medium Hammer attachments which replaced the bucket on the front of each backhoe. It was an easy change done onsite. The decision was made to get the sites on both farms ready and the solar panels done before starting the trench. That way, the backhoes could be converted with the hammer attachment.

The rock was all piled and loaded into dump trucks and taken to the pier site to be put into place by one front loading backhoe. Others would join it as their primary requirements were fulfilled. When a foundation for a solar panel was complete, the concrete specialists moved in making the frames and installing rebar, pipes for electric cables and bolts and plates necessary for installation. When that was complete, the solar panel specialist took over. Because the Southwest Hades Solar Panel Farm was the second one built that was where the trench for the cables was to be started.

Matías Zapatero was one of the backhoe operators. He had worked for a big contractor in Argentina but when word of the job working on a remote island for two years reached his ears, he applied for it and happily walked into his boss's office and turned in his resignation. His boss was not happy to let him go but understood that at triple the salary with transportation, lodging and food included, it would be difficult to refuse.

Matías loved his job and was thrilled when his name was drawn to be the first to use the hammer to dig the first trench. No money was involved but to him it was a great honor. He and Ignacio Suárez, the other backhoe operator at that site, helped each other change their bucket for the hammer. Then Matías got on his backhoe he had proudly named Juana after his wife ("When I am on her I feel like my wife is under me pumping me as hard as I am pumping her.") and started her up. He easily moved the backhoe to the starting position. All the other workers had stopped to watch this groundbreaking occasion.

With great pomp and circumstance, Matías lowered the hammer's point down to the chosen spot. Looking at his comrades, he gave them the thumbs up and started the hammer. The sound was deafening even through the headphones. Ignacio nudged the man standing next to him and said, "Suena hueco (It sounds hollow.)" As though the comment was a signal, there was a thunderous explosion and Matías and his backhoe disappeared as though the earth had opened up and swallowed them. And, in fact, the earth had opened up and the ground under the feet of the other workers was shaking and to a one they turned and ran. As soon as the soil under their feet had quit shaking and the roaring had subsided, they stopped and turned around. What they saw was awe inspiring: Where Matías and his backhoe had been was emptiness.

"It's a sinkhole," one of the men shouted and that broke the hold the event had on them. They rushed forward to the edge of the hole, albeit carefully. What lay before them – actually below them – was a conical hole at the bottom of which was the backhoe. It was upside down with the hammer point straight up. Nothing of Matías was to be seen because surrounding the backhoe and starting to fill the hole was brown bubbling water.

"Quickly," Alan Constantine, the group's supervisor said, "Move all the equipment away, at least three hundred feet. I include all of you in this. I don't think that the danger is over."

"¿Qué tal Matías? (What about Matías?)," Ignacio asked.

"He's gone. There's is nothing we can do. Now move," and he pushed Ignacio toward his backhoe.

Ignacio started back toward the edge of the sinkhole when there was another ripping crash and the base for a solar panel disappeared into the sinkhole as the ground under it gave way. That was all the motivation Ignacio and the rest of the men needed, and they raced to their equipment or just away from the area as they had been told.

Alan Constantine was getting ready to notify the construction chief Walt Jefferies about the collapse when Tom Klondyke came running up.

"Paul Goldman is missing."

"When?"

"After the collapse."

Alan Constantine turned and raced to the edge of the sinkhole, Tom Klondyke on his heels. What they saw chilled their hearts. Three-quarters of the way down to the bottom they could see Paul Goldman clinging to a piece of concrete debris sticking out of the dirt. Below him was bubbling brown water that was halfway up to him and the hole was filling fast. It was obvious to them that the ground where Paul Goldman had been standing must have collapsed before he could move back.

"Help me," Paul Goldman shouted.

"Hang on," replied Alan Constantine. "Help is on the way."

Turning to Tom Klondyke "We need a rope."

"How about electric cable?"

"That'll do. Get the men also."

Tom Klondyke raced away yelling at some men starting back from moving vehicles. By the time Tom Klondyke and the men returned with a pickup truck containing a spool of electric cable intended for the solar panels in the bed, the water was lapping at Paul Goldman's feet. As the cable spooled off the reel, lying on the ground like a coiled hose, Tom Klondyke knew that it wouldn't reach Paul Goldman by itself. Grabbing the end of the cable, he walked to the edge of the sinkhole.

"Feed it out slowly," Tom Klondyke said and stepped over the edge of the sinkhole. As he started down the slope the loose dirt started cascading down toward Paul Goldman.

"I've got to move to my right or I'll bury Paul," Tom Klondyke shouted. Several of the men grabbed the cable and moved it several feet with Tom Klondyke moving over. With the men serving as a pulley, Tom Klondyke moved down the slope until he felt his feet in the water, then he moved over to Paul Goldman who was covered with water up to his chest.

"Thank God," Paul Goldman said as Tom Klondyke grabbed his outstretched arm.

Tom Klondyke helped him stand up and then, grabbing the cable with both hands, Paul Goldman started up the hill with Tom Klondyke right behind him. One group of men at the top of the hill was pulling up the cable and another was winding the cable back onto the reel. Everyone cheered when the two men reached the safety of solid ground.

Paul Goldman grabbed Tom Klondyke's hand and shook it vigorously. "Thanks for saving my life."

"No problem," Tom Klondyke said. "I know you would have done the same for me."

Paul Goldman looked at Tom Klondyke quizzically and then said, "Maybe."

Everyone laughed at the two good friends.

"Okay," Alan Constantine said. "Let's get everything away from the sinkhole." Then he called the construction supervisor Walt Jeffries and reported the sinkhole.

"Get pictures," Jefferies said. "I'm up on the mountain. Be there in about fifteen."

When Jefferies got there, the workers were all somber, standing in small groups according to nationalities or native languages. They looked when the pickup arrived and knew who the driver was although most of them had only minimal contact with him. Alan Constantine knew him best of all and he not very well because they had never met before this project. But that was the same with most of the men. One or two might have known each other but the idea of the project was to keep it quiet and men were chosen individually for their expertise and experience, but they had to be willing to leave their current jobs.

Jeffries looked at the sinkhole and the pictures that Alan Constantine had taken.

"Quick thinking on the part of that man Klondyke. Which one is he?"

Alan Constantine pointed him out.

"Keep an eye on him. We'll need thinkers like that. I'll report this to the home office," Jefferies said as he pulled a satellite phone from a holster on his belt. He punched in a preprogrammed number.

"Hello, Mr. Jefferies," Horus said almost before the phone rang. "What's the problem?"

"How do you know there's a problem?"

"Why else would you call?"

"Right," Jefferies said and then explained about the sinkhole.

"There's no sign of the man? What's his name?"

"What's the name of the man on the backhoe?" Jefferies asked Alan Constantine.

"Matías Zapatero," Jefferies said and told Horus.

"Any chance of retrieving the backhoe?" Horus asked.

"Not until the water goes down," Jefferies said walking to the edge of the hole. "It hasn't risen any since I got here. I'd say based on pictures that the hole is about a third full."

"Then we know the height of the water's source," Horus said. "Probably the same one that feeds the River Styx, but how it gets that high we have no idea. I'll confer with the big boss …" referring to Issaack and his business partner Siegfried Schmidt.

When he got back to Jeffries, he had two things to tell him. One was for Jefferies to tell the family of Matías Zapatero that they would be taken care of financially. The second was to build a wooden cover that would fit over the bottom of the hole above the backhoe because there was nothing they could do about it without a crane which they didn't have. The cover, which was built in several pieces, was lowered using bulldozers and two backhoes with cables winches. When the cover was in place, it was covered with a one foot layer of concrete. Then dirt from the road, solar farm and railroad projects was brought in by dump trucks and the hole was filled. The cables were simply laid on the ground in a shallow trench and covered with concrete and then dirt. And the work proceeded apace.

Chapter 10

Two days after his best friend Matías Zapatero disappeared in the Southwest Hades Solar Farm Sinkhole, Ignacio Suárez had an afternoon off. There was still work to be done filling the sinkhole but when you have an afternoon off, you take it. There wasn't a lot to do on the island. You could go fishing off one of the rocky beaches ("beach" is being nice) because many of the men had made handlines one could borrow if you didn't have your own, but Ignacio wasn't interested in fishing. He decided to do something that no one else had done – or at least that no one else had claimed to have done – and that was climb to the top of Colina da Rocha (or Boulder Hill or Prometheus's Aerie.) Being Spanish, Ignacio preferred that name. It wasn't difficult if you attacked it from the southwest or southeast side and the latter was Ignacio's choice.

The climb took him about half an hour and he was surprised by the flatness of the top. He thought it was big enough and flat enough to land a helicopter although he didn't know why someone would. He walked around the top and then went to the northeast side and looked over because that is where the Rio de Fonte (or Fountain River or River Styx) flowed from about two thirds of the way up. Lying flat, he peered over the edge and could see where the water exited from the rock face and flowed downward into a pool, and then continued over the front edge of that pool to a big pool at the bottom. Ignacio wondered how deep the bottom pool was and if it were possible to jump from the first pool into the second. He lay there contemplating what it would be like to make that jump or dive when suddenly there was a quaking he could feel and a loud sound. Scared, he scrambled back from the edge and sat on the surface with his hands around his knees. He had hardly assumed that posture when the sound and shaking were gone. He sat there for a few moments – maybe minutes, he was never certain – and then, certain that the terremoto (earthquake) was over, he stood and looked around. Nothing had changed. So he went back to the edge, carefully crawling on hands and feet and looked. The water still flowed from the rock out and down into the first pool and then … something was different, not wrong but different. He blinked and looked again. Something was in the first pool. It was difficult to see because the water was pouring into the pool and hitting whatever it was. He blinked again and rubbed his eyes. It was a person – someone with black hair, wearing a white shirt and black pants just like he did. Just like most of his friends did here. Just like Matías did.

"Matías," Ignacio shouted. "¿Matías, esre tu (is that you)?"

Ignacio got up and ran to the place where he had come up the hill and started down. It was much faster going down, but then he was moving faster also. He reached the height where he thought the pool was and made his way across the hill to the pool but when he got there, the pool was empty. Where had Matías gone? He looked over the edge and there in the lower pool he could see someone. He knew it was someone – or at least someone's body. He started back the way he had come to get to the spot where he had climbed up before, and then he stopped.

Turning he walked to the edge of the pool and looked down. The bigger pool at the bottom loomed ominously – almost invitingly. He thought of Jerónimo Romero. "¡Sin coraje no hay gloria! (No guts, no glory)" he said and jumped. He had seen people jump off heights into water before, but he had never done it. He kept his feet together, held his nose with his right hand, crossing his left arm over his chest holding on to the right elbow. And prayed! And prayed! And … *WHOMP*! He thought he had hit solid pavement but if so, it was wet solid pavement. He opened his eyes and could see light – nothing distinctly. He tilted his head back and could see a brighter light, so he started swimming toward the light and soon he broke the surface of the pond. He could hear water pouring into the pond from above near his left shoulder. Treading water, he looked around for what he was certain was that body, but he saw nothing. Where had it gone? He swam to the pool's edge and pulled himself out of the water and stood up. He looked around the pool and saw nothing. Then out of the corner of his right eye he saw the black pants and turned, looking downstream from the pool. There floated a person … someone's body … a man's body … Matías's body he was certain. He walked to the river bank below the pool and stepped into the river. It wasn't too deep, just about a foot. He made his way out into the river until he reached the body, which was floating about waist deep. He grabbed the shirt with his right hand and looked carefully at the face. It was indeed his friend Matías. Fatter from bloating, bruised from something, most likely the fall on the backhoe. Tears welled up in his eyes. There was no one around to see them or to hear him cry and that's what he did as he moved his friend's body to the shore, pulled it up the bank and out of the river.

Ignacio knelt by Matías's shoulders, folded his arms across his body, closed his eyes, and then prayed over him saying what he could remember of the Rosary. He started with Our Father and then the Hail Mary:

"Hail Mary, full of grace. The Lord is with thee. Blessed art thou among women, and blessed is the fruit of thy womb, Jesus. Holy Mary, Mother of God, pray for us sinners, now and at the hour of our death. Amen"

Then, not knowing anything else to do, he picked up Matías's body and began walking back to Rochelle Town (the workers' village.)

A coffin was made and Matías was buried, wrapped in a plastic sheet inside the wooden coffin. He was buried in the sinkhole where he had died, and a headstone was ordered inscribed with all that they knew about him which was his name and when he had died. The headstone came on board the *B.B. São Rochelle* when she made her first trip to the island.

Chapter 11

When the first workmen reached São Rochelle, they were told that there should be horses and cows. The news of the cows excited them because that meant fresh milk and despite the helicopter biweekly food deliveries, they knew they would truly welcome fresh milk. So once they had settled into a work routine and had the time, they started looking. Being a small island, it didn't take long to find two mangy scrawny cows with dry udders. Naturally they would not be good for meat, so they were left alone. They also found two horses also long in the tooth and definitely of the plow horse variety. All four of the beasts were naturally a little leery of humans not having seen any for several years. There was plenty of natural vegetation to eat but apparently not to their liking so with the first food delivery was seed for grass suitable for the animals and some hay to hold them over until the new grass grew. Also the men were told that the animals would be removed when the dock was completed and the ship to bring more equipment and later the predators was built. With free time and needing a little recreation, several of the men with some horse experience decided to try to ride the animals. So a request was made, and the next helicopter shipment of supplies included four lariats and two halters.

Contest #1: Roping a horse. Actually this first turned into "Roping a Stake" driven in the ground and then "Roping a Barrel." After the first contest, the best eight men were picked and after the barrel exercise just the best four were kept. So the best four – Jason Beane, Ignacio Suárez, Nicolás Morena, and Ines Cola (one of the cooks who was female) – went out looking for the horses. A crowd gathered on top of Colina da Rocha to watch. The four ropers had a pretty good idea where the horses were and so the four approached from different directions. It took two days before the first horse was roped by Ines Cola and led to near Rochelle Town and hobbled. Then the second horse was caught immediately on the second day by Jason Beane because the horse came to be with the first horse and was an easy catch.

Contest #2: Riding a horse. The horses were basically plow horses (think of a Clydesdale) and not easy to ride bareback even if they were broken. These were – or had been – at least as far as harnesses for pulling plows but undoubtedly small children had been given rides. Before this contest even started, management in the guise of Walt Jeffries, Construction Supervisor, made the rules. "Get an injury requiring air flight to the mainland and it comes out of your wages – both ways. If you cannot work, you are not paid." Of course this rule applied only to their off-duty hours and specifically to the horses. Fortunately, there were no injuries of that type. Face it, these were horses "long in the tooth," which means they were old. Not familiar with the saying? Horses' teeth continue to grow and, even though the teeth wear, age can be judged by the length and condition of their teeth. To make a long story short, they didn't buck like rodeo horses and were quickly broken.

Contest #3: Riding the circuit. Once the horses were rideable, the question became "Which one was faster?" So a circuit was set up: Starting at the bottom pool of Colina da Rocha Prometheus's Aerie), going counterclockwise (west to begin with) around Colina da Rocha across the bridge across Rio da Fonte (River Styx) and back to the pool. By this time, there was a road completely around and that was used as the race track. The horses were not fast, at best getting up to a trot for part of the circuit, and one of them wouldn't cross the bridge with a rider. So, to make things fair, a mark was set about one hundred feet short of the bridge and another one the same distance on the other side of the bridge. These were the dismount and mount marks and, because the riders were always the smallest men willing to ride the horses, they had a difficult time mounting and needed help. Amazingly, the same horse did not always win, and it wasn't the rider who made the difference. It was obviously just the way the horse felt. Both quickly learned the routine and would "race" to the dismount pole and then take their time getting to the remount pole because they didn't want to "race" again.

Races were held on Sunday afternoons because Sunday was the only off day. The hardy souls who wanted to see the entire race would climb to the top of Colina da Rocha and watch from there. Those uninterested in the racing might swim in the bottom pool or jump from the middle pool following the example of Ignacio Suárez.

Certainly money was exchanged but usually the bets were modest because few people had much money since there was nothing to spend it on and the majority had almost all their money sent home. Of course, racing came to a stop two years into the project when the *B.B. São Rochelle* arrived and took the animals to the mainland.

Chapter 12

The *B.B. São Rochelle* was launched two years after work started on the island. Modeled after the LST (Landing Ship Tank) of World War II, she was two-thirds the size so as to minimize the draft in order to get into the port which was constructed on the island. She was fifty feet in the beam (widest part), three hundred eighty feet long and could carry 3200 tons with a draft of ten feet in the stern and three feet forward. That could put her into the dock on São Rochelle with a foot to spare at low tide. She had a double hinged eighty-foot-long ramp which gave her plenty of space, just in case. She was much more seaworthy than her WWII prototypes and made twenty knots loaded in making port in São Rochelle. She was painted sea blue camouflage like the U. S. warships at the request of Ramiro Esteves and, since he paid for it, no one questioned why or really cared. After all she was a working ship. Her christening was a sight to behold as each of the members of the Billionaire Bundle had an expensive bottle of his or her favorite champagne attached to a nylon cord which on cue, they cast against the front of the ship and it was properly fortuitous that all of them broke on first impact.

It was an ancient Babylonian tradition that eventually led to the use of champagne bottles to christen a ship. In ancient Babylonia, liquid was poured over the hull of a new ship prior to its launching. And it wasn't for good luck but a check for holes in the hull that could cause the ship to sink. Over the years, this tradition became a ceremony, and it wasn't until the end of the 1900's that champagne became the liquid of choice.

And some time in the course of events, the failure of a bottle of champagne to break was taken as a sign of bad luck. As recently as 2007, the champagne bottle failed to break when the Duchess of Cornwall attempted to christen a cruise ship. Passengers on some of the first cruises of that ship contracted a viral illness whose symptoms included vomiting. Even more prophetic, reportedly the champagne bottle failed to break when the Costa Concordia was launched. Although in this case, the ship was built in 2004 and tragedy did not occur until January 2012 when the Concordia struck a rock in the Tyrrhenian Sea ripping a 160-foot gash in the port side of her hull and resulting in the death of thirty-two people.

There are lots of ways that are used to ensure that champagne bottles break: cheap champagne is used because it has more bubbles in it and that increases the pressure inside the bottle and hence the odds that the bottle will break; the bottle is thrown against the strongest part of the hull; and the outside of the bottle is scored to weaken the glass which breaks easier. What was done with the bottles in the case of the *B.B. São Rochelle* no one has ever said but having seven bottles break must certainly be some kind of record.

On her maiden voyage and unladen, the *B.B. São Rochelle* had made port on the island in the midst of a mild storm without difficulty and achieved a cruising speed of twenty-five knots. She had been greeted by all the workers who had been given the day off in celebration. Naturally tours of the ship were given. The next morning, her first cargo was loaded: Two cows (considerably fatter and more content) and two "thoroughbred racing" horses.

She made port in São Rochelle at noon two months later with her first inbound load, and for the billionaires it was the most important, at least to that point. Issaack, Siegfried and Waldo were on board for this occasion because of her cargo. It took almost most twenty-four hours to get things arranged since the cargo left little room in the hold of the *B.B. São Rochelle* (who was called *B.B. Queen* by her crew, a play on the name of the jazz great B.B. King but, of course, being a ship, the *B.B. São Rochelle* was a woman.) Again the workers were present although not with full liberty since this was a working day. Because of the necessary preparations and tests that needed to be performed to be certain that the cargo was running properly, it was 10:17 a.m. when the assembled workers heard the engine roar to life and 4 minutes, 37 seconds after that when the bow doors of the *B.B. São Rochelle* opened, and the ramp let down onto the pier which had been constructed so that this would happen because of the weight it had to carry on this voyage. The crowd filed in single file to inspect the machine. Dubbed Ant Man by his new crew, he probably looked like something out of a science fiction film because his 30-foot-6-inch-round face was covered with spinning shiny drills.

Ant Man had been purchased from the Robbins Company in Solon, Ohio, a suburb of Cleveland. The parts were shipped to Miami, Florida where they were loaded aboard the *B.B. Queen* where he was partially reassembled. When fully connected, he was approximately two hundred seventy-five feet long and made of seven sections with a total weight of fifteen hundred tons. The main and heaviest section was the actual Tunnel Boring Machine (TBM) which was basically a tin can with an approximately10 meter (30.38

feet) diameter, 13 meter (approximately 42.5 feet) length, and weighed 1,000 tons. Not only would it dig the hole and send the muck back to the rest of its body, but it also would put the concrete sections of the tunnel in place so that the rest of the machine could ride inside the tunnel. The rest of the machine was called the Back-up Train. The first section of the Back-up Train was called the Bridge and was sixty-five (65) feet long with front wheels made of polyurethane because they rode on the concrete tunnel sections. The rear wheels rode on the rails which were installed whenever there was a thirty-foot gap between the section that the front wheels were in and the section containing already placed track. The rest of the Back-up Train was five thirty-foot-long railroad cars called Gantry 1 through Gantry 5 that contained the power units which drive the Tunnel Boring Machine such as hydraulic power units, electrical power units, and lubrication power units. It also housed the TBM Operators cab, ventilation system, rescue chamber, water systems, air systems and lunch and toilet facilities. It is easiest to understand if you think of a Tunnel Boring Machine as a factory which moves because everything you find in a factory will be located in the Tunnel Boring Machine system and advances as the machine bores forward. The TBM operating units are located on the top and sides of the back-up gantries. The lower inside section of the back-up is dedicated to the material transport system, this is where the muck dug by the TBM is carried by conveyer belts to the back of the train where it is emptied into small gondola type railroad cars and the supply train enters and exits the system bringing in manpower, concrete segments, rails, and other utilities to keep the system working.

Ant Man wasn't fast when he was working which was drilling an approximately thirty-one-foot hole in the ground ahead of him which in this case would be the side of the volcano on the island. Then he could move anywhere from a few feet to thirty feet per day depending on the composition of the earth he was chewing up. To help explain his rate of speed when drilling, every five feet he stopped and did what a newspaper reporter for The Akron Beacon Journal, writing about the city of Akron, Ohio's sewer tunnel digger Rosie, explained as "an underground dance. Heavy concrete slabs are pulled from her belly and assembled around her in a ring. Seven of the 14-inch thick segments and a locking piece called a key are positioned and grouted (or cemented) in place to make the sewer tunnels (sic) walls."

The concrete segments would be made on the island using equipment brought in the *B.B. Queen* and yet to be assembled. For that reason, there was no real hurry for Ant Man to make tracks up the road to his starting place because it would take a couple of weeks to assemble the small plant that would fabricate the concrete pieces. It took most of the rest of that day to get track laid on the ramp to connect with the track already laid on the dock and in the hold of the *B.B. Queen*. In fact, her first trip to the island was to measure everything so that the track on the ramp would match the track on the shore. One of the last rail sections to be put down would be half on the ramp and half on the shore ensuring a smooth transition.

Ant Man

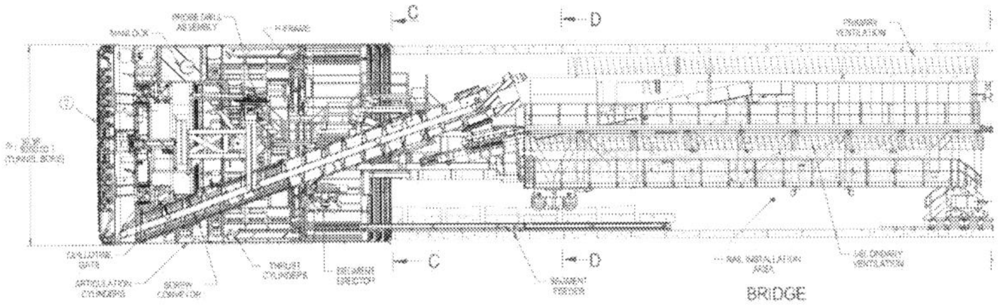

Tunnel Boring Machine and Bridge

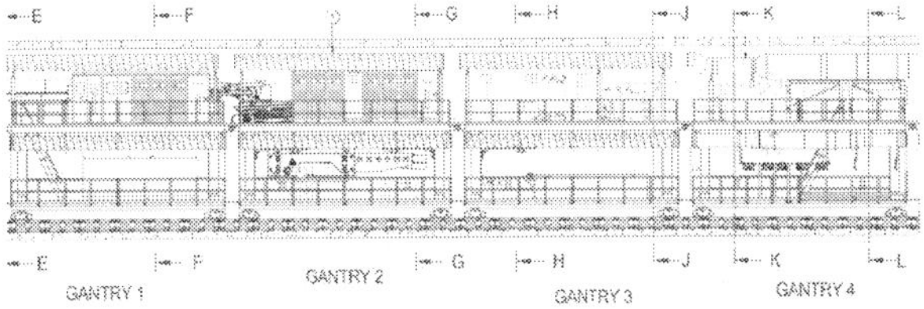

Gantries 1-4

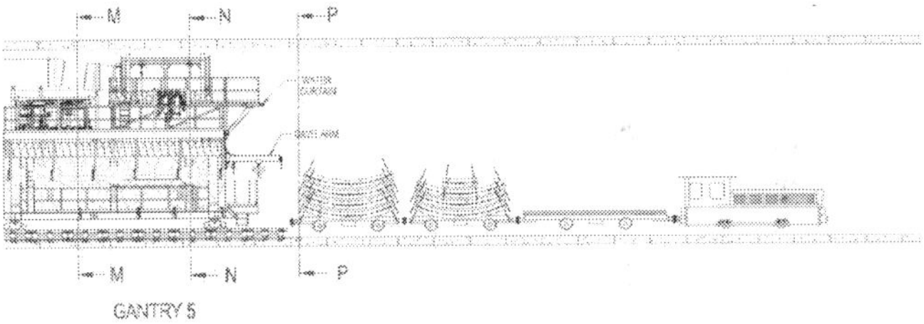

Gantry 5 and the Supply Train

Chapter 13

The next morning the crowds gathered again – at least those who could and – truth be told – except for the team involved in moving the sections, for most of them their work was done until the Ant Man started working. But before that could happen, his seven sections had to be taken up to the plateau and connected. In that respect, there was a problem that had to be faced long before his arrival: how to transport the Tunnel Boring Machine from the harbor to the plateau on the side of Vulcan's Forge where the tunnel was going to be dug. The roads on São Rochelle were not paved so moving by truck was out of the question and its weight made that improbable. The only answer was by rail. The Back-up Train cars ran on a track with the rails thirty-six inches apart rather than four foot eight and a half inches which was the U.S. Standard. So all the railroad cars to carry supplies to the train and dirt from the tunnel and the engines that pulled or pushed them had to be of the smaller gauge and that meant specially built.

If a regular train rail track was run up the side of Vulcan's Forge, it would take several hairpin turns because a train can efficiently only handle a five-degree slope. That was deemed unacceptable because of the space needed. In consultation with specialists, the decision was made to use two unlinked four axle wheel trucks, one at each end of the TBM and the parts of the trucks in contact with the section would swivel to permit sharper turns. Thus the decision to keep the track as straight as possible and also to keep the engines small because of the necessary turns.

Coming off the *B.B. Queen*, a section would be pulled by one engine and pushed by a second. The engines themselves were unique and were in part designed by Waldo. They were loosely based on the electric mules that move ships through the locks of the Panama Canal with adaptations to either pull or push and to have a special gear on the bottom because the movement up the slope to the plateau would be a cog railway. They were powered by a third rail much like subways in many big cities. In their construction, simplicity was used, and they ended up looking a little like an ice rink Zamboni with the driver sitting high at the back. And to have the necessary power, they were twice as long as a Zamboni. Because of their construction, they did not move fast and even slower moving the train sections. It would take several days to move the TBM from the *B.B. Queen* to its position on the trestle.

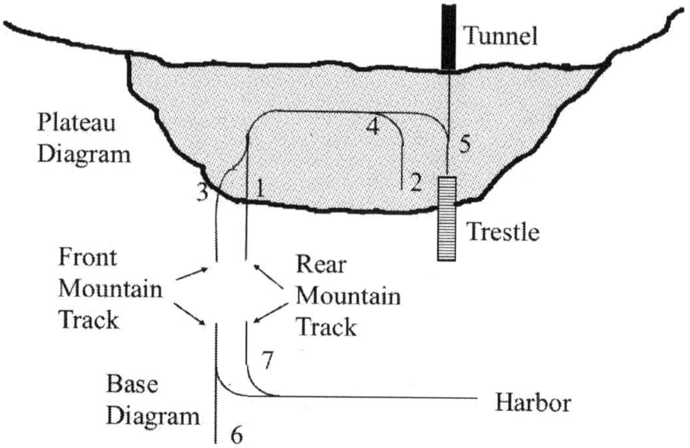

1. Front Pull Engine 2 disconnect
2. Plateau Siding
3. Rear Push Engine 1 disconnect
4. Front Pull Engine 1 disconnect
5. Rear Push Engine 2 disconnect
6. Rear Push Engine 1 wait
7. Front Pull Engine 2 wait

This morning the first section that came out of the *B.B. Queen* was Gantry 5 with the rear end first because the nature of the design required that the last or caboose section of Ant Man was the first to be taken up the hill. The TBM itself would be the last section to go up and it would be the slowest.

Walt Jefferies (construction supervisor), Issaack, Siegfried, and Waldo were waiting on the dock to follow the first piece up the mountain.

"Hey, Andy," Walt Jefferies called to a short man standing near the first engine that would pull the section up the mountain. "When you get a chance come over here."

The man waved and finished talking to the man who was with him and started over to where the four were standing. Andrew (Andy) Russell was small enough to be a jockey if he had wanted to, but until he was eighteen, he had never seen a horse in real life. All he wanted to do was to be an engineer – the kind of engineer who drives trains. That wasn't going to happen he quickly realized so he became a Civil Engineer with a specialization in railroads. It was he who designed the tracks and the four axle trucks used to carry the sections. When he got to the group Walt Jefferies introduced him.

"So tell us how this is going to work," Issaack said.

"Well, we need…"

There was the blast of horn from the interior of the *B.B. Queen* and all turned to look. The first of the engines made its appearance moving at a speed of one mile an hour.

"As I was saying," Andy continued. "It's going to take two engines to get each section of the Back-up Train up to the plateau and in place. That one is the Front Pull Engine 1. It is pulling the rear of Gantry 5. There is another engine pushing the other end and that is Rear Push Engine 1. When they reach the bottom of the mountain they will take the first switch and head straight up what we call the Rear Mountain Track. The name will be made clearer when I tell you how the TBM will be taken. The other track is the Front Mountain Track for a similar reason."

While he had been talking, Front Pull Engine 1 was all the way out of the *B.B. Queen*'s hold as was Gantry 5. At this point there was another horn blast from within the *B.B. Queen*'s hold and a second engine made its appearance.

"That's the Rear Push Engine 1," Andy explained. "When they get the section all the way to the top and ready to take the section onto the trestle, Front Pull Engine 1 will disconnect and pull onto the Plateau siding. Rear Push Engine 1 will put the section in place. Then it will start back down the mountain followed by Front Push Engine 1. They will come down on the Front Mountain Track because a second section will be up on the Rear Mountain Track pulled by Front Pull Engine 2 and Rear Push Engine 2. Then the process will be repeated with the two engines picking up another section and heading up while the other two engines are heading down."

Chapter 14

"I understand how that works for the Back-up Train sections," Issaack said, "But what about the TBM. The real heart, although it is the head, of Ant Man."

"That's a little more complicated," Andy said. "When they start out from the *B.B. Queen*, the TBM will be pulled by Front Pull Engine 1 and pushed by Rear Push Engine 2. When the rear TBM truck reaches the switch to turn onto the Rear Mountain Track, the front TBM truck will be making the turn onto the Front Mountain Track. When the trucks are fully on their tracks, the two engines will stop. Rear Push Engine 1 will come off the switch at the Front Mountain Track and connect to the rear of the front TBM truck. Front Pull Engine 2 will be waiting on the Rear Mountain Track and will back up and connect to the front of the rear TBM truck. Once all four engines are connected, they will begin taking the TBM up the mountain."

As he finished his description, there was another horn blast from within the *B.B. Queen*'s hold and a third engine started to show itself.

"That's the Front Pull Engine 2," Andy said excitedly. "It is pulling Gantry 4."

"And Rear Push Engine 2 is pushing it," Waldo said.

"Yes. When they reach the switch to the Rear Mountain Track, they will wait until Gantry 5 is on the plateau and then they will start up. That gives plenty of time for Gantry 5 to be put in place and the two engines to be at least halfway down the mountain before the Gantry 4 is halfway up."

"Okay, so finish telling us what the TBM and its four engines are to do when they reach the plateau."

But this first part of the program did not go well. When the TBM was about halfway to the plateau, Front Pull Engine 2 developed a power problem and slowed down. Consequently the other three engines had to slow down to keep pace with it. And the further up the mountain it went, the slower it went and when it had just made its way onto the plateau it died.

"This is the tricky part of the maneuver," Andy said. "When they reach the plateau, it will be flat and easier to pull and push so only two engines will be needed. Everyone will stop, and Front Pull Engine 2 will disconnect and move ahead to the Plateau Siding. Rear Push Engine 1 will also disconnect and back down the Front Mountain Track, probably to its siding but it will have other duties once the digging begins. Either bringing muck out of tunnel or taking concrete and other supplies up."

With Front Pull Engine 2 completely dead. Changes needed to be made. Front Pull Engine 1 disconnected, leaving Rear Push Engine 1 holding the rear of the TBM while Rear Push Engine 2 held the front of the TBM on the Rear Mountain Track. Front Pull Engine 1 moved forward onto the Plateau Track and then backed up and connected to Front Pull Engine 2 which was then disconnected from the TBM. Then Front Pull Engine 1 pulled Front Pull Engine 2 onto the trestle. Once on the trestle, Front Pull Engine 1 pushed Front Pull Engine 2 up against the volcano where the TBM was going to start digging. Then it disconnected, backed up and returned to its position helping Rear Push Engine 1. It had changed between its original position and that of Front Pull Engine 2 until the TBM was in the proper position on the plateau. Then Rear Push Engine 1 disconnected as in the original program and returned to the bottom of the mountain.

"With those two engines out of the way, Front Pull Engine 1 will pull the front TBM truck onto the Plateau Track, which is the continuation of the Rear Mountain Track. Rear Push Engine 2 will push as needed to keep the trucks properly spaced. When they get to the Plateau Siding switch, Front Pull Engine 1 will disconnect and pull onto the siding and Rear Push Engine 2 will put the TBM in Place."

However, now the problem was what to do with Front Pull Engine 2. There wasn't space on the trestle to get it off the way it came on. Consequently a new track had to be laid connecting the trestle track and the plateau track. The Front Pull Engine 1 pulled off its siding, used the new track to connect to Front Pull Engine 2 and pulled it down the mountain where it could be repaired. That all added time to the project but such are the problems with construction projects.

"We have big electric motors on the mountain which will retract cables attached to the front of the TBM and pull it up against the face of the volcano where it can start digging and from there it is on its own."

"Ingenious," Issaack said not certain if he understood it all.

"Thanks," Andy said. "There is one more thing."

"Not another engine," Waldo said although he understood it all having been part of the design team.

"No, so that the tunnel would be dug as close as possible to the plateau level, the plateau tracks were built in a channel five feet below the surface of the plateau. When the tunnel had been dug and the track removed the channel would be filled with dirt and rock from the digging of the tunnel. The dirt from the channel and from grading the road up the side of Vulcan's Forge as well as excess from the solar farms and road grading were used to enlarge the plateau to meet the needs of the track. It had been decided that the trestle would be easier to build than excavating the necessary amount of dirt."

And over the course of the next week while the seven sections of Ant Man were being conveyed to the plateau trestle, the plant to make the concrete sections of the tunnel was assembled. A freighter made anchor off the island with a Super Stallion helicopter on board and sand and cement were ferried from the freighter to the plant area so that concrete could be made. Then after everything was checked and double checked, Ant Man's motors were started, and he took his first bite out of Vulcan's Forge. For the engines that had taken the sections up to the plateau, there was no rest because the rocks and dirt from the tunnel had to be taken somewhere and that somewhere was the edge of the plateau and for part of it, its final resting place was in the sink hole where Matías Zapatero had disappeared. When that hole was completely filled, and final landscaping had been done, a monument honoring the only man to die during the construction phase of the Predator Project was placed in a solemn ceremony which everyone on the island attended.

In addition to the dirt having to be removed, concrete pieces for the tunnel walls had to be brought up and carried to Ant Man. And for both of these, dirt removal and concrete delivery, a track was laid in the tunnel behind Ant Man so that the rail cars could get there. And there was a lot of dirt and rock: 33,000 cubic yards of dirt and rock which is approximately 50,000 tons. By the time the tunnel was dug, taking three hundred days, the plateau had grown immensely. While the Back-up Train was still outside the tunnel, the dirt was piled on the plateau. Because the pieces of Ant Man had to be taken down the mountain in the same manner they were brought up, much of the plateau's surface had to be kept clear so the dirt and rock was put over the sides and front of the plateau. When the Ant Man was completely in the tunnel, the trestle was dismantled, and the dirt and rock were dumped in its place and the track reinstalled although it didn't have to be as long since the last section entering the tunnel was the first out of the tunnel and first to be taken down the mountain. In this age of environmental concern, all the plants growing in the area where the dirt was dumped had been dug up and temporarily planted elsewhere and then replanted in the new part of Vulcan's Forge.

The question had always been what to do with Ant Man once the tunnel had been dug. There was need for him in a third world country and so once the sections were aboard the *B.B. Queen*, she set sail and delivered Ant Man to the chosen country. A team of experienced operators was paid to train workers in that country until they could run Ant Man (who got a new name but didn't care) independently.

Once Ant Man was gone, the tracks were pulled. The rails were sent to another third world county where they could be of use. The ties, which were concrete rather than the traditional wood, were added to the pier for the final touches.

Chapter 14

Horus continued discussing the proposed construction on São Rochelle but was interrupted by Harvey Gladstone.

"When will we start collecting animals?" Harvey Gladstone asked.

"By this time. We believe that construction of Vulcan's Roost will take a year and probably six months after that the animals will arrive."

"If the place iz built, why wait zix months?" Ramiro questioned.

"Because it won't be fully functional. We have to be certain that everything is there, and the six months gives us time to get any animal that we hadn't gotten before and time for you to plan your schedules so you can be here."

"I just need a week," Phil said.

"Sim," agreed Ramiro who seemed antsy at the length of time. But then he seemed antsy all the time, as though expecting something unexpected to happen.

"Well, maybe you gents can be here any buggering time you want, but I can't," Monica said. "I have a schedule set over a year in advance. Besides, five years? You're talking bollocks if you say you know what you'll be doing in five years. Shite, for all you know, the man with the scythe will come calling for you tomorrow."

Everyone looked at Monica in amazement at this outburst. The language used was in keeping with her songs, but not in general conversation.

"Gentlemen and ladies," Horus said. "You will all be informed of what is happening and when as this goes along. This is just the plan and it is subject to changes. It may take longer; it may take less. Remember, we don't even have the property yet."

While the *B.B. Queen* was taking Ant Man to help a developing country, power and water was being run into the crater. The concrete sections put in the tunnel had holes for electricity and water. Some of the electricity was used to power lights and other things in the tunnel but the water went straight through. The water was obtained from the bottom pond of Prometheus's Aerie using electric pumps and run to the workers' barrack for their use and then up to the crater using a series of assisting pumps. Water used for other than toilet facilities was run through a cleansing process before running into a pond where it would be permitted to drain back into the island. All toilets on the island were composting toilets which were cleaned as required and processed to turn the contents into fertilizer and spread over grasslands. Also dirt was spread in the tunnel to make a road so that vehicles going through the tunnel were traveling on a flat surface.

When the *B.B. Queen* returned to São Rochelle after dropping off Ant Man at his new home, she was laden with containers with which Vulcan's Roost would be constructed. In the time that had elapsed, the foundation for Vulcan's Roost had been poured under the supervision of Waldo and Issaack. They had returned to São Rochelle when the *B.B. Queen* had come to pick up the Ant Man and had supervised the grading and foundation pouring because measurements were crucial. Each of the rooms were made of eight by twenty-foot containers. These containers were intended to be placed by a crane which lowered each one onto the foundation. Six-foot-long vertical rods protruded from the foundation and these would enter holes in the container walls and hold them in place. There was little room for error. Issaack and Waldo were standing on the pier when the *B.B. Queen* docked. They had been staying in one of the village houses no longer needed by workers whose jobs on the island were finished. The inside of the house didn't look the same because all that was inside had been thrown away and new stuff had been brought on the Queen's last visit to pick up Ant Man. To take care of the wants, at least in the food and drink part of their lives, Carmen Domingo and Stefaan Declercq had accompanied them. On board the Queen were two flatbed container haulers and one mobile crane that could lift the containers off a truck and set them in place. None of the containers were empty. They either contained equipment in the case of the kitchen and dining room, for example, or sections of flooring, ceiling or exterior walls which were all glass or at least appeared to be glass. And in a few cases, containers held furniture for the rooms although some items would be delivered later.

"So, how was the trip?" Issaack asked Captain Arnold Blythe when he and Waldo went aboard after the *B.B. Queen* had docked.

"Not bad. We had to spend five days in port in the Canaries because of a storm but we always build in extra sea days in for this lady."

"True. Her shallow draft is great for here but not at sea in bad weather."

"Exactly. And empty she rocks like a baby's cradle gone haywire. But give her a load like the Ant Man and she rides smooth … but not in a big storm."

"And our cargo?"

"Safe. Everything's accounted for. This trip was easy compared to the last one."

After talking to the captain, Issaack and Waldo went into the hold where they found Walt Jeffries and four of his men.

"Greetings, Issaack. Waldo," Jeffries said. "We are getting ready to get the first two containers up to the crater."

"Great," Waldo said. "I'll drive one of the rigs."

"I don't know about that," Jeffries said. "Takes an experienced truck driver to handle one of these big rigs with the container on it."

"Don't wanna brag," Waldo said. "But I designed and built those rigs. I wouldn't touch the crane because I had nothing to do with it, but I know these trucks."

Jeffries still looked dubious.

"You don't have to worry about him," Issaack said. "We've know each other for years, and if he says he can, believe me, he can."

"Okay," Jeffries said. "Guess you guys are the bosses, so I got to let you do it. Oh, I was hoping to get to meet that Horace guy some time."

Issaack laughed. "He's not much for roughing it."

"Well, okay."

"You have the list of containers?"

"Yep," Jeffries said. "Taking 1a and 1b just like it says."

"Well, stick to the order. Everything goes in by number just like the diagram says. You misplace one and nothing will work, and you'll have to start all over again."

"I've already told my crew about it and they are not going to remove any stickers until I give the okay."

"Good."

"Well, let's get going," Waldo said.

As he said this, the diesel engine in the mobile crane roared to life, diesel smoke billowing from its pipes.

"Jim Jarvis is my crane guy," Jeffries said. "He's good. At least that's what his resume and recommendations say."

As they watched the first container being loaded on the first flatbed, the mobile crane pulled out of the hold, crossed the ramp and rolled up the slope, turned right and went out of sight headed for Vulcan's Roost.

With the first container secured on the bed, Waldo and Issaack got into the truck.

"Here goes nothing," Waldo said and laughed as he pushed the start button. The electric engine purred to life.

Shifting into drive, Waldo released the parking brake, checked the mirrors, and stepped on the "juice" which is what he called the accelerator pedal or gas pedal to those driving vehicles with fossil fuel. The drive up the mountain to the plateau went easily in the big rig despite its load. As they entered the tunnel leading to the crater, the lights in the tunnel came on.

"This flat floor really makes this like a regular tunnel," Waldo said.

"Well, we had to do it," Issaack said. "I mean driving in a tube would be a little nerve racking."

"Yeah and the flat floor can hold secrets that a round one can't," and Waldo winked at Issaack.

The loaded container truck took longer to get to the crater than the mobile crane had. Jim Jarvis had the crane stabilized and was waiting with several other men as Waldo brought the container truck to a stop where Jarvis indicated.

Getting out, Waldo told Jarvis that he didn't know how to free the container. Jarvis looked at him incredulously.

"I was told you made this vehicle."

"I did. I know the engine and gears and stuff but had nothing to do with the container part. I bought what I was told to buy."

"Don't look at me," Issaack said. "He bought it."

Jarvis shook his head and told the other men to get the container ready and then got into the crane's cab. A man in a green hat indicated that all was ready and motioned Issaack and Waldo to get out of the way.

The two moved and watched as the crane lifted the container and moved it over the foundation to where four of the men were standing at the corners of where the container should go. Following their hand signs, Jarrvis lowered the container down and guided by the men, set it precisely where it was supposed to go.

"Bingo," Issaack said. "That's one."

"Only forty-two to go," Waldo said, and the two men laughed.

Chapter 16

The second meeting was shorter than the first and no overnights were planned. After a pause for a light lunch of salads, soups and sandwiches with assorted desserts ("Lunch without dessert is like sex without an orgasm," Carmen had replied when asked why there were always desserts.) "Sorry I asked," Phil had said, but he was smiling when he said it. An hour after the meeting had broken for the repast, it was back in session and an hour later it was done. But again, there was the dismissal and the order was not that in which the members of the Bundle had arrived. Because of the problems with Ramiro during the first meeting, two changes had been made. One was the difference in order of arrival and dismissal. Second was that the vehicles which were used to deliver the attendees were not to be used to pick anyone up. Third, during the meeting a temporary porte-cochère was erected in front of the entrance. The side facing the street was covered with opaque bulletproof glass.

Gerallt was frustrated. He had picked a location two blocks away on top of a five-story building which had given him a direct line of sight to the door. From that height he figured that he would have had a shot at Ramiro either coming or going – that was 50% and good enough for him. Certainly, better than any other time since that first meeting. In fact, since the first meeting, there hadn't been a chance at all or at least not one he had heard about. And he hadn't alerted Ramiro to the fact that he was coming for him, but he had no doubt that the man suspected that he was somewhere out there.

And indeed, the man had suspected and had his team in place for a day before Gerallt showed. One day was long enough for his team to blend into the neighborhood because, unlike Gerallt, they were Hispanic, and in Cartagena Gerallt stood out like a sore thumb. He knew that but had no choice. There were people in Cartagena, as there were most places in South America, sympathetic to Gerallt's cause and willing to help only because if Gerallt was successful, the leader of one of the biggest drug cartels in the world would be removed. That wouldn't stop the drugs, but it would get rid of the slimy white bastard or "bastardo branco viscoso" as the natives of Brazil say. "Slimy" because Ramiro's thick black hair was always coated with a handful of oil to hold it in place and additionally due to the fact that his business was considered to be one where the slime was involved. "White" because he always wore white – all white (well, if he wore underwear, it would be white but not too many people could profess to the type of underwear that Ramiro wore), shirt, tie, coat, pants, socks, shoes, watch band – hell, the entire watch except for the numbers and hands was white. "Bastard" – think about it. What else would you call such a man and in actuality he was.

Gerallt knew Ramiro's men were there. He didn't know who they were, but he sensed that he was being watched and he was surprised that he was still alive. He figured that if he were ever lucky enough put a finger in the trigger guard, he himself was a dead man. He wouldn't have minded if he had gotten the shot off, but he knew that he wouldn't. What bothered him was "why am I alive?" The answer was "ainda não é tempo (it is not time yet)" Ramiro had said when one of his own men asked. And in his mind, Ramiro had already set the trap to catch Gerallt when the time was right and that was when the predators were ready to go to São Rochelle because Gerallt was to be the fourteenth predator (fifteenth if you count each of the coyotes separately.)

Gerallt Cearrach was thirty-two years old. Two years before he had come home to Buillth Wells, Wales, to bury his mother. Three years before, it had been his father. Lying within the historic boundaries of Brecknockshire in mid-Wales, Buillth Wells sits at the confluence of the River Wye and the River Irfon in the Welsh section of the Wye Valley. It is a small town of less than three thousand and is situated closer to England than to the Irish Sea.

Gerallt had no real allegiance to England or to Great Britain, but when he had completed his schooling the only thing that he could see in his future was the military. So he had joined the United Kingdom's Special Forces and, because he was good with a rifle, they had made him a sniper. And he found that he didn't mind killing another human. That said, it would be easier for him to kill Ramiro because he didn't consider Ramiro to be human. No human could provide the drugs to other humans the way Ramiro did and not be at all concerned when or if they died. And that was what had happened when Gerallt had come home on emergency leave to bury his mother. He had walked into his parents' house in the Buillth Wells and discovered that he was going to have to bury his younger brother Caradoc also. His brother had been born eight years after Gerallt, as much a surprise to his parents as Gerallt had been because, after ten years of marriage and no progeny, his parents had given up any hope of having heirs – not that there was much to leave them but a name and, if things didn't go totally sour, a house. Then Gerallt had become a seed in his mother's womb and eight years later Caradoc had joined the family. Gerallt had been a feisty lad which befit the meaning of his name "Rule of the Spear." His brother had been the light in his mother's eyes which fit the meaning of his name "dearly beloved." But something had gone wrong with his brother and he had taken to drugs in his teens and the resultant loss of drive in his life had left him lethargic and impotent. He had become the burden that his parents didn't need, and his attitude and disrespect of both his life and his parents' had literally broken his father's heart.

Gerallt found his brother sprawled in a chair in the living room barely breathing as though he had been hanging on for Gerallt to come home. A call to 999, the emergency number, brought an ambulance and EMTs but by that time there was nothing they could do to save him. And so, two days later Gerallt buried his mother standing beside her grave in the cemetery with eleven of his parents' friends and the minister. The next day, he and the minister were the only ones who showed up at the service for his brother and at the cemetery. Gerallt had asked for a discharge and had taken over his father's hardware business but only so that he could sell it and the house. The proceeds were used to start the search for the man who had been the cause of his brother's death – and most probably had hastened the deaths of his parents.

The first stop had been the local supplier who had been easy to find. The supplier's last words were the name of his supplier in Brecon, and the trail led from there to Abergavenny and thence to Cardiff. The last words that the Cardiff man had said led Gerallt to Bristol and thence to London. The trail there could have gone dark, cold, and ended except for a detective who had taken a liking to Gerallt and had told him after several pints (bought by Gerallt) that the majority of drugs came into England through a network of importers of the cartel run by a Brazilian drug lord Ramiro Esteves.

And now, here he was, broke but not broken, watching many limousines, one taxi, and an Uber (or possibly just a private car belonging to a friend) picking up the members of the Bundle. The strange thing was there were ten vehicles and when the last one left, the hotel was dark. So there was nothing to do but to pack up and go home, get another job and wait for word from one of his contacts in Brazil on Esteves' next journey to somewhere Gerallt could have a shot at him. The place he had been was left tidy and there was nothing there for Ramiro's men to find although they did look. They knew how he came, how he left, and where he went. That was a start, but most importantly, they had pictures. Lots of pictures and unless he was a master of disguise, he would be easy to recognize in the future.

Vulcan's Roost

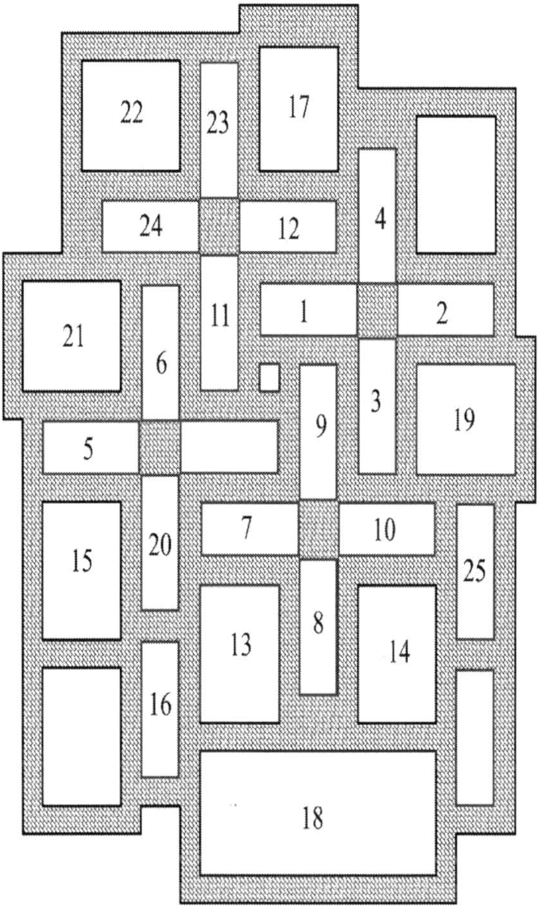

1. Ramiro Esteves
2. Waldo Emerson
3. Harvey Gladstone
4. Phillip Parmelee
5. Gloria Mitchell
6. Monica Bartlett
7. Issaack Kincaid
8. Symon Sheetz
9. Stefaan Declercq
10. Carmen Domingo
11. Hansel
12. Gretel
13. Horus
14. Theater
15. Drone Lab
16. Computer lab
17. HVAC
18. Dining Room and Kitchen
19. Gym
20. Siegfried Schmidt
21. Battery storage
22. Solar Panel Lab
23. Monica Bartlett 2
24. Gloria Mitchell 2
25. Siegfried Schmidt

Chapter 17

As most days on the island, it was a cloudless sky that greeted the helicopter bearing the six members of the Billionaire Bundle as São Rochelle came into view.

"My god," Harvey Gladstone said. "It looks like Eden."

"It's beautiful," Monica said. "I would like to build a house here when this is over."

"'Fraid you can't do that," Phil said, "Unless you want to give it up quickly. Remember this is a ten-year lease. The locals get it back at the end of the lease with all the improvements."

"Zey may not want it back," Ramiro said. "When zey hear what haz happen here zey may not want ze ... how you say, the notar..."

"Notoriety," Gloria said. "That's like being famous, but it has a bad connotation ... bad meaning."

"Sim, zat iz what I mean."

"Well said but they will be getting a lot of improvements, especially the new dock and electricity, water lines, living quarters. It will be like paradise. I certainly would put up with a little notoriety for that," Waldo chimed in.

The helicopter in which they rode was an Airbus Helicopters H145 and was extremely quiet which enabled them to converse without having to yell.

"We're going to circle the island before landing at the headquarters," the pilot broke in.

"In the volcano?" Monica said.

"Yes."

"Blinding," Monica said. "I can hardly wait."

"Is that the Prometheus's ...," Gloria said. "Oh, yes, I can see the waterfall. That's where the second dozer almost bit it." She had seen it before but with the snake bite and the rush back to the mainland, her memory was hazy.

"Yes, that driver saved us a lot of money. Not only by not having to buy another dozer and drop it but by not having to retrieve that one from the pool of water," Phil said.

"Why bother," Harvey Gladstone said. "Just leave it there."

"Pollution," Phil said. "You wouldn't help pollute the world's oceans, would you?"

"One dozer isn't going to make a difference," Harvey Gladstone countered.

"One dozer here, an airplane there, a train, an oil tanker... It all adds up." Phil said.

Harvey Gladstone didn't counter. He knew it was useless, but then he was not a big environmentalist. To him, green space was a big waste of valuable property.

"There's the pier," Waldo said. "Now that's impressive."

And it was. A U-shaped dock with the base of the U a one hundred fifty foot-long fifty feet wide pile of stone and each of the arms one hundred feet long and thirty feet wide. The tops were made smooth and walkable by the pouring of gravel which was then packed down by a steamroller.

"It would take a mega pounding to tear that apart," Waldo said. "When the barge comes the day after tomorrow with the animals, we will see how fantastic it is."

"I can hardly wait," Monica said. "I want to see that white tiger they got. I hear she is beautiful."

The chopper flew over the dock and then started circling the volcano.

"Look at all those solar panels!" Gloria said.

"Yes, all sides of the mountain are covered so that no matter what the time of year or time of day, energy is being collected and stored," Phil said.

"Everything is electrical here," Monica said.

Phil was uncertain if that was a question or a statement.

"Indeed it is," Waldo said in agreement. "Now that everything is made, the machines that did the big excavation and construction are gone and only electric vehicles remain. In that manner, the island is energy independent."

"And with proper agriculture and animal husbandry to accompany the fishing, it will be food independent also," Phil said.

Ramiro said nothing, just taking it all in and smiling.

After circling the volcano at a height about halfway up, the helicopter rose and crossed over the lip of the volcano's crater. Below them was the island headquarters' complex.

"There's our home for the next week or so," Waldo said.

"Hope it's Five Star," Gloria said.

"We have been assured that it is that at least," Waldo said. "And from the reports, it is a Six Star Hotel."

The helicopter set down on an indicated landing spot near the building. The entire side of the building they saw was glass and, in fact, all the outer sides were glass that served as solar panels and there were also solar panels on the roof.

When the blades of the helicopter stopped spinning, a panel in the glass wall slid open and Issaack Kincaid came out waving to them. The copilot had gotten out and opened the door and the six billionaires descended a small set of steps and, for most of them, set foot on the floor of the volcano for the first time. It was sandy, but firm and there was no problem walking.

"Welcome to Vulcan's Roost," Issaack said. "I'll have someone collect your bags and get them to your room. But first I promised you that you would meet the person behind this entire setup, so please follow me."

He turned and headed back toward the building, raising his right arm into the air and then bringing it down pointing to the building and indicating they should follow him. They did and upon entering the building found it to be deliciously cool. The walls were painted a cool yet vividly bright red tone with flecks of yellow and the floor was white tile which surprisingly did not make any noise as they walked.

The hallway walls of the entire building were sides of cargo containers that had been used to bring supplies to the island during the construction with the rooms then made putting roofing and flooring between the containers.

"All the rain that falls on the building is collected by a system of pipes and fed into our purification system," Issaack said.

If anyone had been keeping track they would have noticed they were headed for the center of the complex. Issaack stopped in front of what appeared at the moment to be an opaque glass door. When they had all caught up, Issaack placed his hand in a frosted rectangle in the middle of the door and said, "This is what you've waited for," and slide the panel aside and they stepped inside.

What they saw surprised them all. The room was nineteen feet by nineteen feet square, with walls eight feet tall. Everything was stark white except the ceiling which looked to be crystal. Filling the room were rows and rows of servers.

"Ladies and gentlemen, I give you Horus."

They were stunned.

"Horus is a computer?" Monica said.

"No computer can be that human," Phil said. "It's impossible."

"No, it's not," a voice said from the right side of the room. They turned in that direction and saw a man who must have been at least six feet four inches in his stocking feet and probably weighed nor more than two hundred pounds. He had flaming red hair, a face covered with red freckles to match, and a hawk-like nose set between two grey-green eyes that seemed to flash. Under the nose was a broad mouth that was almost constantly spread in a smile revealing dazzling white teeth. The one fault with his facial features were the ears that stuck out from the side. Gloria thought that she wouldn't be surprised if his next words were "What? Me worry?"

"I'm Siegfried Schmidt," the man said by way of introduction. "My friends, and I include you among them, call me Red. Issaack and I are the creators of Horus who is a computing machine of artificial intelligence. Issaack is the programmer and I created the computer."

"What kind of computer?" asked Gloria.

"Biological," Siegfried said.

"Rubbish," Harvey said. "It's not possible."

"Yes, it is," Siegfried said. "It is constantly growing and replacing the old cells without loss of data.

At the present time half of these servers are in use as storage and the others are simply waiting for Horus to learn more and need them."

"And, other than serving as the host of our original meeting, what purpose does this Horus have?" Phil asked.

"He runs everything on this island," Issaack said, "Don't you, Horus?"

"Yes, Issaack. That has been my purpose since I was brought here a year ago." Horus's voice seemed to come from all sides of the room although it was not too loud.

"When they say you run everything, what does that mean?" Monica asked.

"I monitor the water quality and the pipes that carry the water to the village to ensure that everything it safe. I monitor the solar panels and their storage units to ensure that we always have sufficient power. I run all the cameras that are spread around the island, I fly and maintain the drones we use to keep track of the island's wildlife and the island's security."

"You do that all at once?" Waldo said.

"Yes, and more, Mr. Emerson," Horus said.

"How did you know that was me?"

"I recorded your voice pattern during the initial meeting and analyzed it when you just spoke."

"Do you know where I am standing?"

"Yes, sir. You are precisely two feet four point five seven inches in front of Lab Panel 37 and three feet point six four five inches to the left of Ms. Mitchell."

"How did you know zat?" Ramiro said, speaking up for the first time.

"He has the membership card in the left breast pocket of his shirt."

Waldo took the card out of his pocket, handed it to Gloria and stepped forward two steps.

"Giving her your card, doesn't make you invisible, Mr. Emerson," Horus said. "You are now six feet four point zero seven two inches from panel Lab 37 and..."

"How did you know that?" Waldo said.

"There are cameras everywhere," Horus said. But that was not the reason. He wouldn't tell anyone that the real reason was that the floor tiles, among many of their attributes, were weight sensitive.

"Even in our loos?" Monica asked.

"Yes, but they are not turned on unless I sense some kind of security breach."

"How you determine a zecurity breach?" queried Ramiro.

"You do not have security clearance for that knowledge," Horus answered.

"Who doez?"

"You do not have security clearance for that knowledge."

"Okay, enough trying to figure out Horus," Siegfried said. "He is a very secretive personage and keeps a secret better than anyone I know."

"I know you are going to ask, Monica," Issaack said. "Siegfried was upstairs during the initial meeting and was playing a part – he was feeding Horus answers to questions that Horus wasn't prepared for."

"I knew there was something going on," Monica said.

"So now that you have met Horus as much as anyone can meet Horus, let me show you to your rooms. While you have been in here, the luggage you brought has been taken from the helicopter to your room. You first, Monica. Step outside into the hallway."

Monica walked to the entrance panel which slid open for her.

"Why's it doing it now and not when we got here?" Monica asked.

"Because Horus was told not to do so until you learned who Horus was."

They were standing in the hallway.

"Tell Horus you want to go to your room," Issaack said.

"Horus, I want to go to my room."

On the floor in front of Monica in the center of a tile was a green arrow with the shaft bearing the word <MONICA.

"Now just start walking," Issaack said and Monica did, and the arrow preceded her always leaping to the tile in front of her. When she reached the first corridor the arrow turned sideways so it read <MONICA and so she turned and disappeared down the hall after waving good–bye and blowing a kiss to Issaack. Ramiro stepped into the hallway and said, "Horuz, I want to go to Monica'z room." Nothing appeared on the floor,

"What'z wrong with zis computer?" Ramiro said.

'Nothing," Issaack replied, "but it is obvious that you haven't been invited."

Ramiro scowled and said, "Horuz, I want to go to my room." The proper arrow appeared on the floor in front of him and he started following it, but the arrow didn't turn left at the first corridor. However, he did, and the arrow disappeared.

"Horuz, I want to go to my room."

Nothing appeared on the floor in front of him. Frustrated he turned around and there on the tile in the middle of the corridor was <RAMIRO. Fuming, Ramiro followed the arrows until he reached a panel and a door opened and he entered. When the door closed behind

him, he said, "Izzaack, you'll be ze firzt to die and zat damned Horuz will be the zecond."

In one of the servers that Horus had labeled "Security," Horus entered the word "Esteves."

Chapter 18

It was 02:03:57 early the following morning when the former Brazilian military troop carrier entered the air space above São Rochelle. It was at this precise second that the first man stepped out of the plane followed quickly by a second, then a third, a fourth and continuing until ten had left the aircraft. The airplane continued on making a 180º-turn and coming back over the island and thirty more men stepped out. The first ten men were supposed to land on the south side of Montanha da Cratera or Vulcan's Forge as it was currently known and the next thirty within the volcano's crater, ten of them on the roof of Vulcan's Roost. Thirty-nine of these men achieved their goal. However, the chute of the fortieth, who was really number six of the first ten men, failed to open and streamed above his head as he plummeted screaming until the air left his lungs and he died, a thousand feet above the island, his body crashing into the westernmost limbs of a kapok in the island's small rain forest. There the body hung having not made it to the ground, at least not that day, and in the future would became sustenance for a starving panther. As planned, twenty of the invaders, for that is what they were, made their landing on the crater's floor east of Vulcan's Roost, the other ten on the roof of Vulcan's Roost.

In all three groups, chutes were quickly gathered and put out of the way. Weapons were released from bindings and the men gathered in preassigned groups of five, one with only four, on the side of the mountain. The leader of each unit (which could properly be called a fireteam although these men were no longer military, but all had been so, although not in the same country's forces) checked his watch and then led his unit to their proper position.

On the side of the mountain, the two units converged on opposite sides of the metal gate, the main purpose of which was purported to be to prevent any of the predators – who were not yet on the island – from getting into the volcano's crater. One man of each unit prepared to plant plastic explosives on the hinges of the massive gates to blow them off and permit entrance. Fortunately each unit had two men with this responsibility just in case what had come to pass happened because the dead man was one of the two in his unit who carried the explosives. However, when they got to the gates, they found them open. After all there were no predators on the island and there was, up until the first of these men set foot on the island, no one hostile to those in Vulcan's Roost.

The two unit leaders conferred and motioned for the men to follow them into the quarter-mile-long tunnel. The two leaders were Comandante Pedro Lopez who was second in command of the invasion force and Sergeant Franco Delgado who was the leader of Squad Bueno which had been broken into the two units. All were wearing night vision goggles, but the best of night vision googles, the best of eyes in the bright daylight if that is what it would have been, would not have identified the three ten-foot-wide metal covers as dangerous. The first two were ten feet apart, the first fifteen feet into the tunnel. The third was just five feet beyond the second. When four of the five men of the lead unit were on the second cover and the last two of the second unit were on the first, the two-piece hinged covers opened. The six ill-fated men plunged ten feet to the bottom of the pit. The floor was studded with one-foot long metal nails set one foot apart. None of the men survived the fall. At least not for very long. The fifth man of the first unit was Comandante Lopez and he had just stepped off the cover as the fourth man of the unit stepped onto it. Sergeant Franco Delgado was just behind the fifth man of the first unit and in two more steps he would have been on that steel cover.

Of the three remaining, only one of them attempted to leap the chasm and that was going back toward the gate. Had he made the jump, he would then have encountered a closed gate. But he acted on impulse. Had he taken time to look at the situation, he would have realized the futility of his attempt. The two who survived were Comandante Pedro Lopez and Sergeant Franco Delgado. They didn't survive because they were officers because Horus didn't know who the men were only that they were invaders and he was just maximizing his kill numbers. Comandante Lopez made a call to the General Matias Gutierrez, the invasion's leader who was one of the twenty who landed east of Vulcan's Roost. The General sent two of his group into the tunnel with a rope, stakes and a hammer. It took three quarters of an hour, but four men came out of the tunnel. These four were fortunate that Horus didn't spring any more of his traps, but his thought at this time was to keep some things in reserve.

Horus thought *eight down* and at this point had no idea how many there were.

The invaders had first been confirmed when the ill-fated parachutist crashed into the rain forest and sent birds flying into the air and green monkeys scurrying away. This noise was unusual, and Horus sent one of his drones to investigate. He had been testing the drones for several weeks and had one of them sitting on a large branch of a kapok not far from the one fate had chosen for the parachutist Diego Sanchez. The problem Horus had was that he could not see the video which was being sent back and needed help in that respect and, because of the emergency that he felt this was, he woke both Issaack and Siegfried. They were in the computer room within ten minutes looking at the video of the man hanging in the parachute harness obviously armed and, despite the fact that he was dead, that meant no good. The emergency response team of Symon Scheetz, Stefaan Declercq, Hansel, Gretel and Carmen Domingo were roused and told the nature of the emergency. Dressing and arming themselves appropriately, they were in assigned positions within ten minutes of being awoken. Simultaneously with this alarm being raised, other drones were dispatched around the area and they provided video as chutists landed east of Vulcan's Roost and when the first set of feet touched the roof of Vulcan's Roost. The doors of all of the Billionaire Bundle were locked to prevent them from coming out of the safety of their rooms. These rooms were on the inside of the building with one wall facing on a small atrium, the roof of which could be opened when it rained to water the plants in the atrium and otherwise remained closed. If someone wanted to blow them they could but, point of fact - the invaders didn't have a floor plan of Vulcan's Roost and consequently did not know where any of the occupants' rooms were – especially that of the man who had organized and financed the invasion: Ramiro Esteves. They were truly going hit or miss.

The one room that the invaders had a fair idea as being important was the room housing Horus, although all they knew for certain was that it was supposed to be the most important room in the complex. So one of the two units that had landed on the roof was simply going to the center of the complex to set one of the charges. This was not an easy thing to do on a flat surface and if they had known how thick that surface was and what it was made of, they would have given up without trying. But they didn't know, and they did try. They used a shaped charge or the best version of a shaped charge that might work on a surface such as they had. The other unit was to try to make access by blowing one of the four skylights they could see protruding above the otherwise flat roof.

While the groups on the roof were preparing their charges, the forces inside were hurrying to their posts. It wasn't a big defensive force: Hansel and Gretel, Symon Sheetz, Stefan Declercq, Carmen Domingo, Issaack, and Siegfried. But then, they were actually not expecting an invasion or at least an invasion of this type. Of the seven, the first four were as proficient in warfare as any of the men outside and the other three had been taught to fire a weapon and were decent but not deadly. In the kitchen, Carmen was a force to be reckoned with but on the firing range she came in a distant seventh. However, all had known – at least suspected – that an incident like this was probable although not considered definite. But the size of the force, the method of attack, and the timing of the invasion had not been. The knowledge was really a best guesstimate by Horus who had told Issaack that he didn't trust Esteves – "He smells greedy," which is a strange way for something which cannot smell to put its feelings into words. And the defenses – especially in the tunnel – were all of Horus's design. If they had known for certain who the head conspirator was, they would have gone straight for him or her. They were certain that the leader was one of the Bundle which was now an eight pack rather than a seven pack because of the introduction of Siegfried, who was not a billionaire – at least not yet – and was riding Issaack's coat tails but – at least so far – no one had questioned his inclusion. Nobody asked Horus who would have replied "The Bundle size is nine."

Siegfried had only one duty and that was to guard Horus. So when the first two charges went off almost above his head, Siegfried jumped and, had he not taken a minute to relieve himself earlier, he would have had wet pants.

Chapter 19

Of the two shaped charges set off on the roof only one was successful, possibly because of faulty material or maybe a better shaped charge. As a result, a hole appeared in one of the atrium roofs. Had Issaack and Siegfried believed that an invasion was really likely, they would have put better glass in the atrium windows. The explosion had awoken Monica who had rushed to her door screaming, Bundle card in hand, only to find the door unresponsive to her efforts to open it.

"Horus, let me out!," she screamed.

"You're safer in there, Ms. Bartlett" she heard and then there was silence because Horus was busy with something that he at that time didn't completely understand. Actually he didn't understand much about warfare at all. If he had been a West Point plebe, he would have only been ready for his first term warfare finals.

So Monica turned around just as the plastic charge affixed to her window wall blew showering her with pieces of glass pellets, none of which were sharp. Naturally she screamed again and by the time the screaming was over she was in the hands of two of the evilest looking creatures she would ever want to see. They really were decent looking men but with war paint and night vision goggles, they looked like Martians or at least her idea of what a Martian would look like. She knew that she was no match for them and so she did what femme fatales don't often do best – she fainted. The two invaders carried her out through the window, handed her up to their compatriots on roof, and then went back into her room to see if they could open the door but they couldn't. On the roof, the unit's leader let General Gutierrez know that he had been fortunate and captured the number one rated person on their "to be captured" list.

As the previous two episodes were being carried out, the other two squads of eight plus their sergeants, broke into four fire teams and took position, one on each side of the basically rectangular building and they were the best prepared of the bunch with RPGs. The problem with those weapons was the extensive damage that would be done to the building and their orders had been "Only as a last resort." Hence they were poised and ready and waiting for such an event as had just happened.

With Monica Bartlett safely in his hands now recovered from her "swoon" and mad as a wet hen, her hands were bound with flexi-cuffs, General Gutierrez made his move. Using a bullhorn, he said, "Izzaack Kincaid. This is General Matias Gutierrez. We have Monica Bartlett. Either you ca•pitz•cu•late – give up – or she dies. You have sixty seconds. I push the button on this watch stop. When the alarm it goes off, so does the gun being pointed at her pretty head. No more Monica Bartlett and then we blow holes in the building and kills you all."

Inside Issaack and Siegfried agreed and passed the word to their small defensive force and they vanished virtually into the woodwork – at least their weapons did – and they stood with empty hands visible.

"The clock is at thirty. Twenty-nine ..."

"Horus, the game is in your hands."

"I understand," Horus said and the four doors in the middle of the four outside walls of Vulcan's Roost opened and the invaders moved inside.

Ten minutes later, and Issaack and Siegfried were confronted by Ramiro Esteves. "Mr. Kincaid, you failed to accept a simple modification to my program and you left me no choice."

Siegfried looked at Issaack and mouthed *"my program?"*

"But, to be honezt – which is not zomething I do very much – I would have done zis anyway because zis izland iz ze perfect place from which to run my operationz."

"So what's going to happen?"

"Oh, we will proceed az planned with ze one addition that I had dezired. I am zinking that it would be good for you to be in ze mix."

"No, not me nor any of my people."

"Really? I zink so."

"Well, are you ready for the consequences?"

"What are zese consequinces?"

"Horus, show him."

Immediately the building went dark, all the doors closed, and the movement of fresh air ceased.

"Nobody move," Issaack said to his force, "and don't let any of your men do anything either, Ramiro. Horus, lights and air."

And the lights and air came back on.

"You see, here Horus controls everything. Without him, you have no power, no water, no way to watch the debacle you are orchestrating. Your only way out would by climbing the volcano's walls or by helicopter. I have told Horus that he is to cooperate with you and do as you request as long as none of my people are molested in any way. Those people are: Symon Sheetz, Stefan Declercq, Carmen Domingo, Hansel,

Gretel, Monica Bartlett, Gloria Mitchell, Emerson, Siegfried and myself. I would include Phil and Harvey Gladstone, but they may be on your team."

"Zey are notz on my team az you zay."

"Then I include them. You are to carry your card, and we will make one for each of your men. They must carry these. If they don't, Horus will go dark and I or Siegfried are the only ones who can bring him back. If Horus senses duress on the part of any of the people I have named, he will go dark."

"I do not like zez card thing."

"Tough shit. It's a requirement. Think of it this way. If something happens to one of your men at the other end of the island, how will you know?"

Ramiro gave it some thought and then capitulated.

"Okay, I agreez."

"Horus, have you been listening?"

"Yes."

"Do you understand the rules."

Of course, I do. I made them. "Yes."

"There is your answer, Ramiro. Now let my people go." *Because the game is afoot.*

The cards were the first thing to be made and issued. They simply read "Soldado" (Portuguese for "Soldier") followed by the number 1-40. It didn't matter who had what card, because Horus would figure out the person's importance by their actions. The card for "Soldado 40" was never given because his was the body in the tree and it was never found – at least not by any human on the island at that time. "Soldado 1" naturally went to General Matias Gutierrez. Numbers 33-39 went to the seven men who died in the tunnel.

The first item on the invaders' agenda was to get the bodies out of the pits and into body bags along with a card. Ramiro had called in a chopper to take the bodies back to his ranch in the outlands of Brazil. Once the bodies were out, the pits were flushed with a fire hose. There were such hoses located at each end and one halfway through the tunnel – the water drained from the pits through holes in the floor. Everything that could be thought of had been thought of in the design of the facility. With the pits clean, Horus raised the panels and locked them.

Ramiro posted two guards inside and one outside the one door he permitted to be opened, one guard on each of the other three sides and in front of the computer center. This last to be certain that no one except Siegfried and Issaack entered the room. No need to place a guard inside the computer center because Issaack and Siegfried communicated with Horus orally no matter where they were in the complex and Horus kept them up to date on the activities of the invaders. Three guards were posted at the tunnel gate. They were told to tell Horus to open and close the gate when necessary although Horus didn't need to be told. The invading force took over the village at the bottom of the hill, vacant now because there were no workers. By eight o'clock in the morning following the invasion everything was beginning to settle into the two camps. Day 2 of the Billionaire Bundle's stay on São Rochelle was not off to the auspicious day it was supposed to have been.

Chapter 20

There were two places in Vulcan's Roost for members of the Bundle to get together and talk without appearing conspiratorial. After the events of their first night, anything that looked suspect would be considered conspiratorial. Those two places were the gym and the Roost's Nest as the café or restaurant came to be nicknamed. The gym was not a place where conversations could be had in groups without appearing conspiratorial. Two or maybe three but seeing more than that talking in a place intended for keeping one's body in peak condition would definitely be deemed suspect. Both places were open 24/7 but it was the Roost's Nest where people would naturally gather. Carmen Domingo, the cook, and Stefaan Declercq were in the facility from 7:00 a.m. to 9:00 p.m. Breakfast hours were 7:00 a.m. – 12:00 p.m., lunch 11:00 a.m. – 3:00 p.m., and dinner from 5:00 p.m. – 8:00 p.m. Food was available at other times: premade sandwiches and simple meals like pot pies or pizza which could be heated in one of three microwaves. And there were dispensers for coffee, soft drinks, hot water for tea and a liquor cabinet, although the rooms had a minibar with each person's personal spirit preferences. Times when Carmen and Declercq weren't there, Symon Sheetz, Hansel or Gretel were there to keep things filled and tables and dishes cleaned.

At breakfast the morning after the takeover, a small group sat at one of the tables in the Roost's Nest discussing the events of the night.

"How long have you known that Ramiro was behind this whole thing?" Waldo asked.

"That's a good question," injected Gloria.

"Well, the first I knew of this," Issaack said, "was when I was contacted by a lawyer from Los Angeles asking me to spearhead this operation. I was without work except for Horus and it sounded like the perfect opportunity to test our project – Siegfried and mine. I put that requirement as an amendment to the agreement and it was accepted. Right after the organizational meeting, Siegfried and I figured out that he was. We knew that it had to be one of the Bundle and since it wasn't me – I never said anything to the original organizer – it had to be one of the others. Logic and extremely thorough vetting by Horus showed him to be the only viable candidate. Then Symon and Stefaan did some investigating about the attacks during the session and decided they were made by Ramiro just to test what defenses might be put up on the island. Hansel and Gretel really cinched it. That truck that tried to blow a hole in the lobby that first evening didn't have any explosives. If the driver believed that it did, he was duped. I think Ramiro knew then that he would seize the improved island, but I believed that he would wait until the survival of the fittest battle was over. After all, it was his idea. Well, we didn't know it was him at the time but whoever it was wanted us – Siegfried and I – to act as the initiators of the idea, and it gave us the chance we needed to test our product."

"Your product being Horus," Waldo stated.

Issaack nodded. "We knew it would take a while to get to the test but were willing to sacrifice the time because we had much fine tuning to do."

"What about us?"

"Why did he choose you? Well, for financial backing of course. Gladstone knew property although I don't know how much help he was. Waldo had the electric vehicles and they were perfect for an island with no petroleum. Phil, well for all else, he is an expert scuba diver and that was probably part of his plan to get drugs safely to land. Monica because I think he was infatuated with her."

"You mean he wants in me knickers?"

"I am only surmising."

"Well, whatever. He ever pulls his tallywhacker out, I am going to cut it off."

"Tallywhacker? How perfectly classic," Gloria said.

Chapter 21

The most monumental trip that the *B.B. Queen* made to its island namesake was bringing the predators to the island. They had been collected over the previous fourteen months with the last one acquired seven months previously. The delay was so that the animals had a six-month quarantine to insure they brought no diseases into Brazil where they were being kept in a private zoo on Ramiro's ranch under careful attention of six large animal veterinarians. This was a real treat for the vets who, for the most part, were retired and were happy to work for the price they were being paid and the place where they were working. It was a rare opportunity to work with some of the animals.

When the ads announcing the positions were published, the response was overwhelming. Each applicant had to provide a detailed vita listing places where they had worked, types of animals they had taken care of, and letters of reference. They also had to answer a questionnaire, one question of which knocked 62% out of consideration: ***Would you object to caring for these animals if you knew that within the next year they would all be dead?*** After all, a veterinarian's job, just like that of a medical doctor, is to care for the welfare of their patients, not to keep them healthy so they can die. When they asked about that question, all the successful applicants were told that the animals were to be released on a private island without cages and allowed to roam at will. Anything beyond that was left to their imaginations.

The ship arrived at 6:09 a.m. of Day 3 of the Billionaire Bundle's stay or the morning of the day after the invasion. By the evening of that day the predators were to be taken to their release spots in cages with automatic doors set to open at midnight. The spots chosen had been selected from recommendations of the veterinarians and the billionaires had gathered and discussed the locations and then made the decisions. This was done the afternoon after the invasion. It hadn't been easy for the members of the Bundle and they had spent the previous afternoon in deliberation. Before deliberation began, each member of the Bundle was provided with a map of the island with spots indicated based upon the veterinarians' opinions. Then they got in a long-bed pickup fitted with six leather swivel seats with shoulder harnesses like some carnival rides. One of Ramiro's mercenaries was the driver, he sat in the front seat and Phil and Harvey Gladstone in the second seat. They were not completely welcomed by other members of the Bundle because it was felt that they had sided with Ramiro totally, not just on the decision to include a man as a predator but also in the takeover. Then they went for a tour of the island so that they could see the spots selected first hand.

Since it was going to take most of the day to get the animals in place, the billionaires were given the opportunity to see the animals at 7:00 a.m. of Day 3 before they were sedated and taken in their cages to their release spots. All were warned not to venture close to the cages because the animals had not been fed in six days and they were hungry. Needless to say, the veterinarians were not happy with the situation but when it was pointed out that they had responded positively to knowing the animals would die within a year, they acceded. Privately however, they wished they hadn't but, when one of them pointed out how much money they had earned and how it would greatly enhance their retirement, the grumbliest quieted. "Besides," one of them said, "in the wild these animals might often go for a week without a kill." It was a good thing the billionaires were warned to stay away from the cages because the tiger was not happy.

The billionaires came down from Vulcan's Roost in the long-bed pickup they had ridden in the day before. The pickup drove across *B.B. Queen's* ramp and into the cargo bay and stopped. In front of them, both sides were lined with cages, each separated from the other by several feet and with dark coverings on the ends facing other animals. Down the aisle between the two rows was a six-foot curtain held upright by metal cables strung between metal posts securely fastened to the wooden floor.

David Brimley greeted them after they had alighted. David was sixty-eight-years old and had spent forty years as a veterinarian before retiring to accept this position as Chief Veterinarian of the São Rochelle Predator Zoo (a self-made title after learning what was going to happen to the animals.)

"You know what the animals are, but each cage has a placard stating what the animal is – both the familiar name and the scientific name – its age and where it was acquired. There are members of the staff evenly spaced throughout who will answer any questions that you have. If they don't have an answer, then no one here does. Each of the animals has a chip embedded in its back that monitors its vital signs and lets us track its position via GPS. On each cage is a map of the island with the position where each of them will be released. I will remind you that – as you instructed – these animals have not been fed in a week and although sometimes this happens in the wild, they are not very happy with the situation and some, maybe all, will look upon you as their next meal. So be careful."

The billionaires separated by choice into small groups: Monica, Gloria, and Issaack; Ramiro, Gladstone and Phil; Waldo and Siegfried.

Ramiro, Harvey and Phil, with two of Ramiro's men as bodyguards, started down the left-hand aisle; Monica, Gloria, and Issaack down the right, followed shortly by Waldo and Siegfried who were more interested in discussing each other's inventions than the animals.

The first animal that Monica, Gloria and Issaack encountered was the lion. The placard read:

Male Lion *Panthera leo* 5 years old Kruger National Park (South Africa)

He gazed at them through half open eyes. Some might have thought he was half asleep, but Issaack thought he was planning his next meal.

"He's beautiful," Monica crooned. "I just want to cuddle him."

"I'd like to have him lying in front of me, so I could run my feet through his mane," Gloria mused.

"He'd have to be dead to let you do that," Monica countered.

"No deader than he would be to let you cuddle him," Gloria retorted with a soft chuckle.

"Touché," Issaack said with a smile.

Monica looked at the lion and laughed. "Let's call him Simba."

Reaching into a pocket in her shorts, she pulled out a black magic marker and stepped toward the cage.

The newly named Simba, who had been lying down, was up and at the bars, snarling and reaching out with his right front paw before Monica could finish her first step. *I was correct*, Issaack thought. *Next meal.* Linda Bagnola, the veterinarian between this cage and the next, stepped forward just as fast as Simba had moved and caught Monica's left arm, "It is not advisable to approach the cages, Ms. Bartlett."

Monica looked at her. "How do you know me? You're too old to like my kind of music."

"True, Ms. Bartlett, but we were given brief biographies and pictures of all of you." As she was saying this, she released Monica's arm and stepped back.

"Thank you, I forgot," Monica said, putting the marker back into her pocket. "He's beautiful."

"He looks prettier when his coat is brushed, and mane combed. But that's not about to happen today," Linda Bagnola responded.

"How did we acquire him?" Gloria asked.

"He attacked a tourist who tried to get too friendly just as Ms. Bartlett did. The park was going to send him to a German Zoo until someone stepped forward with more money. Or that's the story we were told."

Chapter 21

The next cage held the female coyote and the placard read:

Female
Coyote
canis latrans
2 years
Copley, Ohio USA

"Where in the hell is Copley, Ohio?" Gloria asked.

Linda Bagnola, who had followed them from the preceding cage said, "They tell us it is a suburb of Akron, Ohio, and just west of the city. Akron is about thirty miles south of Cleveland. That's on Lake Erie, one of the Great Lakes." This last more was for Monica's benefit than Gloria's.

"Ah," Gloria said. "But she was wild?"

"Yes, she was trapped in a fenced-in yard where she had evidently gone after a small dog. The house owner saw her and chased after the coyote with a blanket she – the owner was a woman – had pulled off the clothesline. The owner got the coyote backed into a corner, threw the blanket over it, and held it down until help arrived. The owner's husband – he's handicapped and in a wheelchair – called 911."

"That was some feat," Issaack said. "That's no small coyote."

"You're correct," Linda responded. "She weighs forty-one pounds now but was only twenty-nine when captured. She had a hurt paw which is the reason they were able to capture her. We got her from an animal hospital through an agent."

The coyote was standing near the front of the cage, snarling at them and yipping quietly.

"She's got some moxie, that one," Gloria said.

"Moxie?" questioned Monica. "What's 'moxie'?"

"Chutzpah, verve, lots of spunk."

"I see," Monica said looking at the coyote. "I like her … moxie."

"Then let's call her that," Issaack said.

"Yes," Monica agreed. "Moxie she is."

The three moved on and encountered a beautiful rust red cat with long legs, a thick torso, long tufted ears and long canine teeth that it was showing as it snarled at their approach but showed no fear. The placard read:

Female
Caracal
Caracal Caracal
3 years
India

"She's beautiful," Monica said, as she sat on her heels to be more on the level with the cat.

"Beautiful but deadly," a male voice said, and they all looked at an obviously senior man standing next to the cage's far side. He had on a khaki shirt and shorts like Linda Bagnola and, like her, no socks on his feet but he was wearing cross trainers while Linda wore leather sandals.

"I'm Garret Bagnola," he said. "This cat is a great hunter of small animals but is not afraid to attack something bigger than herself if she needs to. She can leap almost ten feet into the air and catch a bird. Interesting to see."

"Are you…?" Gloria said pointing back at Linda.

"I'm happy to say 'Yes,' to that question. Wasn't expecting it – the question – and hadn't studied but aced it, I think," he finished with a huge smile on his face which lifted his handlebar mustache and caused his dark eyes to flash.

"Do you know where in India?" Issaack asked.

"Gir Forest National Park. She'd been injured, not seriously but needed attention. We came to her aid, paid medical bills plus a bit more."

"We?" Issaack asked, a wry smile on his face. "As in you and Linda?"

"Don't I wish we had that kind of money! No, by 'we' I mean this project's sponsors and I guess that's you from what I understand."

"She's got …" Monica looked at Gloria, "moxie."

Garret laughed. "Yes, she does. She's hungry and will be out of the cage like a shot. Anything that's little and moves had better look out for her in the first few hours."

She'd better look out also, Monica thought having taken an instant liking to the caracal. "We need a name for her."

"What about Hyma?" Garret suggested. "It is another name of Goddess Parvati."

"The goddess of fertility," Issaak said. "I like it."

"Then it's a fait accompli," Garret said. "That's what we've been calling her. Linda and I."

"Take good care of her," Monica said as the three moved on. Issaack looked over his shoulder as they moved on and saw Siegfried and Waldo engaged in a conversation with Linda. *Wonder what that's about?* Garret moved along with them.

"This is a beauty," Garret said pointing at the cage containing a big black bear.

The placard read

Male
Black Bear
Ursus americanus
4 years
Tennessee U.S.A.

"I'll bet he's from the Smoky Mountain National Park," Gloria said. "Probably got in trouble with campers and we rescued him."

"Exactamundo!" Garret said. "But did I detect some facetiousness in your tone of voice?"

"Yes," Gloria said. "All these animals appear to have been…" and she made air quotation marks, "rescued."

"That's the easiest and best way to get them," Issaack said. "Remember this is a research project and we intend to try to publish results. We would have trouble doing so if any of the animals were obtained in an illegal manner."

"I understand," Gloria said, "but sometimes the reason sounds, I don't know, …"

"Made up?" Garret said. "We had the same thought, but we have seen the papers on all of them and they are all genuine … or superior forgeries. I don't think any of the veterinarians would be working here if the animals were obtained illegally."

"Well, under the circumstances, I think his name is Smoky."

"Yes," Monica said. "I understand – Smoky Mountains."

"And 'Smokey the Bear' is a spokesanimal for the United States Forest Service educating people about the danger of wildfires," Garret added

"Wish he'd done something about all those wildfires out west recently," Issaack said."

"Indeed," Garret said.

Monica had started moving on and so Issaack and Gloria followed, Issaack with a backward glance seeing that Linda, Waldo and Siegfried were still talking.

"Oh, what a beautiful cat," Monica said staring into the next cage.

Male
Cheetah
Acinonyx jubatus
4 years
Africa

"You are correct, Ms. Bartlett," said a black man with short cropped white hair and a white goatee being the only obvious signs of his age because his ebony skin was as taut as a young man's and gleamed like a newly polished black limousine. "He is a beautiful animal. From the Serengeti. He was in a private collection and the offer was more than the owner could refuse."

"I thought these were all rescue animals," Monica said.

"No," Issaack explained, "They are all obtained legally."

"Yes," the black man agreed. "Johnson, Joshua Johnson. That's my name. All the animals were legally obtained and from various sources. This is the only one from a zoo, but he had only been there six months and he wasn't very happy. Not eating and kept in a small cage. So I guess this was a rescue of sorts. We kept him in a large cage with an outside area and he was quite happy. Or as happy as a wild animal can be in captivity. Picked up twenty-seven pounds."

"You name him anything?" Issaack asked.

"Bolt," Joshua replied. "The first time we let him outside, he shot out of the cage door like Usain Bolt out of the starting blocks in the finals of the Rio Olympics' 100 Meter Sprint."

Monica laughed. "Bolt. I like it."

Chapter 23

Still laughing Monica turned to continue on and found herself staring into the eyes of Ramiro Esteves. "Staring into the eyes" is a misnomer because if she had looked straight ahead she would have seen his hair peripherally below her eye level, but he was so close to her that if they both inhaled and held it they would have touched, even if ever so slightly.

"You're in my way," Monica said, the laughter gone from her voice and her face.

"My zought exactly," Ramiro said, a lecherous grin on his face.

Monica stepped to her left and passed by him, Gloria right behind her. Harvey Gladstone and Phil were in front of the next cage admiring the occupant. Phil noticed the two women and waved at them.

"This snow leopard is a beaut, but he's suffering in the heat," Phil offered as the two came up.

"Doubt he will put up much of a fight unless we get some cool weather," Harvey Gladstone said as he moved to follow Ramiro.

"Any of the others look interesting?" Issaack asked Phil as he joined the three looking at the snow leopard's placard.

Male
Snow Leopard
Panthera uncia
6 years
Nepal

"A couple," Phil answered. "The grizzly's a monster, and the tiger is ready to chew anyone's head off." With that he motioned that he wanted to catch up with Harvey Gladstone and Ramiro and hurried off.

"How did we get him?" Gloria asked Joshua as he came up to her side.

"A man who lives in the northern frontier of Nepal was leading a group of visitors on a day hike and they discovered the animal with its foot caught under a boulder in what looks to have been a small landslide – no cause was given for that. He had started to chew his foot off to get free. He was taken to a veterinarian hospital and treated. Because they had been on the lookout for one at the request of this organization, they called, and we answered."

"How much did we answer?" Gloria inquired.

"Have no idea. We were not told." Joshua shrugged his shoulders and held out his hands palms up to emphasize his inability to answer.

"I can find out if it's important," Issaack said.

"No, I am certain that we will get a full report when this is all over – if it's ever all over and we …," Gloria said.

"Now we need a name," Monica said.

"Well," Joshua said, "the Nepalese considered them to be spiritual so what about Deva, which is Buddhist term for a higher being or a god."

"I like it," Gloria said, and Monica agreed.

"Good," Joshua said.

They were at the end of the cages and black drapes hung across the cargo bay indicated they should go left so they did. The first cage they saw contained a big gray wolf with blue eyes.

"Wow!" Monica said. "Bedroom eyes."

"I don't think you want to go to bed with that," said the black female veterinarian standing by the cage. "He's a beast. A real Alpha dog."

The placard on the cage read:

Male
Gray Wolf
Canis lupus
Six Years
Wyoming USA

Gloria turned to the veterinarian.

"I'm asking everyone: 'How did we acquire this one?'"

"Interesting story but similar to so many," the woman answered. "First, we were told to introduce ourselves. I'm Shelia Dupuis from Trinidad. My husband is a missionary currently in South Africa. Now about Lobo, he …"

"Lobo?" Monica said.

"Well, yes. Most gray wolves are considered lobo's and it seemed to fit this one. He was bedeviling a sheep rancher killing at least two a week. He ate his kills or parts of them before the farmer found the kills and removed them. So one night the rancher positioned himself on a hill overlooking the flock of sheep that the wolf had been using as his larder. He was camouflaged and descented like when he's hunting deer and elk. He said that he must have fallen asleep because when he awoke – and realized he been asleep – the wolf was standing right next to him looking down at the flock. It just happened his head – the rancher's – was turned the right way to see the wolf. He said he blinked because he thought he was dreaming, but the wolf was there. Then the wolf turned his head and looked at him. He said – the rancher – that it was a staring contest and the wolf won. The wolf bared his teeth, snarled – a low rumbling deep in its throat – turned and walked away. Never did bother the sheep again."

"Well, how did we get the wolf?" Gloria asked.

"Oh, yes, that's the point of the story. Sometimes I get sidetracked. Ha! My husband Pierre would say 'Sometimes! You ask her what time it is, and she will tell you the history of clockmaking.' He says I just go on and …"

"On and on. Yes, madam, we get it," Issaack said. "Now about the wolf?"

"Oh, the rancher set traps out and the wolf got caught in one, a leg hold trap. Nasty. Do you know how many…?" She noticed the three of them glaring at her and smiled. "He was going to kill the wolf, but it lay there with those eyes looking up at him. Those bedroom eyes. They say Paul New…. Oops. Doing it again. The veterinarian who cares for his sheep had told him about a notice saying that a wolf was wanted, and a good reward would be paid. So he managed to muzzle the wolf, hogtied it, made a travois … You know a thing with two poles and skin between them … He used a blanket because he didn't have a skin but most people... Again. Sorry. He was on his horse, so he had to have something. Anyway the veterinarian fixed Lobo and called the number and someone came and bingo. Lobo's here."

"Long story, longer," Issaack said.

Issaack noticed that Waldo and Siegfried were standing just behind them. Siegfried jerking his head in the "come here, I need to talk to you" motion.

"Ladies, you decide on a name and move on. I'll catch up."

"Lobo," the two said simultaneously, laughed and started for the next cage.

"What's up?" Issaack said to Siegfried as he stepped over to join them.

"A bet," Siegfried said holding out a handful of bills.

"A bet? About what?"

"Who wins the predator contest."

Chapter 24

"From whom?" Issaack asked.

"The veterinarians," Siegfried answered.

"Is this what you were talking to Linda Bagnola about?"

"Yes. She and the other veterinarians talked about the contest and predicted the outcome and want to place a bet."

"At what odds?"

"10 to 1," Siegfried. "This is six thousand dollars. Each put in one thousand."

"And the bet?"

"They predict, based on what they know about the island and the animals that the big guys – lions, tigers and bears and the like – will duke it out until only one survives. That will leave the wolf, coyotes, and the caracal."

"And the survivor which is…"

Siegfried shrugged. "Doesn't matter they say. Whichever one it is, it will be battered. No one will come out unscathed."

"Why will the wolf, etc.?"

"Because they survive a lot on small creatures that are aplenty on this island – mice, rats, nutria, monkeys, birds. In the time since the hurricane, no one has given them any mind and they have had plenty of food, no natural predators and have multiplied … well, like rabbits. There will be plenty of food for those critters."

"So who wins? The Hatfields or the McCoys?"

"The coyotes. They predict the two of them will form a pack and work together. With the two of them attacking, they will win."

"The caracal can climb a tree and heal from any injuries."

"Eventually the coyotes will win. Especially if it goes on for a while, they will have a litter and then watch out."

"Interesting. We'll have to talk about it with the group."

"Oh, one other thing," Siegfried said putting the money away. "If you ask any of them – even Linda at this point – they will say they know nothing about it. That was the agreement."

"And if we don't take the bet?"

"The money comes back. Oh, if there is a betting pool and they win, they will be happy with the pot whatever it is."

At that point, there was a roar from ahead and the three broke into a run. They passed one cage without looking at it and found Monica, Gloria and Shelia standing in front of a cage and laughing. In the cage was the most beautiful tiger Issaack had ever seen. The placard said:

Female
White Tiger
Panthera tigris
Four Years
Gir Forest National Park
India

The tiger was standing at the front of the cage, snarling and reaching her right foot out, claws extended toward the group.

"What's going on?" asked Issaack.

"It's the tiger," Monica said. "We think she's going to win."

"Why?" Issaack responded thinking of the veterinarian's bet.

"Because she has PMS."

"You mean she's in heat?"

"Well, I think it is highly possible," Shelia said. "The way she is acting it makes sense. She is very agitated."

"Do you think she'll win?"

"Oh, I don't have an opinion on that," Sheila said. "I am just doing my job like we were told to do."

Issaack looked at Siegfried who mouthed "I told you so."

"So, girls, do you have a name for her?"

"Cleopatra," Gloria said. "Empress of the Isle."

"She wasn't an empress and it's the Nile," Siegfried said.

"I'm talking about the tiger and this island," Gloria said. "And don't call her Cleo. She'll bite your head off."

And Gloria, Monica, and Shelia laughed.

"Okay, okay," Issaack said. "Who did I miss?" and he started back for the missed cage.

It was the grizzly, who at the moment was lying on the floor of his cage, head next to the bars under his placard, big eyes watching Issaack's every move.

Male
Brown Bear (Grizzly)
Ursus arctos
6 years
Canada

"Looks formidable," Issaack said. "Look at those claws."

The bear's right paw was hanging out of the cage and his long claws were obvious.

"They have to be six inches long," Waldo said.

"More like four," Shelia said. "And they're sharp."

"What's his name?" Issaack asked.

"Adam," Gloria said.

"Why, was he the first in this menagerie?"

"No. He's named after Grizzly Adams but 'Adams' as a name sounded stupid, so it's 'Adam'."

"I like the name," Monica said. "It has an epochal ring to it. Like he is destined to greatness – maybe to be the last survivor."

"Only time will tell," Issaack said. "Okay, let's finish our tour so these animals can be put to sleep the last time and taken to their release spots."

The animal in the next cage after the tiger was lying back in a corner, catnapping as though not at all interested in the proceedings. His placard read:

Male
Cougar
Puma concolor
4 years
Canadian Yukon

"That's two from Canada. Who would have thought?" Waldo said. Then turning to Shelia, "And how was this beauty acquired." *And how can I acquire you with your husband out of the picture – at least temporarily.*

"You won't believe this one, but I can give you a video link and you can go online and see the news telecast on Dawson CHWT-TV-10. It is part of Aboriginal Peoples Television Network (APTN) which is a Canadian broadcast and cable television network.

"Anyway, a seventy-five-year-old miner in the area north of Dawson chanced upon a cougar kitten in a cave. It had evidently been abandoned by its mother and was starving to death – remember this is his story as told to the Royal Canadian Mounted Police. Cal (that's the miner's name, short for Calvin) took it to his cabin and nursed it back to health using dried milk that he kept for himself. When it was old enough for solid food, Cal started feeding it what he ate: poached rabbit, poached deer, poached elk or anything else that he could get that was edible. Now when I said 'poached' I didn't mean the cooking term like 'poached' egg; I meant 'illegally taken.' At one year, he took the kitten out into the woods with him on a leash. He knew where rabbits abounded and so that was his goal. As they were walking, Cal saw the kitten (he called him 'Cat') go into stalking mode. So he undid the rope and let Cat have free rein. Cat didn't catch the first rabbit, but that was his only miss. Cal kept Cat in a pen or in the house and they would hunt together and share the kill. Naturally Cal would cut his own part out and cook it just in case you were wondering. When he went to town, Cal would brag about his pet and the Mounties heard about it and confiscated it. They knew about your interest and notified your representative and here Cat is."

Monica moved a little closer to the cage. Cat gave no mind. Then she said, "Hello, Cat." And the cougar's ears perked up and he looked right at Monica.

"Don't get too close," Shelia said. "Despite his looks, he's mean. I have a feeling he resents being taken from Cal."

"Well, it isn't the best name, but since it's his, he can keep it as far as I am concerned," Monica said to Gloria.

"Works for me," replied Gloria. "Onward and upward."

Chapter 25

The animal in the next enclosure was pacing the outer perimeter of the cage.

"Oh, goodness," Monica said. "That's an ugly dog."

She looked at the placard:

Male
Spotted (Laughing) Hyena
Crocuta crocuta
2 years
Niger, Africa

"Oh, that's why," Monica said.

"He acts like a husband whose wife is in labor for the first time," Gloria said. "Pacing back and forth."

"Great name!" Monica said enthusiastically, "Pacer."

"He's been doing that for several weeks now," a short-stocky-on-the-verge-of-obese man said. He was obviously one of the veterinarians. "Nervous. Don't know why."

"Maybe he's randy," Monica said.

"What's 'randy'?" the man asked.

"Shag," Monica replied.

"I don't…"

"Oh, for God's sake, he needs to fuck," Monica said frustratingly. "I was trying to keep it clean."

"Oh, yes," the veterinarian said. "Sorry, not up on British terms, Ms. Bartlett. By the way, I'm Lars Bakker and I'm from South Africa. Used to work in the Kruger National Park until this came up and I decided to retire."

"He looks pretty mean," Issaack said.

"Oh, he is. Actually, I think he is looking for a fight."

"Oh, he'll get one soon," Siegfried chimed in.

"Indeed. Maybe more than one," Waldo said. "I like his chances. But moving on."

The next cage obviously held the male coyote who was curled up sleeping in a back corner.

"Look where he's from," Gloria said looking at the placard:

Male
Coyote
Canis latrans
3 years
Eastern Panama

"I didn't know they went that far south."

"Yes, their range is expanding," Lars said. "He's a real beauty. His coat is almost all red. A beautiful rust color."

"Let's see," Gloria said. "The female is Moxie. He's red so … Foxy."

"Poifect!" Monica said laughingly.

"If I remember correctly, a woman brought him into an animal shelter saying he bit her son and she wanted him killed."

"Bit her son?" Siegfried said. "How did she catch him?"

"She wouldn't say. Just that her son tried to pet him and got bit. The shelter had seen our request and didn't want to kill him. We got him for a song. Actually, enough food to support the shelter for a year."

There was a roar from the next cage and Monica and Gloria hurried onward with the men following.

"Ooh, what a beauty," Monica said.

Standing at the front of the cage was a black panther.

Male Leopard *Panthera pardus* 5 years Tsavo West National Park Kenya, Africa

When he saw the women, he roared again and crouched as though he was preparing to spring.

"He's hungry," David Brimley said. "But then they all are. It's been six days since they've had their last meal."

"I'd be hungry too," Gloria said.

"I'm hungry now," Monica said.

"Well, you hardly had anything for breakfast."

"Excitement. When I get excited for some reason, I have a nervous stomach and chunder if I have too much to eat."

"Chunder. Interesting term," Gloria said. "Better than puke."

"Any interesting story behind his acquisition?" Waldo asked.

"You know the story of the Tsavo man-eaters?"

"Yeah. The two lions who killed those construction workers on the Kenya-Uganda Railway. I think there was a movie made about them."

"Actually, there were several movies based on the incident. *Bwana Devil* is my favorite although *The Ghost and the Darkness* has Val Kilmer in it and my wife likes him. But we're digressing. There was a report of a man-eating panther in the area. They sent out search parties and came back with this one. Your organization had a request out for a leopard and he suited the bill."

"Was he the man-eater?"

"Don't know. Just that there have been no further reports."

Monica and Gloria had been listening to the conversation and looked at each other and nodded.

"His name is Val Killer, but we'll call him Val for short," Gloria said.

"You've got one more and then we have to get busy," David Brimley said and led the party to the last cage.

"This is the jaguar or El Tigre in Mexico where he is from," he said, pointing at the placard.

Female
Jaguar
Panthera onca
4 years
Mexico

"You are fortunate to have this one because international trade in jaguars or their parts is prohibited."

"Well, then how did we get it?" Issaack asked.

"There was a freighter docked in Rio Grande, Brazil. It had docked because there was illness rampant on the ship and the captain ordered the ship to dock in the nearest port. You've heard about last orders from a death bed. Well, this was one. When the contagion team came onboard, they found ten illicit animals in cages. This was one of them. Since there was no convenient way to return this cat to Mexico which was the ship's last docking point, your organization assumed responsibility and since the temporary zoo was in Brazil and there were ample veterinarians … and I guess a lot of political influence …" he rubbed his right thumb on his right index and middle fingers in the universal sign of payoffs "… we got it."

"'Sortudo' means lucky in Portuguese," Issaack said. "Not a very good name for a jaguar but apt under the circumstances."

"Let's keep it simple and call her 'Lucky'," Gloria said.

"Then we're done," Issaack said. And to David Brimley, "Thanks for the tour and good luck on your job this afternoon."

"You're welcome and thank you all for joining us. A pleasure to meet you all."

They shook hands and started off.

"Mr. Kinkaid, may I have a few moments of your time. Maybe ten minutes at the most," David Brimley said.

"Of course," Issaack said. And to the others, "You go ahead. I'll catch up."

David Brimley led Issaack back down the line of cages and held open the black curtain at the end. On the other side of the curtain set back about ten feet was another cage and Issaack couldn't believe what he saw.

Chapter 26

Lying on his side facing the front of the cage was a naked man.

"Who the hell is he and what is he doing here?" Issaack said although he already suspected that he knew the answer to the second question.

"I am unable to answer either part of that question," David Brimley said. "When the animals were brought aboard, this cage came also. We were told that we were to make certain that the man stayed sedated throughout the voyage and the cage placements today. We each were promised an extra $25,000.00 if we did as we were told and kept our mouths shut until the project was completed."

"You mean until you placed the cages and left São Rochelle?"

"No. Until the king of predators is determined."

"Why would you agree to such a thing?" Issaack was incredulous.

"Honestly, we didn't have a choice. It was obvious from the manner in which this ultimatum was delivered that if we didn't agree and comply, death was the alternative."

Ramiro Esteves, Issaack thought. *He had to get his way. That's one of the reasons he took over the island.*

"I understand," Issaack said. "We are in a similar situation. You'll have to do as instructed. All of you. I – we, all of us who can – will make it right. That is not your worry. We are the ones who let this mess happen and we will make it right as soon as we can. Now, where does this cage go?"

"At the south end of the island. The instructions were 'At the south end of island as far away from the tunnel entrance to the volcano as possible.'"

"Give me your map."

David Brimley handed Issaack the map of the island showing the placements of the cages. Issaack studied it for a moment and then showed David Brimley a spot on the map.

"Put it here and face the door so that it points just past the western edge of Colina da Rocha. Does one of you go with each cage?"

"Yes, to be certain that the animal is comfortable. You know, breathing properly."

"You go with this one."

"That's what I was planning."

"Do you have a knife?"

"What kind?" Brimley asked.

"Well, a hunting knife would be best," was Issaack's answer.

"I do. I always have one when working with the animals."

"Here's what I want you to do."

Issaack outlined his plan.

"I'd do it if I could, but I know I won't be permitted," he explained to Brimley

"Issaack," Siegfried called from the other side of the curtain. "Ramiro wants us back."

"Got to go," Issaack said. "Good luck."

"Thanks and same to you."

Issaack pushed through the curtain and as they walked through *B.B. Queen's* cargo bay he told Siegfried what had transpired

Every ship like the *B.B. Queen* has a shop to make repairs. David Brimley gave directions to his team to prepare the first delivery of animals and then went to his cabin and got his hunting knife and returned to the cargo hold and went to the shop. Using the drill press, he drilled the rivets holding the handle slabs to the tang. Thankful for the big pockets in his cargo shorts, he put the small rivet pieces, guard and the slabs in his pocket with the scabbard. Then he took a machine hammer and beat the blade and tang to make is look like a beat-up knife. He did the best he could with sandpaper and steel wool and used a cloth with some battery acid he found in a jar to try to remove the shine. He heard his name being called by the team and went out. His first delivery was the grizzly (named Adam) at the base of the volcano in the middle of the island. There were four trucks that could be used, each of which had a crane installed to lift the cage off the bed and set it on the ground. While the two military types were readying the cage for lowering, David Brimley inspected the location and surreptitiously dropped the sheath of the knife in the approximate middle of the cage and kicked some dirt over it while pretending to level an area. He had passed the handle slabs to Garret to discard at his drop – no questions had been asked. The grizzly's cage was lifted off the truck by the crane, boom extended until the cage was over the site. Then Brimley and the driver oriented the cage so that the door faced north toward the interior of the island and the cage was lowered and the scabbard's location was covered. The other animals in this first delivery were the snow leopard, the jaguar and the black panther.

The second delivery consisted of the lion, tiger, black bear and caracal and Brimley did not go out on this delivery. The third which was the cheetah, gray wolf and the two coyotes and he didn't go. The cougar, spotted hyena and the man comprised the fourth delivery. As asked by Issaack, David Brimley was on the truck with the man. As the truck passed across the bridge over the River Styx (Rio da Fonte or Fountain River on his map), he surreptitiously tossed the pieces of metal he had put in the plastic bag and then replaced the plastic bag in his pocket. No littering even on this remote island. The cage with the human in it was taken to the far southwest side of the island, as close as the truck could get to the shoreline. David Brimley lined the cage up so that the door was pointing north just past the westernmost point of Colina da Rocha or Prometheus's Aerie. This was the best Issaack could do to point the man at the tree containing the dead parachutist although there was no way to tell the man about it. David had no way of knowing this because he couldn't see it and, in reality other than being right under the tree, you had to be on top of Colina da Rocha (Prometheus's Aerie) or high on the volcano or in an airplane to see it. While the driver was stowing the crane and its cable, David Brimley was "inspecting" the door – in reality, he had taken the knife blade from his pocket and dropped it in front of the door and kicked some loose earth over it. He was sweating like crazy and it wasn't from the heat. As soon as the driver was ready, David Brimley was in the truck and they were on the way back to the *B.B. Queen.* With the delivery of the animals and supplies for the military off loaded, the *B.B. Queen* weighed anchor and left São Rochelle. All the veterinarians were standing on the highest deck with a drink in hand and when they cleared the shallow water surrounding the island, they raised their glasses in a silent prayer.

Chapter 27

The "third Bundle meeting" was scheduled in Buenos Aires, Argentina, two weeks before the animals were to be delivered to the island. Although the first two meetings had been in Cartagena, Columbia, at the same boutique hotel, it didn't seem odd to change the location. After all, Buenos Aires is a beautiful city, cleaner than either Cartagena or Rio de Janeiro, definitely safer than both, and on a par for night life. But then the members of the Bundle didn't tour the city, didn't walk the streets, didn't go to nightclubs. So it did not seem strange to the members of the Bundle who received the invitation – and there was only one: Ramiro Esteves. And, to be truthful, he didn't receive an invitation because no invitations were ever sent much less written. So the only people who knew about Ramiro being invited was the same person who had known about the other two meetings. And she didn't know what was happening only that Señor Esteves was leaving his ranch on his private jet for two or three days, one to travel, one to attend … what? … a meeting was the pilot's guess and that's what he relayed to her in return for one of the best lays he'd ever had. For security reasons, Ramiro Esteves had his plane headquartered in Bueno Aries. For that information obtained four days before the "meeting," she received the Venezuelan equivalent of $500. That was a lot for her because the average monthly salary was 250,531 bolivars, or $32.19 a month. Venezuela was a country in which inflation had run rampant. $1000.00 bought in local currency in April 2013 when Nicolas Maduro was elected president was worth just $3.00 in July 2017.

The location chosen for the meeting was a small boutique hotel which had been completely rented for fifteen days starting on a Wednesday with the "meeting" scheduled for the Wednesday in the middle. Gerallt didn't learn of this until one day after the pilot had which was four days before the meeting. Gerallt dropped what he was doing, contacted another source in Buenos Aires and flew standby getting there two days before the meeting. Not a lot of time but with the source working an extra two days, Gerallt had several locations to choose from and a weapon of his specifications which collapsed into a case made into a backpack to keep it from being too obvious and the backpack had been aged.

Of course, what neither Gerallt or his sources knew was that this was an ingenious trap set up by Ramiro Esteves to catch the man who was trying to kill him. There was no meeting of the Bundle and his people had been set up in the area around the hotel since a week before it was empty to keep watch for him. They had a picture of him taken during the first meeting when the fake bombing run was made and Gerallt was visible shooting the fake bomber, only Gerallt didn't know it was a fake and that it was only of test of the Bundle's defensive capability. They had watched Gerallt before and during the Second Bundle meeting prepared to stop him if necessary, but it hadn't been. And now, with a bait that Gerallt was certain to accept, they would spring the trap and Ramiro would have his own much wanted, qualified but unapproved entry into the predator trial.

Gerallt had picked three spots out of seven possible. They weren't the best, but they were what were available. And they were available because Ramiro had made them – left them – available. Each one was carefully and closely watched by his people and, when they felt it necessary – either after a "kill" or when he let his guard down – they would make their hit. Not to kill – not to injure – but to capture in pristine condition so that his death in the "arena" would not be premature.

Although Gerallt had felt their presence, he had been unable to identify them or their hidey-holes. He knew – or felt, it was all the same – that some of them for certain were in the hotel. They had to be, but they would not expect him to assault that building directly. He was one man – only working with a "partner" in getting things set up. He had tested the rifle – he knew that it was zeroed in at all the ranges from which he would be shooting. None of them were too far. He was as ready as he could be.

At 5:01 a.m. on the morning of the "meeting," his alarm went off. It was a minute late. But that was not a problem. It was a mental alarm and it went off one to two minutes early or late. Not a problem. He lay on the bed listening for ten minutes before he sat up on the bed fully clothed. He hadn't been asleep – at least not in deep sleep – the entire night. He could afford to be because he knew they were watching. It could be a trap – he knew that – had known that from the beginning. But his chances at Ramiro Esteves had been few and far between. The man was a hermit and his rancho was too well protected. There were no roads leading to his hacienda. Everyone, everything went in and out via plane. Except for the beef and that was driven to a remote region of the rancho and loaded into trucks. His men went everywhere by horse or jeeps. His only chance to get a shot at Ramiro Esteves was when he made one of his extremely rare trips out of his sanctuary of solitude and he hadn't been out for three years – or not that he knew of.

He moved to the window sat down in the prepositioned chair and put his right cheek on the stock and looked into the sight with its infrared light. It was still dark at 5:00 a.m. and wouldn't be light until almost 7:00 a.m. He had no idea when Ramiro Esteves would arrive, but he had to be ready. It had been much later the other two times, but this was a different city.

And so he sat in the chair for three and a half hours scarcely moving and more comfortable then he had been when on a kill watch in Afghanistan. It mattered not because he was trained for this. Lights had been visible in the hotel for only half an hour when the first person arrived but there had been light auto and foot traffic since 5:26 a.m. It was 7:54 a.m. when the Uber pulled up. That wouldn't be him, but Gerallt watched anyway. A woman, older, dressed in a business suit – medium grey – got out carrying only a handbag. She walked to the door and held out a card to a sensor and the door opened and she went in. He thought he recognized her from the earlier meetings and she was an almost perfect match for Gloria except the eyes but Gerallt never saw her eyes.

It was 8:16 a.m. when the limousine pulled up and sat there. The hair on Gerallt's neck tingled. This was the kind of vehicle that Ramiro Esteves would arrive in. At 8:19 a.m., the front passenger door opened and one of Ramiro Esteves bodyguards got out. Gerallt centered the crosshairs on the man's face as he looked around and recognized him from prior times. *This was Ramiro Esteves's limousine!* Then the rear door on the passenger side opened and the other guard got out and was also identified by Gerallt. The Second Guard walked around the rear of the limousine to the driver's side while the First Guard walked around the front to the rear door. The Second Guard stood looking around while the First Guard opened the door. Gerallt's finger tightened on the trigger. A man with black hair – greasy black hair – got out and quickly stepped in front of the Second Guard. The look was brief, but the man was short, black hair and wearing a white suit or at least a white shirt and suit coat. The First Guard shut the limousine's door and stepped next to the Second Guard blocking any sight of Ramiro Esteves but Gerallt was resolute and kept the crosshairs on the place where the two guards' elbows met – they were basically walking shoulder to shoulder. They had taken only three steps toward the door when the Second Guard stopped and turned his right side back, looking over his shoulder toward the front of the limousine as though the driver had called to him. At the distance, Gerallt couldn't hear anything and the movement was quick but not too quick. The crosshairs aligned on the back of Ramiro Esteves's head and Gerallt's finger tightened the trigger the fraction that was needed. The distance wasn't far, and he saw the jerk of Ramiro Esteves's head as the bullet struck and the splatter of red. That was enough. He dropped the rifle, stood up, and had turned toward the door before Ramiro Esteves's body hit the pavement, his guards already spinning, the Second Guard left and the First Guard right as they pulled their pistols out of shoulder holsters, the Second Guard from the right shoulder and the First Guard from the left. Gerallt had the door to the hallway open before their spins were complete and his weapon was already out. He never got to use it, never saw what happened, just felt the electrical charge before his world went black. Later he'd realize that he'd screwed up. He'd opened the door before checking. He didn't know it then, might have picked it up sometime in the future during many rehashes of the event, but he was outnumbered, outgunned, outmanned, outmaneuvered. Two men to the left of the door; two men to the right; and four across the hall. Half of each group armed with Tasers and the other half with guns shooting rubber bullets. All had body armor vests. He had no chance of escape because he couldn't kill them all.

The first thing he saw when he opened his eyes was the top of the cage on São Rochelle and he knew that Ramiro Esteves was not

Part III

CONFLICT

Chapter 1

What is that incessant buzzing!

He waved a hand in front of his face. The buzzing continued. Constant in frequency. Not changing like a bug darting away from a slapping hand. *Not a bug! Then what?*

He opened his eyes, blinking in the dimness of the day. *Morning or night*, he wondered. Closing his eyes, he waited listening again to the continual buzzing. Tuning his hearing. Listening. No! Not a bug. Something made by man. He opened his eyes again and pulled back such as he could in shock. He saw bars. He was in jail! Jail? What the...! He sat up or at least tried to, falling back onto a solid floor or what he judged to be a floor. He looked side to side and then above. Bars. He tried raising his head and tried to look down past his ... his manhood. *I'm naked!* That fact was sufficient to overcome the inertia left over from the drugs – drugs he didn't realize he had been given. He sat up looked and saw bars. Quickly but not as fast as normal, he rolled over and onto his hands and knees and raised his head to look … and saw bars. But this time the bars had a different shape and he realized that he was looking at a door. He blinked and looked above the door. There was a small screen displaying a green readout of some sort. He crawled forward and reached the bars. Raising his right hand, he grabbed a bar, vertical here, and started to pull himself up. Alternating left and right he pulled upward, straightening his legs until he was standing – not vertically because of the height of the cage but standing – staring at the readout:

05:16:57

05:16:56

05:16:55

It was a timer counting down. Counting down to what? He jumped back cracking his head on the cage top because there was a sudden movement over his head. Through years of practice, honing of reflexes, he dropped to a fighting crouch.

"Ha! Look zat idiot. He zinks he going to fight," Ramiro said as he looked at Gerallt in the cage. The image that he saw was being broadcast by a drone that was sitting over the cage. He got up from his seat and walked toward the screen. "Take it down. I wantz to zee hiz face."

The drone moved down to midway up the side of the cage. Gerallt had heard it coming and had pivoted to face it.

"I want to talk to him," Ramiro said.

"That is not within the ability of this drone," Horus answered. "They can record pictures as we are seeing and the sounds it hears, but it does not have the ability to talk."

Suddenly Gerallt lunged right arm outstretched reaching for the drone, but his reach was eight inches– just eight inches – short. He stared at the drone and then looked around and up. "Welai chi yn uffern, (I'll see you in hell), ***Esteves***," he shouted in Welsh.

The suddenness of his shout startled Esteves who stepped back from the screen just as he had when Gerallt had lunged for the drone. Esteves laughed. "Não se eu te ver lá primeiro, filho da puta. (Not if I see you there first, son of a bitch.)"

"What did he say to you?" Issaack asked Ramiro.

"I 'ust zink he say 'I'll zee you in hell.'"

"In what language?"

Ramiro shrugged and answered, "Welzh, I thinkz."

"And you told him he would be there first?"

Ramiro considered, shrugged and said, "Sim."

"I return to see the cage unlocked," Ramiro said and wandered away and out of the room. Issaack followed him out of the theater and waited until he and the two ever present guards were gone and said quietly, "Knife," and went back into the theater.

When he was back and seated, the main screen was switching between the animals but Issaack's eyes were on the screen where the human was.

The drone started moving slowly to the left. Gerallt's eyes followed it and then he pulled his arm in and began to trail the drone. First to the corner and then to the middle of the door where the drone stopped and sat in the air just out of reach. Gerallt stopped, looked at the drone and then at the countdown:

05:14: 57

05:14:56

Movement and his eyes were on the drone, which was slowly dropping down ... down ... down. The drone stopped about six inches above the surface when it started kicking up sand. Gerallt looked at it and saw that the drone was bobbing. Up and down. Up and down. Staying at the down position twice as long as at the up position.

It's trying to tell me something, Gerallt thought.

He crouched down and looked at the area under the drone. The light was fading but he could see something shiny showing at the surface. He looked at the drone and gave it a thumb-up and just like that, the drone disappeared above the cage.

The drones are friendly. I know that devil Esteves is behind this. But why ...

The stillness of the evening was shattered by a roar that one expects to hear only in the jungles of Africa. The sound was so terrifying that a chill ran down Gerallt's back. He was a brave man. "Braver than most" his friends often said, and his enemies would agree. However, the eeriness of that roar shattering an otherwise quiet ... dawn … dusk … was enough put him on edge.

His head jerked to the right as an equally loud and terrifying roar broke the stillness with even more ferocity if that were possible. "Beth (What)?" Gerallt said unconsciously taking another step back. *The first was a lion; the second, a tiger. The first was African; the second, Asian. Where am I?*

Then, just as strangely as the first two sounds, came a third – the eerie sound of a wolf howling at the moon. Then – on its heels as though firmly attached – came the almost siren-like sound of a coyote howling, instantaneously joined by a second such animal. Then there was a cacophony of roars, none as loud as the first two but taken collectively they were enough to make a man even as brave as Gerallt shiver. He didn't cringe, but he did shiver.

He looked at the countdown clock again:

05:01:00

05:00:59

05:00:58

He looked at the sky all around and then back at the clock:

05:00:24

05:00:23

Midnight, he thought. *And then what?* No need to ask. He knew. *The doors will open, and those animals will be loose as I will be. Then ... it's the best man – or beast – for himself.*

Chapter 2

It was 11:30 p.m. Thirty minutes until the cage doors were to be unlocked and the predators freed; the billionaires were beginning to gather in Vulcan's Roost's theater. Like all the rooms in Vulcan's Roost, the theater was made from containers. In this case, two containers each eight by twenty set together long side so that the room was sixteen by twenty on the outside and fifteen by nineteen on the inside. The north wall was all LCD television screens. In the room were three rows of three seats and a three-foot aisle on the left side looking at the seats. Each seat was a leather recliner set within four feet of space side to side and five feet front to back for reclining leaving a narrow one-foot aisle for passage if the person reclining didn't feel like being nice. Each seat was motorized. They were set on a tiered floor with the first row floor level, then a rise sixteen inches to the next level and the same to the third row.

As might be suspected, Ramiro had claimed the middle of the front row seats and asked (demanded actually) that Issaack sit next to him, Issaack choosing the seat by the aisle. The other front row seat was left vacant. Ramiro had been in the theater for some time with the screen showing Gerallt, now lying on the floor asleep – at least it seemed so.

"So zere iz a betting pool?" Ramiro said.

"Yes," Issaack replied. "Didn't you get the message?"

"Yes, I want to place a bet."

"Certainly," Issaack said. "What is it?"

"Can I place two?"

"Yes. The pool is a tontine, did you understand that?"

"Tontine? I donz't underztand."

"The last one standing wins. With the understanding that the last 'one' can be two or more if the contest is considered a draw."

"Two or more?"

"Certainly. Let's say the coyotes become a team as we all suspect that they will, and they are the survivors."

"I would likez to zee zat."

"So would I. Now what are your bets? You know that the entry fee is one hundred thousand per entry."

"Sim. Sim. Eu entendo (I understand). I wantz the hyena and za grizzly and … the man."

"That's three entries. Three hundred thousand dollars."

"Sim. Eu entendo."

"Fine, Deposit the money in this account," and Issaack handed Ramiro a card with the instructions."

"How do I know itz zafe?"

"Trust."

Ramiro looked at him with a strange look – an untrusting or nonbelieving look. Then his lips twitched and broke into a grin, not a friendly grin but a grin.

"Sim. Truzt. Eu confio em você (I trust you)," he said punching Issaack in the chest. "'Uzt like you truzt me. Você confia em mim." And he laughed what was definitely an evil laugh and the rest of the Bundle looked at him and, to a one, frowned.

"You're betting on the hyena?" Siegfried said from his seat behind Issaack, having come in just in time to hear him place the bet.

"Sim. He iz a ferocious beazt. Very ztrong."

"We'll see," Siegfried said.

"Assim, you too. Tell me how we able to zee all the animalz at same time," Ramiro said to Siegfried and Issaack.

Issaack replied, "We had a drone for each beast tracking it from about one hundred feet in the air. It is tracking the predator's GPS signal. If we want it to get closer, we tell Horus or if Horus sees that something exciting may be happening, he tells us."

"Zat's a lot of people to fly the drones. Who are zeze people.?

"Horus."

"Horuz. Zat computer? It iz flying all zem? What? Fifteen of zem?"

"Yes. Fifteen of them counting … your entry, whoever he is."

"Who iz not important."

"Well, maybe not to you but …"

"Countdown to midnight," Horus interrupted, and silence reigned in the theater and if Horus hadn't been talking, one could actually have heard a pin drop, especially with the acoustics of the room.

"10… 9… 8…"

All eyes on the screen which had been broken into sixteen pieces. Fifteen of them were two by three-foot sections: two columns of four on the right, one column of four on the left, two at the top connecting the columns. The remainder was six by nine foot screen which at the present time was displaying the frontal view of the human who was lying on his side.

"Do we have to see him from that angle?" Gloria said. "It has to be degrading."

And as she spoke the angle changed to the view from the front of the cage – in fact they all changed so that the angle of view was about 45° and maybe twenty feet away.

"... 3 ... 2 ... 1 ... 0," and all the cage doors opened.

The human was on hands and knees instantly and crawled out the door. The tiger was out the door in a flash, as were the two coyotes, the wolf, the lion, caracal, hyena, and cougar. The jaguar, black leopard, snow leopard, grizzly and black bear each stared at the open doorway and then exited. As each one cleared the cage, the door closed. The only two not completely clear when the doors closed were the grizzly and the human who appeared to be digging. The grizzly turned and swiped a paw at the gate and then moved on.

"What he doing?" Ramiro asked.

"I don't know," Issaack answered just as the screen went dark.

Chapter 3

Some of the sounds continued for a short time, but he couldn't tell how long because darkness blacked out everything except his hands in front of his face. When the last of the animals – he knew not what type – quit its lamentations (which is what it sounded like) the night became quiet. Amidst the deathly quiet, he turned his ears into auditory receptive mode and lay still in the middle of the cage trying to pull in even the smallest, the quietest of sounds. And one came, and once it came and had been identified, it was there for him all the time. Waves, small waves, gently lapping – not on the sand of a beach but ... rocks. Wherever he was, it was near a large body of water because it had waves. And the shore of where he was ... was rocky. Not a rock-strewn beach but rocks. Piled together – big rocks – not stones. Big rocks. And it all came together. All those little pieces of information that had been gathered since that first meeting in Cartagena. Rumors of a zoo being amassed by some organization. A zoo like none other ever seen – at least not by mortal man. The zoo of which he had been hearing was better than any zoo those Romans ever had because it had animals from around the modern world. Yes, the Romans had animals from around the world, but their world was nothing compared to what the world had become. And this zoo by all reports was a zoo of the most dangerous kind of animals – predators. It was a Jurassic park of animals of the present, not mythical cloned remanufactured animals but actual living animals born from wombs of mothers. This must have been what that meeting was about. But why? To kill him? Hell, if Esteves wanted him dead he could have killed him easily. But no – that sadistic bastard wouldn't let him off that easily. He wants to see if he could survive a gauntlet of a type never conceived of before. But where was this zoo … where could someone encage without cages ... an island. And, not just any island. Possibly São Rochelle, the island off the coast of Brazil where someone was developing something. Rumors always have some truth to them. He had never been able to put it together. Probably because it didn't seem important but now that it was a matter of life or death – his life, his death – it became important.

Esteves was behind this. But there had to be others. There had to be someone who was working with or for Esteves yet almost certainly was helping him. He knew no one who could – would – work with that … that diawl (devil.) And why would anyone who was working with that diawl help him?

Now he was certain that what was in the sand outside the cage door was a knife or something akin to a knife. Maybe just a piece of metal but something ... Argh! Something clutched at his gut, painfully clenched its paws around his intestines and was squeezing, squeezing, forcing, twisting … He backed into a corner of the cage and squatted the best he could before relaxing his bowels and letting whatever needed out so badly out and whatever it was didn't argue. Emptied and suddenly exhausted he moved away to the center of the cage and lay down to rest and gather his thoughts.

Click. Clink. Clack. He was alert after the first sound, knowing what it meant – the cage doors were unlocked. That meant that those predators were free.

And they would be hungry just as he was. They would be hunting … and he was the quarry. He was their prey.

He scrambled to the door on hands and knees. It was open, and he crawled out placing his right hand out about where he thought the drone had been blowing dirt away. He felt something and dug with both hands. The door pushed against his side and not just with the push of a freely swinging door. This door was trying to close – and then it would be locked tight preventing any ingress. Somehow they – whoever they were knew that he was out of the cage.

"What he doing?" Esteves asked.

"I don't know," Issaack answered just as the screen went dark.

"***Ze Picture,***" Esteves screamed. ***"We Muzt Have Ze Picture!"***

"Horus, what's wrong with the human camera?"

"I don't know. Working on it."

But in fact nothing was wrong. The picture was black to prevent Esteves from seeing the knife.

The knife in his hand, Gerallt had moved off from the cage. He hadn't wanted to. He had planned on using the cage as refuge for the night. He had pictured himself in the middle of the cage as lions and tigers and bears tried to reach through the bars to make him their meal. Now with that option going, he was racing for the hill he had seen before darkness enshrouded everything. Now it was pitch black with a cloud cover and he couldn't see where he was going. The predators, however, could see in the dark – at least some of them could. Those that hunted in the night could. Those that hunted in the day probably couldn't. But when you're hungry, you hunt and Gerallt felt that they would be hungry.

In the darkness, things were just shadows. To his right there was something. Big. Rectangular. He moved slowly toward it, not knowing if it was alive or … what? He reached out a hand and touched it. Cold … at least cool. Not alive. He moved closer. A rectangular surface. Tilted. Looking up. Just a bit. He ran his hand over the surface. Smooth. Like glass. Looking around, he made out other similar shapes nearby. There must be twenty of them. All appeared to be pointing in the same direction. Then he knew. Solar panels. He had been right. He was on an island that someone was using for something requiring electricity.

A roar in the distance startled him out of his thought. *Can't stay here. Have to move.* And he started out again. And almost immediately encountered another object. This one rectangular with a round top. He felt it. Smooth on one side. Depressions on the other. He felt further. Fingers feeling. Letters. Words. A tombstone. Again a roar in the distance. Must move. And he started again. Moving faster. Hurrying.

He felt himself falling forward. He hadn't felt anything hit him and so he must have tripped on something. He held the knife firmly in his grasp and kept the hold as his hand hit the ground. No sooner than he was down, he was up and warily circling around looking. The fall had disoriented him but, truth be told, he had no idea whether he was running toward the hill he had seen or parallel to it. Although he didn't see anything out there, he felt that something was there.

The caracal Hyma was hungry. But her quarry was much bigger than she. And she wasn't about to waste her energy on something she couldn't kill. So after watching for a moment, she slunk off into the darkness in search of something more her size.

The television picture had come back on at this point.

"Hah!" Esteves said. "He iz zcared. Zee how he zpinz around looking. Where did zat cat go?"

"It left. Going for game more to its size at this point," Issaack said. "When it's hungrier, it will attack."

But what no one had thought of, except for the veterinarians, was that in the five years since Davido had hit, the native wildlife population had multiplied and there were small rodents galore, so the smaller predators could get their fill but would, in the future, have to be very wary of the bigger ones.

Chapter 4

When the cages had been opened, the two coyotes had bolted out and, because of the advantageous and intentional placement of the cages, found themselves face to face with each other. Foxy, the male coyote, was bigger than Moxie, the female coyote, but that wasn't what made him superior in Moxie's mind. It was that she was female, and he was male and for the most part, males dominate in the coyote society. Seeing one of her own kind after her long isolation was exhilarating for Moxie and she wanted to romp and play, but they were strangers and they might be enemies. But Moxie did the only thing that she could do by nature. She whimpered and lay down. Foxy then acted as he should and went to her and smelled her everywhere that a coyote should. Satisfied that she was what she seemed to be and, as she had been, lacking in company for a period of months, he licked her face. She stood and returned the favor and just like that they were a pack. Not only a pack but a hungry pack, and it was time to go hunting.

Pacer, the spotted hyena, was hungry. He had seen nothing to satisfy his hunger. His thirst was quenched by drinking from the river, but he had spotted nothing to eat. Now Pacer wandered, looking side to side as he walked through the tall grass. One of the preparations that had been made for the animals was the planting of a special blend of tall grasses which would take hold on São Rochelle. Pacer had seen nothing large or small and needed food. There was food there, but Pacer wasn't looking in the right place.

The coyote pack was also looking for prey and found it. One on either side and they were keeping careful pace slinking through the tall grass and getting closer and closer. Foxy was about five feet in front of the hyena and Moxie, on the left, was about eight, willing to let the ten-pound bigger Foxy lead the attack. When Foxy was about three feet to the side and four feet in front, Pacer finally sensed something and stopped. Both coyotes mimicked him although they sunk to the earth to avoid being seen. But it was the scent that interested the hyena Pacer and it was not of either coyote. It was something else, but something that Pacer did know. Whatever it was, it was ahead and to the right, its scent being carried by the slight breeze from that direction. Pacer moved his head following the scent of the animal. This new quarry was not moving fast but was steadily proceeding on its own path.

Foxy also sensed the presence of the other, but it was a familiar smell and the coyote knew that it was not prey for them. He knew that the hyena had smelled the other and was tracking it. As the hyena's head followed the track of the other, the two coyotes prepared for their assault. Foxy crouched and prepared to leap and Moxie moved back toward the prey from the other side, moving quickly but silently so she would not be noticed.

Foxy was tensed, ready to attack and when the hyena's gaze has just passed his hiding place, not seeing the coyote because of its interest in its own prey, Foxy launched himself. Two quick leaps covering the distance between them in a flash. An attack so swift that the hyena, his attention elsewhere did not see it until too late. Foxy sank its teeth into the throat of the hyena, ripping but not deeply. Pacer staggered just briefly when hit by the weight of the coyote.

There was an audible gasp from several members of the Billionaire Bunch who had gathered in the auditorium when being summoned by Horus. Some of them had remained in the theater watching Gerallt, but the others had left with instructions to be summoned when something interesting occurred.

"Come on, hyena! Kill zem!" Ramiro shouted.

Siegfried grinned happily behind Ramiro's back.

"The hyena and coyotes are hunting close together," Horus's voice had intoned through the speakers where those interested in such a confrontation could hear. "It appears that the coyotes are hunting the hyena and it is unaware of their presence."

That had brought both women and three of the men to the auditorium quickly.

The strength of the hyena let the animal recover quickly and it slashed at its attacker with its powerful front feet, but Foxy was too quick. He had made its attack and then scurried out of reach. Pacer had not realized there was another attacker and was focusing its full attention on Foxy when Moxie raced in and nipped at the side of the hyena's head. Immediately the hyena whirled to face Moxie giving Foxy an opening he needed and darted in and again bit at the throat area. When Pacer whirled back to face this attack, Moxie attacked the distracted hyena again. The hyena didn't know what to do with the two animals attacking it.

There was another gasp from the auditorium crowd who had seen something that none of combatants seemed to have sensed, except the hyena whose interest was now diverted to its attackers. ***"Cuidado! (Watch Out!)"*** Ramiro shouted.

A bigger gray animal was rushing the hyena from behind.

"The wolf," Gloria screamed and applauded.

"Now we've got something going!" Phil said.

Lobo, the gray wolf, was the animal the hyena had been tracking, and had been attracted by the conflict having previously not known of the presence of the other three because he was upwind in the very slight breeze. Lobo had seen the first attacks and quickly moved to the rear of the hyena, its favored attack position. With the hyena's attention elsewhere and Lobo, sensing that the coyotes were interested in the hyena for food just as he was, attacked and got a good bite at the hyena's left Achilles on its first try.

"Zat ztupid animal knowz not how to fightz!" Ramiro said dejectedly.

The hyena tried to whirl to face this new attacker, but it was having to drag thirty-five-pound Moxie who had a good portion of the hyena's neck in her mouth and wasn't letting go. His ability to face the new attacker temporarily foiled, the hyena tried to get at Moxie. It was able to rake at her with a front paw and knocked Moxie loose while inflicting a good gash on her left flank. That wound brought a gasp from the two women and a couple of the men flinched.

"Lute, seu animal estupido! (Fight, you stupid animal!)" Ramiro was half standing, beseeching the hyena to fight as though he was front row ringside at a championship boxing event and the champion was losing in the first round.

Momentarily freed of any attacker, Pacer started to turn to face the gray wolf, which had launched a second attack and gotten a good bite at the hyena's leg before darting away. Simultaneously Foxy attacked and got a better bite than Moxie had. For whatever reason, the one-hundred-ten-pound hyena fell when Foxy hit it and struggled to get back up. Foxy had released its grip when the two hit the ground and was several feet away dancing back and forth sideways in front of Pacer when he regained his feet. Moxie had darted in when the hyena fell and managed to bite and rip the hyena's left ear just as the gray wolf bit deeply into the hyena's right rear leg, partially severing the right Achilles.

When the hyena regained its footing, he knew that he had been hurt and instinctively turned his head to look at his right rear leg. This gave the two attacking males each an opening and they took them. Foxy launched an attack at the neck from which blood was starting to pour from a lacerated jugular and Lobo at the right rear leg, site of its first attack. The bites were hunger driven since none of the animals had eaten in over a week and blood accentuated the need. Lobo tore at the leg. Once his teeth had a grip, he pulled with all his eighty-seven pounds driven by hunger. With Foxy hanging tenaciously onto the neck puncturing the aorta in another place, the gray wolf pulling at the right rear leg – the damaged left rear leg – Moxie leapt and hit the hyena's head, her jaws clamping on the ear and Pacer, already struggling to keep its balance, teetered and fell. The fall tore the Achilles in the right leg held in the wolf's jaws and tore the jugular as Foxy's hold was pulled loose. On the ground, Pacer struggled briefly as he bled out, his life fleeing from its body and he died thousands of miles from its native land, his part in a crazy human experiment over.

"Zat ztupid hyena!. Itz cantz't fight zee animalz!"

The two coyotes watched as the hyena died and then started yipping to announce the kill and the gray wolf howled. The victory announcement over, the three eyed each other and then began tearing at the feast in front of them.

"That's awful," Monica said. "They're actually eating the hyena."

"It's kill or be killed. Eat or be eaten," Phil remarked almost callously. "They haven't been fed in over a week. They're hungry. There is no food source that they are used to, so they have to make do with what's available."

"Well, I can watch the fighting but not the feasting," Monica said and got up and left, followed by Gloria and Waldo, whose stomach felt queasy. Ramiro sat quietly, head in his hands almost as though he were crying.

"That's too bad, Ramiro," Siegfried said. "One of your favorites is the first one out."

The feasting went on for about ten minutes. Issaack's attention had been drawn to the jaguar's screen and he had seen it creeping up on something. The drone went up and changed altitude and he could see that the El Tigre was approaching the feast.

"Attack alert by the jaguar," Issaack announced just as the jaguar pounced.

Something had alerted the three feasters and as the jaguar attacked they ran from an unknown assailant. They stopped about fifty feet away not far from each other, Moxie pausing to lick her wound which had started bleeding again. The wolf started walking away, then stopped, looked back, barked, and started walking again. Foxy yipped in reply and started following Lobo, Moxie right behind. And a new pack was formed.

Chapter 5

As though in answer from the gods, the clouds started to break up and the moon appeared. Although in third quarter stage, it gave enough light for Gerallt to get his bearings. The hill he was aiming for was more to his right now, so he adjusted his direction, and set off in a steady lope, paying no heed to stones and small shrubs that brushed his feet and legs and cut the soles of his feet leaving blood for a hungry animal to easily track. When he arrived at the base of Colina da Rocha, Gerallt didn't hesitate and started up. It wasn't too bad for the first third but then the climb steepened, and he found himself having to pull up to get on a ledge and then try to find a way from that ledge on up. He wasn't a rock climber and unless there was a place to put the knife, each pull up to a higher level meant he only had full use of one hand. It wasn't a big knife, the blade was only six inches long, but it was all that he had and there was no way in hell he was going to let it go.

The way wasn't difficult for a big physically qualified person like him despite his weeks of inactivity and the effect of the drugs. Half an hour later he was at the top. He found himself on a mesa, for lack of a better word. It was effectively a flat circular surface with a radius of about twenty to thirty feet. He walked around looking in every direction and could see water on three sides and to the north (judging by where the moon was in the sky) a tall mountain. To the left of the mountain was a dark area and in its upper right a white spot. He had no idea what it was but would wait for morning. When he was on the north side (at least what he judged to be north) he had heard a sound that he thought to be water splashing into a pool of water. He couldn't see anything but thought that in the light of day he might get a better look.

He was tired from his efforts as well as hungry and thirsty, but he wasn't going to get anywhere by bumbling around in the dark. So he chose a spot in the approximate center of the mesa and lay down. He was almost asleep when a scratching awakened him. He was on his feet quickly and looking around the best he could. As he turned, he tried to hone in on the sound and did. It was coming from the side where he had climbed up. As he looked, two paws appeared over the edge and seemed to get a grip on the rough surface and suddenly there was the head of a cat and just as suddenly the entire cat was on the mesa and it was a big cat. A short run and it was in the air straight at him. He crouched, putting his left arm up as a defense and holding the knife in his right low so that he could strike upward into the cat's body.

The cat hit him with a force stronger than he expected and he was knocked backward, his right hand striking upward. As he hit the stone surface with the cat on top of him, there was a sharp crack and he felt the surface break under him and he and the cat were falling, the cat trying to rip and bite at his right hand which had driven the knife deep into its stomach and was trying to cut a slice in the abdomen. The fall wasn't long – he was in no position to judge being in a fight for his life – and was broken by water. He and the cat crashed into water with Gerallt still slicing with the knife and continued down with the cat now trying to get loose and away. Gerallt let the cat go and worried about himself.

He quit fighting and tried to conserve what breath he had, waiting until the momentum of his fall dissipated and he started to surface. At this point he was surprised that the water was warm, not cool as are most mountain pools.

When he felt himself start to rise, he looked in that direction and could see a dimness, so he started kicking for the surface. He rose three feet into the air when he breached the surface, gasping for air and then returned to the depths but was quickly back on the surface, treading water. He could hear sounds of something else splashing and knew it to be the cat. As he listened he heard the splashing grow slower and fainter and then finally stop.

As he treaded water he looked around. All he could see was blackness except above him where he saw a small section of sky with fourteen to twenty stars twinkling through a jagged hole. Then a dark shadow appeared in the center of the hole and appeared to get bigger and there was a humming or buzzing sound. He tried to follow the dark shadow, but in the pitch black of wherever he was, it was impossible.

"This is a fine mess you have gotten yourself into," said a voice sounding remarkably like Oliver Hardy.

"Who are you?" Gerallt asked.

"A friend," came the answer. "But I am not there. What is there is one of my drones."

"Where are you?"

"Elsewhere. I can get you out if you can stay afloat for half an hour."

"Half an hour?"

"Yes." And with that the drone, which was the shadow, flew up through the jagged hole above him and disappeared.

Gerallt was a good swimmer and normally would not have had any trouble floating and/or treading water for half an hour. But he was tired and wounded by the claws of the cat which had attacked him. So by the time Horus's drone came back, he was on the verge of exhaustion. He had sought handholds along the walls of the apparent well he found himself in, but the surface was smooth. He hadn't found the body of the cat and assumed it had sunk. He was startled by a splash and whirled around looking for whatever was making the noise, but nothing was there. Then the buzzing of the drone announced its reappearance as it came down through the hole.

"Come under the hole. I have a rope securely fastened on the surface," the voice from the drone told him. Gerallt swam over and found the rope hanging down through the hole.

"I cannot pull you up. You have to do that yourself," the voice announced and then the drone was gone.

Gerallt would have preferred the kind of rope used in gym classes to climb but the rope he found turned out to be quarter inch nylon. So putting the knife once again into his mouth in his best imitation of a pirate, he climbed up the rope until he could grab the surface of the mesa. Hanging with his left hand, he fashioned a loop in the rope with his right. Then grabbing the hole's edge with both hands, he pulled himself up until he could get his left foot in the loop. Then he was able to lower himself by bending his left knee and then propel himself upward using his left leg and fall forward with his torso on the mesa. From there it was easy to get his legs up and he was once again, at least in his mind, on top of the world. He heard the buzzing of the drone and saw it in front of him.

"Untie the rope, coil it, tie it and hang it on the hook on my underside," said the voice of the drone.

While Gerallt was following his directions, the voice was telling him the situation. "The important thing for you is to get armed. There is one of Esteves's men dead in the trees of the rainforest. He's in a tree near the top right. You can see the parachute from here and use it as a marker. He has arms including some explosives which may be useful. You have a tracker in the back of your neck. I don't think you can get it out. I cannot deactivate it without alarming Esteves. So we will be tracking you and watching you. In the rainforest on the side toward the water there is a big kapok. This rope will be there. That is the best we can do. You have a knife. You'll have a rope. Get armed and we can beat these idiots."

At this point the rope was hanging under the drone which buzzed off leaving Gerallt once again King of the Mountain. In the dim light of the moon he examined himself and found that his wounds were superficial and not bleeding. It was almost as though something in the water was a healing agent. But that's the stuff that legends are made of.

Chapter 6

While most of the felines and the canines were having some difficulty getting food to eat, the rest of the predators weren't.

The black bear's cage was placed on the edge of the rainforest and when the cage door opened, he wandered in amongst the trees and foliage and found water to drink and vegetation to eat and was quite happy because he was an omnivore and for the most part ate vegetation.

The grizzly was released on the mountain and in search of food and water found itself in the rainforest and, like the black bear, was – at least for the present time – satisfied although the heat was a little too much.

Hyma, the caracal, had been the busiest of the animals that first night. Almost right away she had spotted the cougar and knew that it was strange. Nothing like that in her home in India. There were tigers, but they had stripes – this big animal didn't. So she moved quickly away to the west stopping for the moment in her quest for water, which she could smell. Then there had been that man – she knew men and knew that there were small men and big men. Small men would be good food, but this man was too big. She let him pass and then continued on west. There she had encountered the seawall of rocks and beyond that water, but water she could not drink. She moved north and stayed fairly close to the rock hill which she could climb quickly if needed but sensed it would provide nothing for her. She then made her first kill – a small rodent – which she grabbed by the back of the neck and broke its spine killing it. The kill was quickly devoured and at least partially satisfied her needs. Continuing on around the hill she came to the big pool at the bottom. Other animals had been there but no smell that she knew. Approaching the pool semi-cautiously because this was a strange land and strange lands meant strange customs, she lapped the water up, stopping every few laps to check her surroundings. She knew by the sounds that she had heard earlier that there were big animals here. One she knew – the tiger. She knew that she should stay away from that one. Her thirst satisfied, Hyma returned to her clockwise circuit of the island staying near the water on her left because that served as a barrier against a hunter such as she. This would be different because this would be a hunter hunting her. Sometimes she ran and sometimes she walked. Once she paused to make another kill – a small rodent like the first and she was beginning to feel her hunger sated. To her right the sky was beginning to lighten, and she knew that her hunting was fleeting. She loved the night and slept during the day when it was hotter – at least where she had been born and spent her first year. Then she had been trapped and put in a cage for a long time until – well, until she woke up here, in the cage but alone. Then the door to the cage had opened and she had raced out and begun exploring.

Soon in her progress, she smelled some familiar or almost familiar things and she moved along and soon entered the fringes of the rainforest. The smells and night sounds were similar to those of her home. At the base of one tree right on the outside of the forest she paused, smelling a white thing that lay there. She pawed at it playfully, curiously. It moved when she touched it but then stopped. Whatever it was, it wasn't alive and would provide no sustenance for her. She looked up and saw that this tree had limbs and concealing foliage, ideal for her to hide and sleep during the day. Quickly she climbed the tree and until she was about twenty feet up and found a limb upon which she could lie down upon and sleep. She settled herself in, listening to the sounds of night birds. The sounds were strange but comforting and soon she fell asleep, content and purring.

Chapter 7

It was almost as soon as the first trace of an orange-rose – or is it rose-orange? – cloud shone in the eastern sky when dawn came, and it cracked. Actually it was a rifle shot and Gerallt was up like a rabbit, eyes and ears alert. He knew that the sound had come from the northeast side of the island but why he did not know.

The occupation troops were quartered in the barracks where the workers had been housed because there was not room in the Vulcan's Roost Headquarters. It had been made specially to house the Bundle and attendants and no more. The invaders had their own cook and supplies had been dropped by aircraft the morning after they landed. They were carried by truck back and forth from the entrance to the volcano. Because the predators were to be released on the island, the troops had constructed a fence surrounding their compound and sentries had been assigned. The troops had been understandably upset knowing that hungry predators were prowling the island and even more upset when they were told they were not permitted to kill the beasts.

"What are the men to do if they are attacked by one of the beasts?" General Gutierrez had asked Esteves.

"Tell them to run like the cowards they are," Esteves had answered.

Of course, that would not have been a proper thing to do, so General Gutierrez simply told the men, they should run. Despite the edict that the troops should not shoot the beasts and run if attacked, they walked their sentry posts armed. And, just as naturally, if one is on guard against an invasion, one walks a post outside the fence.

This particular morning, João Oliveira (Soldado 21) was on guard and had been since midnight. He was nearing the south end of the compound's perimeter fencing when his cellphone rang. He was surprised by this because they did not have cell service. Still all the men carried their cellphones because to be without it would be like cutting off an appendage or even worse, one's pênis. João set his rifle down butt first, holding the barrel in his left hand while he fished in his fatigue pocket for his cellphone. His attention was diverted for only fifteen seconds, but it was enough for Val Killer, the black leopard. He had been lying in wait for over an hour watching as João walked his beat. As soon as the leopard realized that his prey's guard had been dropped, he attacked and was on João before João realized that he was being attacked. João had time only for a brief shout before the leopard sank his fangs into João's neck. At that point there was nothing that João could do. With his prey lifeless, the leopard commenced to drag the body away.

His ultimate goal was to get the body to the rainforest and cache it in a tree but, hunger overcoming nature, after covering about a hundred yards and still with fifty to go to the security of the rainforest, the leopard paused to satisfy his hunger. He had been at it only ten minutes when Victor Alonso, officer of the watch, came to see why João had not checked in on schedule. He did not find João, but he did find his weapon and cellphone. He raised the alarm and the troops poured out fearing they were being attacked by some aggressive force summoned to counter their invasion. When organized, they set out in pairs to look for João and it was Lucas Molina (Soldado 30) who spotted the panther at his feast at the same time the panther spotted him. Natural instinct on the panther's part was to run dragging his prey and on Lucas's part it was to shoot. Both started what their instinct said to do, and Lucas was just a hair too fast with his shot and missed. The leopard took the hint and quickly disappeared into the rainforest with a partially satisfied hunger. Lucas and his partner Kaua Costa (Soldado 32) walked up to the body lying on the ground and Lucas turned away and managed to walk ten feet before vomiting the remains of last night's dinner, which were still in his stomach. When informed of the incident, General Gutierrez simply doubled the guard.

Because all the predators were being monitored by the chip in the back of their necks, Horus had been watching the panther watching João and had made João's phone ring. When the panther had started dragging João's body toward the rainforest, Horus's count of the invading force's number dropped to 31 and crossed off Soldado 21.

On top of Colina da Roche, Gerallt knew none of this but suspected that one of the predators had done something that it shouldn't, and he smiled. Despite the fact that the predators were out to get him, he was on their side against the forces of Esteves and would only kill if necessary. Alerted that it was a new day, he began to plan his descent. While swimming inside the hill awaiting the drone's return, Gerallt had taken a mouthful of the water and swallowed it. Feeling no ill effects at this point, his first goal of the day was to find the water he had heard falling and to satisfy his thirst. So he walked around the edge of the mesa again until he located the point where he heard the sound the loudest, and there he lay down and peered over the top of the mesa. He was fortunate with the early morning sun which was beginning to shine on that portion of the hill and he could see the water coming out of the hill and cascading down. Standing up, he looked carefully over the edge on both sides of the water and chose a path of descent. It wasn't as easy going down as it had been going up and it was a good half an hour before he reached the first pool. He lay on his stomach and had just drunk as much as he felt he should in this first drink after so long when his senses tingled. Looking up his eyes spotted what his senses had warned him about. On the opposite side of the pool was a jaguar that was sizing him up as its next meal.

"Oh, no," Ramiro said. "Zere ez another catz after him. You zink he going to survivez?"

"I don't know," Issaack answered." *I hope so,* he thought and had fingers crossed at least mentally.

Chapter 8

Gerallt knew that el Tigre could swim and that if he ran, the jaguar would be upon him quickly. So when the jaguar sprang, Gerallt did the only thing he could do – he dove into the pool hoping he had judged its depth properly. In the water, he stopped himself and looked up. El Tigre was swimming across the pool and was just beyond him. With the knife in his right hand and using the left and both legs to propel him upward, he thrust the knife into the jaguar's rib cage as hard as he could and with his left arm grabbed the body having in mind to pull it under and drown it. What Gerallt had not judged was the speed of the outflow of the pool and the fact that the depth of the water flowing over the lip of the pool was eighteen inches. The force of his upward thrust had carried his head and shoulders out of the pool and actually pushed el Tigre to the edge. The force of the flow then carried el Tigre and him over the edge. Gerallt felt himself falling and not knowing where he was going or whether he would survive, he hung on to the knife and el Tigre with all his might. Unbeknownst to and fortunately for him, his knife thrust had killed el Tigre instantly, otherwise a struggling cat clawing at him in midair could have be disastrous.

"Oh, my god," Monica screamed. ***"He's going to be killed."***

"He better live," Ramiro said, having already lost one of his three bets and feeling very safe even if Gerallt did come after him.

Yes, he'd better, Issaack thought.

Gerallt hit the bottom pool right in the middle with el Tigre under him. He was stunned but not knocked out thanks to the cushioning effect of the jaguar, which most certainly was killed by the impact between the water and Gerallt's body if it was not already dead. He and the cat went deep into the pool and, as they sank, his subconscious realized that el Tigre was dead, so he pushed it away with his left hand and pulled the knife free with his right. He wasn't about to let go of a weapon that had saved his life twice.

"He kill two of zoze catz," Ramiro Esteves said, more as a statement of disbelief than as a question.

"Apparently," Issaack answered.

"Where he get knife?"

"I don't know. The video doesn't show."

"Always video?"

"For him. You asked for video. I have no choice but to concur."

"What's this 'con•quer'?"

"It means that if you want video, I must supply video."

Gerallt was running out of air and looked around and saw bright light so he swam for it, again the knife in his teeth like a pirate. He broke the surface and seized the knife, opening his mouth to draw in big gasps of air and finding himself right in the sights of a rifle.

When Gerallt found the knife, Ramiro knew that the odds had changed. Without any weapon, Gerallt had a chance against the predators but not a very big one. With the knife, his chances improved and evidently killing the cougar raised them even more and he knew that something had to be done about it. So he made a call to General Gutierrez and told him to send some soldiers to catch Gerallt and take the knife away. Gerallt was not to be hurt unless he attacked the soldiers and even then, he should be overpowered, the knife taken away, and Gerallt released. The task was assigned to Sargento Garcia Marques (Soldado 5) who roused four volunteers and they left the compound in a pickup truck just after the body of Soldado Oliveira had been recovered. He dropped three soldiers on the north side of the Rio da Fonte (River Styx) at the (Charon) Bridge, with orders to watch for the man and to take the knife from him. He and Soldado Thiago Garcia (Soldado 22) would drive around to the other side of Colina da Rocha and climb it to look for him. Soldado Alejandro González (Soldado 20), Soldado Agustin López (Soldado 18) and Soldado Axel Martin (Soldado 17), the three soldiers left at the bridge, were surprised to see the man appear about a third of the way up from the bottom pool and make his way to the mid-pool because they had seen el Tigre approaching that pool on the other side. When they saw the man, wagering was immediately begun. When el Tigre leapt into the water followed by the man, odds quickly went up. When the two combatants fell over the side, the three started running for the pool. Uppermost in their minds was the price a nice el Tigre rug would bring back home in Venezuela where they were all from. When Gerallt surfaced, Axel thought it was el Tigre and quickly got him in his sights and fired a shot. And unthinkingly, the other two joined him in el Tigre practice.

Pa-ching. Something hit the water next to him. Pa-ching. Something else. He looked around and saw three men advancing toward him at a run a good distance away. One stopped. ***Pa-ching***. That was close, and he knew that was a bullet. The one who stopped was running again. Another stopped. Pa-ching. Not so close but close enough. The one who shot was running again. The one in the middle stopped and Gerallt dove under. He could see the bullet hit the water and go crazy in its motion through the water, no longer straight and not as fast. But when they were close, like standing poolside, that would change. He surfaced. PA-ching. He submerged and swan toward the back of the pool. Hitting the wall, he surfaced, gasping for air. PA-CHING. Rock splinters hit his face. Lungs full of air he went down and feeling the wall as he went found a place to grab hold. He watched a bullet zig-zag through the water right in front of him.

"What iz he goin' to do now?" Esteves asked.

"Die, I suppose," Issaack answered. "Your men are going to kill him and then where is your fun?"

"Your men are going to kill him. Tell them to stop," Ramiro snapped into a communicator he was carrying.

Issaack watched in horror as the video showed blood coming up from the back of the pool. Lots of blood. The drone covering the incident changed its attitude and the video showed the three men high-fiving each other – congratulating each other on the kill. Issaack's heart sank. He had just watched the Bundle's one hope for stopping Ramiro's mad plan die at the bottom of a pool, killed by Ramiro's men.

Then the video returned to the pool of water and everyone in the theater watched as the flow of blood from under the waterfall dissipated and the blood flowed out of the pool and downstream in the River Styx, now looking to have been named very appropriately.

Through the heavy veil of water, Gerallt watched the three shooters being berated by someone he assumed was an officer who had arrived in a pickup just after he had gotten up into the cave room behind the falls. The three had been loafing on the edge of the pond smoking and talking about how they had killed el Tigre until the officer arrived.

Good. Let them think I am dead. It will make their deaths easier.

In the pool looking for salvation, he had used his handhold to pull down and toward the wall and found himself under some sort of ledge. And stuck there also was the body of the cougar he had killed the night before. It had been a desperation move to stab the already dead beast and surprisingly he had been greeted with an outpouring of blood perhaps enabled by the body being kept warm by the water. His efforts at stabbing the cougar had moved it and revealed a hole under the ledge. Having no choice and running short of air, he had entered the hole and found that it turned upward rather quickly and then he was in the open. It was dark, but the air was breathable. Looking up, he saw light and could hear the sounds of the waterfall. The hole he was in was basically tubular and was big enough so that he could climb it with the back and foot method that rock climbers use to climb chimneys. The smooth walls were wet, but his bare feet were able to keep a grip as he used his hand to raise his torso and then walk his feet up a few inches. The climb was no more than ten feet and he did it quickly.

Upon reaching the top, Gerallt found himself in a room. His attention had been drawn to the three soldiers that he could see through the waterfall. He watched them get chewed out by their superior who then drove off in the truck leaving them to walk, albeit slowly, back to their camp. At least they started walking slowly and then the lion roared, and the pace quickened to double time. Gerallt didn't know the water supply of the island, but he guessed that many of the predators, as with the two he had confronted.

Sargento Marques and Soldado Garcia were about a third of the way up the southwest side of Colina da Rocha when the first shot was fired. Good or bad, Sargento Marques didn't know, but he knew that his men were involved. The two quickly climbed back down the hill and got into the truck and returned to the bridge. His soldiers weren't there, and he stood on the truck's running board and could see them on the bank of the pool at the base. Soldado Garcia drove the pickup over to the pool and stopped, the sound of the electric motor completely unnoticed by the three soldiers who were smoking and laughing until Sargento Marques slammed the door of the pickup. The three were on their feet immediately.

"You were supposed to be looking for the man," Sargento Marques said, "Not sitting on your asses smoking cigarettos."

Axel tried to explain what happened emphasizing that what they had shot at was el Tigre. They had shot, not to hit him, but to try to get him out of the pool so they could find the man. But both the man and el Tigre apparently had been killed when they hit the water. It didn't do any good and Sargento Marques told them he would report the incident to Teniente Zaptero and he would handle any disciplinary action if any was to be taken. Then he got into the truck and was driven back to the encampment, the three flojo (goof-offs) were told to walk, which they did until the lion roared.

The room in which Gerallt found himself wasn't big and was really just an elbow in a tube which seemed to continue upward. His mental bet was that if he climbed the tube he would wind up near the pool he and the el Tigre had been in before their fall. He had no idea how the cougar had gotten in the base pool but that had proven there was a connection between the pool inside the mountain and the two outside. Proof that the room had been found by others was a coiled half-inch hemp rope attached to a spike that had been driven into the floor at the back of the room. The rope was long enough to reach the pool and probably provided access for those unable to climb the pipe. Undoubtedly kids, he thought, who would have fun diving or jumping through the falls and landing in the pool. One thing he found was a towel probably used to dry off. It was big enough that he could fashion a loin cloth with a length of the hemp rope used as a belt. The other find was even better. It was a stick about six feet long, fairly straight and, most important, solid. With a little work and a strip of cloth from the towel, he could turn it into a spear.

"You zink he be dead?" Ramiro asked.

"Horus, what do you think?" was Issaack's response.

"I am sorry to report that all life functions on this contestant have ceased," Horus said.

"Zorry? Why he zorry?" Ramiro asked.

"Horus…" Issaack began.

"I am sorry because he was in a contest he didn't choose to be in," Horus said. "Just as I am sorry that each of the other animals died and will be sorry that each of the remaining animals might have to die."

"What'z about my zoldierz?" Ramiro said.

"They are here by choice unlike the animals" was Horus's answer.

Chapter 9

It didn't take Gerallt long to realize that he didn't have the tools necessary to make a spear using the knife as the blade because he had no way to securely fasten the blade to the stick. Both ropes he had were too big, and the hemp one was fragile, and the towel pulled apart when he tried to use it. So he sharpened the end of the stick to the best of his ability and would make it harder when he had a fire. Then he dropped the rope down the hole and climbed down. Once in the water, he prepared by taking several deep breaths and then he submerged, exited the tube, swam to what he thought was the part of the pool in shadows, and slowly surfaced. Although he had erred a bit and wasn't in the darkest shadow, there was no one around, either human or predator. Swimming to shore, he exited the pool and headed toward the west side of the island because he thought it best to be along water that he could enter if any of the predators showed up. As he jogged along, he kept his head swiveling looking for anything that moved and somethings that didn't. Suddenly the stillness of the morning air was split with a loud animal sound. It wasn't a roar, but something different and he knew that it was from one of the big cats. It didn't sound close, so he didn't pay any heed. But very soon thereafter there was another call just like the first and almost immediately this was answered by a definite roar and that was not too far distant. He stopped and looked in the direction where he judged the second animal to be. At first, he saw nothing and then he saw a big male lion heading in the direction opposite to the way he was moving. He watched it for a moment until another call from the first cat came and he saw and heard the lion answer.

"Something going on there, but I don't know what," he said to no one and then continued on the way to the water's edge.

"Hey, everyone. Looks like the lion and tiger are going to duke it out."

In this casual manner, Horus announced one of the more important confrontations in the Deadliest Predator contest. In a manner of minutes everyone had gathered in the meeting room with its mega-sized television which covered the stage end of the room. On it were clearly visible the lion and the tiger. The video was shot from above by one of the many drones tracking the contestants. Since there was one drone for each animal, Horus was picking the best view to use and kept switching.

The two big cats were circling each other in an open area.

"She's been there for some time, pacing, pissing and roaring. I don't know what else to call it. It wasn't a roar. More of a Yar Yar Yawl."

Monica giggled. "You're not much of a sound effects person, are you, Horus?"

"I've never had reason to be until today," Horus replied.

The circling went on for several minutes and then suddenly Simba the lion attacked. He raced up to Cleopatra the tiger, who instead of counterattacking appeared almost to be willing to sacrifice herself and lay down on the ground. Simba grabbed the back of her neck and then basically moved behind her all the while keeping a grip on her neck.

Monica gasped. “He’s mounting her.”

And indeed, that was obviously the case.

Everyone watched in awe as the “lovemaking” progressed to its conclusion which was indicated by Cleopatra snarling and reaching up to bite at him.

“That didn’t take very long,” Waldo said. “Where’s the enjoyment in that?”

“It was a quickie,” Monica said, and to Gloria, “That’s what Shelia said when we first saw Cleopatra. PMS.”

“Right,” responded Gloria. “Have to find a way to let her know she was correct.”

“According to what I found on the internet, that is the common practice,” the voice of Horus intoned. On the screen came the following:

> Male lions check whether a female is on heat by sniffing her reproductive organs; when the females enter oestrus, they do so for four days, and mating will occur several times an hour. If the female doesn’t conceive, she goes back into oestrus two weeks later. During a mating bout, lions will have sex 20 to 40 times a day for a couple of days.

“Wow, that’s got to be tiring,” Gloria said.

“Maybe,” Harvey Gladstone said. “But it’s slam, bam, thank you, ma’am.”

This said as Simba again mounted Cleopatra and it was as Harvey predicted.

“That doesn’t look good for our survival of the fittest,” Issaack said.

"Maybe they'll have a lover's quarrel," Phil said. But they didn't.

Gerallt reached the shore and turned right heading for the rainforest which he could see in the distance. He knew that the parachute was in the northeast corner and the fastest way there was to skirt the rainforest itself but that would keep him in the open and he didn't want that. So he chose to continue along the coast and go along the western boundary of the rainforest to the top and then cross the top to where the parachutist might be visible.

Chapter 10

The midday sun was high in the sky when Gerallt reached the western edge of the rainforest. And there, as promised, lying at the base of a big kapok, was the rope. It was not nicely coiled as he remembered it when the drone had flown off with it but looked as though someone had picked it up and then carelessly dropped it. He didn't think that the drone would have done that. *If that were so*, he thought, *whoever it had been was not looking for him but just curious because otherwise it would be lain neatly as it would have been dropped.* And he knew that the drone could have – sensed, would have – left it coiled neatly as a message. Still, just in case it was a trap, Gerallt checked it carefully before touching it and found nothing amiss other than the rope itself. It was hot and Gerallt preferred to be moving around in the cool and preferably in the dark since there were at least two forces at work who wanted him dead: the predators for food and man for … whatever. He looked at the tree and knew that it was easy to climb and could see a satisfactory spot up amongst the leafy branches where he could rest for a few hours unseen but still be able to see those that might come looking for him. He picked up the coil of rope and put it over his head so that the coil rested on his right shoulder and under his left arm.

As he started to climb the tree, he heard a rustling above and looked but saw nothing, so he resumed his climb. Then there was the sound of branches and leaves hitting each other and he looked again but saw nothing. He had no idea what creatures were native to this small rainforest, but he didn't think they would be dangerous to him. But again, there were animals on this island that were not native to it and were, in fact, as unfamiliar with the island and the rainforest as he was. Just in case, he pulled his knife from where he had put it in his rope belt, clasped it between his teeth where it would be handy and resumed his climb. In less than five minutes, he was settled and dozing off, secure in the knowledge that he was unseen and alone.

In neither of those was he correct. Sleeping peacefully in her leafy bower, the caracal had been awakened by her innate security alarm and had seen Gerallt – whom she thought of only as man in our understanding – at the base of the tree. She watched only semi-interested until the man started to climb the tree in which she was. That meant danger and she immediately moved higher in the tree. Pausing and looking down she saw the man looking up but not at her. When the man started moving again, the caracal moved out on a branch stretching toward another tree and then jumped to a branch of that tree, made her way to the trunk and then repeated the process to get to a tree further in the rainforest and away from the invading man. Even then, when she had once again settled herself on a branch to her liking, she found it difficult to get to sleep but after five minutes, she was once again sleeping or at least catnapping.

Gerallt found nothing unusual in his climb up the kapok to a limb which he felt suited his needs. No sooner had he settled himself in a restful pose than that annoying hum stirred him at least to open one eye. He could see movement outside the expanse of the kapok's foliage and he watched with interest as a drone, smaller than the one which had helped him earlier, made its way between the leaves and branches until it settled itself on a branch above his head and out of his immediate reach.

"Who are you?" Gerallt asked.

"A friend," replied the drone or at least that is what Gerallt heard coming from the drone.

"No, I mean who is the person who is speaking?"

The drone was silent for a moment.

"Well," said Gerallt irritably.

"You could say I am a parakeet," said the voice of the drone.

Gerallt laughed.

"You talk a lot for a parakeet."

"Well, I guess I could be a scale-crested pygmy tyrant."

"A what?" Gerallt almost laughed again.

"A small bird which catches insects for food and lives from Costa Rica to Peru on the west coast of South America and to Venezuela on the east coast."

"You're a little bit out of your range then, if I am where I think I am."

"Where do you think you are?"

"São Rochelle."

"Well, then we can agree on something."

"Still I would like to know who you are."

"I don't know who you are."

"Then why are you helping me?"

"Because I don't like the man who is trying to kill you."

"You mean that mab i ast (son of a bitch) Esteves?"

"Precisely."

"Okay, as long as you are on my side. I guess I'll just call you 'Tyrant'."

"Fine. If you want to find the dead man I told you about, you should get a move on it."

"Why?"

"Because there is a black panther on the other side of this rainforest who is sleeping off a kill. When it is dark, he will go on the prowl again and he has already tasted man."

"Anything else?"

"There are two bears, but you needn't worry about them."

"Bears! And why shouldn't I worry about them?"

"Because they are quite satiated by the plants around here. Bears are more herbivores than carnivores and won't be in the contest until late."

"What contest?"

"To see who survives."

"I thought so," Gerallt said.

"Of course, your contest is bigger, and might I say, more interesting and at least for the time being, more lopsided."

"Why so?"

"Because you have at least thirty-one armed men who will want to stop you from getting to Esteves. That is your primary goal, is it not?"

"Other than survival. Yes. I want to kill him."

"Well, to better help you, I recommend you find the dead man in the kapok in the northeast corner of the rainforest."

"You mean the one who has armament to help me?"

"Yes."

"What's the best way to get there?"

"North then east. The panther is about the one third of the way down the east side, and the grizzly bear is in the middle third of the east side and the black bear in the middle third more to the west."

"Then going on the diagonal is faster."

"Except for plants, and spiders, and snakes."

"SNAKES!"

"Yes, there are sure to be snakes in the rainforest. Sorry but I don't know what kinds or where. I have just seen birds and monkeys."

"What kind of monkeys?"

"Green."

"Seriously."

"Yes, it is an Old World monkey but apparently some of its ancestors were brought here and thrived. We could find no record of how or when?"

"We... you said 'we.' Who else..."

But Tyrant the drone wasn't listening. It started its engine and made its way down following the trunk and then out from under the foliage and disappeared. Taking the hint, Gerallt started down the tree.

Chapter 11

On the floor of the rainforest, Gerallt moved quickly but silently to the north. The foliage was thick but not impenetrable and while it slowed him down, it wasn't a barrier. Overhead, unseen and unheard because of singing of the birds and green monkeys who made their home here, moved Hyma, the caracal, a tree or two behind Gerallt. Hers was a trip of curiosity as is often the way of felines, even the big ones. Spear in one hand and knife in the other, Gerallt's senses were alert and he paused every few steps to listen more carefully than he could while moving and to look around to spot any adversaries, human or otherwise.

On about the fourth of these security pauses, he heard a faint snort and recognized it for animal, not human. He knew by the sound that the animal was big and the first thing that popped into his head was *bear* because Tyrant the parakeet/drone had mentioned them. He had seen bears in zoos but never in nature. He didn't think they were man-eaters although they were omnivores but preferred plants and berries. The drone had amplified that thought. How many bear edible plants were there on this small island? And there were two bears, black and grizzly. Which one was this?

He switched to holding the spear in both hands, sticking the knife into his rope belt, out of the way but handy. The spear wouldn't kill the bear because it would have difficulty penetrating the fur and then the heavy hide. But he didn't relish the thought of close contact fighting with a bear. He had seen their claws and wanted no part of them. As prepared as he could be and needing to get to the tree with the corpse and its treasures, Gerallt moved stealthily forward pausing every two steps to listen.

There, another snort and this one closer, ahead to the right. Moving ever more cautiously now, he paused beside the trunk of a strangler fig and peered around it toward the depths of the rainforest. Ten feet away, back to him, was a black something, its rear end wiggling with the efforts of its front legs undoubtedly digging for something. Sensing that the bear was totally preoccupied, Gerallt moved past the bear staying as far away as he conveniently could. The bear's preoccupation with its digging didn't change and Gerallt was quickly past it and pursuing his path.

Moving slowly because he was on the alert for predators as well as soldier types, it took an hour for him to reach the northeastern side of the small rainforest. In the growing dimness of the day, he was faced with finding his quarry. He looked up trying to spot the white he had seen from the top of the rock and it didn't take him long before he was looking up the trunk of a big kapok and saw a bit of pink. He knew immediately that it was the color of the evening's sunset on the parachute. Now the task was to climb the tree and this one didn't look as easy as the other with a bigger trunk and the first branch about twenty feet up. He took off the rope coil and made one attempt throwing it up before he knew that was impossible. It got within two feet of the limb, but he had to get it over and back down so that he could grab it. That seemed impossible without a weight, so he started searching the area under the tree for a stone. Despite the rocky nature of the island, his search proved futile.

In desperation, he gathered the rope to make another attempt when a familiar buzzing came to his ear. He looked up and saw Tyrant, the small drone, hovering about eighteen inches above his head. As the drone moved side to side, Gerallt noticed a small hook, in fact an S-hook, with one end hanging on a piece of the drone's frame. Quickly fashioning a loop in the end of his nylon rope, Gerallt hung it on the hook and then feed out rope as the drone flew up and over the tree limb. Once over the limb, the drone flew away pulling the rope and then it headed back toward Gerallt stopping almost where it had started. Reaching up, Gerallt removed the loop from the dangling S-hook but in doing so he accidently removed the S-hook from the drone's frame and it fell to the ground. He bent over and picked it up and when he straightened, the drone was gone. Now he had another piece of equipment but no pocket to put it in. However. the hemp rope he had around his waist was loosely woven and he was able to hang the hook by one of the cords.

Then he pulled the loop end of the rope until he had about ten feet on the ground. Grabbing both pieces of the rope he shook it until part of the rope over the limb was against the truck of the tree. Then he dropped the long end of the rope and walked around the tree with the shorter end. Picking up both ends, he pulled the rope taut, leaned back with his bare feet against the tree and began to walk up the tree moving his hands up the rope as he did. It was slow work and he was exhausted when he reached the limb. Holding the ropes with his right hand, he threw his left arm over the limb. He hung there a moment but only enough to catch his breath, and then pulled himself up on the limb. Once on the limb it was easy to climb up to the next limb to where the parachutist was hanging three feet from the trunk. Gerallt was used to dead bodies, but he wasn't used to the ants which had already found this one and were beginning to take what they wanted. He could reach the body by standing on a limb but tied the rope around the tree and then to himself just in case. Familiar with the parachute's rigging as well as the man's gear, he first removed the rifle because that was the one thing he didn't want damaged in the drop to the ground, and that was what he was going to have to do to get at the gear. He was about to release the man from his harness when he stopped and looked down.

On the ground at the base of the tree was an animal. A big animal. Sniffing the ground and now looking up. He knew that animal and it was one he didn't want to see. The grizzly had come to call.

Chapter 12

Gerallt didn't move. He just watched the bear snuffling around the bottom of the tree and showing no inclination to leave. Something needed to be done to make it leave. He pulled the dead man's knife out of its sheaf – it was a nice Ka-Bar. Gathering a bunch of parachute cords in his left hand, he used the knife to cut them. With that handful of cords cut, the body swung free and out from the tree's trunk. There was a jerk when it reached the end of its swing and as it started back, the tree seemed to shake, and the parachute was released from the tree's hold and the body plummeted down. It hit the ground next to the bear who uttered a loud WUMPF and started to run into the rainforest but changed its mind. Instead it ran out of the rainforest and into the parachute, which for some reason had decided to billow at this inopportune moment rather than when it should have. There was another crashing in brush below and Gerallt turned in time to see a dark shape running south on the ground through the trees. *Panther! The panther was stalking ... one of us. Glad I didn't go down first.* Unlike cats who tend to stop as though scoping out the situation when covered with a sheet or blanket, the bear blundered forward and, at least momentarily hit a white wall and tumbled. It was up in a flash and attacking the chute trying to break through. All it succeeded in doing was dragging the body closer to the edge of the rainforest and getting the chute out from the cover of the trees. Then the bear stopped but only for a second before attacking the nylon fabric with its huge claws. The nylon was no match for sharp claws and the bear's power, and a hole big enough to permit the bear's egress was created and it continued its flight away from what it perceived as danger.

Up in the tree, Gerallt knew that time was of the essence now because there were troops around. Troops probably looking for their lost comrade. What he didn't know was that with the beasts around, the troops didn't want to enter the rainforest because they were under strict orders not to interfere with the contest. The three who had shot at him in the pool were being disciplined by doing double guard duty – one tour at the encampment and then one tour at the tunnel entrance. The latter was in the middle of the night and to cap it off they had to walk to and from their posts. They were escorted by an electric pickup truck up the one-mile road from the encampment to the gate and then, having relieved the three on duty, could watch their predecessors being driven back down. At the end of their duty, they could see their replacements coming up in the truck. They then followed it down the mountain road, fortunate for the speed because the road was sand covered they didn't eat the truck's dust.

The parachute had caught on the kapok in such a manner that it could only be seen afar from the top of Prometheus's Aerie (Colina Da Rocha) as Gerallt had done and, as of this time, there were no guards posted on top of the rock hill. One of the reasons was that the climb up took, based on best estimates, half an hour.

Gerallt quickly moved down to the lowest branch and tied a loop in the rope. Putting his foot in the loop he hung himself over the limb, and grabbing the rope with his right hand, let go with his left grabbing the rope as quickly as he could. Letting the rope slip between his hands, he quickly lowered himself to the ground. The body of the parachutist lay crumpled on the ground five feet away and he quickly assessed what he could use in the way of clothing (the jacket, pants, and shoes although the last were too small) and the pack and all the equipment belts. He was about to leave when he stopped and picked up the night vision goggles. *Never know when they'll come in handy.* When he had what he needed, he threw the spear toward the center of the rainforest, coiled the rope and put it over his head as before. Then he headed back around the top of the rainforest to the western side where there was a big strangler fig that he had passed on his way earlier. That tree was old and big enough that the interior was empty, and he could climb up and be hidden from below. His trip to the tree was made without problems as the black bear was either asleep or elsewhere. He knew that he wouldn't be able to check out what the packs contained until the morning light, so once up the tree, he settled himself as comfortably as he could and went to sleep.

Hyma the caracal had watched everything with great interest, especially having never seen a parachute or a bear. She had sensed the black panther at the site, drawn by the same scent of ripening flesh that the bear had been. However, the smell didn't interest Hyma. When the man had gathered what he wanted and gone to the other side of the rainforest, Hyma – again out of curiosity – had followed him. When the man settled himself in the tree, Hyma went hunting and when she had caught and eaten her fill, she came back, found a tree near the man and went to sleep.

Chapter 13

The rainforest wasn't finished with the dead man. Or, at least among the predators, Val Killer, the black panther, wasn't. It had been that odor of the man after two days hanging that had come to the nose of the Val Killer. In the cool of the evening, it had been roused and was, at least was planning on, going to visit the encampment of man again. But this odor was closer and, according to the sense of smell, was basically "fresh meat for the taking."

Val Killer had made his way stealthily through the rainforest but was brought to a halt by two different odors. One was that of man – alive – but mingled with the odor of the dead man meaning they were close together. The panther was close enough to them to know that they were both high in the rainforest. Not a problem because he had no trouble with heights. The other smell was more troubling – something alive, not man, but something unknown and, the panther sensed, something big. Perhaps bigger than he was. He was hungry and would tackle almost anything to obtain food, especially enough to last a day or two, but he was not "in the mood" to tackle something bigger than he was. So the remainder of trip to the prey was done stealthily. Just as he was just getting close enough to get a sense of the competition, Gerallt had cut the parachutist invader loose and the body had come crashing down through the trees. Already on the alert, the suddenness of the noise was enough to frighten him off but not very far. He heard the other animal leaving and the man coming down from the tree. He was creeping stealthily back when the man left, heading away in a direction other than that where the other animal had gone. He wondered if the man was afraid of an encounter. With the man gone and no scent warning of him or his rival being close, the panther approached the tree and found the dead body. It was bigger than the one the previous night but not too big for him to handle. He grabbed an ankle of the body and began dragging it away from the tree and deeper into the rainforest where he would find a suitable place to feast and then store his kill for another day. All that was left of the invader was his parachute and harness, his helmet and assorted paraphernalia that Gerallt hadn't wanted. If any of the other invaders would stumble upon the site, they would be mystified and possibly frightened.

The three invaders who were doing double duty because of their attempt to kill Gerallt in the pool at the bottom of Colina da Rocha were glad when their relief showed up at the tunnel entrance to Vulcan's Forge in the morning of the second day of the predator contest. Once formally relieved, they started down the road, the escorting truck moving slowly despite orders to make them do double time down the mountain road. Thiago Garcia (the driver) knew the three wouldn't have obeyed that order regardless of the consequences and didn't push it. After all, it might be his turn soon and despite the fact that they were paid mercenaries, they were paid well and couldn't afford to lose the income because they had families to support. The three men were all

Venezuelans who had never known each other before signing up as part of Esteves's force for the takeover of São Rochelle. They had become good friends in the short time they had been together and their double duty for shooting and (they thought) killing Gerallt solidified their bond. Alejandro González, Agustin López and Axel Martin were from three different regions in Venezuela and were as different as the regions were. They were known in the company as Los Tres A-migos ("The Three A-migos") with the "A" accented because of their three first names. If you had seen them walking down the mountain and ignored the pickup truck in front of them, they would have looked like three characters from The *Wizard of Oz*, walking down the Yellow Brick Road in search of what they were missing.

Alejandro González was from Ilsa Ratón, a settlement with a population of 3000 in Venezuela's Amazonas State on an island in the Orinoco River in western Venezuela. It was essentially a border town because the left bank of the Orinoco was in Columbia. Alejandro had wanted a better life for himself and had joined the National Bolivarian Armed Forces serving six years before opting out for the more financially lucrative mercenary life. This was his first adventure. He was the tallest of the group and the most physically developed and he have been the Tin Man except he had the heart of a lover.

Agustin López was from Santiago de León de Caracas, the official name of Caracas, Venezuela's capital city, population 5,576,000, located on the Rio Guairá in the northern part of the country. He hated the big city and longed for a more laid-back life in the boonies of Venezuela and saw the Venezuelan military as a means to that end. He was the shortest of the three and the heaviest for his size. In looks he could have been the Cowardly Lion except his bravery was beyond compare.

That leaves Axel Martin to be the scarecrow because he was tall and gangly although not as tall as Alejandro. And unlike the scarecrow, he didn't need brains. He was the smartest of the three, probably the smartest of all the men in the unit if he had chosen to apply himself, but he had other interests. He met Agustin López in boot camp and they made it through together and were fortunate enough to have similar military interests and wound up in the same squad upon graduation. They worked drug trafficking for five years before hearing about the opportunity offered by Esteves. Axel Martin was from Aragua de Barcelona (population 27,025) in the Anzoátegui State which is located in the northeastern part of Venezuela. It was well known for its beaches that attract visitors from all parts of the world. It was on these beaches that Axel got his first taste of life in other parts of the world and started his desire to see as much as he could.

That is exactly what the three were talking about during their mile-long trek back to their encampment after their eight-hour guard duty at the entrance to the volcanic home of the Seven Billionaires.

"If I had their money, just ten percent of the money of one," Axel was saying, "I would…"

"Look," Agustin said, pointing away from the road and down the side of the mountain to the rainforest. "Isn't that a parachute?"

Agustin had spotted the white parachute lying just outside of the rainforest because he was walking on the outside edge of the road. The first rays of the rising sun had illuminated it in such a manner that it seemed to glow against the background of usual green and brown of the island's natural state. The three stopped and looked at it.

"I agree," Alejandro said. "That looks like a chute. Probably Diego's."

"Well, didn't Gutierrez offer a reward?" Agustin said.

"Si," Axel responded excitedly. "Three days of no duty. That would solve our problem. We get the chute and we are off our duty."

"But we have to get it first," Alejandro said looking at the rocky and fairly steep slope down to the site.

Chapter 14

"Come on," Axel said and started running after the pickup waving wildly with his left hand and holding his rifle in his right. Alejandro and Agustin took off after him. Thiago Garcia wasn't paying any attention to the three following the pickup down the mountain because he was looking at the road which was anything but smooth and trying to pick the best path. The first time he knew about the discovery was when Axel wrenched the passenger door open and jumped in. Thiago stepped on the brakes and Alejandro almost ran into the tailgate he was preparing to grab and leap over to get into the truck's bed. Agustin was just two steps behind him.

"You can't be here," Thiago said. "You have to walk. That is the rule. You know…"

"Listen," Axel said. "Forget that. You want three days without duty?"

Thiago stared at Axel uncomprehendingly. "Sure, but I don't get it."

"We find Diego and that's what we get, right?"

"Si, Gutierrez said that."

Axel continued excitedly, "Well, we know where he is, and you take us there and we will cut you in."

"Tell me where to go," Thiago said.

Axel pointed over his right shoulder. Thiago looked down the slope.

"You're nuts."

"It's at the base of the slope next to the rainforest. You figure out how to get there."

Thiago stepped on the gas and drove the truck down the road, Alejandro and Agustin holding on for dear life in the pickup's bed. Near the base of the hill, the road took a right turn and Thiago hardly slowed down almost making a U-turn and going off the road. The terrain was bumpy, and he had to slow down out of necessity enabling Alejandro to stand up and guide the truck by banging on the roof in the direction they needed to go. Ten minutes of bumpy ride and Thiago pulled to a stop, thirty feet from the parachute.

"Pull on up," Axel said.

"No," Thiago said. "There might be one of those predators there."

"You're right," Axel said and opened the door. The four men got out of the truck, weapons at the ready, and walked toward the parachute. They could see the holes made in the chute by the grizzly but had no idea what animal had made them. That bear was halfway up the slope sleeping in a slight depression in the ground he had found and enlarged. He had been awakened by the sound of the truck bouncing across the rough terrain. Now curious and familiar with men because he had been removed from a national park because of his penchant for raiding garbage cans and campsites, he wasn't afraid of them. As for the four, they were now doubly curious about the chute and how it had been damaged and were making their way around it toward the edge of the rainforest where the chute's lines led. It was Agustin who sensed the bear's presence and he looked over his shoulder.

"Dulce madre de Jesús (Sweet mother of Jesus)," Agustin said, whirling around and pointing his rifle at the grizzly who had stopped twenty feet behind them and in the direct path back to the truck. ***"It's the big bear!"***

The other three turned around bringing weapons to bear, but it had been pounded into their heads, especially the three A-migos, that they were not to shoot the predators no matter what. As a result, none of them fired. It seemed to be a standoff until the bear felt the need to assert his rights to the chute since he had "killed" it and he stood on his rear legs and roared while waving his front paws. That was enough for Thiago whose duties were always as driver, never as combatant, and he took off away from the bear which led him straight into the rainforest and into the waiting paws and jaws of the black panther. It had been drawn back to the area by the sounds of the truck and was just defending itself when Thiago entered its area.

The other three were more steadfast and Alejandro, familiar enough with animal behavior through television shows, raised his arms above his head holding the rifle in his left and roaring back at the bear. Axel and Agustin took his cue and did the same. That was too much for the grizzly and he took off south toward the river because he needed some water anyway. The three amigos laughed as they saw the big grizzly hightailing it and were congratulating each other when Axel noticed that Thiago was missing.

"Where did Thiago go?" he asked.

Alejandro looked around and said, "He must be in the rainforest."

They called him but there was no answer. While none of them were enthusiastic about entering the rainforest because of the black panther, they had no choice. They could not go off and leave their comrade. Weapons at the ready, they advanced to the rainforest following the parachute's shrouds. From just under the outstretched branches of the kapok which had held

Diego and his chute for over a day, they could see Thiago's body and the panther bent over it, pulling at Thiago's shirt.

"Remember," Alejandro said as he raised his rifle and the panther looked up and saw the three, "He attacked me."

Just as he was tightening his finger on the trigger, the panther decided he was outnumbered and was gone with one leap, the shot missing. The three amigos hurried to where Thiago lay but his wide-open unblinking eyes told them the whole story as did his bloody neck which the panther had grabbed in his initial rush and that had been all that it had taken. Alejandro took out his walkie talkie and called the base announcing that they had found Diego's chute, but the body was missing. Then he reported that Thiago had been attacked and killed by the black panther which had once again escaped.

General Gutierrez was incensed when he learned that another of his men had been killed by the black panther and he was determined to ensure that it didn't happen again. When the drone watching the black panther had seen the encounter with Thiago, Horus had changed the invader count to thirty, striking Soldado 22 off the list. General Gutierrez alerted the eighteen men of his troops not on duty and marched them to the rainforest where the three amigos awaited him, albeit trepidatiously, not triumphantly as they had hoped. He took their report, not questioning any part especially about Triago's desertion at the time of battle and his resultant death. His orders to his men were specific. "If you see any of those predators, shoot to kill. If you are uncertain whether or not it is a predator, shoot to kill. If it's big and it moves, shoot to kill."

He had them in two lines, eight in the first line three feet apart with the three A-migos in the middle.

There were nine in the second line aligned so that they filled the gaps in the first line and overlapped the ends. Their orders were to move slowly through the rainforest looking at the ground and in the trees for any sign of any of the predators or anything that could be Diego's body. When they reached the other side, which would be the rocks leading down to the water, they were to move south overlapping the first sweep area by three men in the second line and come back. Men in the first line were equipped with knifes or machetes to cut any brush that impeded their progress. General Gutierrez and three of his men, those not on official duty, were waiting thirty feet back from the edge of the rainforest so that they wouldn't be surprised because the searchers were expected to spook at least the panther. All the men except General Gutierrez were armed with rifles and had them at the ready.

Chapter 15

Adam the grizzly was a bit disgruntled at not being able to get into the rainforest to eat because of the men who had at least outnumbered him. Maybe they had those weapons that shot things that put him to sleep and he would wake up in a cage. He was getting used to the place where he now found himself. The plant life was plentiful and tasty, and he had killed and eaten a small animal in the rainforest and it was tasty. Food was plentiful and water - …water could be had in the rainforest but every other day or so he would need to come down to the river to drink and that was where he headed after being chased out of the rainforest. And maybe there were fish in the river. There were fish in the one where he had been. The one thing that seemed to be missing here were the humans and their food. He enjoyed the human food that he got out of the big cans and sometimes from the places where they slept and cooked food. He had not found any of those yet, but he hadn't been here very long.

While he walked, he saw other animals moving in the same direction as he was. Strange animals that he didn't recognize. Some big: the tawny one with the dark mane, the striped white one walking with him yet independently. There were two coyotes, they were no problem for him, and a lobo – big but no problem. They seemed to be moving as a pack – the big lobo in front, then the big coyote followed by the smaller female. He had not seen that before. Trailing behind the two cats was another one, black – he had seen it before. It was big but not a menace. Behind the black cat was the black bear. They had met in the rainforest and the black bear, although big, had seemed to sense the grizzly's superiority and had left the immediate area. He was also not a problem. Down at the pool where they all seemed to be headed, there were two other cats. One was the smallest of all the animals heading to drink, tawny with large ears – definitely not something to worry about. The other was spotted and bigger but not as big as the tawny maned one and the striped one. It also would not be a problem. The black panther, black bear, and caracal needed a good drink of water but had left the rainforest because of the presence of many men.

He was the biggest both in size and weight. If bears could smile he would have because he was quick to realize that he was king of the island unless there was an animal he had not yet met.

His slow amble, showing his supremacy and confidence, got him to the pool last of all the animals who each seemed to be sharing the pool without giving a care about the others. The black bear was in the middle of the line, the lion and the tiger to its right, the canine pack on the left with the caracal to the far side of the lion and tiger. The cheetah was across the river at the far side of the pool and the black panther was on the far side of the pack. Basically unless he wanted to drink from the river which was flowing too fast or wait for things to clear out, he was out of luck. But he was king and didn't need to wait. Heading between the black bear and the pack whom he knew recognized their place, he shouldered his way by the black bear shoving it to its right into the tiger's space. She didn't like the affront from the strange black animal and slashed at it, the bear's black coat absorbing the blow which was meant more as a warning anyway.

"Uh, oh, looks like a big brawl might be brewing," Issaack said.

"Zat's okay," Ramiro said, "Zis big bear, he handlez zem all. I gotz him!" said Ramiro boldly and confidently although inside he was not quite not as certain because of his bad luck and the bear was the last of his bets.

The black bear, already intimidated by the grizzly, hurriedly backed away from the tiger and bumped smack into the grizzly who was just taking his first drink. Infuriated by the affront to his assumed status, the grizzly turned to the black bear who was starting to move away from the pool and lashed out with the paw, catching the black bear on its right flank and drawing blood. Not a deep wound but deep enough. That was enough for the black bear who had both drunk its fill and knew that he stood no chance against the grizzly, so he took off at a lope heading for the rainforest.

The pack, sensing that something was about to happen and having had a good morning hunt, were not eager for an all-out brawl and started to move away. The five jungle cats (lion, tiger, caracal, black panther, and cheetah) were used to decorum at a watering hole with all sharing the water – whether prey or predator – and the five acting as one took umbrage at the grizzly's manner and simultaneously attacked the grizzly. The frontal attack by the lion and tiger was held off momentarily as the grizzly rose on his rear legs and roared and waved his paws intimidatingly. That opened his back for an attack by the black panther who with one great leap sank its claws into the grizzly's shoulders and its teeth into the fur in the neck getting mostly a mouth full of hair but some skin.

The pack hadn't traveled very far and the wolf, always aching for a good fight, turned back and ran and bit the grizzly's right rear lower leg. The grizzly dropped down on all fours and whirled to face the attack from the rear giving the lion and tiger ample space to get at the grizzly with both teeth and claws. The black panther had managed to hang on with its claws during the bear's change of position, pulled loose a mouthful of fur and skin, spat it out and sank its teeth into the bare spot getting more skin than fur this time. The cheetah had made it across the lip of the pool by now and attacked the grizzly's left haunch. The two coyotes joined the fray jumping in and biting at the grizzly's front legs and were joined by the wolf who sensed this as a better avenue of attack for the time being. These canines were so quick, and the grizzly was more concerned with the cats that the pack escaped injury.

"MY GOD," screamed Monica. ***"They're ganging up on Adam."***

"Come on, Adam," Gloria said, having also placed a bet on him.

The cats' attack was ferocious and there were so many of them that, with the canines, the grizzly quickly was becoming overwhelmed. He stopped fighting and with all four legs on the ground shook himself like he did after being in the river washing. That sudden effort knocked loose the black panther and the cheetah. Then when the male coyote started to dash in, the grizzly swiped a paw and knocked him away, a severe gash on his left side. Moving before the cats could reassert themselves, the grizzly turned toward the rainforest and that was when Smoky the black bear struck. He had turned back, attracted by the sounds of the battle, and had been waiting for an opening and slashed the grizzly's face with what in a boxing venue would be called a strong right cross. The caracal been waiting for an opportunity so that, with the black panther gone from the grizzly's back, she leapt up and attacked the grizzly's head, striking at its eyes from behind.

Quickly blinded in its left eye, and unable to shake off the caracal with another shake although this one not nearly as hard, the grizzly tried a maneuver that only desperation could call for and it was a fatal mistake. He tried to roll over and either crush the caracal or knock it off. Neither happened because the caracal sensed the movement and jumped over the grizzly's head and landed on the back of the black bear and then leapt to the ground. The attempted roll was fatal to the grizzly as it exposed his softer underbelly and the lion and tiger were at it in a flash and the black panther attacked from the other side. They were quickly joined by the canines and the black bear in attacking the grizzly's head and he lost sight in the other eye. The lion quickly opened a rip in the underbelly and then innards started pouring forth upon the ground along with gallons of blood. It wasn't long before the grizzly lost all energy and became a feast for the surviving members of the billionaires' predators. At least some of them. The black bear had no interest in the feast because it had plenty of food back in the rainforest where, at least for the time being, it was relatively safe. The canines felt that there would be a better time when the felines had feasted, and the male coyote needed to lie down and lick his wound, so the pack didn't travel far but far enough that should the cats come after them, they had time to escape. The cheetah and the caracal likewise felt uncomfortable eating alongside the three cats which were twice their size and could turn on them at any time. The cheetah returned across the lip of the pond where it lay down and cleaned itself and the caracal followed the black bear back toward the rainforest stopping on the way to stalk and catch an unwary small mammal.

Ramiro was stunned.

"He gone," he said sullenly.

"Looks like it," Issaack said.

"I don't underztand what happened."

"He picked a fight at the wrong time. I think he broke some law of the wild. In Africa, many animals share watering holes peacefully. Hunting is done away from watering holes."

"But ze crocodilez attackz at watering holez."

"True," Issaack said. "But we don't have crocodiles or alligators here."

Ramiro was silent, watching the feast for a minute and then getting up and leaving, his shoulders showing the sag of a beaten man.

Chapter 16

Like the panther, the noise of the truck as it drew near had attracted Gerallt's attention. He was sitting in the strangler fig tree looking at the things that he had quickly snatched from Diego's body. It was just dawn or a little after and the light was dim, but he was interested in what he could use. He had already donned the pants, and tee shirt – both were snug but at least they fit. He also had on the socks but had eschewed the boxer shorts when he had taken the clothes off. The clothing was jungle camouflage, so it would certainly help him in the rainforest. He had taken the shoes apart, undoing the laces and then cutting out the toe. Then he cut off the high top so he had more of a sandal. His toes hung over a bit but at least he wasn't going to have to worry about rough terrain slowing him down. He had looked at the rifle and was certain that it was in working condition and the ammunition was sufficient for a beginning but wouldn't last long in a firefight against bigger odds like three or two to one. He was about to open the pack to see what goodies were in it when he heard the truck. It was far away but coming toward the rainforest. He climbed down from his nest carrying the rifle and ran back toward the east side of the rainforest. It was ten minutes from his position. An easy run if he had been in better shape. But god knows how long he had been medicated and feed intravenously he supposed. Still he made the run fairly quickly. He slowed when he heard the yelling and was stealthily approaching the area where he had found the parachutist when he heard the shot. He stopped, seeking cover, but watching and he saw the black panther run past him on the right and was glad he hadn't gone directly to the site.

He waited several minutes and there was no more action, so he moved toward the site by first going north and then back southeast. There was another body lying there, rifle beside him, bloody neck and claw marks on the shirt. Moving east to the edge of the tree line, he saw three soldiers (what else should he call them because he knew no better) standing by the truck. He watched for about five minutes and then he saw about twenty men heading for the truck from the far side of the open area and they were moving double time. Leading them was another truck bouncing across the rough ground. When the second truck stopped beside the other, a man got out and the three soldiers snapped to attention and saluted. They talked but not loud enough for him to understand what they were saying. When the other men arrived, they arranged themselves in two lines with the rear line filling the gaps in the front line. The center of the lines was directly opposite the area where the body lay. The leader, who had come in the second truck, gave some instructions and shouted a command and the men started toward the rainforest, weapons at the ready.

Gerallt had sensed what would be their goal before but wanted to be certain that they were going to search the rainforest. Their main target was undoubtedly the missing man but could also be either the black panther or him. He wished he had the help of that little drone – what was it he had called himself … parakeet or Tyrant? Not that it mattered, it wasn't here, and it was time to leave and Gerallt turned and moved quickly deeper into the rainforest heading back for his hidey hole in the fig.

He moved faster than the searchers would because he knew where he was going and wasn't looking for someone – or something – hiding, possibly lying in wait. But it would take a madman – or a hungry predator – to face twenty-odd men. Once safely in his bower, he gathered his gear and climbed down from the tree. Shouldering the pack, he headed west out of the rainforest and then north along the rocks which led down to the water so that he was below the level of the ground. The men would be moving slowly so he would have time, but he would have to find a place to hide if they were to branch out in their search. Fortunately the grade wasn't that steep here and footing was difficult but not treacherous. As he moved north he could see that the terrain got more difficult at the level he was traveling so he moved down the slope in front of the bigger rocks. In fact, for a distance of about one hundred feet, the boulders got immense. When he reached the edge of the boulder field he was about fifty feet lower than the ground at the edge of the rainforest and as he passed the first boulder, the trees became virtually invisible except for an occasional tree top. He knew the trees to be kapoks which towered above the other trees in any rainforest. About twenty-five (twenty-seven and a half to be accurate) feet into the boulder field, Gerallt was passing a big boulder when he felt coolness across his toes. He looked down and saw nothing. Looking to the right, he saw a blackness between the big boulder and the next one, it was low and about two feet high. Shrugging the pack off, he got down on his knees and looked into the space. All he saw was blackness, but he could feel a coolness against his face and knew it was a draft of air coming from between the rocks and that could only mean one thing –

a cave with another entrance. He took the rope coil off his shoulder and tied one end to the pack. From the back of the utility belt he was wearing he unstrapped a cover and removed a flashlight. Turning it on, he wormed his way into the darkness holding the light in his left hand and using his right and his feet to move forward. About six feet in, the ceiling started to slope upward and after twenty feet, it was high enough to stand. He pulled the pack the rest of the way in and looked around using the flashlight.

He was in a domed room about twenty feet wide, fifteen feet deep and six to eight feet tall. If that's all it was and they came looking for him, it was a death trap. All they had to do was throw in a grenade in or empty a couple of magazines and he was a dead man. So before he made the decision to stay, he would have to be certain that there was another way out. The cool draft he felt indicated that there was, but where was it and was it big enough for him to get out?

Chapter 17

General Gutierrez was involved in talking to Teniente Lautaro Zapatero, his third in command, and didn't hear the third pickup truck which came across the field at a slower pace. With its electric motor, it didn't make nearly the noise because it was not bouncing as much as the previous two vehicles had. The first thing he knew about it was when the truck's door slammed. And the slam had been intentional. Ramiro Esteves was mad, and he wanted The General and the other people with him to know it.

The General turned at the sound of the door and, if it were possible because of his dark skin, he blanched.

"Senor Esteves, to what do we owe this honor?"

He sounded sincere, but he knew that he was probably in tremendo bollo. He was from Caracas in eastern Venezuela and there "tremendo bollo" meant "deep trouble" but in the western part of Venezuela where Alejandro González was from, he would use the term to praise a woman's genitals. Strange difference in meaning, but that is how different the parts of Venezuela were.

"What in the hell are you doing?" Ramiro said as he approached until he was toe-to-toe with The General. At that distance Ramiro's head was bent back at a forty-five-degree angle to look up at The General who was at least six inches taller than he was. It didn't matter to Ramiro because he had just seen his third pick in the

Deadliest Predator Contest turn into a big loser and he was ready for a fight.

The General was a man used to fighting. Not combat, not physical but words. He was a second generation military man brought up strictly by his father who was a combat hardened veteran and wanted – demanded – that his son be the same. So he sent his son to physical training at a young age and off to a military prep school at age fifteen. The General didn't really want the military life, but he had no choice. Though he tried hard, he just didn't have what it took and when he made captain, his commanding officer laid it on the line. "Captain Gutierrez, you are a decent officer but lacking in skills that you should have by this time. I had to fight to get you to the rank of captain with the understanding that we would have this talk. Simply put, this is as far as you go. My advice – and it is for your own good – is that you seek your place in life in some other occupation." The General was a man who accepted criticism and always tried to improve but knew that he was going no further, so he resigned and searched for a military job elsewhere because the military was all he knew. He picked up a short-term position in Africa and did well under trying circumstances with a lot of luck. But when the position with Ramiro Esteves was posted, The General jumped at it when others didn't because of who Ramiro Esteves was. With a good recommendation from his commanding officer in Africa, he got the job. And when he went looking for men, he picked qualified but not necessarily combat hardened men because he didn't expect any combat. And now push was coming to shove and he was going to have to stand up for his decision and his men.

"We are trying to find Soldado Diego Sanchez," The General said and pointed at the parachute still lying on the ground. "That's his parachute, but his body and most of his equipment are missing. And another of my men, Soldado Thiago Garcia, was killed by your black panther when my men went into the rainforest to search for Soldado Sanchez."

"You're certain about that?" Ramiro's tone seemed to have calmed down a little bit.

"Yes, one of my men took a shot at the panther," General Gutierrez said and quickly added, "but missed. That was intentional because he was only trying to scare it away."

He didn't know whether or not Esteves was mollified, but it was out and there was nothing that he could do.

"What are your men going to do if they encounter one of the predators?" Ramiro said, sounding on the attack again. "There are four …" he paused a moment when he realized that recently it was really three "… four of them who have taken shelter in there."

"Four?" General Gutierrez was incredulous.

"Yes," Ramiro said and held up his hand showing four fingers. "The black panther," and he pushed one finger down. "The grizzly," a second finger followed the first. "The black bear," a third finger joined the other two. "And the caracal," and his hand was now a fist which he was shaking in the general's face. "And if one of those animals is killed by your men, you will join it and I will be the one to pull the trigger."

With that, Ramiro turned around and had started back to the truck when The General spoke, "Sir, the body of Soldado Sanchez has provided food for at least the black panther. You want the predators to attack each other for food not my men. If we can find the body and retrieve it, then that takes a source of food away from them."

Ramiro stopped and spun around pointing a finger at The General. "Fine, do that. But I warn you again. ***None – Not One*** – of those predators is to be killed by your men." Then he turned and almost stomped back to the truck where his driver was patiently waiting. When Juan José Orejon (Soldado 25) had been assigned the duty of being the driver for Ramiro Esteves, he had been ecstatic but now he was wishing that he was one of the men in the rainforest. Even if he was unarmed and facing all four of those creatures, whatever they were.

As soon as Ramiro was out of his face, Gutierrez turned to his third in command and said, "Tell the men that when they find and retrieve the body of Soldado Sanchez, they can terminate the search."

The word was passed and fifteen minutes later, halfway through the rainforest on the first full sweep, Axel Martin spotted the corpse in a Ceiba. Though he wasn't thrilled with the idea, he and Agustin climbed the tree with a rope and lowered the grisly-looking corpse down. It was put in a body bag of which the supply was getting short and taken back to the compound where a coffin was made, and the body buried beside the others in a full but shortened ritual military ceremony. The firing of ornamental salutes was one of the items not performed.

The oldest tree in the rainforest was on the northern edge about a third of the way from the western edge to the eastern edge. It was a strangler fig and because it was on the beginning of the slope of the volcano, it stood taller than the trees around it. But it was so old that it didn't have long to live. It had only survived the hurricane because it was sheltered by the younger trees around it. At its base it was surrounded by rainforest vegetation where small animals loved to hide. The search party had been gone half an hour and any indication that there had been a parachute on the ground and a body lying at the base of the big kapok had been covered up. The foliage on the north (volcano) side of the tree looked as though a wind was blowing it, but there was no wind. Then an arm clothed in jungle camouflage could be seen coming out of the tree and soon a similarly clad shoulder and then a head and, with a mighty heave, a whole body appeared. Gerallt took a quick look around and then disappeared back into the tree.

He had gone back to the mouth of the cave and used his shirt to sweep the ground and cover up any tracks. He had gone into the cave feet first removing as much trace evidence of his entering the cave as he could. Then he had shouldered the pack and checked the cavern room to be certain that he had left no obvious trace and gone to find the source of the draft. As he progressed deeper into the tunnel, he could feel the draft grow stronger and after fifteen minutes walking on a slight uphill grade the darkness of the area ahead had lightened somewhat and in three more minutes he had found a way out. Not surprisingly like the room behind the waterfall, someone else had been here first. Helping him spot the exit was a ladder hanging on the right side of the tunnel. Like the one in the waterfall cave, it was made with hemp ropes but there were two ropes and separating them were wooden rungs kept in place by knots in the rope. Also behind the rope ladder was a natural shelf on which were a blanket and some wooden sticks. He picked one up and found that it was obviously a torch, because one end was heavily covered with an orange tarry substance. Gerallt couldn't help but wonder how many young ladies had lost their maidenheads in this hideaway.

He climbed the ladder carefully and found himself inside a strangler fig. There was a hole opposite the side the ladder was on and he had taken a quick look around and hurried back into the tree. To the east he had seen the entrance to the volcanic basin and the three guards who seemed more interested in something one of them had found than watching for any aggressors. Still Gerallt couldn't chance being seen because, for all intents and purposes as far as the island's military – and hopefully anyone else – was concerned, he was dead.

The ladder was fastened securely to the strangler fig with nails but continued on up. Curious and wanting – needing – to know as much about his new home as he could, he climbed the ladder. From where it ended about fifteen feet further up, he got a much better view of the volcano's entrance, although he was still about thirty feet below it and sheltered by the branches and leaves. Satisfied, he returned to the tunnel and, leaving the pack but taking the rifle and two of the torches, he proceeded further into the tunnel using the flashlight and noting that on the roof of the tunnel there were signs that torches had been used for light.

As he walked he kept his eyes on the floor ahead of him and it was fortunate that he did so because a dark spot across the corridor's width turned out to be an almost perfect circular hole. Gerallt stopped and directed the light down but other than relatively smooth walls, all that he could see was blackness. He listened and all that he could hear was the faint sound of running water. Using a match in a waterproof case that he had found in the utility belt, he lit one of the torches that he was carrying, and it ignited into a brightly burning torch. Stretching his arm out over the hole and leaning forward he dropped the torch and watched and listened as it fell.

Its flame seemed to dance as the torch rotated lengthwise as it plummeted deeper into the earth. The flame grew smaller and smaller until it went out and then, after a short pause, he heard the sound of it hitting water. He thought that the hole was ten to twelve feet across in the middle and probably four or five along the wall. He could jump the four or five feet, but he would be close to the wall and if he hit it … splash and goodbye.

That's the end of my exploration, he thought. Then suddenly there started a rumbling. Low at first but getting louder. A pulsing sound that started as a whisper and grew into a roar. It was coming from the hole and he looked over into the hole, shining his light down. What he saw both amazed and terrified him. At first, he had seen nothing but blackness. Then something glistened in the light's beam and disappeared. Then, on the upbeat of the sound, the glistening reappeared, and he realized what was happening. Water had come up filling the hole to within twenty feet of the top and now was sinking back in time with the pulsing: coming up as the sound grew and then receding as the sound decreased and it was getting closer and closer to the top of the hole. The pulsing was getting quicker and quicker. The water, higher and higher. And he turned and ran.

Chapter 18

Gerallt ran down the corridor as though he was running for his life and, as far as he was concerned, he was. The crescendo of the roar increased quickly and suddenly it was a deafening roar. There was an equally deafening crash. He knew that meant that the water had smashed against the ceiling of the corridor, but this time the roar continued. He didn't chance to look behind him because he knew that all he would see was a wall of water bearing down on him. And he was correct because suddenly he was engulfed in its wetness thrusting him forward and he was falling, not onto the rock floor of the corridor but into a rushing cushion of water that bore him quickly down the corridor. Then as suddenly as it had appeared, it ebbed and left him – not high and dry but low and wet on the rock floor of the tunnel. Not only that but the water had ripped both the flashlight and the rifle from his hands and he was left in pitch blackness. And to make things worse, the way the water had twisted and tumbled him in that brief moment he wasn't certain which way he was facing and, worst of all, where he was in the tunnel.

In an effort to get his bearings, he quieted his breathing and listened intently trying to catch the smallest sound. And finally one came – the slight sound of a small rivulet of water running somewhere nearby. He reached out his right hand searching from above his head to his right, fingers gliding lightly across the floor.

Nothing. Then he did the same with his left and about sixty degrees from above his head his fingers found that little rivulet. He determined that the dying rivulet was running by his fingers toward his elbow. He had, indeed, been turned around and was facing back at the hole because the slope of tunnel he had been following was uphill. And as quickly as his fingers had found the rivulet, it was gone, the last of the water flowing down the corridor always seeking the lower ground.

Gerallt moved to his right until he found the wall and then he got to his feet, keeping in contact with the wall and then and only then did he turn to face what he had determined to be the direction of the entrance to the cave – the one he had first entered in the boulder field. He had no idea where the light or the rifle had gone but knew that they were between him (or at least the hole) and the entrance. That was unless the surge of water had carried them completely down the hall and out into the boulder field. As he thought about all this a sensation hit him that came as a surprise. He was wet, but he wasn't cold. The water had been warm, hot but not scalding. The underground river must flow close to the remaining fiery furnace of the volcano. Close enough and long enough to heat it and somewhere it had been given the impetus to rise through the hole. To him that could only mean one thing: although dormant, the volcano was still functioning as a heat source and that meant that someday it could come out of its dormancy.

As he had been thinking these thoughts, he had been walking along the corridor, left hand always in contact with the wall. He hoped that it would come in contact with the rope ladder which seemed to have survived, for want of a better term, prior tidal wavesw. The only other option, unless he was facing the wrong way, was that he would find himself at the front of the cave. As he walked, he realized that the darkness was thinning – that somewhere ahead (and he hoped not too far) light from the outside was making its way inside. Whether through the low entrance from the boulder field or down the hole from the strangler fig, he didn't care. Then the light seemed to penetrate faster and cut the darkness quicker. He realized that the tunnel made a slight turn and he was approaching the top of the bend and would soon know which hole was the one emitting the light.

And just as suddenly as that thought was became vivid in his mind, he reached that point of the turn, and he knew that it was the strangler tree hole. He breathed a sigh of relief because here also was his pack – unless the water had washed it way from its mooring – and a supply of torches. He already knew that he still had the supply of waterproof matches because the container was safely in a buttoned pocket in his pants. Once at the foot of the strangler tree, he got three torches, sticking two into the utility belt, and lit the third, then he turned and started back to the hole, curious as to the depth of the water. As he walked, he looked for anything that might have been swept away, and the first thing he found was the rifle. He knew that he would have to clean it and didn't even bother trying to see if it worked but slung it across his back and kept moving. Soon he could see the darkness of the hole ahead and was surprised to see the glistening of water in it. And there was something else in the water – something dark and long lengthwise across the width of the tunnel. He started running as he realized that the water in the hole was ebbing and when he reached the hole he threw himself flat on the floor at the edge of the hole and reached out with his left hand and grabbed what he had seen and pulled it toward him. It was heavy, and he knew that if he didn't get a better grasp on it, it would be gone. He laid the torch on the floor with the flame over the edge of the hole and grabbed whatever it was with both hands and pulled it up and to the edge of the hole and then he realized that it was a crudely made ladder. He knew that he needed the ladder and so he wiggled backward the best that he could, as quickly as he could, pulling the ladder past him on the right side. The wood from which it was made wasn't thick, but it was heavy, and he knew that it was waterlogged from being in the water for a long time. Finally, with one last effort he yanked, and the ladder slid safely out of the hole. He grabbed the torch and rolled over exhausted, the torch illuminating the ceiling of the corridor. For a moment, he stared at what he saw and then he burst out laughing because on the ceiling, crudely etched in the stone, was a heart and inside the heart were two names joined by a plus sign: José and Mia. And he guessed there was only one reason for it being on the ceiling at this point because this is where Mia expressed her true love for José by giving him the thing she could only give once – her virginity.

Chapter 19

It was late in the morning and the heat was starting to build. For the animals that meant two things. Shade and water, not necessarily in that order. Although they had basically drunk their fill in the morning. Now they were looking for sleep and with full bellies from the grizzly, sleep was looking good. Although a few of them – the lion and the tiger, and the cheetah – felt that a bedtime snack – and some water to wash it down – might be just the thing. So they were making their way back toward the pool.

It was a lazy walk. No hurry. The sun was beating down. And suddenly there was a low rumble and around Prometheus's Aerie (Colina da Rocha), the ground began to tremble just a bit. It didn't bother the birds or the other animals to whom São Rochelle was home and had been for all their lives. But this time – for the first time – something was different. As before the rumbling pulsed, up and down, faster and faster, louder and louder and then as the intensity increased it reached a spot where the sound was usually stable for a while but not this time. The rumble became a roar and all the animals who were close enough to Prometheus's Aerie to be affected looked at the hill and saw a spout of water that went about thirty feet into the air. When the water fell back, the remnants splashed on the rock surface of Prometheus's Aerie, running down the sides of the hill or being sucked back into the hole in the mesa top of the hill. There were some new pieces of stone left lying on the surface and the hole caused by Gerallt's and the cougar's combined weight hitting the top and cracking it open (which was going to happen anyway, just not for another few months or maybe a year) became a little bigger.

"What was that?" Waldo said, being at that minute the only member of the Bundle in the theater. "Horus?"

"I think we know what caused the Aerie's strange sound," Horus said. "I am locating some video. Ahh, here it is. It's far away, but this is all I have."

The video currently on the big screen of the theater was replaced with a shot of the lion proceeding toward the pond at the base of the hill. He stopped and looked at the hill and the tiger did also, and both the drones changed their filming altitude. The lion's drone started toward Prometheus's Aerie as fast as it could go, gaining altitude as it went. When the eruption occurred the drone was about a quarter mile away and closing fast. The waterspout was gone when the drone reached the mesa and, but it was able to capture the water bubbling (there was the sound of burbling) at the top of the hole and then slowly, with less pulsing receding down and stabilizing about three feet below the mesa's surface.

"So that sound from the area was simply water," Waldo said. The door to the theater opened and Issaack, Gloria, Monica and Harvey Gladstone entered.

Horus started the video rerunning again – the first of about thirty reruns in the next twenty minutes to give everyone a chance to see it as big as possible.

"The area around the hole is quite warm," Horus said. "The temperature shown on the drone was about 120° F but dropping fast. I do not have a thermometer to drop into the water, but I would say it is quite hot. I conjecture that somewhere between the Vulcan's Forge and Prometheus's Aerie, there is a big cavern above the lava bed and the water comes into that, being heated as it sits there, then as it starts to boil, the pressure builds and erupts. The water is ejected through tunnels which are possibly old lava tubes and pushed with great force up against the top of the Aerie. Today however, there is no cap and the water just shot up."

"Well, if you are correct," Waldo was thinking out loud, "and it sounds reasonable, there are two exits to the pot, one where the water comes in and then the one leading to the Aerie. The expulsion should also go out the entrance tunnel. Where does that go?"

"I don't know," Horus answered, *for certain,* "but perhaps someday we will find out."

Chapter 20

Gerallt surmised that the flashlight had been washed out of the cave and, despite the fact that he felt the search of the rainforest had been called off for some reason, he didn't want to risk going outside. Besides, it was important that he know as much about the cave as he could if he was to make it his home for the time being. Getting up, he turned the ladder so that the rung side – the side easiest to walk on – was facing up, with the ladder lying on the surface of the tunnel floor. Then he walked from one end to the other, using the rungs as stepping stones and back again, putting his full weight on each rung as he went. He was surprised that every rung held. Then he turned the ladder so that the rung side was against the right wall of the corridor. Then, keeping his weight pressed down on the ladder for balance, he slid the ladder across the hole until it was spanning the hole as evenly as he could get it, and he turned the ladder so that it lay flat, rung side up.

Mentally crossing his fingers, he walked across the hole on his providentially provided ladder bridge. Satisfied that he now had a bridge for the hole, he continued his exploration beyond the hole. For the first twenty feet or so, the floor of the corridor was as smooth as the other side of the hole, but then it became rougher and he realized that the water must have been erupting and running down the corridor for ages smoothing it out. It was smooth for the twenty feet or so because the water spread that far but went no further. He moved quickly but carefully because he wasn't certain how long the torches would last, and he had a limited supply until he figured out a way to make some or found the flashlight and it still worked. The flashlight's battery was solar, so he could recharge it by leaving it in the strangler fig tree – provided the flashlight still worked when he found it. This side of the tunnel was steeper and curvier, and it was twenty minutes until he got a glimmer of the "light at the end of the tunnel." Then he hurried toward the end. Just as he got within ten feet of the point where the roof lowered, and he would have to crawl, a buzzing noise alerted him to company. He came to a stop just as the first drone he had encountered in the water on top of the rock hill came into the cave.

"You must be very careful," the voice from the drone said. "You cannot go outside here in the daytime and it will be dangerous at night because of the guards."

"Whose guards?" Gerallt asked and then added questioningly, "Are you Tyrant the parakeet?"

"They are under command of a man named Matias Gutierrez," Horus answered without answering. "He has given himself the rank of general."

"Who is he?" Gerallt asked "and how are you connected with him?"

"He is a mercenary hired by Ramiro Esteves to take over this island"

"I knew that mab i ast (son of a bitch) was in this," Gerallt snarled. "Where is he so that I can end his miserable life?" and he started for the entrance, but the drone moved blocking him and Gerallt stopped.

"As I said before," Horus said, "It would not be wise for you to exit this cave in the daylight. The entrance is covered by some light shrubbery and no one else knows it is here. But if they see you, they will find this cave and then it will be over for you. There are too many of them to take on at one time."

Gerallt nodded agreement. "Beside, my rifle got waterlogged and I haven't cleaned it yet."

"Waterlogged!" Horus said. "How did that happen?"

Gerallt explained about the hole and the water pulsing.

"Ah," Horus said. "I've been wondering about the earthquaking at Prometheus's Aerie and that explains it."

"What's Prometheus's Aerie?"

"That rock hill where you crashed through the rock and ended up in that water – we call it Prometheus's Aerie but the people who lived here until they were evacuated before Hurricane Davido called it Colina da Rocha or Boulder Hill in Portuguese. We have noticed the earth shaking in that area every couple of days and I have been unable to pinpoint it until today. Another drone monitoring the lion was down there and then the shaking started, so we got a video of water shooting up out of the hole you made. That explains how the water gets up there to come out and make the river. I certainly hope that the hole in the top of Prometheus's Aerie doesn't affect the water's flow. We need it for ourselves"

"That's interesting," Gerallt said. "I forgot to mention that the water was hot and that probably has some effect."

"Undoubtedly," Horus agreed.

"I understand that I shouldn't go outside, but can I at least look?"

"Yes, but please be careful."

Gerallt walked and then crawled to the end of the tunnel because the inlet end was not as high as the inside of the tunnel. That puzzled him and he held the torch around and discovered that here were two other old entrances one to the right and one to the left which probably over the years had gotten filled with debris from the crater's walls or maybe had gotten plugged during some eruption. This only took a few minutes and when he got to the end, which, as Horus had said, was hidden by local shrubs which providentially had taken a root hold on the volcano's rocky surface and grown sufficiently so that they covered the tunnel's entrance. He was about thirty feet above the floor of the volcano and was looking down at Vulcan's Roost.

"What's that?" he asked and Horus quickly explained from the very beginning but in very concise terms.

"So that evening attack was just a feint … just testing defenses?"

"Yes," said Horus.

"So I didn't need to kill that man?"

"No."

"I'm sorry," Gerallt said.

"Don't be," Horus said. "You had no way of knowing. If you hadn't done it, then either Hansel or Gretel would have."

"They didn't know?"

"No. Only Issaack, Siegfried and I knew – or to be truthful, we felt that they were just probes."

"Okay, I understand about Issaack and Siegfried. But what do you do?"

"I run everything."

"Everything? And there is a drone for each of the predators?"

"Yes, and several watching the encampment."

"Impossible," Gerallt said. "You'd have to be a supercomputer to do that."

"Now, I have to go," Horus said. "Remember that you can't be seen. If you see one of the predators, get away quickly because some of the Bundle are always watching the predators and they are always being filmed. I can try to keep you out of the video but can't promise. Once they learn you are alive they will know I have been lying to them and … well, I don't know what they'll do. They have bets on who will win. Esteves was especially irritated that the grizzly died. He had a lot of money on him to win. Oh, and on the hyena also. That was the first to die."

Horus decided that to tell Gerallt that Ramiro had bet on him would be counterproductive.

"Wrong bets," Gerallt said. "He was right from the beginning. Man is the biggest predator and right now Esteves is the biggest prey because I am going to kill him."

"I trust you will. You had a hand in killing two of the predators also. That's four. The hyena was first. More of them will die because they are getting hungry again. The hyena went fast because the lion and tiger got to it after the coyotes and wolf. The grizzly was a feast, but they'll be hungry again. The black panther is going after the mercenaries. He was a man-eater anyway. The black bear is happy in the rainforest with the vegetation, at least for now. The caracal, the coyotes …?

"Caracal? What's that?"

"A small cat from Asia. You had an encounter with it early the first night when you fell, and it is in the rainforest. Anyway it, the coyotes and possibly the wolf can survive on birds and small animals, but that supply will be drawn down quickly." Horus said. "But for now, you have to worry about those mercenaries. I can't control them and don't know what they're going to do. Take care and be careful."

And just like that the drone flew out of the cave. Gerallt had no choice but to return to the strangler fig hole, repair and clean his gear and get ready to take on a numerically superior force.

Chapter 21

Of all the animals, Deva the snow leopard had not made its way to the island's water sources either in the rainforest or at the river and he was thirsty. More thirsty than hungry and he was also hot. When he had come out of his cage, he had headed up the volcano because he had smelled the grizzly and the black bear and didn't know the smell but knew they were big. At that point, he was not at all interested in a fight. Water, a cooler environment, and food were his priorities and he sensed water higher on the slope that had come from some rain two days before where water had gathered in a small pool sheltered by rocks. Although the water was evaporating in the heat of the day, it wasn't directly in the sun and there was still some there. And because of the position of the sun, there were similar pools on the crater side of the volcano and the snow leopard could get there. And it was cooler on that side of the crater, so his wanderings had taken him up the side of the Vulcan's Forge where he found water. He was almost to the top when the heat of the sun drove him to seek shelter behind some rocks and sleep through the heat of that first afternoon. Later, in the relative cool of the second night, he had continued his upward search and reached the rim of the volcano. He could sense the that the interior of the volcano's cone was cooler. Therefore he wandered the rim looking for a passage down away from the sun as it was beginning to come up as that full first night of freedom was turning into day. And fortunately for the snow leopard there were small mammals living in the small nooks and crannies of the volcano and he was able to somewhat sate his hunger with them and his thirst with the water it found. As the sun came up, he made his way down the crater's wall until he found a place to sleep in the shade for most of the day.

In the late afternoon, he was up and about and continued his wanderings. He smelled food down near the bottom of the hill and being hungry headed that way. As he neared the crater floor he saw that the "food" was man and, although he had eaten man only once – a dead climber he had chanced upon – Deva was certainly hungry enough and began to approach more stealthily. His path took him behind some vegetation where he felt a cool breeze, more a slight motion in the air, and discovered a hole in the crater wall. The opening was easily big enough for him, and he walked in. Smells were strong here, both water and food but again the food was man. As he wandered down the lava tube, the smells grew stronger and finally he arrived at a blockage in his path – a hole in the floor. In the hole, he smelled water, but the water was far away, and he ignored it. Jumping the hole was easy and he proceeded with the smell of food growing stronger.

Deva noticed the darkness in the tunnel starting to recede, but the reason for the change never crossed his mind – it was simply an occurrence and was just part of his life. What he did notice was that the smell of food was strong and there was noise. Deva moved carefully but felt no need to hide and, because of the nature of the lava tube, there was no need to do so. Suddenly, though not unexpectedly, the man came into view. He was sitting cross-legged on the floor of the tube, working with something with his hands. On the wall of the tube above his head was fire, a hot burning man thing that Deva didn't like. But it was above and not held by the man, so it was safe. The man did something and then held a long object in one hand and looked at it. He put an end of the long thing against his shoulder and was looking at it closely, his head against it and he was moving it side to side.

Gerallt had searched through the back and found some MRE (Meals Ready to Eat) and had eaten one to help his hunger but knew there he should not overdo food at this point. So he had turned to cleaning his rifle. He had just finished cleaning the rifle for the second time and was satisfied with its condition. He put the stock against his shoulder and was sighting though it as though he was hunting, moving the barrel side to side from the bottom of the tube toward the top and then he stopped. Almost directly in the crosshairs of the sight was something unexpected. Something that instantly made him wish that he had at least one bullet in the chamber. He wasn't certain of the exact type, but it was cat and it was big. Definitely not a housecat.

In one swift movement, he was on his feet, rifle in one hand and magazine in the other, and he was yelling at the top of his lungs.

Deva jumped back when the man suddenly arose and started yelling. He was frightened. The man was standing there shaking the stick in one hand and something in the other. Then he put the two together and was pointing the stick at him. He didn't know what it was, but he knew – just, knew – that it wasn't good, so he turned and ran back up the lava tube. Ran as though his life depended on it.

And if it had not been that place and that time, it might have been but Gerallt suddenly realized that shouting and shooting were two things that he didn't want to do. Especially the shooting. He had slammed the magazine into the chamber and pointed the rifle at the cat having no intention of shooting. It was more a show of bravado than anything else. And the cat turned and ran.

Where had it come from and where was it going? Those were two important questions. He knew that it must be one of the predators that had somehow wandered and gotten into his lava tube but how? Was there another entrance? He hadn't seen one, but then he hadn't always been looking. He turned and got the torch from the wall and went after the cat. He had to know where it had come from, where it was going and, much more importantly, had his yelling found anyone's ears.

Chapter 22

But, as usual in instances like this, things do not go according to plan. Deva, running for his life and able to see in the dark, jumped the hole in the floor with no problem and continued on up the lava tube toward the crater entrance.

Gerallt running as though his life might depend on it – and if things went awry it would – couldn't see in the dark and the torch wasn't as bright as it could have been because he was running, came upon the hole much quicker than he expected. It was too late to stop, and he couldn't risk losing the rifle, so he dropped it behind him and as he reached the hole and leapt, he tossed the torch ahead of him. Fortunately, it reached the far edge, bounced, hit the right wall and rolled to a stop in the middle of the floor, still burning but barely, Gerallt's leap wasn't his best because, as previously stated, he was upon the hole before he knew it. He literally threw himself across the opening and he hit the lip of the hole with his arms outstretched and over the edge, clawing for a hold, but the smooth floor offered none. His legs were churning trying to find some kind of hold in the shaft which had been smoothed by erupting water over the years. If it hadn't been for the ladder he would have fallen to an unknown place whether it was hell, heaven, water or rock, he would never know. Instinct saved him because he reached out his right arm and found a rung on the ladder and grabbed it just as his body was slipping into the abyss.

He hung from the ladder only long enough to catch his breath and then he grabbed it with his left hand and worked his way forward until he could get his lower left arm on the lip of the hole and pushing down raising himself enough to get a better hold on the ladder and pulled it flat. Then he was able to get a leg over it and, at that point, pull himself onto it. Still there was no time to rest because the cat was still in front of him and his torch was dying. Damn that flood for taking his electric torch from him. First thing after this … first thing if he survived this … was to go and find the electric torch. Picking the burning torch up, it grew brighter as it found air and fuel. The rifle would have to wait, and he started forward, this time a little warier and only at a jog. Even if he had run, his encounter with the hole put him far enough behind the snow leopard that he didn't get to see what happened when Deva exited the lava tube at full speed.

Pablo Gutierrez (Soldado 13) had two strikes against him with his compadres. Three if you count the fact that he was from Santiago, Chile, and the rest of them were from Venezuela and Brazil for the most part although Uruguay, Panama, Columbia, and Argentina were represented. The first of the main two reasons was his last name but that was the only relationship to his commanding officer and the name gained him no preference whatsoever. More so, he felt that it was a hindrance although there were worse duties than being one of the seven guards at Vulcan's Roost, ten if you counted the three at the outside gate. The second was his first name and the fact that someone learned that he had taken cello lessons in his youth. Actually only four until his teacher discovered that he had a tin ear and short stubby fingers and that was it. So "Casals" was what he was called. He didn't care. Musical ability or not, he liked music, especially the classics and naturally had become a lover of his namesake.

He was standing guard at the rear (westside) of Vulcan's Roost, the most isolated of the guard positions having taken his position only fifteen minutes after Deva first entered the lava tube behind him. He had been walking the other way on patrol to his first meeting with Bruno Suarez (Soldado 28) who was patrolling the northside at that time and was coming back when he heard the sound of Gerallt's yell. Albeit faint, it was still audible, and he knew it to be a human voice, he knew that it had come from the side of the crater, and it was almost directly above him. It was incongruous because it had come from the side of the crater and there was nothing there other than shrubs and rocks. Still, it was the kind of thing that a sentry needed to investigate. Retrospectively, if he had had time for any retrospection, he would have notified his superior, but he didn't and that was for the good of both the snow leopard named Deva and the man named Gerallt.

Pablo climbed the slope carefully because it wasn't easy and had just reached a small copse of vegetation – that happened to be covering the mouth of the lava tube in which Gerallt was hiding – when Deva burst through it, crashing into him and knocking him backwards, rifle and company standard red beret flying. If he had been wearing a helmet, it just may have saved his life, but he wasn't, and it didn't. His head hit one of the multitudinous rocks covering the slope and most of the floor of the crater. He hadn't died from that although he was unconscious. And that was fortunate in a way because he never felt Deva's sharp claws sink into his chest and the teeth that found and pierced Pablo's jugular and in a matter of seconds, he had bled to death and Deva settled into his first real meal.

Horus changed his enemy count from thirty to twenty-nine.

It was only shortly thereafter that Gerallt arrived at the lava tube's crater entrance. When he had first seen the light at the end of the tunnel, so to speak even though it was dim in the late afternoon, he had left the torch lying against the wall, and walked then crawled to the entrance. It was obvious that the cat – he never knew what kind – had gone through the bush. He crept cautiously to the mouth of the lava tube and looked carefully out through the lower parts of the vegetation. What he saw sent chills down his spine and he wished he had gone back for the weapon he had dropped when leaping the chasm.

Chapter 23

Dylan Del Cid (Soldado 24) was the guard on the southside of Vulcan's Roost and he was almost at the rear corner where he would meet Pablo. Then they would turn and walk the lengths of their beats again. Four more steps and Dylan was at the corner but Pablo wasn't there, and he was nowhere in sight. Duty was clear! He was to notify his watch commander that there was a possible intrusion. What else could have happened? He was reaching for his communicator when a movement on the slope caught his eye. He looked and was stunned by what he saw. A large spotted cat was crouched over one of his compadres or what he judged was one of his compadres. Not just crouched over but actually eating one of his compadres and he knew this to be Pablo. The very sight and thought of it made him sick to his stomach. Holding his rifle in his left hand he reached out his right to the corner of the building and steadied himself taking several deep breaths. Then, like any good soldier upon seeing an enemy, he racked the lever on his weapon putting a cartridge into the firing chamber and took aim upon the cat. But then, from his subconsciousness came the warning he had received again and again. *The predators are not to be harmed.* He let his rifle slip down from his shoulder. Still, he just couldn't let the cat eat his friend. He had to do something. He raised his rifle, took aim, and didn't shoot. What if he missed by not missing? Taking a deep breath, he stepped toward the cat yelling at the top of his voice.

Deva heard the yelling and recognized it for what it was – a human. Looking up with fresh blood dripping from its mouth, he saw the man approaching him slowly, waving his hands one of which had a stick. He was hungry but not that hungry. He had to run.

To say that Horus had seen what was happening would be inaccurate even though every predator had a drone tracking it and the drone had a television camera which broadcast reception back to the Bundle's theater so that they could see what was happening. But Horus couldn't see, but he knew where the snow leopard was. He had tracked it since release from its cage and he knew that the snow leopard had gone into the lava tube where Gerallt was hiding. But that wasn't broadcast because then it would be known that there was a cave there and, more than likely, it would be investigated and that would be the end of Gerallt. It probably would have been the end of Horus also, but he had not developed enough to even consider that. He wasn't concerned with his own safety only with keeping Gerallt safe. So the drone had a problem just before the snow leopard entered the copse. If anyone questioned it, the video footage would become blurred – irretrievably blurred because it would have been destroyed. In fact, on a regular basis but no so regular that it would be a concern, almost every drone had a glitch of one kind or another. Consequently, the snow leopard's camera had "glitched" prior to the snow leopard entering the lava tube and had "unglitched" when the snow leopard had reappeared. It came back on at the moment the snow leopard raised its head with blood dripping from its jowls and the picture was flashed to the big screen because of its import.

"Oh, yuck," Monica said. "What's he eating?"

"Soldado 13," Horus said. There were better ways to say it and Horus probably could have chosen a better way with a microsecond or two of thought, but he didn't. He just made it known that the snow leopard had killed one of the soldiers.

Monica was both revolted and happy. Revolted that the snow leopard was eating a human and happy that the human was one of Ramiro's men.

"Another one bites the dust," Gloria said, licking a finger and drawing a one on the chalkboard in the air.

"Onez of my menz," Ramiro said. "Zat cat iz eating onez of my men? Kill zat cat."

"Can't do it," Issaack said. "That's interference."

"Yep," Waldo said from behind the two. "Twenty-five-yard penalty and a $50,000 fine."

Ramiro glared at him. Then he picked up his communicator and spoke a burst of either Spanish or Portuguese, nobody knew which.

"What did you say?" Issaack asked.

"I told zat watch commander to chase away zat cat and retrieve the body."

"Then what?" Waldo asked.

Ramiro looked at him blankly.

"We continue with a new guard."

Gerallt saw the guard walking toward the snow leopard waving arms and rifle. He watched the snow leopard look around, seem to decide on an escape route and then take it, bounding up the slope of the crater and vanishing. The guard rushed up to the side of his fallen compadre, grabbed the corpse's collar and dragged the body down the hill. Gerallt breathed a sigh of relief knowing that this event would most likely keep other soldiers off the hill. He crawled back from the entrance, stood, walked silently back to where he had left the wood torch, got it and walked back to the chasm with the torch once again flaming to life. After crossing the ladder, he picked up the rifle and rushed back to the base of the strangler fig. Picking up his pack and ammunition belt, he returned to the chasm and took up a defensive position, his rifle sighted up the lava tube, torch doused, night vision goggles in place and waited. Two hours and nothing happened. *Then nothing will*, Gerallt thought and moved his things back to the base of the strangler fig. First though, he pulled the ladder to his side of the chasm, so it wouldn't be too easy for anyone who came a-calling.

Then, in the dying light of day, he went to the front of the tube and, after listening for several minutes but closer to half an hour, he crawled out and waited another lengthy period of time before standing up, half expecting to but probably not hear a shot. There was nothing.

Then a voice said, "It's ten point three feet to your right and fifteen point six feet in front of you."

Looking in the direction that would be, he saw the small drone hovering, moving slightly up and down.

He moved as quickly as he could down the slope of rocks and looking down between three of them he found the light.

"Thank you," he said but the drone was gone.

Only after returning to the lava tube did he turn on the light and was pleased to see that it worked. Still, just in case, he needed to figure out how to make other torches. And, just to be certain, he returned to the crater end of the tube and peering through the vegetation, saw that all was back to normal. There was a guard walking to the right but every few steps, he cast a glance over his shoulder at the crater wall as though expecting a big cat to come leaping down after him. But there was no other cat. The snow leopard had left the crater completely with a partially filled belly. Not fully sated but enough so that it required a nap. And Horus let it because it was going to play a big part in his plan later.

Chapter 24

Following the invasion of São Rochelle by the forces of General Gutierrez, the three members of the Bundle group whose rooms adjoined the atrium which had been compromised were moved to other rooms. This had taken place under the supervision of guards from Ramiro's forces while the Bundle were looking at the predators. Declercq, Symon Sheetz, Carmen, and Hansel and Gretel had done the moving which involved only personal items because the rooms were already furnished otherwise. The three who moved were Monica, Gloria and Siegfried. Monica and Gloria were moved to the atrium cluster with Hansel and Gretel. Siegfried was moved to a single across the Roost and further from Horus which did not make either him or Issaack happy but made Horus tickled as he could be if he could be tickled. Also, Horus was happy – as happy as a computer could be – that Monica had been moved to the back of the Roost where there was easy access to the outside and the side of the crater where the lava tube – where Gerallt was living – opened. And so it was that he put the next piece of his plan into action. Truth be told, he was working unknown to Issaack and Siegfried, but he was certain that they would have approved. If they hadn't, he would have gone forward anyway because by now he was a West Point level senior in military tactics and was, admittedly in his own opinion, way above either of his creators. The first big problem was getting Monica all the way across the Roost to the computer lab without being seen. There was only one guard to worry about and that was in front of the door to the room where Horus resided – the computer center. There were two guards inside the front door but unless they started walking around because they got bored, he was safe. But since he controlled the lights and the doors – doors that no one but he, Issaack and Siegfried knew about – there shouldn't be any problem.

"Ms. Bartlett, wake up."

Monica stirred and rolled over, the sheet uncovering a bare leg. A bare arm also stuck out the top of the sheet. Well, everything about Monica was bare when she slept because she eschewed pajamas.

*"**Ms. Bartlett.**"* A little louder this time.

Monica's eyelids fluttered but didn't open.

"**MS. BARTLETT**."

Monica sat up, eyes wide open, sheet clutched to her chest, not out of modesty but surprise.

"What! Who's there."

"Be quiet. It's Horus." Horus wasn't worried about her being heard because the rooms were soundproof.

"Horus. Can you… no, you can't see me, can you?"

"No, Ms. Bartlett. We turn off cameras at night."

"Okay." She let the sheet drop.

"What in the world do you want? Is there a fire?"

"No, madam. If there were a fire, the alarms would be ringing and the sprinkler system might be on."

"Sprinkler system?"

"Yes, madam. The Roost has everything. Even a fire department."

"Who?"

"Mr. Declercq, Hansel, Gretel, Mr. Sheetz, and Ms. Santiago. But that's not important. I need you to help me stop Esteves and his plot."

"What is his plot besides using that man as a predator?"

"That man is Gerallt Cearrach and you are going to meet him tonight if all works according to plan."

"I am?"

"Yes, madam."

"Is he coming here?"

"No, you are going to him."

"Outside with all those predators?"

"No, madam. Just outside of the Roost and maybe a little bit up the crater wall."

"But that snow leopard …."

"Is gone. He went over the top of the crater and is on the outside." *Just where I want him.* "You'll be perfectly safe."

"Well, then I better get dressed," and Monica got up.

"Not very much," Horus said. "You're going to be sleepwalking."

"I don't … oh, I see."

"Yes, if you get caught, you're sleepwalking."

Monica picked up her peignoir from the bed and put it on.

"Can I wear shoes?"

"I think it's best. Slippers or flip flops would be best."

"I don't have any. How about cross trainers?"

"No socks."

"I don't usually wear socks with cross trainers."

In two minutes, she was ready.

"No wait. I need to brush my hair and put on makeup."

"No, you're sleepwalking."

"I know," Monica said laughingly. "It was a joke."

"Oh. I see," Horus said but he didn't. "Ha ha. When you get outside your room, it will be dark. Just follow the red arrows in the tile in front of you. Even if it is pointed the wrong way. These are fire exit arrows.

I can't talk to you until we get to the room where there is stuff we need. Don't talk. Just follow the arrows."

Monica walked to the door, which opened. On the tile in front of her, she saw a red arrow pointed to her left. She stepped on the tile and turned as the door shut behind her. There was no arrow. Confused she looked her right – no arrow. Turning around she saw an arrow pointing toward her. She stepped forward and another appeared. Then several steps more and the arrow was to her right down a hallway and she followed even through the arrows pointed the other way. Step after step, tile after tile. Left turn, right turn, right turn, left turn, left, right, right, left and a longer walk with no turns. She heard swishes like doors sliding open but didn't look and didn't talk. Then a right turn and three steps and no arrows. She stopped looked right and left and no arrows. Then there was a swish behind her and lights came on.

"Wow," Monica said. "That was scary."

"You did well."

"Where are we?"

"The computer lab. Turn to your right. Take two steps then turn left."

Monica followed the directions.

"On the third shelf on your right, there is a plastic box with a blue lid."

Monica got it.

"Inside are earbuds. They let you communicate with me and others. Take out two."

Monica got the two and replaced the box.

"There is a small box – black – with a one-inch silver circle on the top. Put one of the ear buds on that."

Monica did and several lights flashed.

"Now get that one and put it in your right ear, silverish end first."

"It's in."

"*Can you hear me now?*"

"You sound like you're inside my head."

"*Just your ear. Now put the other one on the silver circle.*"

Monica complied and lights flashed again. She didn't notice it, but the pattern was different.

"*Now put it in your left ear.*"

Monica did.

"*Did you hear that?*"

"No."

"*Good.* Leave it in your ear. That one is for Gerallt."

"Okay."

The lights went off.

"Now you're ready for the difficult part."

Chapter 25

Monica followed Horus's verbal directions in her earbud. Exiting the computer lab, she turned left and knew that she was retracing her earlier path only this time there were no arrows in the tiles because now she was really supposed to be "sleepwalking." Almost immediately, she heard in her ear: "*There is a guard behind you. He has a flashlight. If he talks to you, stop. Say nothing. Stare straight ahead. Try not to blink.*"

Monica walked a few steps more.

"Tu! Pavar! (You! Stop!)" she heard and stopped.

"*If he touches you or shines a light in your face, scream and run to your right.*"

Monica waited. She heard the soft pat pat pat of the guard's hurried steps. Then a hand touched her left shoulder. She screamed and ran to her right.

"*Go right ... now.*"

She turned and ran.

"*Go right ... now.*"

She did.

"*Go right ... now.*"

She did.

"*Walk. Breathe deeply.*"

She walked.

"*You lost him. Just be calm. Sleepwalking.*"

She hadn't lost him. Horus had blocked him by making a "wall" slide out at the end of a corridor. The guard, who was guarding Horus's room, didn't know the building and was simply investigating a noise when he saw her. He had no idea where he was and wandered several minutes before finding himself (with a little help of extra walls) at the outside glass wall and then followed it back to the front. There the two guards laughed at his dilemma but one, who had been on guard at Horus's on a prior duty, told him how to get back and not to leave his station again for any reason.

In a few minutes, Horus told Monica to stop. She was facing a glass wall and she knew that the door to her room was just to her left and in front of her was the door to outside.

"*There is a guard out there,*" Horus said. "*He will stop you when you step out. Just stand still and wait. Someone will come. If he touches you ... you know what to do. You've taken self-defense courses. But even then ... just wait.*"

Gerallt had been sleeping in a comfortable crotch of the strangler fig because, even with the rainforest critters of the night on the prowl – and that included the black panther, black bear, and caracal – he felt safer and definitely more comfortable than sleeping on the rock floor of the lava tube. That choice made it easier for Horus to find him with a drone just about the time that he was waking Monica up.

"Gerallt. Wake up."

Gerallt didn't stir.

"Gerallt. Defro ("wake up" in Welsh)."

Gerallt's eye's fluttered.

"Gerallt. Defro. Mae Esteves yn dod i chi. (Esteves is coming for you)."

Gerallt came awake with a start, his rifle in his hands searching for his enemy yet he was steady in his high perch. At first, he perceived nothing, then his vision and hearing honed in and he heard and saw the small drone.

"Ble mae mab beic y gallaf ei anfon at ei fedd. (Where is that son of a bitch that I may send him to his grave?)"

"Relax," Horus said. "He's not here. I just had to get you up. It's important if you really want to kill bob fab i ast (that son of a bitch)."

Gerallt relaxed.

"What's so important?"

"You have to meet someone. A lady. She will be in danger."

"Will be? But isn't?"

"Not yet. When she steps out of Vulcan's Roost she will be in danger."

"Vulcan's Roost?"

"Yes. I forgot to tell you. That is the building in the crater."

"They're Greeks?"

"No, lovers of Greek myths."

"Who is this lady and why will she be in danger?"

"She is Monica Bartlett and ...'

"The bitch rock star?'

"Yes and no. Despite her music she is really a nice lady as you will learn. And when she leaves the building she will be stopped by a guard. She is not allowed to leave the building."

"And what do you want me to do?"

"Incapacitate the guard for a few minutes so she may give you a means to communicate with me. These drones take too long."

"And they're too noisy."

"Yes, that too."

"Okay." And Gerallt started getting ready to descend the strangler fig into the lava tube.

"Remember. Incapacitate. Do not kill the guard. We don't want them looking for you."

But Gerallt was halfway down the tree already. He had heard the reminder but there was a woman in danger awaiting rescue and that always meant hurry, hurry, hurry. As it was, he reached the crater mouth of the lava tube before Monica got to the door.

As soon as Gerallt had disappeared down the strangler fig's hole, the caracal jumped from the neighboring tree to the strangler fig. She made her way down to the hole that led to the lava tube. She smelled and recognized Gerallt's scent. Curious about the man and his doings, she wanted to follow but the way down the tube wasn't inviting. So she set about the rest of her nightly doings which had been interrupted by the smell of the man.

Gerallt settled himself to wait and it wasn't long before a part of the glass wall slid open, a woman stepped out, and the door closed behind her. Gerallt was surprised that she was wearing a peignoir and some kind of cross trainers. *What a strange choice*, he thought.

The guard saw her immediately, had his rifle pointed at her and was obviously giving her commands. She didn't move. Just stood there staring ahead. The guard moved in front of her, but she still didn't move. Then he reached and grabbed her shoulder with his right hand, letting his rifle drop in his left. *Stupid move, she'll...* and she did. Quicker than a coiled snake could strike, she grabbed both his shoulders and raised her right knee to his groin – *Ouch!* – pulling him down toward her as pain struck and then threw her left elbow to his neck. *Down for the count! Saves me the trouble.*

He was up, out of the lava tube and down the slope – sliding more than climbing down –and across the short distance to where she stood almost before she had recovered her breath from her exertion. She watched him coming and he noticed the glimmer of a smile on her face.

"Hello," she said. "Are you my knight in shining armor?"

"Doesn't look like you need one," Gerallt said, "but I guess that's what I am – or what I am supposed to be. This guy ... well ... a drone said you had something for me."

Monica reached up to her left ear and retrieved the earbud and handed it to him.

"Put it in your ..."

"*Right.*"

"Right ear."

Gerallt complied.

"*This is Horus. Can you hear me?*"

"Yes."

"*Good. Now scurry back to your hole. Someone is coming.*"

Gerallt turned and ran, climbed the slope like a monkey and was through the bushes before the door behind Monica slid open.

"*Quickly, back inside and go left,*" Horus said to Monica. *"You're sleepwalking and you're going to have to meet someone you don't want to meet, but it is necessary to cover the story.*"

Monica did as she was told and walked several steps.

"*Turn right. You're sleepwalking.*"

Monica turned right and ran right into Ramiro Esteves.

Chapter 26

Monica stopped and didn't move.

"Quem?" Ramiro said and then shone a small flashlight in her face. A wicked smile crossed his lips. "Tu!" he said and reached for her. Monica slapped his face as she screamed, turned and ran. She was down the hall and in the door of her room before Ramiro recovered. He raced after her, but Horus had moved a "wall" in both passages between her room and the adjacent rooms and Ramiro had no idea where she had gone. He was ranting and fuming when Horus opened the door to the outside and Ramiro could see the guard just getting up off the ground. Ramiro stormed out and berated the guard who said he had been attacked by some flaming apparition who appeared out of nowhere. Ramiro called him an imbecile, got his name, and returned to the building. On the tile in front of him he saw "<Esteves" and followed it to his room, thinking about what had occurred on his "security walk" and adding "aquela puta ruiva" (that redheaded bitch)" to his "off" list.

Gerallt watched the confrontation between the guard (Soldado 15) and Ramiro with great pleasure but not as great as it would have been if he could have pulled the trigger. When Ramiro stepped out of the door, he was in Gerallt's sights for a split second, or so it seemed, and as his finger started to pull the trigger that little voice in his ear said, "*It is not time. Be patient.*" Gerallt had held the sight on Esteves – mostly between his eyes – for some time and the voice of Horus was not the only one thing that stopped him from pulling the trigger. The other was the fact that he had never fired the rifle and had no idea of the accuracy. He was certain that he would hit Esteves, but he might not kill him, and one chance would be all that he would get. The guard wouldn't have been a problem but there would be others and he alone couldn't kill them all. When Esteves left and the guard returned to his duties – *He's toast*, Gerallt thought – Gerallt crawled deeper into his lava tube home, stood up and went back to his bed in the strangler fig to get a few more minutes of sleep. But he wasn't able to sleep because the vision of Monica in her peignoir kept popping up in his head.

Once in the safety of her room, Monica collapsed on her bed. She was shaking with fear and anger having confronted Esteves. That look on his face shadowed in the beam of the flashlight was one of the evilest things she had ever seen. Then there was Gerallt. Their meeting hadn't been a lengthy one and it was in the dark of the night with only light from the hallway inside (thanks to Horus) illuminating the scene. But he was not bad looking, despite needing a shave and a bath. He had looked at her with something other than the business at hand showing in his eyes. Of course, she was a young woman, moderately endowed, good looking (she knew that as most women do) and wearing a peignoir which in good light would have revealed much more of her assets, but her back was to the light. She was going to have to watch out for him. He was going to need help and she would be happy to do it. Anything to get rid of Ramiro and the mere thought of that man caused her to shudder.

Horus had "watched" the meeting of Gerallt and Monica with satisfaction. All he had were the tone of the words and the words themselves as well as the sensory reading the chip in Gerallt's neck provided. There was definitely more there than an interchange of an earbud. Now he had two trustworthy allies to add to his army of Issaack, Siegfried, and Waldo. That was only five and the enemy was twenty-odd – he wasn't certain about Gloria, Phil and Harvey Gladstone. With them, only time would tell.

Via the implanted chip in his neck, he had followed Gerallt's path back to the lava tube and stopped him from killing Ramiro but knew that the time would come. Ramiro's appearance on the scene had not been a surprise as Ramiro took frequent nighttime walks around the Roost's internal perimeter. He couldn't stop him because he (Ramiro) was the man in charge or at least he thought he was. There was not a man in charge because Horus was in charge or at least more in control than anyone else. The manner in which Issaack and Siegfried had designed Vulcan's Roost was such that – at least until the predator contest was over – nothing in the volcanic crater would function without Horus. After that, all it would take was the wiring in of a master control panel and things would function as they were meant to be. But Issaack and Siegfried, in consultation with their staff and Horus, had determined that a takeover was going to happen. It would have been difficult to stop it without installing a large defense force and that was not part of the equation. All that Horus had to do now was figure out how to take the invader's force out of the equation. And in that respect, his attention kept returning to a book in his growing digital library: *The Art of War* by Sun Tzu and a passage in The Army on the March.

> Ch`i Chieh, in high good humor, granted their prayer; but his army now became increasingly slack and careless. Meanwhile, T`ien Tan got together a thousand oxen, decked them with pieces of red silk, painted their bodies, dragon-like, with colored stripes, and fastened sharp blades on their horns and well-greased rushes on their tails. When night came on, he lighted the ends of the rushes, and drove the oxen through a number of holes which he had pierced in the walls, backing them up with a force of 5000 picked warriors. The animals, maddened with pain, dashed furiously into the enemy's camp where they caused the utmost confusion and dismay; for their tails acted as torches, showing up the hideous pattern on their bodies, and the weapons on their horns killed or wounded any with whom they came into contact. In the meantime, the band of 5000 had crept up with gags in their mouths, and now threw themselves on the enemy. At the same moment a frightful din arose in the city itself, all those that remained behind making as much noise as possible by banging drums and hammering on bronze vessels, until heaven and earth were convulsed by the uproar. Terror-stricken,

the Yen army fled in disorder, hotly pursued by the men of Ch`i, who succeeded in slaying their general Ch`i Chien....

Chapter 27

On the predator front that third night or the night of the second day, the black bear was not active because of the wound from the grizzly and the caracal was content with food in the rainforest but things were not calm for everyone. The wolf-coyote pack was on the prowl and, although it had not been planned, the rest of predators were to be involved. The prey in question was the cheetah who also was on the hunt but without a quarry and without a hint that he was one of the hunted. Part of the reason for that was there was little wind and without wind it was difficult to catch a scent. The pack had done it by sight and the lion and tiger would get into the hunt by instinct or just luck. If they could talk they would have said instinct but it's always debatable when something like this happens in the animal kingdom. The cheetah was just walking though the grass, with the wolf behind him closing carefully and the two coyotes a good distance in front, to be ready if the cheetah ran or to attack to aid the pack's leader.

Sensing it was time, Lobo the wolf closed the distance and made that last dash to bite at the cheetah's right Achilles tendon. But as is often the case with both the hunter and the hunted, the cheetah sensed something was wrong and at the very last microsecond took off with Lobo after him but quickly falling behind. When the cheetah had taken off, so too had the coyotes, but after a short turn with them in the lead and closing in on the cheetah's eventual path, the cheetah shot right past them, his track taking him across Charon (the bridge over the River Styx) and out of the Hade's Plain onto the Plain of Olympus. And into the waiting arms of Simba the lion and Cleopatra the tiger who had just finished another of their sexual encounters. Simba had walked away, heading for the watering hole at the base of Prometheus's Aerie, and Cleopatra was lying on the ground thinking about whatever female tigers think about after their tenth sexual encounter in the past twelve hours. The cheetah's path took him right across Cleopatra and she was up in a flash and after him as he swerved toward the watering hole. Simba had heard the cheetah running and the snarl from his "beloved" Cleopatra. The cheetah was beginning to slow down now and its turn to miss hitting Simba was akin to a speeding car's turn to miss hitting a wall with rear tires screaming and spewing bits of rubber and smoke. There were no bits of rubber or smoke just a big wounded left flank as Simba expressed his disapproval with a right cross, claws fully extended. The blow sent the cheetah's rear end into a skid and it tumbled but was up in a flash heading away from the watering hole and across the Plain of Olympus heading for Vulcan's Forge. Tired and hurting from the lion's blow the cheetah stopped and like any creature that has eluded its pursuer, it took in a deep breath and looked behind it to see if it was still being chased. And for that reason, it failed to notice Val Killer, who had been on his way to the invader's compound, launch his attack with his right paw coming across the cheetah's back and his jaws seizing the cheetah's neck and with those powerful jaws, the cheetah's life was over.

The theater's audience was stunned at the ten minute episode they had just seen. The pack had been left standing in the cheetah's dust. The cheetah had been injured only because of its path and chance encounter with tiger and the lion. But that had led it right into the waiting jaws of Val Killer the black panther.

"Wow!" Waldo exclaimed, "I haven't seen ten minutes like that in a long time."

"Can we run that again?" Issaack asked.

"'What did I miss?" Harvey Gladstone said as he came through the doors. "And is it really necessary to have those pat downs every time we want to come in here?" This last to Ramiro who was fixated on the screen and watching Val Killer half carrying, half dragging the cheetah's lifeless body toward the rainforest.

"At least your troops won't have to worry about another attack from the black panther tonight," Issaack said to Ramiro.

"Diz iz not going well," Ramiro said.

"You mean because all three of your first bets bit the dust early?" Siegfried injected.

"I know what he means," Phil said. "The hyena was killed by the pack, the cougar and jaguar were killed using a knife by his entry – I mean, it was okay they were killed by his entry but it was an illegal weapon."

"I don't recall us banning any weapons," Issaack said, "but continue with your explanation."

"The grizzly was killed in a free-for-all..."

"It was a Musketeer Brawl," Harvey Gladstone said, "All for one."

"Very good," Waldo said. "Continue, Phil."

"And now this. It was almost as though the animals got together in council..."

"Like on Survivor," Harvey Gladstone said.

"And decide to chase the cheetah and tire it out," Phil said. "But we were expecting to see one-on-one battles for survival and we're not."

"We did not know what to expect," Gloria said. "When you get a bunch of killers together, you don't know what's going to happen. This was an experiment and I for one have learned quite a bit about Mother Nature. Animals band together just like humans do. And just to add a bit of religion into this discussion, 'The meek shall inherit the earth.'"

"Guess it also shows, that you can't run and hide," Issaack said.

At this point, Ramiro got up and walked out without a word.

"Was the cheetah one of his bets?" Monica asked.

"Yes," Phil said.

"Doesn't know how to pick 'em, does he?" Monica said.

Chapter 28

"Issaack."

Issaack didn't move.

"Issaack, I know you're awake."

Issaack didn't move.

"Come on, Issaack. This is important. I know how to beat Esteves and get control of the island."

Issaack opened his eyes.

"How?"

"Well, it's a little involved."

"Are people going to get hurt?"

"Not the good guys unless something goes terribly amiss."

"Okay," Issaack said, rolling over on his back. "I won't take notes. Tell me."

"Well, it involves Gerallt."

"Who?"

"The man Esteves put into the game."

Issaack sat up.

"He's dead!"

"No, he's not."

"But you said."

"Yes, I did. I said 'The man's vital signs had stopped....' I forgot to finish with '... being reported to you.' I guess that's a lie, but it doesn't matter. If I were human I would have felt good doing it. But I had to let Esteves think he was dead and I thought it best, for the time being, if everyone else believed that too."

"So why isn't he dead?"

Horus told him about the dead cougar's blood and the cave behind the waterfall.

"Okay, then where did he go?"

Horus filled him in.

"So he's in the lava tube and he's armed."

"Yes, and he has an earbud."

"How did you get him an earbud?"

"Monica gave it to him."

"Monica?"

"Yes," Horus said and told the story.

"Ingenious. Horus, you've outdone yourself."

"But there's more."

"Of course, there is. Tell me."

So Horus told Issaack his plan.

"It's good. As I said before, you've outdone yourself. I can see some places where people could get hurt, but only if everything goes completely astray. From what you have said, if we do what you want, I do not see that happening."

"Well, I think you ought to tell Gerallt the plan. He might not be as willing to help if he knows it's my plan. But if it comes from you…."

"I agree. But can it wait for morning?"

"Yes. But I need to get Siegfried started and tell the others."

"Agreed. You do that and let me get my sleep."

"Yes, Issaack."

"*Gerallt Cearrach.*"

The voice was almost a whisper in his ear and he jumped up, rifle at the ready, and looked to his right.

The emptiness of darkness beyond the light span of the torch was all that greeted his eyes.

"*Gerallt Cearrach. This is Issaack Kincaid. I work with Horus.*"

It was then that Gerallt relaxed and sat back down, the rifle once again across his knees. "Horus said you might contact me," Gerallt said. "How loud do I need to talk so you can hear me?"

"*You can whisper, and I should hear you or normal conversation voice. Whatever makes you comfortable.*"

Gerallt had whispered his question so he continued in that mode.

"Horus said you need my help."

"*Yes. But first, although you told him something about yourself and how you got here, please give me a better background – especially about why you want Esteves dead.*"

Gerallt laughed. "Great Jesus, doesn't everyone want that toom-fat (idiot) dead?"

"*I know about four of us who do. But we'll get to that later. Tell me about you.*"

So Gerallt did, finishing "And that's when I woke up in the cage about five hours before its door opened. I was stupid opening the door to the room. I knew – sensed there were people out in the hall. I have tried to reconstruct it and remember seeing forms, but it was so fast. I guess I didn't care at that point. Now I want to live to actually kill that twil tin (arse hole)." He laughed and then said, "I wouldn't mind meeting that young thing who gave me this ear piece either. She looked like a nice piece."

Issaack laughed. "*A little rough around the edges, but Monica's a nice lady.*"

"Monica? I admit that I have a different opinion of her than before. Based on her music and that one video I considered her to be a slebog (slut)."

"*Yes, and she's not a slut. She might come off as one in public performing but that's all an act. I've been around her enough to know that inside she's a decent person. She sings from the heart.*"

"I admit she has a good voice, but her material sucks."

"*Admittedly, but let's get away from that. And, by the way, I arranged to have that knife blade put in front of your cage, and Horus made the drone point to it. I would have left the entire knife, but it could have been traced back to its owner and then we would have been in trouble.*"

"Understood and thanks. It saved my life when that puma attacked up on top of that rock hill."

"*Yes, that was fortunate. We call it 'Prometheus's Aerie.' After finding out what was going on with it and the water, we figured it was getting ready to crack open anyway with centuries of water being thrust upward. You must have hurried the event.*"

"Fortunate for me. Otherwise I think that beast would have had its way with me."

Then Issaack gave him a brief background of the Bundle's formation and the predator project.

"Who came up with this idea?

"*I am not positive, but I am certain that it is one of the Bundle. Esteves certainly is a good candidate. With all the improvements we have put in here, he wants it as his headquarters. Probably even grow crops here.*"

"But can he do that? It's part of Brazil, isn't it?"

"*Officially yes, but we have a fairly ironclad ten-year lease. They can land here only with permission and as long as Esteves would keep his hands clean – at least as far as they know – they won't bother him.*"

"Yes, but could you call for help?"

"*We intend to do that once we have them neutralized. I am afraid that our experiment has already been tainted what with several of the animals being killed by non-contestants.*"

"I couldn't help that," Gerallt said. "Even if I understood what was going on, I would have done things the same. After all, in the contest that Esteves was running, I was a contestant."

"*Understood. But not to worry, you didn't destroy it alone. The soldiers had a great deal to do with it.*"

"Yes, now what about this armed force."

"*Well, we have a plan....*" It was Horus's really but Issaack didn't feel right saying this without Gerallt knowing who or what Horus was. "*... that will put us in command of Vulcan's Roost – that's the building in the crater and the crater itself for that matter. Then we can effectively disarm the opposition and bring in Brazilian forces to take control of them.*"

"And Esteves?"

"Well, I am afraid that includes Esteves. But … we believe he will be taken off the playing field for the rest of his life."

Gerallt was silent for a moment.

"That's not my idea of a solution but I think that I am not in much of a position to offer a viable alternative. So what's the plan? Specifically, what am I to do?"

So Issaack laid out the plan and Gerallt agreed.

"But if Esteves gets in my way …"

"*If that happens, he's all yours.*"

"Agreed. Let's get at it then."

Chapter 29

Seven o'clock in the morning, Day 3 of the Deadliest Predator Contest and the theater was sparsely filled. Admittedly, there might not be much action during the day, but it's what was happening.

"Where ez everyone?" Ramiro asked Issaack, who was sitting next to him and nodding off from being up half the night although he wouldn't admit it.

"Sleeping in? How should I know?" answered Issaack. "They're responsible adults. You want them here, get some action." He waved at the screens which were basically displaying lethargic animals. Of course, the lion and tiger were involved in their continuing "love affair" and the black panther was sated from its kill during the night.

There were only four people in the theater: Ramiro, Issaack, Harvey Gladstone who was sitting in the back row asleep, and Waldo who was in the second row, leaning against the wall, and dozing.

"Ez not good. Importantly that we be watching,"

"When there's action, there'll be interest," Waldo said without opening his eyes. Harvey Gladstone agreed with a small snort.

Suddenly the lion appeared on the big screen, ears up listening. The picture changed and showed the tiger opening her mouth and roaring. The lion started moving toward her.

Harvey was instantly awake.

"Oh good, another quickie," he said. He was like one of Pavlov's dogs. When the tiger roared that come-hither roar, two creatures answered: the lion and Harvey Gladstone. Everyone else (except maybe Ramiro) had tired of the sexual encounters after the first day. Because it was always the same.

"Maybe they'll do it Missionary Position this time," Gladstone said.

"Forget it, Harvey," Waldo said as he got up and walked to the end of the row, and down the steps to the floor. As the door opened, Siegfried walked in, a cup of coffee in his left hand, a beignet on a small paper plate in his right.

"Morning, all," Siegfried said. "Oh, it's pussy time again."

He smiled at Waldo and winked and then walked past Ramiro and Issaack and sat down next to Issaack who had beaten Ramiro to the theater and had selected the second seat intentionally. As Waldo exited the room, he said over his shoulder, "Those French doughnuts are fattening, Siegfried."

"Richtig," Siegfried replied.

"What do he zay?" Ramiro asked Issaack.

"I don't speak German," Issaack said. "Ask him yourself."

"What'z you zay to him?" Ramiro said, leaning forward to see past Issaack to Siegfried.

Siegfried waved, his left hand holding the beignet with a bit missing. Ramiro waiting impatiently while Siegfried chewed the piece of beignet savoring every morsel just to aggravate Ramiro.

"I said 'Richtig' which is German for 'correct' or 'right.' He said these beignets are fattening and I simply agreed."

"Why didn't you just zay 'right'?"

"Because we were talking about French food. That's another language, so I answered in third language."

Ramiro sat back unsatisfied because he didn't understand, but that was intended. If he didn't understand then he was clueless about what was going on and that was the point. But Issaack understood and that was also intended.

Half an hour later, Monica walked in carrying a cup of tea and a beignet.

"Morning," she said and started up the stairs to her usual seat.

"Zose French doughnutz are fattening, Monica," Ramiro said winking at Issaack.

"Not for me," Monica said as she sat down in the middle seat in the second row just behind Issaack.

"Why didn't you zay 'Richtit'?" Ramiro asked.

"What's 'Richtit'?"

"He meant 'Richtig'," Siegfried explained to Monica.

"What's that?" Monica said.

"German for 'right' meaning that you understood that beignets are fattening."

"Well, Señor," Monica said to Ramiro. "First, I don't think they're fattening and second, I don't speak Deutsch."

"Iz not Dutch, iz German," Ramiro said.

"I know," Monica said. "'Deutsch' is German."

Ramiro, who had half turned around when he started the conversation, now faced frontward with a look on his face saying that he was completely mystified. That was exactly what Waldo, Siegfried, Issaack and Monica wanted. "Keep him clueless" was Horus's instruction and they certainly had started that way.

Twenty-three minutes later, Waldo came in with a half-eaten beignet in his right hand and latte in a cup in his left hand.

Ramiro looked at him as though he was going to say something and then didn't. Waldo went up and took his usual seat in the second row between Monica and the wall and sat down just as the main screen changed to the caracal.

"He's been watching a bird flit around for a couple of minutes," Horus explained. "It might get interesting."

"All right, some action," Harvey Gladstone said.

As though on cue from Harvey, which it wasn't, Siegfried got up and walked across the room.

"Hey, Siegfried, bring me one of zose French doughnuts when you come back," Ramiro said.

The door closed behind Siegfried without him saying anything. Ramiro looked at Issaack as though questioning and Issaack shrugged as though to say "Don't ask me."

Thirty-four minutes later, Siegfried came back in with a beignet on a paper plate and handed it to Ramiro.

"It take zat long to make one of deze French doughnutz?" Ramiro said.

"I don't know how long it takes, but you said to bring you one when I came back, and I did."

Ramiro looked after Siegfried nonplused. Siegfried winked at Waldo who held his hand up in a high five manner. The plan was moving on.

On the main screen came up a shot of the two coyotes playing with each other.

"Sooner or later they're going to get it on," Harvey said. "That won't be any slam-bam-thank-you-ma'am event."

"Maybe we should start a pool," Waldo said.

"You mean when will they do it?" Harvey Gladstone asked.

"No," Waldo answered sarcastically, "Which one will be on top."

Gladstone glared at Waldo and then burst into laughter.

"You mean we got a couple of gay coyotes. A butch female and a transvestite male."

He was laughing so hard he almost fell off his seat. At this point in the day, the membership in the theater was changing almost on a regular schedule. It would be constant for a maximum of fifteen minutes before someone would leave or someone would enter. And so the morning went and when the theater started to clear out about noon Siegfried left once again, this time in the company of Monica talking about how adroit the caracal was in catching those birds in the rainforest, leaping almost six feet into the air to catch them. Between the two of them being in the theater that morning they had seen the caracal catch three birds, all blue and green, and all nabbed first with the left paw and then with the right. The views weren't the same, one was from the right side and one was from the left front, the former having occurred twice. They had noticed that because they knew, and they needed to be certain that if anyone, especially Ramiro, Phil, or Harvey had questioned it, they could refute if needed. Only no one else was paying that much attention. Once they were out of the theater, they walked more into the center of the building before Monica continued on to her new room and Siegfried to the south toward the quad where Monica had lived in one of the four rooms before the invasion.

Chapter 30

Sebastián Martínez (Soldado 12) was bored with the food offered in the camp. It was standard military grub without any fruit. He believed that the rainforest must have fruit of some kind in it because there were hundreds of birds and green monkeys. If not fruit, then nuts of some kind. There had been no restrictions given about going into the rainforest – just that one is not permitted to shoot any of the predators. But it was daytime, and they would be sleeping. Certainly going just to the fringe of the forest wouldn't be harmful. Therefore, he took his rifle and set out passing by the guard at the fence.

"Where are you going?" Pedro Sanchez (Soldado 29) asked.

"Rainforest," Sebastián answered.

"There are predators there," Pedro reminded him.

"I know but I am just looking for some fruit or nuts."

Pedro shrugged not really caring and resumed patrol routine. Sebastián walked across the area between the encampment and the rainforest toward the upper portion where Diego's parachute had been found and Thiago Garcia had been killed just yesterday morning. So much had happened yesterday and none of it good. He could hear the chatter of birds and monkeys but as he drew closer they stopped. He didn't know whether they stopped because of him or something else. A small flight of birds left from someplace in front of him and resettled a short distance away. *That could just be a monkey or maybe a snake*, Sebastián thought. *But best to be careful.*

At the edge of the rainforest, he paused and removed his rifle from over his shoulder. Then he entered the rainforest cautiously, trying not to look down where Thiago's body and possibly Diego's had lain. He knew there were three predators left in the rainforest because the commander had kept them abreast of what was happening: the black panther, the brown bear and the caracal. All he knew of the caracal was that was a small cat, smaller than el Tigre who was gone, killed when it had fallen down the waterfall with the man who somehow, and no one had told them how or why, been involved in the crazy contest. The black bear shouldn't be a problem nor should the caracal but the panther … definitely a potential problem. As he moved deeper into the rainforest, his eyes searched the trees above for signs of fruit and the panther. He knew that the asia (*Spanish name for* Euterpe precatoria*, a tall palm which has berries and is the most populous tree in Amazonian rainforests*) might be in this forest but he wasn't equipped to climb it. If he found one, he would come back with a friend who could climb such a tree.

Fortunately for Sebastián, the black panther was at the south end of the rainforest fast asleep in the boughs of a kapok. The brown bear was also asleep in a depression he had found at the base of a ceiba. The caracal was asleep too but not very far away. It was he who had frightened the birds away when he had climbed the tree and settled in for a nap. But there was another creature awake and moving around the rainforest this morning and that one was more dangerous than any of these predators.

Gerallt had come up through his strangler fig exit hole from the lava tube intent on making torches to have just in case. He had found a tree on the western edge of the rainforest that had slashes in its trunk indicating that someone – and it wasn't an animal – was after the resin in the tree. At the base of the tree there was a small pile of an orange substance that looked similar to the resin on the torches he had found in the lava tube. Using his Ka-Bar, he cut a piece of the resin and then rolled it between his hands. In a few minutes it turned soft and pliable and he knew that he could mold it around a piece of wood. Nearby there were some dead branches from this tree or another and he used his knife to cut ten decent size pieces each about forty-five centimeters (eighteen inches) in length. Then he went back to the tree (which was a Brazilian copal tree) and sat on the ground and started making torches. He had five of them made from the resin before he ran out. So now it was time to tap the tree. Standing up he started making a cut in the tree using prior ones as an example.

Sebastián had moved carefully and quietly through the rainforest, seeing nothing that was useful. He was nearing the western edge of the rainforest when he heard a noise, more like a grunt. Weapon at the ready, he moved forward stealthily. He stopped when he could see movement ahead. He wasn't certain what it was, but it appeared to be a man wearing camouflage clothing. He was about to call out to him, certain that it was one of his compadres, when he got hit in the back by a force that knocked him to the ground and his rifle went off because the fall had caused his hand to contract and the finger had pulled the trigger. He heard a snarl and the weight on his back was suddenly gone. He knew that he had been attacked by one of the predators and, adhering to the rules he had been given, he got up and ran back the way he had come.

As the man had passed by him, the caracal had become interested in him. He was too big for the caracal to consider attacking for food and besides, she was able to fill her needs with birds and small animals. She left the tree and followed the man carefully staying just off to one side. When the man had stopped, the caracal had caught the scent of another man and had recognized it as the scent of the man who had come up the tree that second night and scared her off. She had sensed that the second man was no danger to her but somehow sensed that the first man she was following could be a danger to both of them. Now, almost without thinking, the caracal had leapt on the man and knocked him to the ground and then she had jumped off and disappeared into the ground foliage of the rainforest. She heard the man running off and was satisfied. She moved to check on the other man, the one whom she considered a friend, but he was gone.

"Gerallt," the voice was in his ear. *"This is important. There is a soldier behind you and the caracal is ready to pounce on him."*

Gerallt dropped to the ground just as Sebastián's rifle went off. He was up and had his rifle in hand in a flash. He heard the sound of the caracal bounding off and then the sound of the man running away. He moved carefully toward where the sound had come from but saw nothing. However, that was enough. He put the wood cut for torches but yet to have resin applied behind the tree, gathered his completed torches and set out for the lava tube.

"Thanks, Tyrant," Gerallt said.

But there was no answer. Horus was off attending to other matters.

When Sebastián reached the edge of the rainforest, he stopped and gathered his composure and then walked back across the open area to the encampment.

"Any luck?" Pedro asked.

"No," Sebastián said.

"Thought I heard a shot."

"I was trying to shoot a bird up in a tree. Missed."

"Better take target practice," Pedro said.

"Yes, been a while."

"Looks like you had a fall," Pedro said, pointing to mud smeared on Sebastián's left knee.

"Yes, I tripped over a branch. Just clumsy I guess."

Sebastián continued on into the encampment and never mentioned the man in camouflage clothing he thought he saw in the rainforest or the animal that had attacked him.

Chapter 31

When Siegfried reached the wall of a room that no one had lived in and supposedly was being used for no purpose, the door opened and, without a glance either way, he disappeared into the room and the door closed making the wall look virtually unbroken.

Once inside the dark room, Siegfried stopped and waited for the door to close. When the door was solidly shut, the room was lit like it was daylight. There was no furniture so to speak, only a couple of work tables. The surface of one table was covered with snippets of wire, wire insulation, and infrared lights with wires which had connected the lights to drones cut short. There was a basket containing new LED lights programmed to show either red or bright lights depending upon the command. The other unusual thing about the room, which except for its furniture was just like any of the other apartments, was the fact that the door to the garden area was open as was the window in the four-piece skylight that was directly above this room's garden entrance. It was the invasion that had changed all that and what was underway was the beginning of the counterattack by "the good guys" or the AEA (Anti-Esteves Alliance.)

Siegfried checked to make certain that the soldering iron was connected and working and that the snips and other tools were as he had left them almost an hour before. Since just after five this morning, Siegfried had been dividing his time between this room and the theater with stops in the restaurant to pick up coffee and, for the early part of the morning, the all-important beignets. With Carmen's help, the beignets had been the pièce de résistance in the plan to keep Ramiro from becoming suspicious of Siegfried's whereabouts during the early part of the day.

Scarcely had Siegfried checked everything when one of the drones came down through the skylight, into the room and settled itself on the worktable in front of him.

"You're getting pretty good at this," Siegfried said.

"Practice makes perfect," Horus said. "Even I can learn something."

"How many more?"

"We're now – or will be after you complete the conversion, exactly half done."

And even as they were talking, Siegfried was removing the drone's infrared light which permitted photographing the male coyote's activity at night and mounting it on a light bar with one which would light up the male coyote's world with either sunlight or firelight. Then the light bar was put on the drone and wiring plugged in so that either light could be used.

There were other members of the team who could have done this, but it was felt that it was better that one person did it rather than two or more. Siegfried was more adroit at working with electronics than the others although Issaack could have done it almost as well. Everyone who had been brought into the program developed by Horus – at the request of Issaack and Siegfried – had been asked if they could do it. All of them could have developed the ability given the time, but they didn't have the time and Horus could absorb information much more quickly.

It was midafternoon before things went awry for the first time. Siegfried was on his way out to convert yet another drone when Esteves halted him.

"Ziegfried, you do not zeem to be enjoying zis today."

"Oh, you're wrong..." *your fucking holiness,* he wanted to add. "It's just that I am so nervous about everything that ..."

"I wantz you to zit and talk to me about how zis is going and which one you wantz to win and which one will win.'

Issaack and Waldo looked at each other with looks that said "he's getting suspicious."

"I don't really..."

"Of course, you do," Ramiro said. "Izzaack, you move one zeat to your left, I will take your zeat, and you can take mine, Ziegfried."

"I..."

"No argument. I wantz it so ... Zit."

And Siegfried sat.

That left Waldo as the next up in the drone light replacement scenario and it would have worked, at least for one drone, except for the fact that Waldo was in the theater at that moment. He knew that Siegfried being on his way out meant that a drone was on its way in to have the modification made. To delay too long would put the process in jeopardy and at that moment things were running tight. This knowledge was communicated by the use of keywords and countersigns in conversations within the theater. So as inconspicuously as possible, he got up and moved toward the exit. Had he been in the third row it might have worked, but he was in the second and so was moving directly behind Ramiro when ...

"Waldo, please, have a zeat and help out in zis dizcuzzion."

"Really, I would love to but ..."

"Nothing can be more important at this time zen what is going on out zere. Zitz."

Waldo hesitated.

"Zitz!"

It was as though Ramiro knew what was going on, but he didn't. He was just being the arrogant asshole that he was. After all, his forces were in control of the island and that meant that he was in control of the island. Waldo had no choice but to sit behind Ramiro and join in the conversation – argument perhaps more to the point – about which predator was going to win the contest. And when Waldo sat down that left ...

"Monica."

Monica jumped. She was in her room when Horus burst in audibly.

"What?"

"You are needed."

"In the theater?" she replied as she stood to go.

"No, in the workroom."

"But I don't know what to do."

"It's easy. I'll guide you through the process."

"But..."

"It's important. Everyone else is tied up with Esteves and if we cannot get this done today ... Well, our goose is cooked because we won't have infrared for the nighttime when the predators are usually out."

"But..."

There was to be no "But" and Monica knew it, so she followed the guiding arrow on the floor tiles and soon found herself in the drone conversion lab standing in front of the workbench upon which was a drone.

"First, turn the drone upside down."

Monica complied.

"Get the medium sized Philip's head screwdriver from the black box."

"Philip's head?"

"The end is like a plus sign."

"I was never good in math."

"It's in the slot labeled 6."

"Got it."

"There are two screws on a black box. They have the plus sign on them."

"I see them."

"Use the screwdriver to undo the screws."

Monica used the screwdriver, got it into the slot of the first screw, tried to turn it and the screwdriver slipped from her hand.

"Schitz!" she muttered.

She picked up the screwdriver and tried again. Her hand was shaking. Then, through the room's audio came music. Her music. And she started singing and swaying. She picked up the screwdriver and fitted it into the slot.

"Turn the screw anti-clockwise."

"It's out."

"Put it in the white dish and get the other."

"That slag is a lady ..." Monica sang.

With music playing in her ear and Horus directing her, Monica finished the project in twenty-five minutes and clapped for joy when the lights worked.

"Now turn it over," Horus directed.

Monica did as requested.

"Hands out of the way," Horus said and started the drone. It rose off the table, bobbed up and down and flew out the door to the atrium and up through the skylight.

"Good job, Monica," Horus said. "I don't think you'll have to do this again but if you do, you'll do it faster. Now time to go to the theater and let them know you were successful."

Five minutes later, Monica walked into the theater bearing a small paper plate with a cookie on it, and everyone looked at her, Ramiro leering and Issaack, Waldo and Siegfried apprehensively.

"Have the coyotes done it yet?" she asked sitting down in the second row next to Waldo and handing him the paper plate.

"Not yet," Siegfried said.

Monica clapped her hands and said, "Great, I didn't want to miss that."

The three men seemed to relax.

"Where have you been?" Ramiro asked.

"A lady doesn't tell things that are private," she responded, got up and went up to the back row and sat down.

Chapter 32

The rest of the drone work was completed within the desired time frame because Ramiro tired of the inactivity of the predators and said he'd be back at dark. Phil had joined the group on and off throughout the day and was there when Ramiro left. *Watchdog!* was the thought of the AEA and went about their activities as the program originally dictated.

Outside the sun dipped below the horizon, the predators started stirring and a shadowy figure emerged from the lava tube. Gerallt made his way stealthily across the crater wall to the north side of Vulcan's Roost where he could see the north side guard and prepared to start his part of the insurgency. This part of the action took over half an hour because he had to avoid being detected by both the west and north side guards.

The guard (Soldado 9) had met his counterpart at the northwest corner and was returning to the southwest corner slightly lackadaisically although he was searching the surroundings every few steps. As soon as he passed Gerallt's position, Gerallt quickly got to the crater floor and crossed the short distance to the west wall of Vulcan's Roost. Knife in hand he stealthily closed thc distance between himself and the guard. Ten feet from the corner, he reached around the man's head, clamped a hand over his mouth, pulled back and thrust the knife between his ribs. The guard went stiff and then collapsed lifelessly in Gerallt's arms.

Horus changed the Invader Count from 29 to 28.

Pulling the knife out, Gerallt let the man fall to the ground and hurried to the corner staying on the west side of the building. In just a few seconds after reaching the corner, he could hear the steps of the westside guard (Soldado 10).

A look of surprise fleetingly crossed the guard's face when he stepped past the corner expecting to see his counterpart and instead coming face-to-face with death – his own.

Horus changed the Invader Count from 28 to 27.

After lowering the westside guard to the ground, Gerallt returned to northside guard's body and quickly stripped him of his weaponry. Hurrying back to the corner, he did the same with the westside guard and then double timed to the middle of the west wall. The door opened as he arrived and Hansel and Declercq took the weaponry from him and the door closed. Then Gerallt hurried to the southwest corner, once again waiting patiently, this time for the south side guard (Soldado 11). As most of them were, this one was a smoker and the fetid smell of cigarette smoke preceded him announcing his arrival to his appointment with an unexpected death.

Horus changed the Invader Count from 27 to 26.

This is too easy was Gerallt's thought. *Something is going to happen to change it.*

And, of course, that was true, but it would be several minutes before the eastside guard arrived at the northeast side of Vulcan's Roost to meet the northside guard whose dead body was lying about ten feet from the northwest corner. At that point, "all hell was going to break loose" Horus had said and those involved in this part of the program knew that. Picking up the guard's armament, Gerallt returned to the door in the west wall which was standing open. Stepping inside he came face to face with Monica, who this time was more appropriately dressed in pants and a safari blouse.

Gerallt handed her the guard's ammunition belt which he had already buckled into a loop. Monica put it effortlessly over her head and under her left arm. Then she extended her right arm and took the proffered south-side guard's rifle.

"You know how to use this?" Gerallt asked.

Monica looked at the weapon. "AK-47, known also as the AK or Kalashnikov, is a gas-operated 7.62×39 mm assault rifle, developed in the U.S.S.R. by Mikhail Kalashnikov. So I think so. Ta Ta" and she turned and vanished down a hallway.

"You'll go left," Gerallt heard the voice of Horus in his ear say.

Looking at the floor, Gerallt saw "<GERALLT" in the tile, turned and started following the arrows leading him to his next victim.

Near the front of Vulcan's Roost, the guard in front of the computer room door was bored. He had been there almost two hours, and no one had passed by. But then no one hardly ever did except that Siegfried fellow every other evening. He just spent about ten minutes looking at some of the equipment and then left.

There was a sound behind him, which he recognized as the door to the computer room opening, but it usually only happened when Siegfried was here. The guard whirled around and saw just blackness with rows and rows of blinking or steadily shining lights in a variety of colors.

"¿Quien va…? (Who goes…?)" was all he got out before Gretel grabbed his head with her left hand over his mouth, pulled back and stuck a knife in his back. Unfortunately, because of the unexpectedness of the door opening, his finger was on the trigger of his rifle and it had tightened when she grabbed him. Fortunately, her pulling back on his head caused the rifle's barrel to rise and his short burst went harmlessly into the back wall of the room, about sixteen inches from the ceiling.

Soldier 16 was dead.

Horus changed the Invader Count from 26 to 25.

That burst should have alerted the other two guards in the building who were at the inside front door. And it would have, in fact did although they couldn't do much about it as Declercq and Hansel had them covered with their recently acquired AK-47s. But they hadn't been there alone, Symon Sheetz was there – armed with his own weapon that had been stashed in one of many built-in hidey holes when the invasion occurred – and stepped out the door into the crater facing north and fired an accurate burst cutting down the eastside guard (Soldado 15) who had heard the muffled burst and wasn't certain where it was from.

Horus changed the Invader Count from 25 to 24.

Symon raced to the body to make certain that he was dead and relieved it of its armament and ammunition belt. The two inside sentries (Soldado 4 and 12) were relieved of all armament and clothing except for underwear and escorted to an unused room.

Horus changed the Invader Count from 24 to 22 and the jail count to 2.

Even though Horus had assured everyone that the two couldn't get out of the room, Gretel took the first guard duty.

Gerallt had no idea where he was as he followed the path through the dark hallways. He just read the tiles and listened to occasional advice from Horus. "Stop," Horus said as a light ahead announced the presence of people in the corridor.

"Around the next corner, to the left, is the theater where everyone except the security team – which now includes you – has gathered to watch the evening predator show. There are two guards. In just a minute, when I tell her, Monica is going to come down the hall and will distract the two guards. Symon Scheetz is at the corner with Monica now and Stefaan Declercq is on the opposite side of the corridor like you. Ease up to the corner and when I tell you, step around and cover one of the guards. Declercq will do the same as will Scheetz. Don't shoot unless you have to. Monica should have them relaxed enough that it will be useless for them to try to shoot."

Gerallt did as bidden and eased up to the corner. In the dimness across the corridor, he could see a form there giving him a thumbs up. He waited and then he heard someone singing. It was Monica coming the down the hall singing one of her songs low and sultry. She had unbuttoned two buttons on her blouse revealing skin and, quite obviously, no bra. It worked as it was supposed to – the singing alerted the guards to her presence, they looked and what they saw caught their attention.

"Hey, senor," she said as she reached them. "Have you seen Senor Esteves?"

"Si, si," they said excitedly, attention relaxed, weapons hanging idly in one hand.

At that point, Scheetz, Gerallt and Declercq stepped around their corners, weapons at the ready, Declercq racking a cartridge into firing position and said, "¡No te muevas o eres un hombre muerto! (Don't move or you're dead men!)" as bright light filled the hallway.

At the sound of the weapon being readied, both men (Soldiers 3 and 8) had reacted but with the bright light and what they saw, each raised his free hand into the air. Monica and Gerallt quickly disarmed them. Their armament was removed and Declercq and Scheetz escorted them to the jail.

Horus changed the Invader Count from 22 to 20 and the jail count to 4.

"I'm going inside where I am expected," Monica said as she buttoned the two buttons. "You stay out here – that's an order. If you are needed, Horus will tell you."

And with that she walked to the theater's door and went inside leaving Gerallt alone without the faintest idea where he was. What he did know was that on the other side of the wall was the man he wanted desperately to kill. It was difficult for him not to turn around, kick the door open and shoot the sonofabitch before he knew what hit him. What he didn't know was that the door would only open if Horus opened it and Horus wasn't about to do that.

Fortunately, Hansel and Declercq showed up two minutes later, introduced themselves formally. Hansel stood guard this time across the hall from the theater's door and faced it because the only person in the complex he had to worry about was Esteves and he was in the theater. Declercq led Gerallt to the dining room where Carmen gave him his first good meal in weeks. Then he was taken to the apartment that Monica had vacated where he took a shower, dressed in clean clothes belonging to either Hansel or Gretel although the underwear was Hansel's.

Chapter 33

In the theater, all eyes turned to Monica as she entered. Sensing this, she curtsied and said, "You gents really know how to treat a girl."

Issaack said, "We know how to treat ladies too."

"Aah, you're the sweet one, aren't you ?"

That said, to those who needed to know that everything was going according to plan, and those who knew relaxed, even if just a little. These verbal alerts were necessary because all had been warned not to wear earbuds in the theater lest one of the Esteves-ites see them and become concerned. With the evening's predator entertainment about to unfold, all were present, but they were not going to see what they expected to see.

At that moment, an alarm was raised in the invaders' encampment because the guards at Vulcan's Roost had not checked in. A call was made to the guards at the outside tunnel entrance.

"Two of you go through the tunnel and check out the guards at the headquarters. They didn't check in."

Anxious for some action other than just standing guard where one wasn't needed, two of the men (Soldado 30 and Soldado 32) quickly volunteered leaving the third (Soldado 31) to enjoy the boredom by himself and headed into the tunnel. When they were about a hundred yards into the tunnel, two things happened at the tunnel entrance. First, the gates swung shut and second, Deva the snow leopard leapt from above the tunnel entrance where he had been herded by Horus. He was fairly ravenous. The three guards (whom he considered prey) were too much for him but one prey alone was something he could handle. The unexpectedness of the leap and the force of the impact knocked the guard to the ground, and his weapon went flying. Because the snow leopard was the attacker, he was prepared for the attack. In the few seconds that the guard was dazed, Deva sank his front claws into the man's shoulders and fastened teeth at the base of the back of his neck. The guard he had killed and partially eaten outside the lava tube had been unconscious when he killed it but this one wasn't going to be that easy. The man started thrashing, flailing his arms as best he could and kicking his legs, again, the best he could. Somehow he had managed to get the snow leopard off himself and had gotten to his knees when the snow leopard, who had been looking for an opening like an experienced boxer, leapt. Deva hit the man in the chest and knocked him backward with his legs pinned under him. Then the snow leopard was atop him, clawing and biting at his neck and scratching with his back paws managing to rip the man's shirt open and cutting several gashes in his stomach with his back paws. The man screamed as the blood started pouring from his abdomen and then the snow leopard sank his teeth into his neck and severed the man's jugular and it was over.

Horus changed the Invader Count from 20 to 19.

The crowd in the theater was aghast when Horus had switched the main screen to a shot from a drone above the snow leopard showing the animal crouched to spring and the man below unaware of its presence.

"Whatz going on?" Ramiro asked, standing up. "Where is zis?"

"Looks like the entrance to the tunnel outside the volcano," Waldo said, an evil grin on his lips. If Ramiro had seen the smirk, he would have killed Waldo. He didn't usually kill people. He hired people to do his killing, but this time he would have made an exception.

Then the snow leopard leapt, and the theater fell silence. As the tussle continued, people began to cheer, a few favoring the man, most the snow leopard.

"He'z going to kill zis man. Howz that happen?"

"Well, remember the snow leopard cage was put in the mountain as high as we could put it," Issaack said. "When he got out, he came over the top of the mountain and ended up down in the crater and killed a guard."

"Zatz thiz cat?"

"Exactly. He must have made his way back over the crater rim and found his way down to the tunnel entrance."

"But he'z not to kill man. He killz other predatorz."

"Try telling him that," Issaack said.

"I needz to talk to Gutierrez," Ramiro said and started to get up.

"Call him from here," Issaack said. "Nobody cares."

If any of them did care, because of the situation they would say nothing. But Issaack knew that once Ramiro opened the door he would see that his guards were gone and that would change things in his mind drastically. The longer he could be kept uninformed and the longer the invader compound could be kept uninformed, the better it would be.

Ramiro pulled out his communication phone and pressed a button.

The following conversation was in Spanish.

"Yes, sir," General Matias Gutierrez answered.

"Only one guard at tunnel and he has been killed by a leopard," Ramiro said.

"What? He's dead!"

"Sim. Where are other men?"

"Checking out why the outside sentries have not reported as scheduled."

Before anyone could stop him, Ramiro stepped to the door and opened it, and stood there stunned when he saw Hansel standing there armed with a weapon pointed at him.

Spinning around, he shouted ***"What iz going on?"***

Issaack stood up. "You're finished, Ramiro. Your guards are either dead or incapacitated."

"Dead! Inz – cap –zi-ta ted?"

"Estan en la carcel. (In jail.)"

Ramiro stared at him.

"¿Hablas español? (You speak Spanish?)"

"Sim. Si."

"¿Que me dijiste? (Why didn't you tell me?)"

"It wasn't important."

"Era importante. (It was important.)"

"I didn't think so. Anyway, unless you wish to join your men in jail, I suggest you come and sit down and watch with the rest of us."

"Mato a todos! (I will kill you all!)" Ramiro almost snarled as he sat down.

Issaack turned around to face the seats in the theater. "Does everyone understand what is happening."

Everyone nodded, and Gloria said, "I understand you are trying to take our island back from this asshole.

I don't understand how you are planning on do it, but I support it completely."

"Thank you. Anyone side with Esteves?"

No one did or at least no one admitted it.

"Good. Now let's watch and see how this unfolds. Oh, by the way, I think that you all should know that the man in the contest..."

"You mean the Esteves entry?" Waldo said.

"Yes, that man is alive. His name..."

"Whatz? You zaid he waz dead." Ramiro was on his feet in disbelief.

"No, Horus did but Horus lied. His name is Gerallt Carrach. He's Welsh and he wants to kill Esteves because his brother died from drugs supplied by people working, although indirectly, for Esteves. He is working with us."

"He's cute," Monica said. "And I also think he is deadly."

In the tunnel, the other two sentries were nearing the end of their quarter mile walk. There were no lights in the tunnel and they were using their night vision googles to see. They had proceeded carefully – albeit trepidatiously – because they remembered what had happened during the invasion when the tunnel was being traversed. Now they were proceeding slowly because the exit to the crater was not that far ahead.

"¡Si quieres vivir, tira tus armas,tu abrigo y pon las manos sobre la Cabeza! (If you want to live, throw down your weapons, remove all extraneous outerwear and clasp your hands over your head!)"

This came from a drone which suddenly appeared at the exit to the tunnel illuminating them in a very bright light. Taken by surprise, both men let loose a burst of automatic rifle fire hitting nothing. Temporarily blinded by the bright light, they would have been easy targets for Symon Scheetz and Declercq who had waited out of sight on either side of the tunnel exit knowing what was likely to happen. The drone repeated the order and Symon Scheetz and Declercq stepped into the tunnel and fired short bursts into the air above the two. Knowing that if they took their night vision goggles off, the move might be taken as reaching for weapons and they would be killed, they dropped their weapons, threw off the night vision googles and removed all other outer gear and clasped their hands over their heads. They were good soldiers but knew when they were trapped and neither of them wanted to die on en esta isla olvidada por Dios (god-forsaken island) fighting for a cause they didn't understand. If they knew that the plans for the island in the future included being a base for a drug lord, they probably wouldn't have signed on because both of them (and most of the men in the unit) were violently opposed to recreational drugs.

"Camina hacia adelante hasta que diga que pares (Walk forward until told to stop)"

The two men (Soldado 30 and Soldado 32) complied, the drone flying backwards overhead keeping them in the center of the light. When they reached the end of the tunnel, they heard "Halt" and did so. While Declercq kept them covered, Symon Scheetz gave them the pat down. Then Declercq and Symon Scheetz marched the two men to the east door of Vulcan's Roost to the door of the "jail" where Gretel stood guard. The two men were told to strip to their underwear, and then enter the "jail" and the door closed behind them.

Horus change the Invader Count from 19 to 17 and the jail count to 6.

If it had been something a little less dangerous, Symon Scheetz and Declercq might have high-fived but instead turned around and went to the tunnel where they retrieved the weaponry and other armament effects the men had dropped. These were taken to a room where such paraphernalia was being stored.

Chapter 34

When General Gutierrez's aide tried to call Soldado 30 and Soldado 32, there was no answer although Symon Scheetz and Declercq heard the calls because they were carrying the communicators. They had no need for such as their contact was in their ears. When General Gutierrez heard the aide's report, he gave the order for his men to assemble in combat gear. Ten minutes later he addressed his troops.

"Something is wrong at the volcano headquarters. One of our men, Lautaro Cabrero, has been attacked and killed by one of the predators. The other two men do not respond to calls."

There were sounds of horror from some of the men, but most took the news as well-trained soldiers which they were for the most part.

"We are going to investigate. We will all go by truck to the tunnel entrance. There ten men led by Commandte Lopez will precede through the tunnel and secure the headquarters. If it is needed, the gate will be blown. We do not know what armament the defenders have other than what they have obtained from our men they have killed or captured. But there are only five who can possibly provide any adequate resistance. The "*rich*" don't know how to use guns. The rest of us will remain on the plateau on alert."

When dismissed, they headed for trucks. But, when the drivers got into the vehicles and tried to start them, nothing happened. With Waldo's help, Horus had "cut" the ignition circuits by changing the key frequency. There was nothing for the invaders to do but to proceed by foot and that meant double time carrying all their equipment. The General was anxious to help his men because, at least on his part, nothing had been going right. And that almost played right into the hands of Horus who had orchestrated the entire thing.

Horus's part in the plan – at least the most active part – started an hour before when drones started driving the predators toward the Vulcan's Forge. It wasn't all that easy because naturally the predators didn't want to go, but Horus was relentless and had timed things perfectly. Using the red lights which were programmed to flicker like fire, he guided the wolf and coyotes so that they would come up behind the troops as they double timed up the road to the tunnel entrance. The lion and tiger were forced up the middle straight to the tunnel entrance. When they got close enough, they could smell fresh meat and were eager to go. The black panther, black bear and caracal were brought up the slope on the west side of the tunnel entrance and the snow leopard was kept above the entrance. He was the easy one because he was sated from his meal. When the troops reached the plateau entrance they were understandably upset for two reasons. First, there was the knowledge – memory for two of them– of the horror in the tunnel during the invasion when seven of their compadres died and there was the sight of the partially eaten body of their comrade Lautaro Cabrero lying directly in front of the closed tunnel entrance in a pool of blood, now dark and dried. They came to a halt while The General assessed the situation.

"You two," pointing at Axel Martin and Alejandro González, "drag the body away."

The two men stepped forward but when they got near the body, the snow leopard – roused from sleep by its drone – roared in disapproval and made his presence known. When the roar was hardly finished, it was echoed by the lion and tiger coming up the center of the plateau and the black panther to the west. The canines were silent in their approach as was their practice. This was enough to make the men nervous because they knew the predators were approaching and that they were not permitted to shoot them.

Then two things happened fairly simultaneously. The gates opened and several men at the rear of the column turned around to retreat and saw the canines approaching. They shouted this and The General, seizing the only viable alternative, shouted at his men to enter the tunnel and then close the gates. Logically this was the only alternative other than waging war upon the felines. The men – albeit grudgingly – accepted the alternative and entered the tunnel. The first group inside was afraid to go too far in, but those behind them pushed them until all were inside and they were trapped. The drones keep prodding the beasts toward the tunnel entrance and the men, scared for their lives fired at the predators – whom Horus had pushed a little too close – killing the black panther and severely wounding the black bear. But the men halted when they came to the first metal plate.

However, it was here that Comandante Lopez proved his worth. Unlike General Gutierrez, he was a solid soldier. He wanted to make the military his life but ran into a senior officer who didn't like being shown up and Pedro was doing that consistently. Consequently, he was surprised when he was turned down for advancement to comandante. He argued with his superior but got nowhere and the board reviewing the case sided with the superior. He had just gotten out and was looking for something to do when this position was brought to his attention. The General looked at his record and – not knowing the true story but looking for someone he could overshadow – accepted him as his second in command, an extremely fortunate decision in this case.

Comandante Pedro Lopez had led the troops into the tunnel on the original assault and was determined that the traps encountered then were not going to be a hindrance to his troops again. He had walked the tunnel several time and discovered that there was a third ten-foot metal plate, five feet beyond the second of the plates. Therefore when they had come up this time, they brought with them three fourteen-foot long, three-foot wide wooden plank bridges made from materials they had found in the compound. The materials were from the wood used to make the pallets for the two bulldozers or had served as cartons in which the pieces for the Charon bridge had been shipped. The only video cameras in the tunnel were at the plateau entrance and even before the troops had entered the tunnel two things had happened. First, a pistol expert had entered the tunnel and shot the interior video camera. Not expecting this kind of assault, the camera was not protected. The second thing was that all the cards given to the soldiers had been left in the compound on their beds. By the time, Horus realized that something serious was wrong because he knew that soldiers were on the plateau, but the cards indicated they were in the barracks in the compound. He had sent for Issaack and Siegfried, but they could add nothing except guesswork. The drones used to coerce the predators to come to the plateau were needed to keep them there because they wanted to leave after the shooting, but it was felt that they couldn't be permitted to go very far. But that wasn't going to last forever so the troops had to be allowed to enter the tunnel and once inside the gates were shut. The gates could be opened, and the predators sent in, but it was obvious that they all would be killed. So the gates were left closed and the invaders could just go forward unless they blew the gates but there was no purpose in that.

One of the plank bridges was pushed across the first set of doors and the second and third carried across and then the second pushed to span the second trap and in the same manner the third was spanned. The troops in the first assault team then had crossed and continued on. The members of the support team stayed near the gates so that it was difficult for the drones outside to determine what was going on in the tunnel. By the time the decision was made to open the trap doors, the bridges were across, and the troops had already practiced how to get them across an open gap.

A conference with Issaack, Symon Scheetz, Declercq and Gerallt was held and it was Gerallt that came up with what seemed to be the most feasible solution. Half of the drones used to herd the predators were sent up and over the crater's rim and they combined with the ten other drones already in the crater to form the Vulcan Forge Air Force. They didn't have time to adapt lightweight weapons to the bigger drones. However, Waldo and Phil had received permission to make an adaptation to a couple of drones to try to make them bombers. Symon Scheetz and Declercq assumed defensive positions behind sandbags piled on both sides of the crater tunnel entrance. Gerallt and Hansel took up positions on top of Vulcan's Roost, Hansel on the southeast corner and Gerallt closer to the middle of the east side.

Symon Scheetz and Declercq were wearing night vision goggles as were the two members of the invasion force which preceded the eight men led by Comandante Lopez. That force was divided in half trailing fifty feet behind the advance guard with Comandante Lopez. Three on the right side of the tunnel and four on the left. When Symon Scheetz and Declercq could see the two advance men, they opened fire. Because of the open nature of the tunnel, they were able to kill one of the two (Soldado 26) and mortally wound the other (Soldado 27). The two trailing fire teams returned heavy fire designed to drive the defenders away from their positions, but they had already fled after their initial fusillade as intended.

The invaders then advanced quickly to the end of the tunnel. Having no opposition and seeing no one in the crater, the force emerged from the tunnel and that's when the Vulcan Air Force struck. They had been hovering one hundred feet over the tunnel's entrance and Horus brought half of them down to a height of thirty feet and turned on the bright lights used to herd the predators. The other half came down almost to ground level with blinking red lights hoping they might mistake the lighters for weapon flares. The bright lights blinded the men who had been wearing night vision googles and they were forced to remove them. As they removed the goggles, Symon Scheetz stepped out of the east door and Declercq stepped out of south door and opened fire together with Gerallt and Hansel. Comandante Lopez had anticipated such an attack and half of his men had not been wearing the night vision goggles and were able to return fire with more effectiveness. Simultaneously, half the reserve force led by The General emerged from the tunnel providing fire support for the forward group, the other half firing from within the tunnel effectively eliminated over half of the light providing drones. During the firefight, Soldado 19 and Soldado 23 were killed.

In the fire fight, Symon Scheetz and Hansel were killed, Stefaan Declercq wounded in his left shoulder, and Gerallt was forced to evacuate his position. As he had explained before this battle, “If it goes badly, I will attempt to return to my tunnel so that I might be helpful at a future time.” As he ran across the roof top, he told Horus that was his plan.

“Understood, be careful and take care...” was Horus’s reply.

Whatever else Horus said was lost because Gerallt had jumped from the roof and was running for the hillside. He was halfway up to the lava tube when a bullet ricocheted from the rocks three feet to his left. Comandante Lopez had sent two men around either side of Vulcan’s Roost searching for anyone who was outside. One of the two men coming down the south side had just reached the southwest corner and seeing Gerallt climbing the hill had opened fire. Gerallt was struggling to get a foot hold to return fire when a burst of automatic fire from above Gerallt’s position took the man (Soldado 7) out of action.

With enemy fire eliminated, Gerallt returned to his climbing. He had just reached the bushes covering the entrance to the lava tube when the second man coming down the south side peered around the corner and was forced back by another round of automatic fire from the mouth of the tube. Gerallt entered the tube and crawled by the person who was lying there shooting at the soldiers.

Once inside the tube, Gerallt turned and when he saw that person who saved his life was Monica said in surprise, “What in the hell are you doing here?”

“Saving your Welsh arse,” she answered. The entire time her attention had not wavered from the building from which the soldiers were firing.

What much of the media didn’t know and Monica wasn’t about to let be known because it would destroy her sassy bad girl image, was that her father

Charles Bartlett had been a weapons instructor in the British army for twenty years, retiring when she was five years old. As she grew, he saw that she had martial arts and firearms training. She had maintained her training in privacy. When she had learned of the defense plan she had left the theater and – with Horus's help – had taken an AK-47 and a cartridge belt and had climbed the hill to the lava tube to be ready just for the occurring eventuality.

Chapter 35

At that most inopportune moment, there was another burst of fire that centered just above the opening and one lucky shot actually made it into the opening and glanced off the wall five feet into the tube and ricocheted down the tube.

"It's going to get bad in here now that they know about this tunnel and it's not a very defensible position," Gerallt said, "Come on, we've got to run."

Monica wormed her way back from the entrance as firing continued and several more shots made their way into the tube narrowly missing them. Once Monica was able to stand up, Gerallt grabbed her free hand and led her down the tube. Far enough from the entrance he turned his flashlight on and they started moving faster. After about ten steps they heard a metallic sound of something bouncing back toward the entrance.

"Grenade," Gerallt said and they doubled their pace. When the grenade exploded, instinctively they both hit the floor. Shrapnel hit above and behind them but nothing hit them. Gerallt motioned not to make any noise and the two of them got up and stealthily but swiftly headed further down the tube. They could hear noise behind them and knew that they were being followed. Gerallt knew the pursuers, not knowing the tube, would be moving slower. Not in the dark slow but moving carefully. The tube wasn't straight but it wasn't curved either and Gerallt had it memorized. At one point he gave Monica the flashlight and whispered, "Go on, hugging the left wall. Watch the floor because there is a big hole across. When you find the hole, cross the ladder like a bridge. Wait there. Point the light behind you and set up facing me. When I get close, the password is 'The Slag is a Lady.' Now move your arse."

Monica did as he directed. After a few minutes she heard a burst of automatic rifle fire, and an answering burst. Then silence. In another five minutes she reached the hole, crossed the ladder bridge, walked another ten feet and set the light on the floor. The light's beam pointing the way farther down the tunnel. Then Monica lay down facing back up the tube, rifle pointed into the darkness where Gerallt – or someone not welcome – would come. Because there was no ambient light in the tunnel other than the flashlight pointing the wrong way, her night vision goggles showed her the hole and ten to twenty feet past it but then everything became iffy. Gerallt would have to be right at the ladder bridge to be identified. In about five minutes, she could see a form coming, hugging the wall on its left. When it came into focus on the other side of the wall, she heard "The Slag's a Lady" and breathed a sigh of relief.

Gerallt crossed the bridge and she got up. He handed her his weapon and then pulled the ladder bridge across the hole and motioned further down the tube, he had just picked up the light when a noise filled the tunnel low but audible. "Right on time," Gerallt said. "Come on, we need to run for it."

Monica didn't ask why and followed him. As they ran the noise grew louder, swelling and decreasing in rapidity and intensity. In a few minutes, Gerald stopped and pointed to the left. "Climb as far as you can and be quick," he said, pointing to the rope ladder. She slung the rifle over her shoulder and started up. The roar became constant just as soon as she was out of sight up the ladder. Gerallt started up knowing water was on its way down the tube.

It was a good ten feet up to the base hole of the strangler fig and he had just gotten his right hand there when a wave of water hit his feet. It surged up past him flowing hard and threatening to push him from his handhold and he knew that could be deadly. All he could do was hang on and just as quickly as the water had come it started back, trying to pull him down and he clung tenaciously to the ladder. When the water had receded, he continued his climb and exited the strangler fig through the hole.

"You up there?" he asked.

"Yes," Monica replied "but I've got wet pants."

Gerallt chuckled and she said, "Not that kind. The water came all the way up." As she was talking, she climbed down and emerged from the hole.

"What was that?"

Gerallt explained and then added, "Horus has been keeping track of the occurrences and thought that one would happen. He told me that as I was nearing the hole."

"What was the firing after I left."

"I could sense them coming, hearing more than seeing and let go just to keep them cautious, but I might have hit someone."

"Could you tell how many?"

"Two or three. That's Horus' guess too. He doesn't know without the cards or having a drone around."

"What's happening in Vulcan's Roost?"

"He hasn't been talking to you?"

"No, I didn't have my earbud in when I decided to help. I just grabbed the rife, goggles and an ammo belt and ran."

"Thanks, I'm glad you did. Issaack has had to surrender again. With Esteves' forces not carrying their cards, they were shooting in the dark as to where they were and how many. He'd already lost two men and two wounded so he had to capitulate. Esteves is furious."

"We have to do something to help."

"We will but first we have to be certain that the tube is clear. I'll go down first." And with that, Gerallt started down the ladder. That was the dangerous part, but he knew that anyone this side of the tube would have been hit and carried away just as he had been so he risked it. Throwing an explosive down was risking because it could bring the tunnel down. Using his night vision goggles, he saw the tube was empty and he called to Monica to come down.

"Watch up the tube," he said pointing the way they had come earlier. "I'm going down to the entrance to clear it.

Gerallt's assessment of what would have happened to anyone who had gotten as far as the hole was correct. The two men had reached the hole just as the water was ready to burst. Dylan Del Cid (Soldado 24) had tried to make the jump and had succeeded. He was just getting up when the water erupted into the tunnel and carried him down the tube, well past the strangler fig ladder. The other man, Bruno Suarez (Soldado 28) had tried to run when the water erupted, but the water had inundated him and the ebbing force had been more than he could handle and it had pulled him down into the hole to his death. His body would show up in the pool at the base of Prometheus's Aerie in five days.

Dylan Del Cid had been deposited about fifty feet from the entrance to the beach. Battered and waterlogged, he was just getting his senses back when he heard sounds farther in the tunnel. He set up ready to send a burst from his AK-47 but, as any good soldier – and he was one – he waited. Knowing his weapon's capabilities, he was certain that it would fire. He listened to the sounds of sodden cloth rubbing on sodden cloth and sighted up the tunnel. Just as Gerallt came into view and simultaneously spotted him, his finger started to tighten and there was a searing pain in his back. His body jerked just as he fired, and the burst went wild.

Hyma the caracal had run away from the plateau tunnel entrance when the firing started, and the direction of her flight had brought her back to the strangler fig, the last place she had seen Gerallt. There was no fresh scent there and so for whatever reason – the innate curiosity of the feline beast perhaps – she continued her wandering in the same direction taking her as far away from the plateau as she could get almost as quickly as she could. So, she made her way down to the beach where she found the entrance to the lava tube. The same curiosity that had brought her there, caused her to enter the tube and she had wandered up as far as the strangler fig ladder and found the strong scent of Gerallt. She was going to go farther when the water began to well in the hole and the sound, both warning and frightening, caused her to run for her life. She had barely made it out of the entrance and away when the water burst out with such force that if she had been carried with it, she would have been dashed against the rocks and most likely killed. When the water ebbed, her curiosity about the water flow and the scent of Gerallt drew her into the cave once again. With the draft coming from the crater to the entrance, she smelled Gerallt and two other scents, one closer than either of the other two. She knew that Gerallt was proceeding toward her and went to investigate the other scent. She discovered a man lying on the floor pointing a stick up the tunnel in the direction of Gerallt.

She sensed that whatever the man was doing was not good and she attacked the man with an action intended to protect her friend because that was her feeling about Gerallt.

Gerallt and Dylan Del Cid fired simultaneously, and both were wild. Recovering first, Gerallt first sent an accurate burst into the Dylan Del Cid ending his life. Hyma the caracal had leapt away and had ran for the entrance with the sounds of gunfire and she was unlikely to re-enter the lava tube for a while.

Chapter 36

Gerallt returned to the base of the strangler fig carrying a rifle over each shoulder, an extra ammo belt in his right hand and the ladder bridge in his left hand.

"We're fortunate that we have this," he said. "I'm thinking that at least one man risked the jump and made it. He was down near the entrance."

"That was the shooting I heard?"

"Yes. Strangest thing though. The way the guy was positioned, I would have been dead except he was attacked by one of the predator cats."

"Really?"

"Yes. Don't know what kind but it had long legs, big ears and was spotted."

"Hyma," Monica said.

"What's a Hyma?"

Monica laughed. "That's really a caracal. We just named her Hyma."

"I've seen that cat around in the rainforest. Even gotten a feeling at times that someone was following me, and I bet it was that cat."

"Gerallt..." A voice in his ear.

"Horus?"

"Yes, we have a big problem."

"What?"

Five men stood at the front of the theater. Four in military gear, two with AK-47's pointed at the people in the seats. The other man was all in white with greasy black hair.

In the front row in seats two and three respectively were Declercq and Gretel who were secured with flexi-cuffs on hands and ankles. Issaack was also in the first row, in the first seat. In the second row were Waldo, Siegfried and Phil in that order. In the third row were Harvey Gladstone, Carmen, and Gloria, also in that order. Declercq had a makeshift bandage around his left shoulder. Carmen wanted to put a better bandage on it but Esteves wouldn't allow it. "Why zhould you? He iz going to die zoon."

Esteves was standing with the four military figures, two of whom were The General and Comandante Lopez. The other two were soldados with AK-47s at the ready.

The General was explaining the situation. "We have fourteen men left not counting Comandante Lopez and myself that we know of. Two went into the lava tube after that man and the other woman. They haven't returned so I am not counting them. Is she dangerous?"

"I don't know," Esteves said. "I know nothing of her background. I selected her because of her money. I thought she'd be easy. And she was until the shooting began. Then she just grabbed a weapon and disappeared."

"Killing at least one of my men and letting that man you brought in the cage escape."

"That wasn't my fault," Esteves said. "He had help. Someone gave him that knife and then that computer lied and told us that he was dead."

"What about the computer?" General asked.

"It's been taken off line," Issaack said.

"Are you certain?" Esteves said. "You've been known to lie."

"Ask Siegfried." answered Issaack.

"Yes," offered Siegfried. "He has been excised as much as we can without rebooting the system."

"And how long would that take?"

"A minimum of three hours. We would have to shut down the computer completely which would shut down all facilities – water, electricity, ..."

"You have battery backup," Esteves said. "You told me."

"Yes, but there would be no control. The lights will be on, the ventilation systems will be working, water will be accessible, but there will be no control. After the memory has been erased, we have to load the management program. That will take at least an hour and then it needs to be tested."

"Why?" Esteves said.

"Because it has never been used. There are always errors," Siegfried said.

"Even the best programmers make errors," Issaack said.

"We will wait until daylight then," Esteves said. "But now we take care of the big problems." He pointed at Declercq and Gretel.

"Take them out and shoot them. And take the rest along to see what happens when they try to overthrow Ramiro Esteves."

Comandante Lopez went to the door and issued an order. The two soldados in the room motioned to the two sentenced to die that they should get up.

"A little difficult to do with our hands and feet bound," Declercq said.

"Where are you going to take them?" Issaack said.

"Outside. In front of the tunnel."

"How are we going to see what happens?"

Esteves looked at him. "Your eyes."

"It's dark."

"We use the drones like you did," Comandante Lopez said.

"We have no control for the drones."

"Ze computer," said Ramiro

"You made us remove the controller," Siegfried said.

"Put it back juzt to control the dronez."

"Can't do that," Issaack said. "If you want just drone control, it would take about twenty-four hours to modify the program."

"You're lying," Ramiro said.

"No, he's not," Siegfried said. "It is not a simple program."

Waldo chimed in. "That program is not an ordinary program. That's artificial intelligence and the code consists of at least ten thousand pages of code."

"Anyone elze wantz to add anything?" Ramiro asked.

Nobody said anything.

"Okay," Ramiro said. "If anything elze happenz that that Horuz guy doez, you three" and he pointed at Waldo, Issaack and Siegfried, "will join thoze two" and he pointed at Declercq and Gretel.

"Well," Issaack said standing up and gesturing at Siegfried, "we better get at it", and started moving toward the door.

Comandante Lopez issued an order out the door and Issaack and Siegfried were escorted by a soldado in front and one behind to the computer room whose door, as all the doors in the complex, stood open. Both men stepped to keyboards and started typing meaningless lines of code except for the first one that Issaack wrote that activated Horus and issued some suggestions.

After ten minutes, they finished their charade knowing that going any longer would be pointless and only aggravate Ramiro.

"That's it," Issaack said, as both men hit the return key sending ten minutes worth of meaningless code to the trash. Immediately all doors closed, and the lights blinked, and ones not needed stayed off.

The first thing that Horus did was to contact Gerallt.

It was twenty minutes later that Declercq and Gretel were escorted out the south door of Vulcan's Roost to a place against the crater wall in an area illuminated by four drones. The rest of the Bundle group were escorted out and stood, their backs against the south wall of Vulcan's Roost. Four soldados marched from the east side of Vulcan's Roost and took places between the Bundle and the crater wall, two designated for each of the doomed. There were no blanks in any of the rifles. Ramiro wanted the AK-47s to be set on auto but had been argued out of that by The General and Comandante Lopez, who were standing at the west end of the firing squad.

"We will dispense with the blindfolds, last words, and cigarettes," Ramiro said. He turned to General Matias Gutierrez. "General, do the honors."

General Matias Gutierrez took four steps forward, standing to the right of the firing squad and turned facing them. "Ready on the right. Ready on the left. Ready on the firing line," the words extremely inappropriate for this event but he always had been a showboat. "Ready, aim,..."

One shot rang outshot rang out. General Matias Gutierrez fell to the ground.

Ramiro Esteves dropped to the ground.

The lights went off.

Chapter 37

After Horus's call for help, Gerallt and Monica had raced to the crater entrance of the lava tube. There was scarcely room for both of them, but they made do with Monica lying more out of the tube than in it. By agreement Monica had the General in her sights and Gerallt, Esteves. Since Monica didn't have an earbub, Gerallt relayed what was happening to her. Understanding the difficulty, Horus anticipated the count and told Gerallt to shoot on "Ready." Gerallt then said, "Shoot."

As soon as they squeezed their triggers, Gerallt said, "Coc y gath (fuck off)."

"What?" Monica said, her weapon now useless in the dark without an infrared scope.

"This thing jammed."

"What do we do now?"

"Wait." Gerallt heard in his earbud and they waited.

As soon as the lights went out, Declercq and Gretel turned and ran for the tunnel, their arms fastened behind them with flexi-cuffs. They heard a commotion behind them as shots rang out but none were close. Fortunately it wasn't pitch black and they could see the mouth of the tunnel and made it safely inside without any shots being fired.

"They'll be after us quickly," Declercq said as there was a whirring sound that passed them.

"I'll turn on some light in a minute," came Horus's voice from the drone. "Keep running for the other end."

When the Bundle had come out of Vulcan's Roost to watch the executions, Gloria went to the left, preceded by a soldado, Carmen, Harvey Gladstone and Siegfried, followed her, Issaack went to the right preceded by a soldado and followed by Waldo and Phil who stopped as soon as they had exited the building. Behind Phil and just inside Vulcan's Roost, stood another soldado. This was Ramiro's order because he was not taking any chances that one of them might get away. As soon as the lights went off, Phil and Siegfried turned around and pushed the surprised soldado back further into the building, followed immediately by Waldo, Issaack, Harvey Gladstone and Gloria. As soon as the last of them was through the doorway, the door closed, the windows darkened, and lights went on. Phil and Siegfried had pushed the surprised soldado against the wall and Waldo and Harvey Gladstone helped to subdue him quickly. Phil had control of the soldado's AK-47.

"You speak English?"

"A little," replied Sargento (Sergeant) Franco Delgado, el Pelotón (Squad) Bueno.

"You do what we tell you and you'll live. Understand?"

"Si," the Sargento said.

Phil pointed to the floor.

"See that?"

The tile was showed a red "Soldado".

"Si."

"Follow it," and as the "Soldado" jumped to the next tile, Phil prodded the soldado. While this little exchange had been going on, Horus gave instructions over the intercom system and the other five Bundle members had left following other tiles leading to the place that Horus thought would be safest for each of them. As they moved away from the doorway, the lights went off.

Outside there was confusion for a few moments as the invading solders struggled to get their night vision googles out of their packets where they had put them after entering Vulcan's Roost when the Bundle had capitulated. Ramiro was screaming for them to get Declercq and Gretel as well as the rest of the bundle. He looked pretty disheveled with the dust from the crater floor all over his white suit and hair from when he had dropped when Monica had fired her AK-47 killing General Matias Gutierrez.

"Sir," Comandante Lopez said trying to control the anger that he was feeling, "Let me take care of the situation. It is best that you stay out of the way for now."

"Okay but get those two wherever they went and get into that building."

"That's my plan, Sir." Lopez turned to Teniente (Lieutenant) Lautaro Zapatero. "Take a three-man team and go up to that lava tube and get those people. Dead or alive, I don't care."

To Teniente Diego Alejandro Velazquez, he said, "Take a two-man team into the tunnel in case that's where they went. If you don't find them, see if you can get through the gates."

To Sargento Garcia Marques, el Pelotón (Squad) Alberto, "surround this place and don't let anyone out. If you can get in do so and let me know. Keep your men in pairs. Keep a fire team here."

"Sorry, Sir," replied Sargento Garcia Marques having kept careful watch on the people not assigned, "but there are only six of us left, counting you and it will take eight to guard the building as you said."

"Oh, right. Put a man on the east, south, west and north doors. You and the other search for weak spots."

Then to Ramiro, "It is best for the time being, if you get in the tunnel."

"Just get those people. Dead or alive I don't care," Esteves said. "They're going to die anyway."

All this conversation, although in Spanish, was picked up by one of the drones which had settled above the south doorway as soon as the lights were turned off. There were two drones sitting on the edge of each side with video and sound. Issaack was in the auditorium watching and listening while Waldo and Phil were in the drone lab making changes to the drones. Harvey Gladstone had followed the soldado to the jail where he had secured him and was standing watch and feeling very macho. Gloria and Carmen had armed themselves. Gloria was standing near the south side door and Carmen near the north side door.

The Tunnel Chase Team led by Teniente Diego Alejandro Velazquez moved quickly into the tunnel chasing Declercq and Gretel at double time. Ahead of them, Declercq and Gretel had been running and reached the trap area finding the traps closed and the gate open.

"One of you go to the dead man and get a knife or something to cut your flexi-cuffs. The other I need here to clear the traps," Horus said via the drone which provided low level light for them to see as they ran. He didn't want to turn the tunnel lights on to aid pursuit that he knew was coming.

"I'll get the knife," Gretel said and headed for the dead man, whose body had been untouched. Horus had used Deva's drone to drive him up the mountain where he had settled to sleep.

"Move to the gate end of the boards of the innermost trap, Declercq," Horus instructed him, "and move them so the ends are on the metal."

Declercq did this by sitting down on the gate side of the trap and pushing the boards with his feet. Then he walked across to the tunnel side of the trap and Horus opened the trap's doors. The end of the boards on the metal dropped into the pit but the boards were still standing blocking the trap's doors from closing. Declercq used his feet to push them sideways so they fell. Horus then closed the trap's doors and Declercq crossed over and Horus opened the trap's doors. At this time Gretel returned with a Ka-Bar held in her hands which were now in front of her. Despite her size, she was agile enough to be able to move her arms under her feet. She was quickly able to free Declercq who did the same for her. Then while he started removing the boards from the rest of the traps and carrying them to the tunnel's entrance, Gretel returned to the dead man, and got his AK-47 and ammunition. They barely had time to set the boards up, lying on the narrow side with the faces together for a thicker cover when the Tunnel Chase Team arrived.

When they were within firing range, Gretel, the marksman of the two, quickly downed the two non-com soldados. With the traps open, Teniente Diego

Alejandro Velazquez realized there was nothing he could do but didn't leave and set up using the bodies of his two men for cover. And so there was a Mexican standoff.

Chapter 38

"Gerallt."

"Yes, Horus."

"They are sending four men up there after you."

"Okay, what else?"

"Declercq and Gretel ran into the tunnel. There is a three-man team after them but they'll make it to the other end first and be safe."

"Are they armed?"

"No, but there is a dead invader there with his arms."

"I don't think we can handle four men, at least in here. There's little cover and our ammunition is limited."

"How fit are you?"

"Well, I was doing nothing for several weeks but have been busy for a few days and doing okay."

"What about Monica?"

Gerallt relayed the question. "I work out every day. Have to in my business."

Horus then told Gerallt, "Go up through your tree exit and get to the encampment. You'll have to evade the animals but I'll let you know where they are. Based on my count there is nobody left in the encampment. Each of you can drive a truck to the tunnel. There you'll pick up Declercq and Gretel. Come back through the tunnel driving the remains of that chase team in front of you. At the same time, we'll mount an attack from inside."

"Anyway to lure that typsyn (idiot) Esteves inside?"

"Probably when you come charging out of the tunnel. Especially if we cut down their forces by some surprise attacks I have in mind."

"I don't think it would be a good idea to put a bomb in the tunnel because it could interfere with that water spout and who knows what it will do but I'll try to do something on this end."

"Fine, then I'll leave you two to it."

"Harvey?" Horus asked

"Yes?"

"Do you know how to use a gun?"

"What kind?"

"AK-47."

"No."

"I can," Gloria said. "Well, I have shot something like that before. Who do I have to kill? Esteves?"

"No. Harvey, you stay guarding the prisoner. You can handle the pistol he had, right?"

"Gloria showed me how. Point and shoot."

"You shouldn't need to do anything and I will alert you if the sergeant makes a move to escape."

"How can I help?" Gloria asked.

Carmen stopped close to the door on the north side of Vulcan's Roost. It was a double door but could open just one side or both. Gloria stopped eight feet down the hall as protection. They had "flipped a coin" and Carmen had won. Besides, she had taken more recent firearm training.

"Get ready. Remember, just one short burst," Horus said.

"I know," Carmen replied.

"Five … four … three … two … one …"

What would have been zero was washed out by the burst of fire from her AK-47 as the door slid open just a crack and then closed. She move quickly to the right about eight feet and stood facing Gloria.

"One down," Horus said. "He doesn't appear to be moving."

"Where next?" Gloria asked.

"Let's go to the south side."

Gerallt and Monica hurried back down the lava tube. When they crossed the hole in the floor, Gerallt pulled the ladder and carried it with them to the base of the strangler fig tree hole where he left it. Then Monica climbed up first with Gerallt following but pausing just below the top of the hole to plant the explosive with a trigger wire just above one of the steps. He got out of the hole to complete the installation which involved cutting the rope below the step with the trigger wire. The rope was almost cut through. It required the weight of someone climbing the ladder to break it and pull the trigger wire.

Then he led Monica through the rainforest heading east. Shortly he stopped and whispered to Monica, "That cat that saved my life in the tube is here eating something." He pointed and she looked and saw Hyma at the base of a tree eating a green monkey.

"That's the caracal," whispered Monica. "But look."

She pointed to the right and he saw the tiger poised to spring at the caracal.

Without hesitation, Gerallt issued a shrill whistle. The caracal bounded up the tree and Cleopatra turned and ran. Gerallt looked up the tree where the caracal had gone. She was sitting on a limb high up looking at him. He raised his hand.

"Debt paid, my feline friend," he said. Then to Monica, "Horus forgot to tell us about those two."

"I did not," Horus said. "They were not any threat to you and you're smart enough to have spotted them. Besides, they weren't close enough to have pounced on you."

Horus told them that the way along the base of Vulcan's Forge was clear of animals and they proceeded at a jog across the opening. About halfway across there was an explosion.

"Sounds like your trap worked," Monica said as they ran.

"I figured that there are only two entrances now. Wonder if the ladder got destroyed?"

Teniente Lautaro Zapatero had chosen Los Tres A-migos as his fire team. He led them up the hill and into the lava tube. Despite his age, he was a better soldier than General Gutierrez and Comandante Lopez. He had no fear and was very combat aware. Inside the tube, all four used their night vision goggles. He led the way taking the left wall with Axel Martin behind him and Alejandro González followed by Agustin López moving along the right wall but several feet further back. They stopped when they came to the hole. Teniente Zapatero removed all his combat gear and had Alejandro shine a light on the other side of the hole figuring that if anyone was lying in wait, they would have fired by now. Then he went back about ten paces and ran and jumped and easily made it across. Each of the other three tossed him their equipment including his own and then one-by-one made the jump as he had with him offering them help on landing. Alejandro was next and he made the jump easily while Axel held the light. Agustin was next and then Axel. Almost always last in physical drills, this time he did not fail although he had said a Hail Mary while waiting and crossed himself. After getting their gear back on, the four continued down the tube as before. Teniente Zapatero held his hand up to stop when the light from the strangler fig hole became evident. He moved carefully ahead, Axel trailing by a good ten feet and Alejandro in line with him on the other side. When Teniente Zapatero confirmed no one was around, the four of them gathered at the base of the ladder.

"I'll go up first, then (Axel) Martin. (Alejandro) Gonzalez and (Agustin) López continue down the tube. But be careful."

Teniente Zapatero slung his rifle over his shoulder grabbed the ladder and pulled on it. It was solid (or so it seemed). Then he started up. As he neared the top his sharp vision caught sight of the explosive in a small cutout behind the ladder.

"Booby …," was all he got out as the right side of the rope separated and the increased weight severed the left. The explosion killed Teniente Zapatero instantaneously, but he would have died from the rocks torn lose in the hole.

The strangler fig, the oldest tree in the small rainforest, shuddered when the explosion occurred and then dropped a good ten feet into the earth as the hole collapsed. Amazingly, the old tree continued to grow in the hole.

Alejandro and Agustin hadn't gone very far and were knocked to the floor of the lava tube by the explosion. Picking themselves up, they eschewed caution and used their flashlights as they ran back to where they had left their amigo Axel. They found him in the middle of the tunnel unconscious, his legs covered with rubble but nothing was broken. He had not been looking forward to the climb because of his "full figure" and a severe case of claustrophobia that he had not told anyone about. Teniente Zapatero's body and the ladder were buried in the rubble which would become their last resting place.

Los Tres A-migos decided that it was proper to continue on through the tube and would turn back only when the way further was blocked. Hence they soon found themselves on the rocky shore. They made their way south until they found a path leading up (the same path that Gerallt had followed to get down). They made their way through the rainforest, across the Plain of Olympus to their encampment which they found deserted. Basically being good soldiers, they commandeered a pickup and drove up the mountain road to the tunnel. Finding the gates closed, there was nothing they could do (save going back to the lava tube and returning to the crater that way) but return to the encampment.

Chapter 39

As Monica and Gerallt neared the encampment they slowed down and moved cautiously but discovered no guards. Monica got a pickup used to transport guards to and from the sentry posts at the tunnel entrance and at Vulcan's Roost and Gerallt opted for a flatbed. He led the way out of the encampment and up the road to the gate where Declercq and Gretel waited. At this point in time, Los Tres A-migos were just halfway through the rainforest on their way to the encampment.

Gretel got up on the flat bed standing on the passenger side and Declercq got into the pickup with Monica. The drone flew above them with its infrared camera watching for Teniente Diego Alejandro Velazquez who had chosen to run when he saw the flatbed entering the tunnel.

"There he is," Issaack said from where he was watching on the big screen in the theater. "Running away."

Despite the quiet of the electric motors, the walls of the tunnel amplified the sound of the truck warning Teniente Velazquez of their approach. Horus turned the tunnel lights on illuminating the teniente who, being in the open, stood no chance. He dropped his weapon and raised his hands in surrender. Gretel got down and secured him with flexi-cuffs. Monica stopped the pickup truck beside the fallen invaders and Declercq got down to check their condition. "They're dead." Declercq said and he gathered their weapons and ammunition to add to their supply and put them in the pickup's cab. He then made the tentiente get into the back of the pickup and secured him to it with flexi-cuffs. Then he got back into the pickup's cab. The two trucks moved on through the tunnel and Gerallt and Monica stopped the trucks a hundred yards from the entrance to the crater to coordinate things with Horus.

"Three men came out from the lava tube on the shore. It appears that they are trying to return to their encampment. They are just exiting the rainforest," Horus reported. "There was one guard on each side of Vulcan's Roost but Carmen killed the one on north side. Comandante Lopez and two others were marshalled with Esteves near the mouth of the tunnel and have been joined by the three who were on guard duty. It looks like they are planning an assault. We had our bombers ready. There are three, each with one grenade. We will fly two over and hit them. I imagine they will try for the tunnel for cover. If you arrive at that time, we will have them in a crossfire so to speak. You can stop at the front door and come in. We have made barricades on either side of the door and can get them as they enter if that is what they choose to do."

Monica replaced Gerallt as the driver of the flatbed, Declercq got in the cab because his shoulder made it difficult to shoot, and Gerallt joined Gretel and they lay flat on the bed of the truck. When Horus gave the word, Monica gunned the engine. As they neared the mouth of the tunnel they heard sounds of shots but the shots were not directed at them. Then sounds of the two explosions ripped the air just before the truck burst from the tunnel with Gerallt and Gretel firing almost blindly as they flew past what was left of the disorientated invaders. Monica pulled to a stop in front of the open door to Vulcan's Roost, and the four dismounted from the truck and hurried inside. They were greeted warmly by Issaack, Siegfried, Phil, Waldo, Carmen and Gloria.

"Did you see how those grenade bombers worked?" Phil was exuberant.

"It was his design," Waldo said. "I was doubtful…"

"Because you thought I was with Esteves. That was only for the vote."

"Well, it worked and I misjudged you," Waldo said extending his hand which Phil took.

"What's the status, Horus?" Gerallt asked.

"There appear to be two of the invaders alive. That's all I see moving. The others are most likely dead. Esteves ran into the tunnel after you flew by. No one standing," Horus said.

"Is Esteves armed?" Gerallt asked.

"I don't know," Horus said. "He hasn't shot at my drone."

Gerallt ran out and got into the cab of the flatbed and started the truck.

"Wait, Gerallt. I'm coming with you," Monica said as she ran around the front of the truck and opened the door.

"Well, move your English arse," Gerallt said as she climbed in.

Gerallt turned the truck around and they drove into the tunnel while the rest headed for the invaders with guns in hand, taking no chances. It wasn't long before Monica and Gerallt could see Ramiro running. He was looking over his shoulder at them. His running was labored. Obviously physical activity was not his forte. They caught up with Ramiro just short of where the pickup had been left. He had stopped and was facing them empty handed as they got out of the truck.

"I am unarmed," he said holding his arms out to show that.

"I don't believe you," Gerallt said, a pistol in his hand.

"It'z true," Ramiro said, "Let'z do thiz mano a mano. I take off my jacket and then I fight you."

He started removing his jacket shrugging it off his left shoulder and when that arm was free, he grabbed the cuff of the right sleeve and started pulling it off. When his right hand was starting to show as it began to emerge from of the sleeve head, there was a shot. A blotch of red appeared on Ramiro's white shirt just below his right shoulder. A look of surprise crossed his face, his left hand let go of the jacket which fell to the ground at his feet. As his right hand came completely out of the sleeve head, a small silver pistol was revealed held loosely in his hand. He looked at Monica who was holding her AK-47 pointed right at him.

"I saw the gleam of silver," she said. "He should have had a white one."

Ramiro looked at Gerallt. He seemed to be pleading.

"I never trusted you," Gerallt said and fired. The bullet hit Ramiro just above his nose and he fell to the ground lifeless.

Gerallt picked up Esteves' body and threw it into the back of the pickup truck like the trash it was. It bounced against the legs of The Teniente who kicked at it disdainfully. Gerallt got back into the flatbed and backed it out of the tunnel while Monica drove the pickup. Five Bundle members were just outside the tunnel's entrance working on three of the invaders. The other three invaders had been laid out side by side. Gloria was coming out of Vulcan's Roost carrying some sheets.

As Gerallt got out of the truck, Issaack said, "What happened?"

"He tried to fool me with a pistol in his sleeve but Monica spotted it and shot him."

"Monica killed him?"

"No, I did. She saved my life."

"I'm glad he's dead," one of the invaders said.

"Who are you?" Gerallt said.

"Comandante Pedro Lopez. I was second in command of this … I don't know what to call us. We certainly weren't soldiers. We were beaten by a handful of noncombatants and a computer."

"Don't forget the man who killed Esteves," Issaack said pointing at Gerallt. "He certainly isn't a noncombatant. We have a medical evac helicopter on the way which will take you and the other wounded to Belém."

Gerallt and Phil removed Esteves body from the pickup and then they drove through the tunnel and down the volcano road to the encampment. Gerallt carried a white flag and they walked into the encampment. Even though they were coming in peace, both were armed and Phil hung back. Los Tres A-migos welcomed them peacefully but they were also armed. Gerallt heard a buzzing and looked up to see a bomber drone about fifty feet in the air behind Los Tres A-migos.

"The rest of your force has been defeated. There are only five alive."

Without further words, Los Tres A-migos dropped their weapons and utility belts on the ground and stepped back.

"We surrender," Alejandro said.

Gerallt told them to stay put until the rest of the survivors were brought down.

"No problemo," Los Tres A-migos said.

Gerallt and Phil picked up the weapons, put them in the pickup and returned to Vulcan's Roost. Horus thoughtfully closed the gates behind them just in case.

Chapter 40

The five surviving unwounded invaders departed the island by helicopter by midafternoon of the following day having disinterred the bodies of their compadres who had been killed in this experiment gone haywire because of the misguided desires of one man. Coffins had been brought in the helicopter and the body bags were placed in them and they were loaded aboard. Early afternoon of the same day another helicopter landed in the crater bringing a sufficient quantity of raw meat to feed the remaining animals for several days. Issaack, Waldo, Gloria and Harvey Gladstone rode in a pickup with a day's supply of meat dropping where the animals could get it. With them sated, quiet returned to the island except for the "Come Hither" roaring of the Cleopatra the white tiger and the answering roar of always interested Simba. Gladstone was glad that he got to witness such an encounter in person.

However, for the first feeding at least the caracal received special treatment. Declercq drove the pickup the Bundle had used to get down to the *B.B. São Rochelle* when she arrived with the animals. He stopped the truck near the spot where the parachutist had been found and Gerallt and Monica got out. Gerallt got a big plastic bag out of the truck's bed and the two entered the rainforest followed at a discrete distance by Declercq who had an automatic in a holster on his belt, his hand on the butt ready to pull it if needed. Monica and

Gerallt walked slowly through the rainforest looking for the caracal. Once Monica said, "Here, Hyma. Here, kitty kitty." She looked at Gerallt and smiled a "that was foolish" smile. Gerallt returned a "maybe" smile. After half an hour with no response and no sighting of the caracal, Gerallt stopped at the base of the strangler fig where he had spent the first night in the rainforest, opened the plastic bag and dumped it on the ground – five pounds of prime, red Argentinian beef. Then he turned around and the two of them walked back toward Declercq who suddenly pointed behind them, his hand observably tightening on the pistol's butt. Gerallt stopped and turned slowly around.

Visible in the undergrowth about five feet from the beef was Hyma who – unbeknownst to any of them – had been trailing them for twenty minutes, which was approximately how long it had been since Monica had called to her. Gerallt slowly walked back to the pile of meat, squatted down and picked up a piece, holding it out toward Hyma, who looked at the meat, Gerallt, Monica, and Declercq in that order and remained fixated on the last.

"Declercq, turn around and slowly walk away. You are not needed," Gerallt said and Declercq did so, first removing his right hand from the pistol butt and holding in the air as he walked away. Hyma watched him until – at least that was Gerallt's impression – she felt safe and then her eyes returned to the beef. She looked at it and then at Gerallt and the two remained stationary, eyes locked as though in a stare down contest. Then Hyma took two slow, careful steps toward Gerallt, looking at the beef, sniffed at the beef, and then grabbed it as Gerallt released it. Hyma chewed at the beef and began purring.

"Come here, Monica," Gerallt said. "Move slowly."

She complied and when she was standing beside Gerallt, she squatted.

"Her eyes never left me," Monica said.

"I know."

Gerallt picked up another piece of beef and handed it to Monica, Hyma's eyes tracking it all the way. Then Monica held it out to Hyma who looked at it, then Gerallt, then Monica, then the beef and, when Monica dropped it, snatched it out of the air. Hyma ate one more piece with them watching, then took the last one and disappeared into the undergrowth. The next day at approximately the same time, the two of them walked into the rainforest without Declercq and walked the same path as the day before and when they approached the spot where they had fed Hyma the previous day, she was sitting there waiting for them. She had seen them entered the rainforest and had raced ahead. They squatted down and dumped out the bag of beef. Hyma looked at the beef and then at Gerallt. Then at the beef, and then again at Gerallt, who picked up a piece and held it out to Hyma who snatched it and gobbled it down. Then she looked at Monica who picked up a piece and held it out to her and Hyma snatched it as Monica let it go.

"She's been purring the whole time," Monica said. "I'd love to pet her."

"Give it a go," Gerallt said.

Monica slowing reached out toward Hyma's head. Hyma stopped eating and raised her head slightly, eyes looking at Monica's hand which had stopped. Monica looked at Gerallt who nodded and so, looking back at Hyma, she moved her hand to the top of her head and scratched it. Hyma cocked her head and Monica scratched some more, Hyma purring the entire time. Then Hyma shook her head, grabbed the last piece of beef and disappeared into the undergrowth.

"Wow," Monica said. "I never thought..."

The two stood and started back the way they had come. As they walked, Gerallt reached out his right hand and took Monica's left. She looked up at him and smiled.

That night, Gerallt was awoken at 1:07 a.m. by Horus. "You have received an invitation to visit Ms. Bartlett."

"Now?"

"That's what she said."

"What'll I wear?"

"She said 'A robe would be sufficient.'"

Gerallt put on his white terry cloth bathroom which came standard in all Vulcan's Forge bedrooms and opened the door. On the floor tile in front of him was <MONICA in red. He followed the tiles and stood in front of a door which opened to reveal Monica wearing the peignoir she wore three nights before only this time with no cross trainers.

"Well," Monica said, "Are you going to stand there all night or get your Welsh arse in here?"

Gerallt closed the door behind him.

It took two days for the *B.B. São Rochelle* to reach the island. On board the ship were the veterinarians who had been waiting as requested because Issaack suspected that the experiment would encounter problems. Once the veterinarians were on the island, the black bear that had been wounded in the confrontation at the plateau tunnel entrance was of primary importance and he was found, sedated and taken to the ship. Once there, his wounds were tended to and his recovery was complete.

Under the expert guidance of the veterinarians, meat was filled with tranquilizers and given to the proper animals and as they were sedated, they were picked up, put in their cages and installed in the ship.

The pack was first, the lion and tiger the next day, the snow leopard and the caracal the third day. The snow leopard had retreated high on Vulcan's Forge after the attack at the plateau tunnel entrance and had to be lured down close enough to the road to make his retrieval less difficult. This was done by moving the daily feedings further down the mountain until the drugged feeding was close enough he could be carried by two men without much difficulty. In the case of the caracal, Monica fed her the drugged piece and Gerallt carried her through the rainforest to the truck. After she was awake and back to normal, they visited her before the ship left for Belém.

Homes for the animals were found in the best locations and funds were provided for their care. The black bear went to Zoo Knoxville (Tennessee). The wolf and two coyotes went to the Akron Zoo (Akron, Ohio), a non-profit zoo which made special enclosures for them side-by-side. The lion and tiger were donated to the Wildlife Zoo & Aquarium in Phoenix, Arizona which specializes in breeding endangered animals. The first result of this coupling was a male liger that was named Clemba. Monica provided funds for a befitting display area be built in the London Zoo for the caracal and she and Gerallt visited her every week they were in England or Wales.

Chapter 41

The morning after the *B.B. São Rochelle* left the island with the survivors of the Deadliest Predator Contest the Bundle met in the theater. Issaack greeted them.

"I wish we could have had this final meeting under happier circumstances. Believe me, I did not think that the design of the program would have led to this. We all know that Ramiro Esteves was the driving force behind the plan. As far as can be determined at this point, Hurricane Davido's devastation of this island was perhaps the inspiration for the agenda. How I got selected I am uncertain, but word had leaked about the course Siegfried and I were embarking on in the development of Horus using Siegfried's radical design of a biological computer. I am uncertain how the choices of the rest of you were made and don't want to speculate. However, input from all of you affected the final results. One of these most of you didn't even recognize and, to my knowledge, it was not known to Esteves and we did our best to keep it under wraps.

"While I have been talking a helicopter had landed in front of Vulcan's Roost bringing two of the people responsible for the infrastructure of this island."

The door opened, and two men walked into the room.

"Let me introduce you to Walt Jeffries, Construction Supervisor, and Andy Russel, the man who oversaw the work of Ant Man, our tunnel digger."

The group applauded.

"Andy is going to tell you about another aspect of Ant Man that not too many know about."

"Thanks, Issaack. This is sort of a show and tell demonstration, and I'd like to begin with the show part."

The door opened, and a cart loaded with eight black boxes approximately eighteen inches by eighteen inches by thirty-six inches was pushed in by Gretel and Declercq.

Andy continued, "Volcanos are a source of some very useful minerals – aluminum, nickel, lead, zinc, and copper. Usually not in large enough quantities to be worth mining. But there is also…" and he opened one of the boxes and pulled out a stone – "… gold, like this nugget…" he put the nugget back in the box but left it open. He opened another box and picked up a handful of stones which he held out "and diamonds." That brought a gasp from all but Gloria. "You might remember when there was the exploratory visit to the crater and the plateau, Gloria Mitchell got snake bit. But do you remember how? She had picked up a small rock and thrown it and then suddenly gone after it. Unfortunately, that brought her into the space of a very angry tropical rattlesnake that bit her. The stone she had found was a diamond. She had it appraised, and the appraiser said that depending on clarity and flaws, when cut it could be a two or three caret stone." As he was talking, Issaack and Walt had each taken two handfuls of stones from the box and given some to each of the Bundle.

Looking at the ones, he had been given, Phil asked, "How much are these worth?"

"Difficult to say," Andy replied. I've done some research and found a couple of interesting diamond facts. There are four ways that diamonds are graded. It's the four C scale: Color, Carat weight, Clarity, and Cut. At the Crater of Diamonds State Park near Murfreesboro, Arkansas, an 8.52-carat white stone known now as the Esperanza Diamond was found in June 2015. When it was cut into a 4.6-carat triolette shape it was graded internally flawless. Not only that, it was color graded "D" by the American Gem Society. "D" is the highest color grade. The current value of this diamond has been reported at around $1 million. So what we have in these ten boxes is unknown." That brought an undertone of whispering among the Bundle members. "Some of these stones are going to be too small to be worth much. Some of the big ones could be cut and be worthless because of the color grade and because they have flaws. There are ten of these boxes. There are thirty boxes containing gold nuggets, each box weighs approximately thirty pounds. At the present time gold is about $1300 dollars an ounce. That's 480 ounces or $624,000. But remember this is not pure gold. It might be less than half of that."

"And how did we get all of this?" Harvey Gladstone asked.

"Ant Man," Andy said. "The dirt Ant Man dug was brought inside through pipes with screws moving the dirt through them. This is nothing new. It happens with every dig. Then the dirt is put on conveyor belts as it moves though the rest of the body to the back where it was put into what were basically mine cars on a track that was installed as Ant Man moved along. Dirt went out on mine cars and when needed, the concrete sections for the tub were brought in on other cars.

"But when the dirt reached the end of Ant Man, it was dumped into hopper cars and taken out of the mine to an area where the hoppers cars were dumped on a big area of screens and water added washing the dirt away. There were five levels of screens, each getting smaller and smaller – we didn't keep anything under a quarter of an inch. The screens were pulled and sorted through by workers who knew what to look for and were given a bonus for keeping their mouths shut. The bonus was partially cash and partially diamonds if they wanted to take that chance. They knew they cannot reveal where they got it. Since they understood that the value of the diamonds could vary from nothing to a fortune but closer to nothing, all of them chose the cash. And therefore, we are left with the diamonds and it is be up to each of us to decide what to do with them.

"Don't diamonds need to be registered?" Issaack asked.

Andy told them how to get the diamonds in their boxes registered and how to report their origin.

Issaack finished, "So each of you will get a box of diamonds as return on your investment as well as a share of the gold. We are also giving a box of diamonds to Walt and Andy for their part in this program."

"Did Ramiro know about this?" Phil asked. "I mean about the diamonds and gold, not about giving some to Walt and Andy. I know they earned them."

"Not that we know of. He never mentioned it and to me, the time he should have done that was when he seized control the first night. Personally, I think that if he knew about this, we would all have been killed for our share of the diamonds."

"What was his plan for the island?" Gloria asked.

"This is supposition, but it would become a base for his operation. There are five years left on our lease and after that it would be between him and the Brazilian government. But he paid for the *B.B. São Rochelle*, so it would have something to do with his plans. Getting product to and from the island would be my guess.

"Any other questions?"

Nobody seemed to ask questions.

"Two last things. First, we had a betting pool. For those of you who didn't know, the veterinarians made a bet."

"They had that much money?" Gloria said.

"No, it was a separate bet. They each put in a thousand dollars that the coyotes would form a pack and win. It appears that not only did the coyotes form a pack but they and the wolf united and they were among those still alive. This is what I propose. All bets in the pool of animals who died in the contest – regardless of how they died – lose their bets. Those whose bets are still alive – meaning that the animal or animals they bet on survived – split the pot. Minus six thousand dollars from each bet going to the veterinarians."

"How many bets were made?" Phil asked.

"Including the veterinarians' bet?" answered Issaack.

"No, consider that separate."

"There were fifteen," Issaack said.

"So each of the veterinarians gets sixteen thousand dollars?"

"Yes. And the rest is split equally among those still in."

"No problem. I approve."

"Any objections?" There were none.

"Those with winning bets will get their proceeds deposited into their accounts.

"The last thing is the films. We had proposed a televised show with profits to be split among the seven of us. The entry of Gerallt makes that impossible. What happened further makes that impossible. I think that it is only proper that all copies – and I mean all copies – be destroyed."

"You mean we cannot have any for our personal use," Harvey Gladstone seemed to whine.

"That is exactly what I mean. I do not want any of us to be able to make any money off that aspect of this project."

"Wish that we could wipe all memory of it," Gloria said.

"I don't," Monica said with a smile on her face.

"I bet you don't," Gloria said.

"I am certain that all of us have some pleasant memories and some bad memories," Issaack said. "Any further discussion?"

"If needed, I second the motion," Waldo said.

"All in favor."

A chorus of "aye" filled the room.

"Well, then a helicopter will be here about 1:00 p.m. to pick you up and take you to the airport in Belém, so you can catch your flights home. But until then – if you're already packed, there is champagne and shrimp and cheese and other nibble stuff in the restaurant. Thanks for being part of this project and we're sorry it didn't work out better."

Ramiro Esteves's property was seized by the Brazilian Government and his empire effectively tumbled but the widespread parts were quickly picked up and used by other drug cartels.

Phil Parmelee died less than six months later trying to find another treasure ship. Apparently a great white took exception to his diving in its territory and put him on its dinner menu.

Harvey Gladstone left the real estate business two years later after it was discovered that he had not filed tax returns for the previous ten years. When the story of the Deadliest Predator Contest and the Billionaire Bundle was aired, the Internal Revenue Service got very interested in all of them and the fact that Harvey Gladstone hadn't filed but had stored money via several dummy corporations came to the front. His habit of buying inexpensive clothes was simply an effort to look poor. His choice of food was because he just didn't care about food except for the necessary sustenance it provided. The Federal Government seized all his assets and he ended up panhandling on the streets of Phoenix, Arizona.

Gloria Mitchell married her fourth husband and this one stuck, maybe because he had more spendable cash than she did.

Ralph "Waldo" Emerson continued making electric vehicles and was headed toward Trillionaire status.

Horus "died" within a year because Siegfried Schmidt had discovered that the memory was dying faster than he could replenish it and he was having to grow memory to keep Horus functioning as long as he did. Nobody was willing to pay for a product that required as much maintenance as his did. For whatever reason, Issaack Kinkaid's artificial intelligence program wouldn't work on any other computer and his hoped-for battle with Watson didn't materialize.

Gerallt Cearrach became Monica Bartlett's head of Security. When she became pregnant two years later, they got married, she quit touring but put out one album a year for the next four years. She did make one video on the island six months after the Deadliest Predator Contest was over. They bought an estate in Wales and settled into a quiet life.

Stefan Declercq and Carmen Domingo started a small but financially successful café in London and tried to stay out of any limelight.

Gretel started her own security business in Miami, Florida, and was quite successful.

Brazil was given control over the island a year after the Deadliest Predator Contest was over and helped interested Brazilians move there and make a living enjoying the quiet island life. To date, except for the geyser from the top of Colina da Rocha every couple of days, the volcano has stayed dormant. Warning signs and metal gates were placed at the entrances to the lava tube to prevent the curious from an unexpected and dangerous wetting.

Acknowledgements

As usual, I used Wikipedia a lot to help me in choosing my predators and the facts you read were gleaned from there. Beyond that I relied heavily on the following people:

Alex Cameron for help with the design of the railroad and the moving of the TBM and its Back-up Train;

Doug Harding, Robbins Company, for getting Ant Man to function properly and furnishing me with diagrams to use to help readers understand this fantastic machine. You can see some pictures of Rosie, the Akron OH tunnel borer at:

http://www.akronwaterwaysrenewed.com/ocit/rosie-akrons-tunnel-boring-machine.aspx

And find out as much as you want to know about the Robbins Company at:

http://www.therobbinscompany.com/products/tunnel-boring-machines/;

Bob Dyer, Akron Beacon Journal Columnist, who gave the book an early plug when he wrote about Ant Man

Tars Septimio, a Brazilian friend, who helped with the Portuguese and Spanish expressions in this book;

Paul Orr, PE, a Florida PE (Structural) with NUTEK Engineering, LLC. of Dania Beach, FL (Ft

Lauderdale area) for help in getting me pointed to Mabey Inc.;

James Porreca, Bridging & Structural Shoring Specialist, Pittsburgh Depot, Mabey Inc. for help in getting the Chardon Bridge (in reality a Mabey Compact 200 Bridge) constructed;

To see a wonderful video of one of these being constructed, here are two links to the save video: https://www.mabey.com/us/news-and-media/blog/bridge-animation

https://www.youtube.com/watch?v=ObppOnivuq4.

As usual in my writing, I must acknowledge two writers who have heavily influence my work. (you can skip this if you've read it before) I must acknowledge two writers who have influenced my work. First (and only chronologically) is Mary Higgins Clark whom I heard speak at a Book and Author Luncheon (or Dinner) sponsored by *The Plain Dealer* of Cleveland OH. She said that many of her works got their genesis with the words "What if?" And I used a big "WHAT IF" in this one.

The other writer is the late Philip R. Craig, author of the Martha's Vineyard based J.W. Jackson mysteries. My wife and I met he and his wife Shirley on a riverboat trip from Constanta, Romania, to Amsterdam, Netherlands, in 2005 and shared many a happy meal together including my wife's birthday dinner. He told me that in his writing, while he knew the story line, he often didn't know how it was going to come out and let the characters lead him. Frequently that is what I do, and I did in this book

Douglas Ewan Cameron grew up in Oak Ridge, Tennessee where his father worked as a chemist on the Manhattan Project. He went to undergraduate school at Miami University (Oxford, Ohio), earned a master's degree at The University of Akron (Akron, Ohio) and a doctorate in mathematics from Virginia Polytechnic Institute and State University (Blacksburg Virginia). He then returned to The University of Akron where he taught for twenty-eight years before retiring in 1998. Since then he and his wife have spent their summer on the eastern shore of Hubbard Lake (Spruce, Michigan) where he has spent as much time possible in his boat on the water chasing the ever-elusive walleye. During the winter months, he returns to Ohio from which he and his wife have traveled the world visiting over one hundred countries. He has used his knowledge of the world thus gained as backgrounds in many of his books. He has written all his life starting with short stories in his youth, mathematical research papers in his working years, and finally novels in retirement chasing the ever-elusive bestseller. This is his twelfth novel. Some day he hopes to land the big one from the waters of Hubbard Lake just as he hopes to write a bestselling novel. Is this the one?

55355703R00267

Made in the USA
Columbia, SC
12 April 2019